Dedicated to Rachel, who helped me on my own journey.

PART 1

CHAPTER 1

The Great Union
Shadow is where we will return.

She opened the book, her eyes wide with intrigue as she carefully flicked through the old, frail pages.

"What does it say?" Jimmy asked.

Joan stayed silent as the words filled her mind. At first, they seemed chaotic and formless, but as she gazed at the pages, their meaning became clear. She sensed an invisible force drawing her away, but was powerless to stop it.

"Joan?" Jimmy asked, concern in his voice.

Her eyes appeared to glaze over and darken, as if a shadow had fallen upon her. She drifted into a trance and spoke in a low, emotionless voice. "It wasn't a sound or a melody, but a thought that swept through the vast emptiness before time and space. Creation was inherent in the void, and it was inevitable that *they* would emerge."

"You're freakin' me out," Jimmy said as a cold chill wrapped around him, causing him to shiver.

She continued speaking, ignoring Jimmy's words. "Life exploded in the beginning, though it was finite in the end. The idea was formed: the Great Union—birth, death, rebirth." She paused, gazing blankly at the page as if she were hearing something or someone that Jimmy couldn't perceive.

They stood silently as he wondered what to do next when a scream echoed in the distance. This only made Jimmy shiver more as a cold chill ran down his spine. He went over to the old broken door of the cabin and tried to close it, but it offered no security.

"We need to go, Joan," he said, peering out into the night surrounding them.

"However," she continued, her voice grim and foreboding, "Light extinguishes truth, burns away the origin, for it is in the emptiness thought is created. The Great Union is the great lie, *He* has come to me, *He* has shown me truth." Joan lowered the book and looked blankly at Jimmy, her eyes completely black. "We are forever trapped."

Those last words echoed in Jimmy's mind as he caught Joan's gaze. "We are trapped," he whispered, his words falling dead in the heavy atmosphere that threatened to suffocate them.

Joan's voice suddenly rose, now vicious and spiteful. "*He* underestimated the strength to be found in life, the one light in a sea of perfect beautiful darkness that refused to be extinguished." She suddenly looked pale and frightened, and her voice dropped low and trembled as she whispered a name: "Daniel."

Jimmy grabbed her by her arms. "Joan, snap out of it, now!"

Her voice abruptly erupted and screeched, "We come from Shadow and close our eyes to the burning Light, and Shadow is where we will return!"

Joan's body suddenly writhed and contorted as she convulsed, causing Jimmy to struggle to keep her in his arms. Her screams echoed through the room, a high-pitched wail that filled the air with terror. Suddenly, her body went limp and she fainted, and all fell into an eerie silence. Then the door burst open. Jimmy turned, heart racing as a howling wind shook the cabin.

"Jimmy, wake up, we need to go," Joan said, waking Jimmy from his dream.

With a sudden jolt, Jimmy sat up on the sofa, his eyes wide with shock. The familiar walls of the house surrounded him, and he realised that he had dozed off while Joan had been busy packing.

"I have a bad feeling about this," he said and shook his head.

CHAPTER 2

A New Journey
Like a fragile petal opening, feeling the first rays of a warm sun.

He was overwhelmed with curiosity as his eyes darted from one blurry image to the next. This new foreign landscape that encircled him conjured strange feelings. His senses were alive and acutely aware of his surroundings: sounds roared, smells tickled his nose, and the cool air on his skin tingled and made him shiver. The sensation of panic instinctively grew, and he started to cry out. This new world overwhelmed him, and he desperately reached out to find the same warmth and comfort he was torn from.

"Hello, my little boy," he heard a whisper, looked up, and his gaze anchored on the deep blue eyes looking lovingly at him.

"Shhh," she said softly and pressed him close to her.

He fell silent, though many voices surrounded him that he could not understand. The world swirled about, begging to be noticed; however, his stare did not falter. As he lay there, he felt the warm embrace that held him tight, and he experienced a feeling of safety. He was home. For the first time, he smiled, and a warm smile echoed back.

He was overcome with peace, and his eyes flickered in a vain attempt to stay open. He felt a loving kiss on his forehead, and his heavy eyelids could no longer resist the urge to close, and slowly, the scene faded from him.

It is inherent in us, the deep need to turn over every rock, to look around every corner, to find that ultimate answer. It is that struggle that pushes us forward, as we search for that elusive prize, revealing the eternal dream. Life must continue.

Simon picked up Daniel and looked at his child, examining every feature, every frown, every dimple on his perfect face. He looked at Susanna and smiled, his eyes watery with joy.

"How did we do this?" he said, his voice wavering.

Susanna beamed. "Would you like me to

explain to you about the birds and bees?" she jested and smiled lovingly.

Simon rolled his eyes and laughed. "No, I think I have that covered. Thanks anyway." He gently handed Daniel back to his wife, and she adjusted Daniel's blue wrap. "You are beautiful, you know," Simon said, looking at her.

"I'm a mess," she said, leaning back into the fluffed pillows.

"A beautiful mess," Simon said, kissing her gently. "I love you."

"I love you too."

"I think it may be time for Mum to sleep now," came the voice of a midwife as she entered the room. "Why don't you treat yourself to a coffee, or perhaps go home and have a sleep," she said to Simon.

Simon turned to protest but, seeing the stern look on her face, decided that maybe he did need some caffeine in his system. He gave Daniel and Susanna a kiss and reluctantly left the room. He made his way down the stairs, through a long corridor to the canteen, which was located near the entrance to the hospital. He was greeted by a middle-aged man standing at the counter complaining that he didn't like the coffee and that he wouldn't feel the need to complain if they bought a better coffee machine. The staff member had a painted smile spread across her face and vacant eyes as she recalled a rather pleasurable encounter with one of the electricians working on site earlier that morning. Eventually, the man was asked to leave, and everyone clapped in appreciation.

When Simon finally managed to get a coffee, he found a place to sit by a window. He felt the warmth of the morning sun and could hear the sounds of birds singing melodiously. The long night started to take its toll, and within minutes, his eyes were closed, and he was fast asleep.

Simon, Susanna, and their new baby, Daniel, left the hospital exactly one week after he was born. They sat in silence as Simon drove. Susanna sat back resting, gazing out the window and watching the clouds drift by, whilst Daniel slept soundly in the car seat. As they drove to their house, they saw her parents, Louise and Paul, already waiting by the door to welcome them. Simon had called ahead to let them know they were on their way. He pulled the car to a stop, and at that moment, relief hit him. They were finally home.

Susanna carried baby Daniel inside, cradling him as she went. Louise followed Susanna whilst Paul helped with the bags. Paul, in particular, seemed to be in his element, bustling around the house, making sure everyone was okay, until Louise gave him a cup of tea and told him to relax, sit down, and keep Simon company.

They sat silently for a while. "You know, Simon, when I first met you, I had my doubts," Paul said, eyeing Simon suspiciously. "However, I am not too proud to admit I was wrong."

Simon grinned. "Thanks?" he said awkwardly.

"No, no, you have made Suzy happy. I mean truly happy." He stretched out his right hand to Simon, and they shook. "Congratulations, son, you did well."

"I love Suz, she... Well, she's perfect," Simon said, looking over at the bedroom door where Susanna and Daniel were resting.

Paul placed a hand on Simon's shoulder. "It's been a long day, son, and I don't think a cup of tea really captures the moment."

The doorbell rang, and Simon's parents, Keith and Marge, stood there. They hugged their son and peeked into the bedroom to see their grandson. As the day passed, their small house was soon packed and lively with friends and neighbours who wanted to welcome them back and see the new arrival. Louise and Marge made food for everyone while Keith, Paul, and Simon chatted over a drink about the latest football scores. However, Susanna stayed away from the celebrations, just wanting to spend some time alone with Daniel, loving the new life she had brought into the world.

Louise stayed for a few weeks to help out before returning home. At last, the house was truly empty and they were alone, just the three of them. They could finally start to relax and settle into the new normal with baby Daniel.

Daniel was a happy baby who rarely cried and was quite content to spend time alone. When Susanna was busy doing house chores, he found great amusement in trying to suck on his toes. Eventually, he'd grow tired and lay looking about the new world he found himself in, studying the strange shapes and colours caused by the soft light of the summer filtered through the window, dappling the walls with its light. Susanna watched him, gurgling and blowing bubbles, quite happy and content; she was captivated by his unfailing curiosity. She marvelled at how his eyes lit up with every new experience and discovery. She was sure that Daniel would face the world with courage and optimism, and that he would never lose his playful spirit.

It was a warm Sunday morning. The sky was a deep shade of blue, and the sun peaked over the horizon, its golden rays spread across the sleepy town beneath it. Birds sang familiar songs in the trees, and people slept in late, content to enjoy a lazy day. The streets were empty save for the occasional passerby, and everything seemed to move in slow motion. A gentle breeze rustled through the leaves, and the sound of a distant church bell echoed in the air.

"It's a beautiful morning," Susanna said, opening the curtains.

Simon rolled over and pulled the duvet over his head. "Yeah, and let's keep it outside of the room."

She threw a pillow at him. "It's a lovely day.

Let's go out."

Simon groaned in response. She leapt on top of him, and he let out a louder groan. "Okay, okay, I'm awake." He spun around and rolled on top of her. "You're lucky I love you." Their lips softly met.

A cry rang out from another room.

"I'll go," he said, rolling out of bed, "you make the coffee."

Simon opened the door to Daniel's bedroom and found his son crying in his cot. "Woo," Simon said. "Good morning, my stinky boy. I think someone needs changing." He scooped him up in his arms and brought him into the living room. He laid him down on his changing mat and proceeded to carry out a well-practised morning routine.

Susanna came in with coffee and toast and set them down on a small table that had been pushed to the side of the room. She knelt beside them and put her arm around Simon. "I love you," she whispered and smiled at Daniel.

The sun shone down warmly on them as they made their way to the park. The canopy of the cloudless sky seemingly stretched to infinity, and the trees that lined the roadside swayed gently below, causing the sound of rustling leaves to fill the air.

They soon reached the park and sat at their usual spot by the lake. They watched the world slowly drift by, taking in the beauty of the scene. The lake was still except for the occasional tiny ripple caused by a few ducks swimming along, drifting peacefully in search of food. The sun glittered on the water, causing the colours of its surface to shift hypnotically with the changing light. Daniel's parents sat in silence for a while, listening to the peaceful sounds, each lost in thought.

"Do you ever miss it?" Simon said.

"Miss it?" Susanna answered while checking on Daniel, who was asleep in his pram.

"The travelling." He paused. "The fight."

"No, not really." She looked sombrely at Daniel. "We did what we had to. We couldn't go on. In the end, well, you know where it leads."

"I know, but we had some adventures, didn't we?" he said, watching her.

"I'm happy. This is our biggest adventure," she said, smiling. She turned to him. "Just look what we made."

Simon looked at Daniel. "You're not wrong. I'm a father now."

"Welcome to the party. I'm glad you finally made it," she mocked kindly.

"You know what I mean, sarky!" he said, rolling his eyes.

"I know," she said, and leaned over and kissed him on his cheek.

They sat quietly for a while, enjoying the peace.

"Zack called the other day," Simon said casually, breaking the silence.

"I told you no!" Susanna said, instant anger in her voice. "We are out. It has nothing to do with us anymore!"

Simon sat quietly, staring into the lake. "I don't think anyone can ever be out," he said sombrely.

"I'm going." She abruptly stood up and started to walk away with Daniel. "Are you coming?"

Simon sat there, still staring into the lake. "I may sit for a bit."

"Fine!" Susanna turned to go, but stopped and

looked back. "We have Daniel now. We have to protect him."

"I know, I know." Simon looked up at them and smiled. He stood up, walked over to her, and embraced her warmly. "I know," he whispered. "We will stay out of it."

...

Daniel ran across to the swing and stood there, arms stretched up, jumping up and down whilst making demanding squealing sounds. Simon followed, picked him up, and lowered him onto the seat.

"Hold on tight," he said as he pulled the swing back and pushed.

Daniel shot forward; in his imagination, he was soaring, almost touching the sky. He screamed with delight as his father pushed him higher and higher. Daniel stretched out his arms as the swing reached its highest point, and for that brief moment, he felt as if he was flying. The sensation made him giggle, but then he burped, and the contents of his stomach flew out of his mouth and down his jacket.

Simon slowed the swing carefully, took Daniel out, and stood him on the ground. Daniel couldn't say many words at three years old, but he made his discomfort known.

"Yucky!" he said, trying to wipe the partially digested food from his jacket.

"No, Danny." His father gently grabbed his hand. "Let's find Mummy."

Susanna sat on a bench chatting to another mother, enjoying a welcome break.

"Mummy!" Daniel said and ran over to hug her.

"Danny." She held him at arm's length. "You mucky pup, what happened?" She turned to look at Simon, who smiled awkwardly and looked for wipes in their backpack.

He pulled out some baby wipes and started to clean the jacket.

"I have a spare in the bag," Susanna said.

"You think of everything," Simon said, pulling out a clean jacket.

Before long, Daniel was running around the park again, closely chased by his father. Susanna sat on a bench and watched them running about. She was happy and content with her life.

"I'm gonna get you!" Simon said, acting like a monster. "Roar!" he screeched and stomped his feet.

Daniel screamed and ran as fast as his little legs could move. It was only a second that his father's attention was drawn away from his son, the briefest of moments, but when he looked back, Daniel was gone. Instant panic erupted, and he frantically ran forward, scanning every inch of the playground in search of his son, but he wasn't there. Susanna noticed that something was wrong and rushed over.

"Where's Danny?" she said desperately.

"He was here," he answered. "Look over there." They ran in a desperate search in opposite directions.

Daniel had left the playground and was walking amongst the nearby trees. He looked back and saw his parents rushing about, but he giggled, not realising their panic, and continued exploring.

"Hello, Daniel," a low hiss came from behind a tree. It sounded kind, but beneath the surface, malice lurked.

Daniel stood still, transfixed on the noise,

curious who was calling him. The figure of a person slowly stepped out from behind a large tree. They were cloaked in a long, billowing robe that seemed to swallow up any light that touched it. A deep hood was pulled over their face, obscuring any features from view.

"Don't be scared," they said, kneeling down level with Daniel. "Come here, I have something to give you."

Daniel stood frozen. He felt a chill in the air and shuddered. He instinctively knew something was wrong, "Go away!" he shouted. "I don't like you!"

"Now that's not nice, is it?" their voice slithered, its tone deliberate and false.

The robed figure stood up and faded away in a smoky mist. The vapour hung in the air for only a moment, when suddenly a shapeless horror burst forth. Its shadowy tendrils spread out like a contamination, devouring the light. Then it rose in the air, creating a canopy of night as it loomed over Daniel with cruel intent. A cold mist fell about him, plunging him into an empty blackness.

"You must not be," the voice said, cold and harsh now. "You cannot be. The cycle must end!"

The air grew thick and frigid, and Daniel started to cough; his tiny lungs were filling with an invisible toxin that burned. Tears streamed down his face as pain overtook him, causing him to instinctively cry out for his mother. He attempted to run, but his legs gave out and he crumpled onto the ground.

"You must not be," the voice repeated. "You cannot be. The cycle must end!"

Suddenly, in the darkness, a white light erupted, bright and blinding. It cut through the blackness with razor-sharp precision. There was a hideous scream as beams of pure white sliced through the black veil, shredding its hold and allowing the warmth of the world to flood back in. Claw-like hands grabbed Daniel, but he was shielded as his father covered him. The claws tore into Simon, and he shouted in pain. Susanna's brilliant glow shone brighter and exploded in a kaleidoscope of colour, and in an instant, the blackness was gone, and they were in the park under the tree.

Simon was lying on the ground but heaved himself up. "Danny! Danny!"

Daniel lay still, his skin grey and his body

limp. Susanna had run over and kneeled beside them. "Quick! Get him out of the shadow and into the sunlight!"

They moved Daniel out from the shade of the tree into the sunlight. Within seconds of the sun touching his skin, his colour started to return, and he opened his eyes to see his parents looking anxiously at him.

"Danny?" his father whispered.

The Shadow had left no trace in Daniel's mind, but his parents bore the scars of its visit. They knew that there was nowhere to hide, and an everyday life was something they may never be destined to have. They lived in fear, knowing they could not escape its dark desire and that their son was its mark. The seasons changed, and they watched Daniel grow, but they remained vigilant, waiting for it to return. It was when Daniel was five that their wait was over.

...

There was a flash. Zack and Simon were down. Only Susanna stood against the beast, and she would not back down.

Then, in an instant, life changed forever.

...

The day started like any other in the small town of Sanly. Daniel was up first, went downstairs, played with his toys and sang quietly to himself. At five years old, he was an average child who behaved and misbehaved as you would expect. His eyes, however, were wise beyond his years.

Susanna glanced at the clock and hastily threw on some clothes, knowing her boss wouldn't be happy if she were late to work again. Simon had already left for work hours before. She went downstairs and peeked into the living room, smiling as she took in the sight of her son lost in his own world. He hadn't noticed her presence, and before she disturbed him, she pulled out a small camera and snapped a quick picture, wanting to capture the moment.

She went over to Daniel, who warmly hugged his mum when he noticed her. They went through their regular morning routine, and within thirty minutes, they were out the door and driving to the nursery. She dropped Daniel off and, as usual, he ran away, vanishing in a swath of kids, wanting to find his favourite toy, a small action-man doll.

The day passed drearily for Susanna. It was quiet at the office: no one chatted, and work was slow. Eventually, the time came to leave. She went to the shops to pick up a few bits for dinner whilst Simon collected Daniel on his way home from work. All in all, it was just another day.

Susanna arrived home, and when she walked in, her mother was there. "Mum?" she said, surprised to see the unexpected visitor.

Louise approached her daughter and gave her a big hug that lingered.

"Everything okay?" Susanna asked, feeling a little confused by her mother's behaviour. "Where's Dad?"

"Oh, he's at home, still writing that book of his," her mother answered.

"Oh, you okay?" Susanna asked again.

Louise smiled softly. "Yes, yes, all fine. I just… Oh, it's nothing."

They walked into the living room to find Daniel play-fighting with his father. Toys were scattered all over, and the TV blasted loudly.

"Ah, there are my boys, chaos as usual."

Susanna laughed and walked over, carefully navigating the minefield of toys, and turned the TV down.

"Mummy!" Daniel cried out and leapt from his father into his mother's arms.

"So what are you doing here?" Susanna asked again, now worried about her mother's strange behaviour. "Dad okay?"

"Everything is fine. I just wanted to see my grandson, that's all," Louise answered, unconvincingly. However, Susanna didn't push her mother further and let the subject go.

The evening passed pleasantly. Daniel eventually went to bed after dinner, and Susanna, Simon, and Louise sat down with hot drinks and played cards. Suddenly, the doorbell rang, breaking the happy mood in the room.

Louise looked startled. "Oh no, it can't be," she said worriedly.

Both Susanna and Simon looked at her, startled and confused.

"It's Zack," she said as the doorbell rang again.

"It can't be," Simon said.

"Impossible," added Susanna.

"I know it is, I…" She trailed off. "I know this is strange, but I dreamed it last night."

Susanna looked at Simon with an understanding born of hidden knowledge.

"You can't go. Please say no!" Louise pleaded.

The doorbell rang again, followed by a loud knock, which woke Daniel. Louise stood up and went to see him. They went to the door, and to their shock, Zack was there. He was out of breath, panting heavily, and he looked drained.

"It's here. I can't stop it. It's close." He stumbled onto his friends, who caught him and brought him into the house. They sat him down on the couch. Susanna quickly went to the kitchen and brought back a cool cup of water, which Zack eagerly drank.

"What happened?" Simon asked.

"It's found Daniel. I tried to stop it, but it was stronger. I don't know how, but…" He coughed violently, and black liquid splattered onto his hand. Susanna rushed away and brought back another glass of water.

"We have no choice," Simon said, looking at Susanna. "We have to protect Daniel."

"There is another way," she said cautiously.

"No, that has to be the last option," Simon insisted.

"We have to go now before it gets here," Zack said weakly. He lifted himself up and staggered from the house.

"We have no choice," Simon said. "Zack needs us. We have to go!"

"I am not leaving Daniel," Susanna said.

"We'll leave him here with your mother. He'll be safe," he said.

"I know he will, but…" She trailed off and went to go to Daniel.

Simon grabbed her arm. "No time, we have to go now! This is the only way we can protect him!" he shouted.

"Last time, then I am out! Either you agree or leave me now!" Susanna said, the ultimatum clear.

"Okay, okay. Then never again, I promise," Simon said, desperation filling every part of his body.

"There is another way," she said, looking gravely at him.

Simon went pale. "I said no! Please, no."

...

The three stood together, facing a dark beast that had arisen from the blackness surrounding them. It appeared to them as a mass of writhing tendrils brandishing razor-sharp claws. It was a manifestation of the Shadow's malice and evil intent, its appearance made to create terror in all that stood before it. The beast was an ancient force created from the deepest void on the outskirts of the eternal nothingness, where true death exists. Its purpose was to consume all life and extinguish Light from the world. The beast should not have existed; it was the manifestation of corruption. It was an insult to creation.

The monster surged forward and frantically lunged, slashing with its claws and whipping with its tendrils. Simon dodged and kicked at it, which had little effect. Susanna clasped her hands and uttered words, each syllable unleashing power that grew and exploded in bright colourful rays that pierced down from the sky, striking the creature. It recoiled, but her attack was ineffective.

Zack started to chant an ancient prayer as he walked slowly towards the beast. Simon screamed out to him to stop, realising his intent. The creature filled Zack's head with repulsive images of horror, whispering depravity into his mind. However, his will did not falter, and glowing energy grew around him with each step towards the creature. The beast appeared unnerved, but only momentarily, because it lowered itself to the ground, and its body dissolved into a dense fog that shot straight into Zack's chest in a spear-like fashion. He was thrown back and engulfed in the gloom and was gone.

The beast screamed violently and writhed about, appearing to mock their attempts to stop it. It roared out with an unrelenting ferocity that made the ground shake. Simon pulled out a book from his backpack, placed it on the ground, and started to read a passage, but a hideous tendril materialised and swooped at him, striking him with force and throwing him into the blackness.

Susanna stood alone in the clearing, a solitary figure surrounded by a swirling vortex that threatened to consume her. The shadows crept menacingly, closing in with each passing moment. She could feel their icy fingers reaching out to grab at her, and she shuddered with fear as she stood her ground against the encroaching darkness. She fought against the seeds of doubt sowed in her mind by the creature. It urged her to run away, whispering words that conjured images of loss and defeat. Still, her heart would not abandon her son. Suddenly, the darkness swamped her, and the air thickened. She gasped for breath and fell to the ground.

Susanna awoke in bed; she was sweating, and her heart beat violently. She took a moment to calm her thoughts and drew a deep breath. What a terrible nightmare, she thought. She looked to the window, and the sun streamed in, warming the room, indicating that it was the start of another day. The horror of her dream faded quickly with the warmth in the room, and she felt a sudden thankful calm.

She looked at the clock on the bedside table and realised that she was going to be late for work. She leapt from the bed and hastily rushed through her morning routine. Simon had already left for work. She quickly rushed downstairs, peering into the living room to check on Daniel. He was sitting with his back to her, playing with his toys.

She smiled. "It was all just a dream," she whispered.

She entered the kitchen and was greeted immediately by the comforting smell of coffee. Simon was standing there, preparing the morning drinks. Susanna was surprised to see him.

"What are you doing here?" she said, walking over and wrapping her arms around him.

"I decided to take the day off," Simon said. "So, I thought I would make you a coffee. I was going to bring you breakfast in bed."

"The last time you cooked, the fire brigade turned up!" she laughed.

"I did apologise," he said and kissed her.

"Go and see to Daniel, I'll sort this," she said. Simon went off to the living room.

As she readied breakfast, her thoughts drifted to the people and places in her life. She thought of her family, her friends, and the summer days spent in the park by the lake. She thought of the place she grew up and the town she now called home. Through it all, she was filled with a deep sense of contentment and joy. Her life had its ups and downs, but her heart was at peace. She was happy. She sang a soft, low song as she cooked, barely above a whisper. Her simple song was filled with gratitude, and as the melody floated around the kitchen, it expressed what words could not.

"Danny! Simon! Breakfast!" she called out.

She heard Danny laugh, but no one answered. She thought they were play-fighting again. "Danny, Simon, breakfast," she repeated.

Still no response. Susanna went to the living room and stood by the door. Simon wasn't there, and Daniel was still sitting where he was when she first came down.

"Danny, breakfast," she said softly, looking around the room for Simon.

Danny didn't move. He sat there with his back to her, giggling, and appeared preoccupied.

"What do you have there, Danny?" She walked over to him.

As she knelt, her eyes widened in horror. Her mouth went dry, and her heart hammered in her chest. She screamed and stumbled back onto the floor.

"Mummy," Daniel said.

"No, please, no!" she screamed, tears streaming down her face.

He stretched out his hand; he held what looked like a beating heart. It was raw and glistening with blood as it pulsated with a dreadful rhythm. She looked at Daniel's face: claw marks were scratched across his eyes, which were torn and bleeding with a black tar-like substance. Daniel smiled, and his black teeth were tainted with bits of red flesh.

"Daniel!" she screamed and stumbled from the room.

She desperately ran into the kitchen and grabbed a knife, not knowing what to do next. She stood there shaking with fear and despair. Suddenly, she felt her arm being grabbed. She turned violently and stabbed out. In a single instant, she was back in the clearing. Her heart sank as she saw Simon lying on the ground, writhing in pain, a knife wound piercing his side. He clutched the wound and struggled to keep his blood from gushing out. She knelt and desperately tried to stop the bleeding. Tears began streaming down her face as blood spilt out over her hands.

"This has to be a nightmare," she cried. "I'm sorry, I thought…"

"I'm okay, I'm okay," Simon said, clearly in horrendous pain.

"I thought…" She looked confused.

Simon summoned a smile. "It's okay. Go, save Daniel. Take him away, far away,"

The creature screeched, and its grotesque laughter echoed about them. They both felt a burning pain, as though it scraped their soul.

"I love you so much. Look after Daniel." Susanna stood up with a precise determination.

"No! Run, please!" Simon tried to hold onto her, but the pain was unbearable, and he folded over.

She walked from Simon and stood alone in the clearing as though she was challenging the beast. It took the bait and rose high in front of her, towering over her. It was a grotesque amalgamation of broken limbs, twisted and contorted, pulsating malevolent energy. Its eyes were black as sin, emanating a hatred born from the deepest layers of reality where Light could never exist. Its tendrils snaked out, creating a canopy of dripping venom that burnt the ground where it touched. It opened its mouth, revealing layers of razor-sharp knives and a blackened tongue that begged to taste Susanna's flesh.

Susanna fell to her knees and clasped her hands in prayer. "Efanu, light that is Light. Efanu, that is life that is Life. I freely give my blood so that my blood may live. Efanu, hear me. Efanu, grant my prayer."

Then, in a loud snap, the beast came down on Susanna, and she was gone. The beast roared in laughter as fresh blood ran from its mouth.

"Susanna!" Simon cried out; all hope left him.

The beast approached him, and an evil smile spread across its shadowy face. It filled his mind with despair, images of Susanna's suffering and Daniel's death.

Simon broke. "I am lost. All is lost," he said, and collapsed.

Suddenly, the beast screamed. It writhed

about and twisted in agony. A small shaft of intense light burst from it, emanating from somewhere deep within its body, then another and another. Its wails were agony to hear. Then, as quickly as it had appeared, it exploded in a shower of bright sparks and flames, leaving behind a charred crater and a foul stench.

It was gone. Daniel was safe, for now.

...

When he would fall into a deep dream, lost in some distant world, she would come to him, always by his side, keeping him safe, but always just out of focus, and as he stared out into the emptiness, deep blue eyes looked back at him, always leading him back home.

She looked down at him. "Daniel," she whispered, her voice carried on a dream. "Daniel, I love you."

Daniel's thoughts wandered aimlessly, lost in a sea of confusion and uncertainty. He felt a deep yearning for a sense of direction, purpose, and a desire to find his place in the world. As he traversed the vast expanse of his mind, he explored different possibilities, searching for a glimmer of hope, or perhaps a spark of inspiration. Yet, despite his efforts, he could not shake the feeling of emptiness that gnawed at his soul, leaving him adrift in a sea of endless dreams.

He was always searching, until...

CHAPTER 3

Daniel
Life is a fleeting moment.

Daniel's existence was a fleeting moment in the grand scheme of eternal creation. He experienced joy and sorrow, love and loss, triumph and defeat, much like everyone else who lived before him. He was not a hero or a villain, but just another flawed human being trying to find his way in life.

Everyone has their own journey to walk, run, or ramble through, often going unnoticed. However, Daniel's journey *was* noticed, and though many wished him only happiness, there was one who took a more sinister interest.

Shadow is to Light what Light is to Shadow.

Daniel's early life was much like any other child until his mother died when he was only five. As he grew, he was left with only vague memories of her. He could recall odd moments, a smile, an embrace, but those were hazy at best. His father used to show him pictures of her and tell him stories about her life before he was born. They had travelled worldwide, crossing oceans, exploring jungles, and even visiting old Mayan ruins. As a young boy, he imagined his parents as treasure hunters, searching for lost artefacts from ancient civilisations. His parents were inseparable, always by each other's side, and their life was an endless adventure. However, when Daniel was born, that all changed. His father told him that settling down and starting a family was their greatest adventure, and that his mother loved him very much.

His father tried to bury the pain of loss he felt, but the death hit him hard, and he sank into a depression that would stay with him until the end of his life. When Daniel was older, he pressed his father for answers, but he refused to talk about the circumstances of her death. All he would say is that monsters lurked in the shadows.

His father lost all passion for life, and the wonderland he once lived in faded into a harsh, cold, empty reality. His world had become consumed by Shadow where once there was Light. Unable to cope with his grief, he withdrew from the world and those around him, collapsing into his work. An emptiness fell over him, removing all colour from his life. He forgot about joy, love, and eventually his son.

Daniel eventually spent most of his time living with his grandmother. His father often went away on long trips, sometimes for months at a time. She was a good, kind person, though a little strict sometimes. She lived in an old Georgian townhouse in Bath, Somerset. Daniel always felt a sense of magic whenever he visited her house. It looked ancient and needed a little repair, but it sparked his imagination. He treasured his time spent there, as his grandmother would often spoil him, and she enjoyed the liveliness a young boy brought to her life. He loved exploring her old house; she had spent many years collecting all sorts from all over the world. Her house had no rhyme or order but an eclectic charm that intrigued and perfectly fuelled his imagination.

Daniel particularly enjoyed retreating to the attic, where he'd immerse himself in long-forgotten memories. It was an Aladdin's cave filled with charming relics—clothing from the past, odd trinkets, unusual statues, and many books. However, what captured his attention most was the old photographs of his parents. His father had stored everything that reminded him of Susanna there, boxes piled with clothes, memorabilia, and any memory of their life together. He sometimes felt his father wished he could pack him away too. Armed with only a flashlight, he'd sit for hours pawing over old photos of his mother's youth, arranging them chronologically from her birth to the most recent. Her entire life, so fleeting, was laid out before him. Whenever he stumbled upon a photograph of his parents in a far-off place, he would let his imagination run wild and conjure up elaborate stories of their travels. He created a scrapbook, with each page holding a photograph and a few words scribbled down about the adventure he had imagined. This was how he remembered them, full of life.

It was decided that Daniel would permanently live with his grandmother. His father made the difficult decision to sell their family home and move into the old house with them. While Daniel was filled with excitement about the new arrangement, it also served as a bittersweet reminder that his childhood home was now a part of his past. Like leaves falling from a tree, one chapter of his life had ended, which left a lingering feeling of melancholy.

He never spent much time with his father, but it was something that he longed for. He tried to get his attention whenever his father was home, but he always appeared preoccupied. Nevertheless, Daniel's fondest memory with him occurred one particular year, during the school holidays.

His father returned after being away much longer than usual. Still, Daniel noticed that something about that trip seemed different from the other times. His father was excited about something, but he wouldn't say what. While at home, he spent his days buried in his laptop and studying what Daniel thought were musty old papers. He tried to get his father's attention, but no matter how he tried, his father would push him away, saying things like "not now" and "maybe later." His grandmother would often find him asleep on the floor just outside his father's study, and she would gently wake him and put him to bed.

His father rarely left his study unless he needed to. When he returned, he would quickly lock the door behind him. On one occasion, he rushed from the room and inadvertently left the door open. Daniel snatched the opportunity to peer in while his father was away. He saw piles of books and papers spread all over the small room. There were unusual statues and plaques adorned with strange symbols. He picked up one of the papers, written in a text he did not recognise. The characters were scratched into the parchment, yet they stood out as though each symbol penetrated his mind.

"It is a language that has long been forgotten," his father said, standing at the door, carefully watching his son.

Daniel dropped the paper and went pale with fright. "Sorry, the door was open," he said, expecting to be scolded.

His father pondered the situation for a while, which seemed like a lifetime to young Daniel. He walked over to his desk and sat down.

"There are monsters lurking in the shadows, son," he said.

Daniel gulped and stood staring, daring not to speak.

"When your mother died..." He paused. "Well,

I saw things that I never want you to see."

Daniel nodded his head, though he didn't understand.

"Go," his father said.

Daniel turned to run out of the room, but his father stopped him. "I have something I have to do," he said, looking away and staring out the window. "I don't know when I'll be back."

Daniel swallowed the lump in his throat that threatened to spill over. He could read the worry in his father's eyes and the weight that seemed to crush him. He wished he knew what to say, but he stood motionless.

"How about you come with me? I must meet someone, but afterwards, let's do something together." He turned to look at Daniel. "What do you say?"

Daniel was shocked by his father's words but smiled broadly. "I'll tell Nan. When are we going?" he said eagerly, unable to hold his excitement.

"A few weeks yet, I think." His father smiled warmly, something Daniel hadn't seen for a long time. "Now, close the door, please."

Daniel rushed from the room to find his grandmother, slamming the door behind him.

After several weeks of impatient waiting, the time came for his father to leave. However, Daniel was looking forward to his father's departure this time because he would be going with him.

His grandmother had packed for Daniel; she covered every eventuality. In his case, besides a plethora of clothing, there were plasters, bandages, emergency contact numbers, and even food and drink. He said a rushed goodbye to his grandmother, then dragged his suitcase to the cab waiting outside, eagerly clambered in, and waited for his father to join him.

As he sat there gazing out the window, lost in imagination, he noticed his father and grandmother talking, but there were no smiles. He felt something was wrong, but the joy of finally leaving with his father outweighed any concern.

"Where are we going?" he asked his father when he entered the cab and sat beside him. Daniel realised he had no idea where his father was taking him.

"You'll see." His father smiled.

They stepped out of the cab and into a bustling scene of travellers from all over the world. Daniel's eyes widened as he heard snippets of conversations in languages he didn't recognise. He felt excitement and curiosity as he wondered where these people came from and where they were going. He followed his father to the check-in counter, where they handed over their passports and luggage. Then they made their way to the gate; high above was a sign that read *Paris, France*.

Daniel couldn't believe he was about to visit the same place that Andrew Mulkinny, a boy in his class, had just visited with his parents. Andrew bragged that his parents always took him away to the best places and often showed the class pictures of him on massive rides at various theme parks. Daniel was not amused. He didn't like Andrew at all, and thought he was a royal pain who looked down on everyone else. Daniel now intended to top him, because when he returned, he hoped to have some pictures of his own to show to his classmates. He smirked, imagining the look on Andrew's face when he realised that he had outdone him.

They found a place to sit overlooking the runways and made themselves comfortable;

they had several hours before their flight departed. Daniel was given some spending money and told he could explore the nearby shops and kiosks. Still, he was warned to stay close and return within an hour. However, he returned within ten minutes, bearing a few magazines and a sizable gift bag brimming with sweets.

"You weren't gone long," his father said, surprised.

"I didn't really want anything," Daniel said.

"I can see," his father said and laughed, looking at the armful Daniel was carrying.

"We going to France?" Daniel said, contently sucking on a gobstopper.

"Yes, we are off to Paris. I thought we could go to the theme park there," his father said.

"That would be so cool!" Daniel excitedly replied. "Andrew in my class was boasting about it," he said, disgruntled. "I never thought that I would ever go too!"

His father smiled. "I'm glad you're happy." He paused and sounded sombre. "We will have to meet someone first," he added, "after we arrive."

Daniel looked at him and was about to ask who, but his father interrupted.

"Before you ask, it is someone I haven't seen since your mother..." He paused, and a strange expression grew across his face. "Since..." He didn't finish his sentence or elaborate on the person they would meet, and he would say no more about it.

Daniel stared out the window, mesmerised by the sight of the aeroplanes as they landed and took off. He imagined they were giant silver birds landing and then soaring, climbing above the clouds, leaving the world and going to some far-off planet. Daniel made up stories and adventures about the people hidden inside; he wondered where they were going and if any of them would ever be coming back. He imagined some could be going to a magical place where dragons and fairies lived.

A sense of exhilaration and fascination coursed through him as his imagination burst into life, and he couldn't help but wonder what lay beyond his familiar town. The possibilities seemed endless, like a vast sea waiting to be explored. It was as if he had been given a key to a secret door, and he couldn't wait to unlock it and see what lay on the other side. His heart raced with anticipation, eager to discover all that the world had to offer.

However, his thoughts were anchored on the theme park where, he heard, you could ride on a roller coaster that went upside down. Daniel slipped into a daydream as he slowly made his way through his bag of sweets.

"You'll feel sick if you eat all that," his father said, quickly stealing a cola bottle.

"Nah," Daniel answered as he stuffed another sweet in his mouth.

After a long wait, they finally boarded the plane and settled into their seats. Daniel watched the world outside the window shrink as they soared into the sky. *I'm in the belly of a silver bird*, he thought, and looked about anxiously. However, Daniel felt a wave of drowsiness wash over him as he listened to the soothing sound of the engines. He drifted into a dreamless slumber, unaware of the passing time.

After they touched down and the plane stopped, his father gently nudged Daniel. "Wake up, sleepy. We're here."

Daniel yawned and stretched his arms. He was surprised to hear an announcement over the

Tannoy: "Welcome to France." He looked out the window and saw a sign that said *Bienvenue en France*.

After they had left the airport, Daniel's father remained quiet during the drive to the hotel. His father's silence didn't worry Daniel; he was more fascinated by the new sights and sounds of the city, especially the signs written in a language he couldn't read. He remembered his French lessons and realised he hadn't been paying attention in class. He expected he would have felt like a stranger among the people here, but he realised they were not so different from him. They all had hopes and dreams, fears and worries. He smiled and thought, *people are people, no matter where they are*.

They checked into the hotel and went up to their room. As soon as they entered, his father disappeared to the bedroom, closing the door behind him. Daniel heard him dialling a number and whispering something, but he couldn't understand what he was saying. A few minutes later, his father came out and told him to get ready.

As they left the hotel, Daniel trailed behind his father, admiring the scenery around them. The street was bustling with activity, and lined with small shops that sold a variety of items, from clothes and meats to flowers and more. However, it was the irresistible smell of freshly baked bread that caught his attention and made his stomach growl. Many of the buildings were old, but their intricate stone architecture was a testament to their rich history and grandeur. They towered high above, each telling their own story and making their presence known with an impressive beauty.

The busy street was a melting pot of cultures, with tourists and locals alike hurrying from one shop to the next. The cacophony of voices and footsteps echoed off the buildings, creating a symphony of city life. The storefronts were bursting with vibrant colours and intricate designs, luring in anyone who walked by. But to Daniel, it was more like the Venus flytrap that he had seen once in class, enticing unsuspecting prey with its alluring facade. He couldn't help but feel a sense of sadness as he watched them, lost in their own worlds, unable to appreciate the simple joys in front of them.

They passed a talented musician strumming his guitar and singing loudly with a fierce passion. Daniel's father gave him some coins to give to the young busker, who flashed a grateful smile in return. With each step, Daniel felt increasingly immersed in this new world he was experiencing alongside his father. He was happy, and he never wanted the feeling to end.

They walked for about half an hour before stopping at a café. Above the door hung an old wooden sign: *Fin du voyage*. A small brass bell rang as they opened the door. The interior was small with rustic decor, with dark overhead beams and yellowing walls covered in old photos showing different scenes from a Paris now long gone. A handful of wooden tables were scattered about, draped in plain tablecloths, each with a small vase holding a freshly cut flower.

Daniel's father told him to pick a table and he would bring over some drinks and food. Daniel scanned the room and found a corner spot with a window view. He sat down and waited for his father to join him. He wasn't hungry; he felt tired despite sleeping on the plane. He wondered who his father was meeting and what they would talk about. His father had been acting strange since they'd arrived in France, which made Daniel feel uneasy about the whole situation. He had enjoyed the journey, but anxiety grew inside him as he waited in the café for this mysterious visitor.

His father came over carrying a small tray. He handed Daniel a soft drink and a sandwich. Daniel smiled but looked uneasy at the sandwich; it looked a little fancy for his tastes, and he poked at it with his finger. His father placed a hot cup of black coffee on the table and sat down.

"We're here to meet someone who…" he paused and turned towards the window as though he was looking for someone, "who I hope can help me with something that is very important."

"Help?" Daniel asked inquisitively, but his father remained transfixed on the entrance and did not hear his question.

Just then, there was a slight ringing sound, and the cafe door opened, and an odd-looking man walked in. He had an unkempt appearance with wild and scraggly hair that looked like it hadn't been brushed for weeks. He had a quirky fashion sense and wore a long, old coat that looked like it had seen better days. Daniel caught his gaze, and the man's intense, mad eyes locked onto him. His facial features were sharp and defined, with high cheekbones and a thin, pointed nose. Daniel stared wide-eyed, unable to move. However, the man suddenly smiled broadly, and though he appeared to be a bit peculiar, he radiated a warmth and kindness that instantly put Daniel at ease. His father jumped from his seat and rushed over to him, and they embraced as brothers would.

"Zack! How are you?" his father's excited voice carried across the cafe.

"Good, good. Nice to see you again, Simon."

Daniel thought that Zack's gruff voice suited his appearance perfectly. They sat down at the table. Daniel stared at Zack and wondered if he was an actual wizard.

"This is Daniel," his father said with pride.

"Daniel," Zack said, studying him. "You look a lot like your mother."

Daniel smiled at hearing this but remained silent. He listened as his father and Zack talked about many things, often drifting back to when Daniel's mother was still alive. They joked and laughed; it was a side of his father he had never seen before. Daniel looked around the cafe at the other people in there.

Some quietly read books, while others were buried in their papers. Couples were laughing and joking with each other whilst others sat intermittently, breaking the silence between them with a passing comment. He watched quietly while sipping his drink and wondered how his parents would have acted if they were both here.

There was another clanging of the bell above the door. It swung open once more, and a couple entered with a pram. Daniel watched as the man and woman spoke quietly, exchanging a kiss before she headed to the counter. The man leaned towards the pram and smiled caringly. They then sat at a table at the opposite end of the cafe.

A moment later, she went to where the man sat, carrying a tray of drinks and a couple cakes. They looked like the perfect couple; they laughed together and seemed comfortable in each other's company. The baby started to cry a little, so the woman leaned over and took it out of the pram. Daniel stared as she cradled the baby in her arms. The baby seemed to love being held. As he watched, he wondered what it would feel like to be held like that.

A couple stood up to leave, lingering for a

moment in front of Daniel, blocking his view of the baby. He turned back to his table and took a sip of his drink. When he looked again, the baby was being held over her mother's shoulder; she gently rubbed its back, and it gave out a loud burp. Daniel chuckled. The baby looked up at Daniel, and he could tell it was a girl with deep blue eyes. She just stared at him, and he stared back. They were locked in each other's gaze. Daniel felt that he knew her, but that was impossible.

For the briefest of moments, he was no longer in the café, but standing on the top of a hill, and standing in front of him was a woman with deep blue eyes. He went to speak but found no words, and then she smiled. Suddenly, he was back in the cafe, staring at the baby as before. Without any thought, he stood up out of his chair. It was like he fell into a trance and started to walk over to the little baby, and then he felt his father's hand on his arm.

"Where are you going, Danny?" he said, looking in the direction his son was walking.

This snapped him out of the trance he was in. "Oh, just to the toilet," Daniel said, confused.

"Okay, I think it's over there," he said, pointing

to the rear of the cafe.

Zack stood up, shook Daniel's hand, and told him to enjoy the theme park, suggesting some rides he should look out for.

Daniel made his way to the toilet and stood in a cubicle for a while. He felt confused about what had happened with the little baby; at ten years old, this was too much for him to handle. He decided to forget about it and concluded that it was all just too weird for him to process. By the time he returned to his father, the couple, the baby, and Zack were gone. He sat back down.

"Did he help?" Daniel asked.

His father looked surprised at the question. "Yes, he will help," his father said, sounding like a small weight had been lifted from his shoulders.

Daniel and his father walked outside, and his father turned to him, looking thoughtful. "I only want to protect you. There is something that I cannot say, something that…" he looked strained, "that we found, something…" He awkwardly smiled as his words faded. "Just know that I love you, son, and always will."

Daniel didn't know how to respond and

smiled awkwardly. His father knelt in front of him and hugged him. "It will be okay in the end," he said.

"It's okay, Dad," Daniel said, smiling awkwardly at him.

He gave a little laugh. "Yes, it is." He paused. "Yes, it is, son." He wiped away a tear. "Now let's find that theme park."

...

When Daniel was eleven, his father started to spend longer periods away, sometimes many months at a time, and these long absences hit Daniel hard. He often sat alone outside school at the end of each day. He watched kids being picked up by their mothers and fathers and pretended he was in their place. He watched parents hug their kids, playfully rub their heads, and warmly smile at them. However, in Daniel's imaginary world, he was receiving that attention. He imagined what life would have been like if his mother were still there, and that was his parents waiting to take him home. Long after everyone had left, he would make his way back, often lost in a fantasy world far removed from his reality.

He missed his father and felt lonely without

him. He loved his grandmother dearly, and she did her best to fill the void left by Daniel's parents, but it was an emptiness that lingered and could not be filled. He often skipped school, and his grandmother was called in to talk to the headmaster on several occasions. Rather than scolding Daniel, she would take him to the park, and they would sit on a bench by a lake and feed the ducks. They talked for hours about life and his future, but the conversation would drift to her past. She would tell him about the times she was in school and the many mischiefs she and her friends used to get up to.

"Life's not so bad, Danny," his grandmother said, throwing a piece of bread in the air only to see a seagull swoop down and snap it up before it could hit the water. "It's for the ducks!" she raised her voice, scorning the seagull, who looked indignant.

"I know, I know," Daniel said, swinging his legs. He went to throw a slice of bread into the lake, but his grandmother stopped him and tore it into smaller pieces. He took those pieces and shared them equally with the excited ducks under the watchful gaze of his grandmother. "What was she like?" Daniel finally said after he had thrown his last piece of bread.

"Your mother?" his grandmother said, sighed, and then a broad smile was drawn across her face, and she chuckled. "She could be a little terror at times, but the most caring person I ever met."

Daniel looked at his grandmother curiously.

"Well, your mother was the perfect student. All the teachers loved her." She paused to scowl at the seagull stealing bread from the ducks. "Until…" She trailed off.

"Until?" Daniel asked.

"Oh, yes, until she met your father!" she said sternly, but then her expression softened. "They were a pair: inseparable, mischievous, and perfectly matched."

"Dad doesn't say much about her. Well, he says nothing." Sadness spread over Daniel's expression, and he stared blankly at the ground, trying to kick at a small clump of grass.

"Ah, your father, well, he's…" She hesitated. "Anyway, I'm happy to tell you." His grandmother gestured for him to stop fidgeting with the grass. "They first met when they were around thirteen or maybe fourteen," she mumbled, scratching her head as she tried to remember.

"Nan? I get it. They were young," Daniel said, eager to hear more.

His grandmother frowned at him.

"Sorry," Daniel said, avoiding eye contact.

"That's okay, Danny." She offered a reassuring smile. "When they first met, I was not too happy, I can tell you. Some scallywag dating my daughter," she said playfully. "But your dad has his charms, and I grew very fond of him, but I think your grandad may have taken a little longer to warm to him." She laughed and then sighed.

They stayed quiet for some time, lost in reflection, while the ducks squabbled over the last bits of bread bobbing on the water's surface. The gentle waves on the lake lapped against the shore in a soothing rhythm that instilled a feeling of calmness.

"I like it here," his grandmother said.

"So do I, Nan," Daniel replied, enjoying the sun's warmth.

"Your mother was a caring soul." She paused as a memory filled her mind and she grinned. "I remember a time when I thought we had a mouse infestation. Me and your granddad tore the house apart looking for a nest. It was quite the palaver, I can tell you." She smiled. "Well, it turned out that our little Susanna had brought home an injured mouse, nursed it to health, and decided that it should live with us. So, she made quite the nest in her dollhouse." She broke out into a chuckle. "Needless to say, the mouse didn't stay long, and your grandad was not amused. He grounded her for two weeks."

Daniel listened intently, absorbing every word as his imagination recreated the scene, moment by moment. He loved the stories that his grandmother told him. They gave him a window into a happier time. He sat back and looked up at the blue sky. He watched as large white fluffy clouds formed different shapes; he thought one looked like a duck and laughed to himself.

"What's so funny?" his grandmother asked, looking at him curiously.

Daniel pointed to the cloud high above. His grandmother laughed too. "That looks remarkably like a duck, wouldn't you say?"

On some occasions, Daniel found the courage to run away from home. He imagined elaborate schemes for how he would travel around the world and find his father. However, he would end up at the train station, staring at all the destinations, wondering where to start. Finally, it would get late, and he would turn away, defeated, and return home, feeling disillusioned and empty. He returned only to find his grandmother waiting for him with chocolate cookies, a hot drink, and a warm embrace.

When he was much older, he often thought fondly of his time with his grandmother and regretted that he had put her through so much worry. He would laugh to himself, now realising that she was right most of the time.

When Daniel was sixteen, his grandmother passed away, and his home life became empty. His father had inherited her house, so Daniel's daily life continued. However, despite his friends, his sense of loneliness grew without his grandmother there. He missed her company, the stories that used to captivate him, and even how she sometimes scolded him.

After she passed away, his father's preoccupation with work only intensified. He appeared oblivious to any of Daniel's needs, often leaving him to fend for himself. Daniel would regularly hang out with his friends at their ageing camp and stay at Robbie's house on weekends whenever he could. However, when he was back home, the feeling of loneliness was overwhelming, and he would retreat to the attic to look through the scrapbooks he had made when he was younger. It was in those brief moments that he found a sense of happiness amidst the bittersweet memories.

When Daniel's father was away, Mrs. Fredure, a friend of his grandmother's, stepped in to help with the household tasks and daily meals. Despite her kindness and gentle nature, he found it hard to interact with her. She reminded him too much of his late grandmother and stood as a constant reminder that his grandmother would never be coming back. Nonetheless, Mrs. Fredure came to their house every day like clockwork, always trying her best to comfort him.

The memory of his last conversation with his father lingered in Daniel's mind like a dull ache. His father had promised it would be the last time he left and that things would be different when he returned. But those words were empty promises, as his father never did come back. This realisation hit Daniel hard, leaving him with a sense of abandonment and confusion. Phone conversations became sporadic, brief exchanges filled with strange questions about dreams and shadows.

Eventually, it was decided that Mrs. Fredure would move into the house permanently to care for Daniel; this decision only confirmed to him that his father would not be coming home again. The once comforting walls of their home now felt empty and cold. The weight of the truth settled heavily on Daniel's mind as he tried to come to terms with his father's broken promise.

"I guess monsters do lurk in the shadows," Daniel whispered into the darkness as he lay staring up at his bedroom ceiling.

...

Daniel awoke bright and early and ran downstairs to a breakfast of pancakes and golden syrup waiting for him on the kitchen table.

"Happy thirteenth birthday!" his grandmother said, warmly hugging him, "My, you are getting tall."

"Oh, Nan." He sat down and started on the food. "Do you think Dad will make it back today?" he said with a mouth full of pancakes and syrup dripping down his chin.

"Don't speak with your mouth full, please," she said sternly.

"Sorry," he answered with his mouth full.

His grandmother turned away and started washing some dishes, wanting to avoid eye contact. "I am sure he will do his best."

Daniel polished off his pancakes, then rushed into the living room to be greeted with many presents. He quickly scanned the room, looking for one particular present, but it wasn't there. He sighed and started unwrapping his gifts, each of which he carefully inspected before moving on to the next.

His grandmother had rushed in and stood by the door watching, not wanting to miss the event. Daniel scooped up his farrago of toys and placed them on the dining room table. He sat down and started to play with them.

"I have one more for you." She smiled and gave Daniel an old camera. "This was mine, but I want you to have it. I hope that it will capture those happy memories." She gave him a warm hug. "Oh yes," she added, "there is one more, you know," she said with a broad cheeky smile. "Garage, perhaps?"

He leapt from the table, ran outside across the garden to the garage, and slid open the heavy door. A brand-new Chopper stood, shiny red with three gears of pure power. A card was taped to it: *Have a happy birthday, love, Dad.* The card meant he wasn't coming, and his heart and enthusiasm sank.

His grandmother walked to the garage to find Daniel sitting solemnly on the floor.

"Now, Daniel Halton, I will not have a moody teenager sulking in my garage, especially on his birthday," she said, pretending to scold him.

He shrugged. His grandmother went over to the bike. "Right," she said and awkwardly sat on the bike. He looked up, not sure whether he should laugh or panic. "Here we go!" His grandmother pushed off and flew down the road.

He watched agape, quickly got to his feet, and chased her down the road, shouting, "Stop! Stop!"

...

Robbie walked around the bike, scratching his chin. Every now and then, he would lean in for a closer look and make a grunt of satisfaction.

"Yes, yes," he finally said after several minutes, "I can see that this particular model is red."

Daniel laughed. "Is that all you have to say? Red?"

"Well, it is, isn't it?" Robbie said, grinning. "Let's have a go then."

Robbie climbed on the bike and raced off down the street, swerving in and out of parked cars and coming to a skidded stop just out of Daniel's sight.

"Hey, Danny!" Samantha called out and ran over to him.

"Oh, hi, Sam," he said, trying to see why Robbie hadn't returned.

"Happy birthday!" she shouted and proceeded to sing that well-known birthday song.

Daniel waited patiently for her to stop. "Yeah, thanks."

"What's up with you? Anyway, don't worry

about that." She produced a small box that she was hiding behind her back.

"Oh, thanks." He took the package and tore away the neat wrapping. Samantha watched eagerly, waiting to see his reaction.

He opened the box, and it was a torch. Samantha jumped up with excitement. "Thanks," Daniel said again.

"Thanks?" Samantha growled.

"Yeah," Daniel said, inspecting the torch.

"That is no ordinary torch, you know. It is the Z-Max." She waited for the reaction, but it never came. "The Z-Max!" she shouted, bursting with excitement.

Daniel rotated the torch in his hand. "Looks like a nice torch, thanks," he said.

"Oh, really!" Samantha said, then stomped her foot and crossed her arms with a huff.

Robbie returned and jumped off the bike, trying to pull some stunt that didn't work, causing him to fall. Daniel rushed over to his bike, looking for scratches or any damage.

"Robbie!" he shouted angrily.

"What? I'm fine. No damage done, calm down," he said dismissively. "Oh hi, Sam. How's it going?"

"Robbie, that was a gift from his father," she said sternly.

"Oh," Robbie said more apologetically. "Sorry, mate."

"Doesn't matter," Daniel shrugged. " Anyway, how did you know it was from my father?"

"Nan," Samantha said. "Your Nan spoke to my Nan, who spoke to me," she said with a smile.

"What's that?" Robbie said and took the torch from Daniel. "Ooo, a Z-Max, nice."

"See, it's a cool present!" Samantha said.

"I never said it wasn't," Daniel retorted.

"A very cool present; however, not as cool as mine," Robbie added.

He vanished into his house, returned with a small package, and eagerly gave it to Daniel. "Open it, open it!"

Daniel opened it, and it was a flint pack, some strips of wood, and string. It was a fire starter set. "Cool, thanks."

Samantha huffed. "Yes, that is cool. I just got a thanks!"

"Party later?" Robbie asked.

"Nah, I don't really want any fuss," Daniel said.

"No fuss? It's your birthday. We have to celebrate," Samantha insisted.

"No fuss," Daniel demanded. "I have to go. Meet at the base later? Around five?" Daniel said.

Robbie and Samantha both agreed. Daniel climbed on his bike and rode home. Robbie and Samantha watched, then turned to each other and mischievously smiled.

"Party at the base then," Robbie said.

"Party at the base," Samantha agreed.

...

He was running late; his grandmother baked him a cake and invited friends to celebrate Daniel's birthday. He sat there listening to three elderly ladies talk about when they were thirteen, then sang him a happy birthday and watched him blow out the candles. Only then was he allowed to leave.

He raced down the road on his bike, along

the tarmac, throwing spray into the air as he splashed through a puddle running off one of their neighbours' drives. He flicked the gear down to second and leant into a turn so hard he nearly fell off his bike. He entered a lane at the back of the houses that lined his street and peddled hard until he reached the end. He turned onto a smaller dirt path, which ran alongside tall trees with long branches that swayed eerily in the wind. The lane narrowed, and the bushes brushed against the sides of his hands as he held the bars. He pushed through it and squeezed his body in as tight as he could until he reached the edge of the small wood, where he had to lift his bike over a low wooden fence and wheel it along a muddy path that only the local kids knew.

Eventually he came to a clearing, and in the middle was an old, large, dead tree. Its bark had been burnt away long before they had discovered the place. Under it was their makeshift base, more a collection of random pieces of branches, leaves, and a battered piece of blue tarpaulin that someone had dumped at the edge of the woods. It looked like a poorly made teepee.

"Hello?" he called out. He looked about but couldn't see anyone. Suddenly, he was struck with terror. "No, no, please, no," he said.

A familiar song rang out from behind the tree. A second later, the procession appeared. "Happy birthday to you, happy birthday to you," they went on relentlessly in their goal, "Happy birthday, dear Daniel, happy birthday to you!"

They all laughed as Daniel played dead, lying still on the ground.

"Get up," Robbie said and lightly kicked Daniel's foot.

"Ow, okay, I'm alive." Daniel got up to see not only Robbie and Samantha, but Richie, John, and James were there too. "Hi, guys," he said.

They nodded in recognition. Samantha rolled her eyes. "Please, now, who's for cake?"

"Cake?" Daniel said.

"I am prepared," she said smugly. She vanished for a moment inside the base and came out with a tray of cakes, crisps, and a bottle of orange Tango. "Your favourite." She smiled.

They all helped themselves to what was on the tray. Samantha handed out the cups and poured a little drink into each.

"A toast," Robbie said, "to Daniel!" They all cheered and drank. "Right, let's build that fire!" he said excitedly.

Robbie sent everyone in the group off to find dry wood despite Samantha's objections. He had every intention of making use of the gift he had given Daniel. After about thirty minutes, everyone eventually returned. However, Richie was not happy because he had slipped and fell into some mud. He skulked for a while, but Samantha gave him the last piece of cake, and his mood brightened.

Robbie pulled out a small booklet simply called *Camping*. He was meticulous as he flipped through the pages, carefully studying the diagrams and directions. Robbie would look up occasionally and point to a specific location where and how he wanted the firewood placed.

Daniel watched him work with care and grace; he thought it was like watching an artist, or perhaps a budding young arsonist at work. However, he was oblivious to the attention, purely focused on the task at hand. Several times, Samantha sighed in disapproval. She made it very clear that she thought this was a bad idea. However, when

Robbie had finally finished, they all stepped back to admire what they had built. Even Samantha was reluctantly impressed.

"Now," Robbie announced, "the birthday boy, who carries the power of fire, must fulfil his destiny," he roared as though he were at some ancient ritual.

"I must obey," Daniel feigned hypnotic compliance, walking over to the strategically placed pile of wood and dry leaves. He knelt at the designated opening and took out his fire starter kit when he heard a loud voice shriek behind him.

"And what do you think you are doing?!" A small girl barged into the clearing, flanked by two slightly taller girls. They were each dressed in a girl guide uniform.

"Who are you?" Daniel said in surprise.

"I am Jessica, and that doesn't matter. Do you know you shouldn't be starting fires?" she said ferociously.

"Look, little girl. We will do whatever we want. This is our base, so go far away!" Robbie said confidently.

"Oh really?" came an unexpected reply. "I'm

not scared of you, Robbie." She smiled smugly. "I know who you are. I've seen you in school."

Robbie blushed slightly. He didn't expect Jessica to stand her ground. Before long, mayhem broke out, and the two sides started arguing, first about the fire, then who had the right to be in the base, then who had the right to be in the woods, then school sports, and it went on and on.

Eventually, Daniel had enough. "Okay!" he shouted as loudly as he could. "Okay!" Everyone stopped and looked at him. "Jessica, being in the girl guides means that you know how to build a fire properly?"

Jessica and her friends all nodded with an air of superiority. Robbie looked away indignantly, and Samantha gave him a stern look to behave.

"Okay, how about you help us with our fire then?" Daniel said, to Jessica's surprise.

"Oh," Jessica said. "Well, as you asked, okay, but we have to follow my rules."

"I can't stand that girl," Robbie whispered to Samantha, who vehemently agreed.

...

He had grown accustomed to not seeing his father, now feeling indifferent towards him. It had been several years since he had left, with only sporadic phone calls from various places around the world. The last time they talked was when he was eighteen. It was the usual unexpected phone call. He said that he was taking a small chartered plane to an island somewhere. It was a routine flight, and his father had taken this trip several times before. However, he sounded more present than usual, and somehow his tone was softer.

"I am proud of you, son," his father said.

"Are you okay?" Daniel asked, concerned.

"It will all be okay in the end," his father cryptically answered, and then the line went dead.

Daniel and his father never spoke again after that moment. He often wondered if his father knew those would be their final words. His body was never found, nor was the aircraft he had been in. After several months of searching, his father was declared dead. The house, all his belongings, plus a considerable sum of money, passed to Daniel.

He sat on the bottom step of the stairs in

the empty house and looked around. Though his father hadn't been there, there was always a glimmer of hope that he would one day return, but his death signified an ending. Memories of his childhood flashed through his mind. He saw his grandmother playing catch with him, his friends running about chasing each other, and he saw himself running to the door to greet his father whenever he came home.

Daniel looked at the study door and realised he had avoided that room ever since he was a young child, and it had been many years since he last found the courage to peer in. Daniel went over to the study and slowly reached for the handle. He felt nervous, as though he was ten years old again. His hand felt sweaty on the brass knob and slipped slightly as he tried to open the door, which was locked as expected. He knelt in front of it and peered through the keyhole. He saw part of his father's desk; it looked neater than he remembered.

Daniel recalled that his grandmother used to keep a box of keys in the attic. Her key box, as she used to say, was an old blue Royal Dansk cookie tin; Daniel had long ago eaten the original contents. He thought perhaps there was a spare. Daniel went up to the attic and started to search for the box of keys.

While searching, he found an old photo that he had never seen before of his father, mother, and a much younger man. Was that the man they met in France all those years ago? What struck him as strange was that they were all standing by the tree in the clearing where he had built a base as a child. That made no sense to him. What were they doing there? As he studied the photo, he noticed that the old tree looked alive, not the husk that it was when he and his friends used to play there.

"Ahh, there you are," he said aloud, his attention drawn to a box poking out from a shelf.

He took the box and went back to the study. He sat on the floor and opened it. To his dismay, there were possibly over a hundred keys. He let out a long, slow sigh and started testing each one in the lock. After about an hour, the lock clicked, the door creaked open, and he sheepishly entered the room.

His father's desk dominated the small room. It was plain but made of solid wood, giving it an elegant air. To the left, a bookcase sat from floor to ceiling. It was full of various books, most of which looked old and worn. On the opposite wall hung a painting of a grassy hill. In the distance, there were fields of flowers. The sun hung low, but the colour made it look like morning. Underneath the painting was an ornate wooden cupboard. It had two large doors on the front. Daniel went over, knelt, and opened them. Scrolls and old parchment fell out to the floor. He picked up a rolled-up parchment and unfurled it. He saw the same scratchings and symbols that he'd seen as a child; it still meant nothing to him.

Daniel sat with his back against the desk, and emotion overwhelmed him. He buried his head in his hands and started to cry. Tears poured from him as he released his hurt, frustration, and loneliness. He screamed, hurling abuse at the world, wanting it all to end, wanting his life to end.

Suddenly he felt a hand stroke his head. "You'll be okay, Danny," his grandmother said. "Don't stay here lost in memory and pain. She is out there, and she is looking for you."

Daniel felt the warmth of his grandmother, and his pain subsided. He slowly looked up, hoping that it wasn't just a dream, but he was alone. He knew he couldn't stay there; he had to go.

"Who is out there?" he whispered. "Am I finally cracking up?" He chuckled morbidly.

With the help of his friends, he spent the next month clearing out the house. Daniel moved all his father's papers and books into storage. He sold most of the furniture and ornaments but kept many items that had personal meaning. The house was sold, and he moved into a small flat in Bristol.

Daniel tried to leave behind everything that connected him to his old life. However, he carried a deep sorrow in his heart since his grandmother passed away, worsened by his father's disappearance. This sorrow seemed to haunt him like a dark presence lurking in the shadows, taunting him with its evil thoughts but never showing itself. He felt it encircling him as though he was prey. He started experiencing recurring nightmares: He was standing by the tree in the clearing where he and his friends used to play. He was a young boy, and the tree looked tall and full of life. He had a feeling that something was stalking him. Night after night, he would hear a terrible sound that seemed to be getting closer and closer, causing him to wake up in a cold sweat.

He grew anxious about sleeping and tried

to stay awake, but eventually fatigue overwhelmed him, and he fell into a dream. That's when he finally saw what was hunting him. It had no distinct form as it remained hidden by a shadowy veil. Only a mass of black tendrils that writhed out of the darkness and twisted like venomous snakes revealed its presence. They hissed and spat a poison that burned and filled the air with rancid odour. It reached out, slithering across the ground in search of Daniel.

Daniel stumbled back in fear and fell to the ground as the creature approached. He desperately tried to drag himself away, hoping to find an escape. Then, a dim light revealed what lurked in the blackness. It had no eyes on its hideous, decaying face, and its mouth was stitched closed with wire, a thick, black liquid oozing from the wound. It sensed his fear and pain and whispered sinister words into his mind. Its purpose was to spread evil and chaos wherever it went. It was a monster born of hell, and it was hungry for Daniel's soul.

Just as it was about to strike, a bright light flashed and it retreated, letting out a grotesque scream. He looked up, and his father, mother, and the man from the coffee shop stood between him and the beast.

The creature howled in agony as a brilliant flash pierced its rancid skin. It twisted and turned in pain and fled from Daniel, who was paralyzed with terror on the floor. He lifted his head and saw his parents and the stranger standing before him, shielding him from the monster. The creature lunged again, its whip-like appendages striking out at them. The stranger was caught and dragged into the shadows, disappearing.

His parents clasped each other's hands and chanted words he could not comprehend. Suddenly, they burned with a luminosity that radiated from them, and as they spoke it grew brighter. The monstrosity uttered a hideous cry of agony as if its soul was being torn apart. It pounced one last time, lashing out at them. Daniel's parents did not waver in their resolve.

Their light suddenly intensified forming an impenetrable barrier that radiated power, enveloping them in a protective shield of pure energy. As the creature clashed with the light, it exploded into a shower of sparks and screams, as though it had been obliterated from existence.

Then, all was quiet.

His mother knelt by her son. "Time to sleep,

my sweet little boy. The monster lurking in the shadow has gone."

Daniel opened his eyes, and a feeling of peace and calmness washed over him, all dread gone. The horrors that had haunted his sleep for so long had left his thoughts; not even a fading memory remained. Instead, he dreamed of happier things: love, joy, and wonder. He felt a new sense of purpose and direction in his life. He was ready to face the day with a smile.

They would sit together on a small hill blanketed in soft green grass. They held hands and gazed at the sun as it peeked over the horizon, painting the clouds pink and gold. A gentle breeze would caress their faces, carrying the scent of flowers. They always turned to look at each other and smiled. They were in a dream world where everything was vibrant, mystical, beautiful, and full of hope. Daniel could see flowers of all shapes and colours around them, some glowing or sparkling. He felt a connection with nature and with her as if they were part of something bigger and more wonderful than themselves. He knew this moment was precious and wanted it to last forever. She became everything, his beginning and end. He instinctively knew she existed and was out there, and he knew he had to find her.

As the years passed, life slowly found its rhythm and normality settled in. The sun rose and set, the world continued to spin as it had since the beginning of time, and daily life continued. Still, the feeling that something was missing lingered long after the pain of loss lessened. He felt unable to decide exactly what he wanted to do with himself. He wandered from job to job, making enough money to travel but forever searching. When he was home, he loved spending time with his friends whenever he could. They were the constant in his life, and he felt alive and free in their company. They always knew exactly how to cheer him up. However, there was a restlessness that he could not shake, the recurring dream of the mysterious woman who had captivated his heart.

There were many times that he swore he saw her in the crowds. But whenever he tried to follow, she vanished like a ghost. He couldn't shake off the feeling that she was real and that he had to find her somehow. He felt a powerful longing to pursue her, even if it meant leaving everything else behind, to follow her no matter where it would take him.

...

Samantha had always loved Cardiff; she called it "Little Bristol." The opportunity arose by chance for her to move there. The owner of the flat where she was staying in Bath fell into financial difficulties and was forced to sell, leaving Samantha desperate to find somewhere new. At the same time, they were making cutbacks at her place of work, and she was made redundant. This was a bittersweet pill. Samantha enjoyed her work; however, she received financial compensation, which meant she didn't have to work for a year if she chose.

The strangest thing happened: Samantha was sitting at a cafe, staring blankly at nothing in particular, wondering what she would do. A waitress bumped the table, spilling the contents of her tray over Samantha. There were many apologies, and Samantha was taken to the staff room to clean up. Two staff members talked about how they hated working there and wished they could leave and start afresh. A newspaper was spread across the table, opened on the job page.

When Samantha came in, they went quiet and promptly left the room. She was given some towels to dry herself. The manager came in with two coffees and sat at the table. She was a young woman who looked too young for the job.

"I am so sorry," she started to say. She pulled the newspaper over and started inspecting the jobs, lingering on each, imagining a new life.

Samantha smiled politely and continued to rub herself down.

After a moment, she turned the newspaper around to face Samantha. "Look at this," the manager said, pointing to a job advert. "If only I had the qualifications needed."

Samantha leaned over. The advert read: bookkeeper needed, flexible hours, apartment available for those wishing to relocate, pay negotiable.

This was too good to be true. "May I take this?" Samantha asked.

The manager shrugged, finished her coffee, and left Samantha to her thoughts.

...

Robbie has always looked for new opportunities from a young age, even if they involved danger or breaking the rules.

He fancied himself as a visionary, always dreaming of the next big thing.

Robbie had a knack for business since he was a kid. He turned the playhouse into his own little enterprise, renting it to his classmates for a small fee. He collected candies, chocolates, and cookies as payment for every quarter of an hour they spent inside. This lasted a month before the teacher noticed the queue forming and promptly ended his thriving business efforts.

He had a talent for influencing people and knew how to charm them. Robbie had many ambitious plans; he was going to be the head of a great business empire, and it was going to be the biggest and best. Clients from all over the world would compete for his services. However, his imagination turned out to be very different from what fate had in store for him. It was his time in university when he would find the one person who would be his match, an encounter that changed his life forever.

"I'm going to be late!" Robbie shouted to anyone who could hear him as he dashed through the crowded hallways racing to a lecture. He barged into other students who were inconveniently loitering, blocking his way. As he pushed past, several rude words were hurled at him. Robbie sheepishly grinned and yelled apologies several times as he dashed along. This was a very important class, a mock exam that he was warned, in unambiguous terms, not to miss.

Robbie sprinted towards his goal, his heart pounding in his chest. He had dodged and weaved through the crowded hallways, ignoring the shouts of, "No running in the hallways!" and the annoyed glares from the other students. He was nearly there, he could almost see the door to the classroom. Robbie rounded the final bend and collided with a young girl running breathlessly in the opposite direction. She had also been in a hurry and had left behind a wake of annoyed and bewildered students.

They collided with a loud thud, and both tumbled to the floor in a flurry of curses. Their books and bags soared into the air and clattered down all about them. They both sat there for a second, stunned by the impact of what just happened. Robbie suddenly blushed when he heard a familiar voice.

"You!" Jesicca shouted when she realised who had run into her.

Robbie stared at her in disbelief. "Out of all the people, you had to be the one!" he exclaimed.

They glared at each other, and then Robbie started to chuckle.

"What's so funny?" Jessica snapped.

"Well, I don't have to rush anymore. I think I've blown my exam," Robbie said, leaning on the wall.

Jesicca's expression softened. "Me too, I think."

Robbie got up and helped Jessica to her feet.

"Sorry you missed your exam," he said while collecting her books.

"Well, it was as much my fault. I'm sorry too." She smiled sweetly.

Robbie looked at her and felt something stir inside him. He was drawn to her in a way that surprised him as much as it would later surprise his friends.

"Can I treat you to a coffee?" Robbie asked, trying to sound charming.

"That would be lovely, thank you." She smiled.

...

Samantha was so excited about the idea of Daniel moving to Cardiff. She thought it would be a wonderful change for him instead of staying isolated in Bristol.

"Cardiff has so much to offer," she told him. "It's a vibrant city, full of friendly people and plenty of opportunities. You won't regret it."

"Perhaps when I'm back home…" Daniel said, and the phone cut out for a second.

"Don't worry about finding a place to stay," she added. "You can crash at my flat until you get settled. I have a spare room and everything."

"I appreciate it, Sam, but…" His phone failed again.

A few minutes went by, and Samantha's phone rang again.

"Sorry," Daniel said. "I'm using a pay phone, and it's eating up my money."

"Okay, so when you're back from Hong Kong, will you move?" Samantha said eagerly. "Robbie and Jess have already found a place," she quickly added.

"When I'm back, I'll come stay, and we'll see what fate brings."

CHAPTER 4

The Eternal Kiss
Moments never last, no matter how you hold on.

"You'll be late!" Tom Lament snorted. He was a short, slightly chubby man with a round face and eyes always darting about as though he was constantly looking for something to complain about.

Robbie smiled dismissively but did not say a word and kept his eyes fixed on finishing his work before leaving for the weekend. He did not like Tom; in fact, nobody in the office particularly liked Tom. He was known as the "Always Watching Guy" and was avoided wherever possible. Unfortunately, Robbie's work cubical was next to Tom's after he drew the short straw at an office party.

Tom would take immense pleasure in pointing out others' shortcomings, especially if he turned out to be correct. It was a well-known fact that Tom was not to be trusted;

just making the wrong comment or the slightest misplaced remark would find your name in what became known as his little red book of horrors. Of course, Tom tried to hide this from his co-workers. Still, secrets are difficult to keep in a small office, especially when a cleaner happened upon it one evening and found their name underlined twice in red ink with the comment, "lazy and doesn't wipe my bin out."

"You'll be late!" Tom repeated gleefully, his little round face grinning broadly.

Robbie usually loved his job, working for a brand advertising company. He was great at inventive ideas, and presentations were his speciality. Usually, he would work late if needed, but today was one day he had to be home on time. He hastily switched off his PC, grabbed his coat and bag, and rushed to the lift lobby, ignoring Tom. He had planned to leave the office early that day, no later than lunchtime; however, his boss had other plans. He asked Robbie to finish the final edits on a project he had been working on. His boss was desperate for the work to be completed before the weekend. It was scheduled to be shown to a client on Monday morning, and many careers were resting on the results of that meeting. So Robbie ended up working through his lunch break, running late, and, to top it all, having to listen to Tom's irritating remarks.

Robbie pressed the lift call button, waited, pressed it again, waited a little more, and then hammered it repeatedly whilst eyeing the stairs. He looked at his watch. *Blast, she's going to kill me*, he thought. He decided to take the stairs to the car park; however, the familiar ping of the lift doors opening caused him to swiftly about turn and run to the lift. A few people clambered out as he squeezed in. He awkwardly shuffled his way to the rear corner of the tight, crowded little metal sweat box. Robbie didn't particularly like small spaces; why he tortured himself daily by using the lift was often a topic of discussion with his friends.

The lift doors started to close. Robbie thought he heard his name being called out but chose to ignore it as only one thing was on his mind: to get home. He had promised Jessica that he wouldn't be late. Nonetheless, she had doubts, as timekeeping wasn't something he was particularly well acquainted with.

His desperation to be on time came about when they decided to have a small bet, thanks to the excessive consumption of alcohol a few evenings before.

"I am rare...rarely...rarely late!" Robbie said, slightly slurring his words. He felt motivated by the power of drunkenness and a desire to prove Jessica wrong.

"Oh, really? You can say that to me, despite being late on so many occasions I've lost count?" she said confidently and sat back, arms crossed.

"I won't be la...laa...late!" He laughed cockily.

"Okay, a small bet then?" She smiled deviously.

"Lay your terms, wooo...womaaaan!" Robbie said, wobbled, and fell over.

"If you are late, even by a single, little, itty bitty second—"

"I won't be," he interrupted and burped.

"So sure of yourself, aren't you?" Jessica said, shaking her head. "You will do the cooking, cleaning, ironing, washing up, and every other house chore for six months!" She waited for his objections.

"What? Are yooou ma...ma...ma... crazy?!" he slurred, lying on the ground.

"I knew it," Jessica mocked. "You, Robbie, are full of it."

"Right," Robbie retorted, struggling to sit up. "I accept your ter...terms, and if I win, you will dooo what...whatever I ask for a period," he paused in thought, "of twenty-four ent...ent... entire hours!"

Jessica smiled confidently. "Agreed."

Robbie gulped hard.

The bet echoed through Robbie's mind, and he regretted ever agreeing to a wager where there was no way he could win.

Then the lift started to move. It went up. Robbie groaned loudly as he glared at a young man who had pressed to go up. The young man avoided eye contact, pretending to read the emergency procedure guide on the wall.

"Would you mind pressing the car park, please?" he called out to two women who blocked the call buttons. They appeared preoccupied with a new brand of lipstick that one of them was now wearing and were oblivious to Robbie's request.

"Excuse me!" he called again, a little louder, then made a coughing sound, causing a young girl standing near him to back away. He reached over and pulled on the sleeve of one of the women, who turned, looking somewhat disgruntled at the interruption.

"Car park, please," he said, feigning politeness.

One of the women, who looked put out, falsely smiled in return. She pressed the car park call button and then returned to her conversation. The lift climbed from floor to floor, and people shuffled in and out of the hot, sweaty box. Robbie turned his back on the others squashed beside him and pressed his face onto the cool lift wall. *When will this end?* he thought and laughed out maniacally, which got the attention of some of his fellow travellers, who seemed to sympathise with the sentiment.

Eventually, the lift headed toward the car park and salvation, though it moved irritatingly slowly. The doors pinged open, people moved in and out, and then the lift lingered for what felt like an eternity before continuing downwards. Robbie's annoyance grew, especially as the small ticking watch that clung to his wrist relentlessly reminded him of how late he would be. He reached the ground-level car park and leapt from the lift in a hail of apologies as he barged past others leaving with him. He didn't stop to look back as he ran, feet slapping against the concrete floor as he raced to his car.

"Where are my keys?" he mumbled as he frisked himself down. A mild panic washed over him when he didn't find them in any of his pockets. *I hope I haven't left them on my bloody desk.*

There was a loud jingle from his trousers. "Thank the heavens!" his voice echoed around the car park as he pulled his keys from a pocket he had previously checked. He hastily unlocked his door, chucked his bags onto the passenger seat, and sat in his car. He glanced at his watch and groaned, then reassured himself that there was still time. The thought of the chores he had agreed to do filled him with dread. *Damn my foolish pride*, he thought, laughing in disbelief. "Why did I have to open my mouth!" he mumbled to himself, shaking his head as he started the car and ground it into reverse.

Suddenly, a pair of hands slammed hard on the roof by the driver's side window, and a panting red-faced man pressed hard against the glass. His spread-out squashed features didn't disguise the familiar face of his manager, Jasper Cockering. Robbie jumped from the window in surprise; the engine stalled as it bounced back, coughing, and the car abruptly stopped. He sat there glaring at Jasper, who appeared to be oblivious to Robbie's annoyance.

"What do you want?" Robbie said, frustration mingled in his tone, heart still thumping in his chest.

Jasper stepped away from the car, took a deep breath, straightened up his clothes, and regained some composure. He was in his early fifties, a short, skinny man. Some would characterise him as stick-like. He wore thick round glasses that enlarged his eyes, creating an almost comical appearance. Jasper was the sort of man who, due to his slight stature, wouldn't be noted entering or leaving a room. He was always overlooked, hence not being considered for any promotions. He was a quiet yet considerate man; however, since Jasper hit his fifties, there was an air of nervous desperation about him, specifically regarding work. He started to notice that he was constantly being overlooked for any promotion in favour of his younger and taller colleagues. This obviously didn't fill him with any sense of self-worth, but instead sent him into a panicked meltdown. This not-so-irrational fear of losing his job drove him to work late nights at the office and most weekends. He had missed his son's graduation, family parties, and even his family's Christmas dinner. However, the final straw for his wife was when he forgot her birthday, which didn't end well for his marriage.

"I needed to talk to you before you left for the weekend." Jasper's muffled voice had a tinge of despair as it penetrated the car.

Robbie frowned, looked at his watch, then at the clock on the dashboard just to be sure and shook his head. *I'm not going to get home on time*, he thought and sighed heavily. Jasper motioned for Robbie to wind down his window, clearly wanting to talk. He reluctantly pressed a button on the driver's door and watched, losing all hope, as the window slowly lowered.

"Hello, Jasper." Robbie sighed, feeling utterly disheartened. "Could this wait? I really need to go."

He shot him an apologetic look. "Sorry, buddy, I just heard that Coltair is going for the same promotion as me." He had an uneasy expression drawn on his face. "Has anyone said anything to you?"

Jasper believed the meeting scheduled on Monday would be the break he was waiting for. He also secretly hoped that this promotion would justify all the time he had spent away from his family and somehow save his shattered marriage, but little did he know his wife had been having an affair with Geoff, a man half his age and twice his build at a local gym, which she visited every Thursday, to "keep fit."

Unfortunately, Geoff's brother knew Simon, who worked at the gym, who knew Susan, who was married to Reolf, who was the mechanic who fixed Eddie's van, whose wife was the hairdresser, who told Tom's wife, who told Tom, who wrote it in his book... Truly unbelievable, Robbie thought.

Robbie shook his head and sighed. "No." He shrugged.

Jasper looked at him intently. "I heard that a few people in our office said that my..." He paused. "You do know it's all just rumours and lies," he said. "Probably that Coltair... If I was younger!" He didn't finish to say what he would have done. Still, Robbie guessed a young, even less muscular and skinnier Jasper probably wouldn't have done much.

"I haven't heard a thing," Robbie interrupted. "Pay it no attention," he lied poorly, and Jasper looked at him suspiciously.

Jasper was possibly the only person on the floor who didn't know about Tom's book of horrors.

"It'll be fine," Robbie lied, feeling sorry for Jasper, knowing full well that everyone was talking about his wife's affair, and in a small office, gossip flows like alcohol at a hen night. A lot!

"Really? Is there something I should know?" Jasper may have been naive about office culture, but when he got a scent, he could be relentless.

"Jasper," Robbie stated abruptly, "perhaps best to ask Tom, better still, about his red book." After he said the words, he instantly regretted it, realising the commotion that would erupt next week. However, that was for another day. Right now, his only concern was to avoid months of house chores.

"Tom?" Jasper said, thinking briefly. "I like Tom. He's one of the good guys, but I will have a quiet word." He smiled, looking content with Robbie's reply.

"Cool," Robbie said. "So, bye?" Robbie went to start his car, only to be waved to stop by Jasper.

"Right, about this meeting." His tone now sounded slightly unnerved. "I really need this to go well."

Robbie smiled reassuringly. "Our last campaign went well. It was a success. We always deliver."

"Yeah, it did go rather well, if I do say so myself." He paused as a sense of accomplishment washed over him, then coughed uncomfortably after seeing the expression on Robbie's face.

"Obviously a team effort." Jasper smiled awkwardly.

"Yeah," Robbie rolled his eyes. "Look, I'll come in early to check everything is okay, but now I'm going home," he said in no uncertain terms.

"Thanks, Robbie." Jasper smiled gratefully. "I appreciate it."

Robbie nodded, started the engine again, and slipped it into gear.

"Sorry, go, go, have a good evening." He waved

Robbie away. "We got this!" he called out, clasping his hands in victory above his head as Robbie hurried off.

Robbie waved his arm out of the window as he drove away. He felt an adrenaline rush surge as he sped out of the car park, swerving around corners like a stunt driver in an action movie. He drove at breakneck speeds through the streets while checking his watch every few seconds. His grip tightened on the wheel as his desire to not have to do the cleaning for months fuelled his acceleration. Robbie made the most of every shortcut, every back road, rampaging through the streets like a man on a mission. Finally, his house came into view, and he slammed on the brakes just in time to not plough into the bins. He leapt from his car.

"I'm early, I can't believe it. I'm actually early," Robbie said to himself as he ran for the door. "Half a bloody hour!" He laughed aloud, oozing with excitement. "I actually won!"

"I'm home!" he called out, whilst casually strolling through the front door. A wide grin spread across his face, accompanied by a very smug feeling.

"You're late," came the reply. "I'm upstairs."

Robbie looked at his watch; it had stopped about an hour ago. "Bloody thing, that's it. I'm getting a new one," he grumbled.

Disheartened, he returned to the car and parked it properly, gathered his coat and bag, and returned to the house. He made his way upstairs, where he could hear Jessica singing to a tune playing on the radio. He opened the bathroom door, and his mood instantly lifted as he looked in longingly at her as she fussed around with her makeup. Her long, slender body beckoned invitingly, covered only by a slight dressing gown that clung to every curve.

"Get ready," she said whilst ushering him away. "We are going to be late."

Robbie grabbed her firmly around her waist as he stood behind her. He leaned in and kissed her neck, breathing in her familiar scent. She arched her back and tilted her head, enjoying the warmth of his breath.

"I love you," he whispered.

She grinned. "And I love you too."

He reluctantly left her and jumped into the shower; a moment later, she peered around the tinted curtain. "Hurry up, and maybe I will treat you later." She looked him up and down, smiled seductively, then slapped him on his bum. Robbie flinched. "Oh, I left some clothes for you on the bed," she said.

Jessica went downstairs and poured herself a glass of red wine. "Do you want a drink?" she called up.

"Yeh, I'll be down now," came a faint reply.

She poured Robbie a Jack Daniel's and sat on the couch, placing the drinks on the low wooden coffee table in front of the sofa. A few moments later, he entered the front room. He wore slim-fit black chinos, a button-down fitted shirt, an elegant waistcoat, and leather brogues.

Jessica turned around. "Looking good," she said with a seductive smile painted on her lips.

"Why thank you." He grinned and brushed himself down.

She waited, looking expectantly at Robbie. "And do you have something you want to say?" she eventually said. She had been looking forward to this moment all month, wearing her new La Camisa dress.

"No," he said, smiled, took a sip of his drink, and pretended to fiddle with his watch.

"No?" she said, surprised.

"Well, er…" He paused and glanced at her. "You look okay," he said, continuing to play about with his watch.

"Okay? Fine!" Jessica folded her arms and looked away irritated. "I guess someone will be sleeping alone tonight!"

Robbie laughed, walked over, knelt in front of her, and gently held her hand. "Jess, you are perfection. You are beauty beyond beauty. You are the angel who stole my heart." He lovingly kissed her gently on her hand.

She blushed subtly, enough for Robbie to notice. "Thank you," she whispered and smiled softly.

They sat on the sofa and made themselves comfortable. "So, what time is the cab coming?" he asked, reaching for his drink.

"About half an hour, I had to change the time because someone was running late." She acted cool.

"This watch stopped again," he said, pointing

to his watch to reinforce his point.

"I told you to change it," she replied.

"Well, I've had it for years. I like it," he said, now defending his watch like an old friend.

"I'm not saying throw it away. You've had it fixed, what, twice now?" she said.

"Three times," he mumbled.

"Three times. Perhaps a new one now, babe?" she asked softly.

"Okay, okay, I'll get a new watch," he conceded, took it off, shook it a couple times, and put it down on the table, accepting defeat. "Anyway, what is the time?"

A car pulled up outside, followed by a hoot. "Time to go." She smiled. "Must be the taxi."

Robbie opened the rear door for Jessica and then jumped in next to the driver, an older man who glanced suspiciously at him. Robbie grinned broadly and cracked a joke, which brought no reaction.

"24 Besden Road, please, mate," he said. He looked at the driver for a moment. "You have quite the poker face."

"Robbie!" she hissed as she nudged him hard in the back.

"What?" he said, undeterred. "What did I do?"

Robbie spent the journey talking to the driver, though the driver didn't talk back, only offering a feigned smile and nod at the appropriate times. The taxi soon pulled up outside Samantha's house. Robbie leant over and tooted the horn. The taxi driver finally spoke, but only to tell Robbie he would be walking if he did that again. Robbie sat back and apologised, then sniggered quietly to himself, receiving a stern look from Jessica.

Samantha came out, hurrying down the path. She opened the car's rear door and climbed in next to Jessica.

"Where have you been?" she said, looking flushed. "You were meant to be here an hour ago!"

Robbie smiled. "Hi, Sam," he said, then returned to instructing the taxi driver how, with a bit of advertising, he could have a fleet of his own taxis. The driver stared blankly out the window, wondering how he ended up here and regretting his life choices.

"Well, someone was late getting home," Jessica

said, looking at Robbie.

Samantha sat back, shook her head, and laughed. "Robbie, are you ever on time?"

"I have been known to be early," Robbie answered, glancing over his shoulder, which ended his conversation with the driver, who smiled in relief.

"He was even late on our first date," Jessica reminded him.

"That wasn't me. I got delayed, and I had to walk," Robbie insisted. "However, nothing was going to stop me from reaching the most beautiful woman alive."

Jessica smiled and blew him a kiss.

"Unfortunately, she wasn't about, so I—" he added and laughed.

Jessica slapped his arm before he could finish. "You're lucky I love you," she said.

"I know I am," he smiled smugly.

...

The taxi pulled up near the club, and they all got out. Robbie paid, gave a tip, and offered his business card. The driver feigned interest and promptly put the card in his glove box to be forgotten until he rediscovered it a year later, crumpled it, and threw it in the bin.

"Look at that queue," Jessica grumbled, exasperated.

"It'll be fine." Robbie's attempt at reassurance was met with a glare.

"I told you not to be late," came Jessica's irritated, mumbled voice. "We'll be queuing for hours."

Robbie rolled his eyes and thought it best not to respond.

"Now, both of you behave, or I will have to put you both in the naughty corner."

"Me and Jess? Alone in the naughty corner? Does that mean I get to be naughty?" He grabbed Jessica and stole a kiss.

Her mood lifted, and she pushed him off, laughing. "Sometimes, Robbie, I could really…"

"Wait till we're back home." He smiled lewdly.

"Oh, get a room, please," mocked Samantha.

They hastily rushed over to join the end of the

queue.

"This is going to take hours to get in here," Jessica sighed, her shoulder slumped.

"Patien—" Robbie decided not to finish his sentence; he recognised the look on Jessica's face all too well and knew best to say nothing. He sighed and pretended to take an interest elsewhere.

"Did anyone catch the show last night?" Samantha piped up.

Jessica looked at her. "What show?"

"*The Money Shot*?" Robbie sniggered.

"Child," Samantha said.

Jessica ignored Robbie. "Can you believe it, the last question he got wrong," Jessica said with certainty. "We all know that coffee comes from the coffee bean, kinda obvious."

"Sorry, light of my life, but you're wrong," interjected Robbie.

"Sure I am," she mocked. "A hundred thousand pounds," she added, thinking of everything she could have bought. "A holiday, probably a cruise around the Med, then come home to the house fully redecorated, new kitchen. Oh, perhaps a pool too."

"A pool? In our garden? Can you imagine going for a swim, looking up, and seeing that grumpy git next door leering out his bedroom window? No, thank you." Robbie shuddered. "We would move," he added.

"Move to a house with a pool." Jessica smiled.

"Anyway, you got the question wrong."

"No, I didn't. Stop trying to get one over on me," Jessica retorted.

"What part of the plant does the coffee bean come from?" Robbie asked.

"Obviously, it is a bean that grows on a plant," she said confidently. "A coffee plant, I guess."

"Nope," responded Robbie.

"Look, say what you want. You won't get me this time." Jessica glared.

Robbie laughed. "I ain't trying to get you. It comes from the coffee plant's fruit." He looked to Samantha for support, who just shrugged.

Jessica laughed. "Fruit?"

"Yep, it would be more accurate to call it a

coffee seed," Robbie added smugly.

"Sam?" Jessica, too, looked for support, but Samantha just shrugged again.

"He's right. It's a seed," came a voice from someone who was taking an interest in their conversation. "Saying coffee comes from coffee beans is like saying a car comes from a car dealership; technically true, but not completely accurate."

"Thank you and shut up, please," Jessica retorted sharply whilst she stretched to see where this unwelcomed confirmation came from, but with no luck, she slumped back down.

"Rude!" the hidden voice responded.

Robbie sniggered. "I think it was meant to be a trick question."

"I guess you didn't see the end of the show?" Samantha said, trying not to laugh at Jessica's expression.

Jessica remained silent.

"No, Jess missed the answer and only caught him losing all that cash," Robbie added.

"Oh," Samantha said.

Her phone beeped, and she rummaged around her handbag looking for it. Silence fell as Robbie and Jessica stared at Samantha, waiting to see who had sent the text, both happy for the distraction. Samantha read her text and chuckled. She looked up to see her friend's faces staring expectantly at her and laughed coyly.

"Well?" Jessica asked.

"Well?" Samantha answered.

"Was it?" She paused. "Well, was it him?"

"Who?" asked Robbie.

Samantha smiled and blushed ever so slightly. "Oh look," gesturing to the front of the queue, "we're finally moving," she said, escaping the subject.

"At last!" said an excited Robbie.

After another thirty minutes of a slow shuffle, they worked their way to the main entrance, where a burly bouncer was barring the way. He had a bored, indifferent look etched on his face, born from years of standing at many different venues. He stepped aside and beckoned them in. Robbie smiled as he passed, but the bouncer ignored him.

The nightclub was alive with energy. People were packed tightly in a writhing sea of bodies. Laughter, chinking glasses, and thumping music filled the air and strobe lights set the atmosphere alight.

"Now, where's Daniel?" Samantha said, finding it difficult to see farther than a few metres.

"He said he would meet us by the bar," Robbie added, raising his voice to be heard above the music.

"Over there, by the bar." Jessica pointed to the far end of the bar.

Jessica and Samantha headed to the cloakroom to check their coats as Robbie pushed through the tightly packed crowd to Daniel.

Daniel turned as he felt a slap on his backside, almost spilling his drink over the girl he was chatting to. He smiled awkwardly and thought, *Robbie has arrived*. He turned to see his friend grinning broadly.

"Danny!" Robbie opened his arms for a hug. "Give me a kiss, birthday boy!"

He stepped in and tried to kiss Daniel on the

cheek, who shrugged him off whilst looking uncomfortable in front of the girl he had been trying to chat up.

Robbie laughed. "Sorry we're late, mate," he said. "You know Jess, always running late."

Daniel laughed and shook his head. "So, were you held up at the office?" he said, knowing his friend well.

Robbie feigned injury. "You wound me." He clutched his chest. "But yes, Jasper chucked some stuff on my desk that I had to get done. Sorry, mate."

"No problem." Daniel smiled and made brief introductions, "Lucy, Robbie. Robbie, Lucy."

"It is very nice to meet you, Lucy." Robbie smiled warmly and bowed. Daniel rolled his eyes and chuckled.

Lucy grinned. "Hi," she said, looking a little awkward now that Robbie had arrived.

"Where are Jess and Sam?" Daniel asked, looking towards the entrance.

"Coats?" Robbie shrugged. "So, birthday boy, what can I get you to drink?"

"I'm good, thanks," Daniel answered, raising

his glass.

"Cool, a double JD, coke and ice, and Lucy?" Robbie said, ignoring Daniel's refusal.

"No thanks." She smiled awkwardly and looked across to the other side of the club to where her friends were standing.

Robbie leaned on the bar, squeezed in, and joined the sea of despairing faces, each trying to make eye contact and catch the bar staff's attention. However, they appeared to be in no immediate hurry as they chatted about a band they all went to see a few nights back. They slowly meandered from person to person, only showing a vague interest in what they were doing. *A sense of some urgency would be nice*, Robbie thought.

"You never said it was your birthday," Lucy said, looking a little put-out. Daniel shrugged. "So, how old are you?"

"It's my fortieth," Daniel said, feigning indifference. "Anyway, age is just age. You're as old as the girl you are feeling," he joked. "So how old are you?"

Lucy did not answer or smile.

"Forty?" she eventually said.

"Yeah, forty," he said a little defensively.

Jessica and Samantha walked over. "Danny!" Samantha said and gave him a warm hug.

"Hello, birthday boy," Jessica added, following Samantha's hug with a kiss on his cheek. She stepped back. "You don't look a day over forty," she jokingly mocked.

Daniel laughed, then uncomfortably looked at Lucy. "Oh, this is Lucy, guys, and Lucy, meet Jess and Sam, my sane friends." He chuckled, and Lucy smirked.

The air thickened uncomfortably as they stood there in silence. Samantha looked at Jessica and mouthed, "What's up with her?" Jessica shrugged.

"So, drinks?" Samantha asked.

"Robbie's at the bar," Daniel answered, "I'll go give him a hand." He moved over to Robbie while he squeezed past his friends and looked at them, pleading for help.

"So, Lucy," Jessica started, "how do you know Daniel?"

Lucy turned to Jessica. "Well, we just met tonight." She acted uninterested.

"So?" Samantha added. "Do you like him?"

"You can't ask that. They just met," Jessica intervened but continued. "So, do you like him?"

Lucy squirmed and looked back over longingly to her friends.

"Sorry, he's a bit old for me, really, and I know he's your friend, but he's a bit…" she lowered her voice to almost a whisper, "well, odd." She shifted uncomfortably. "Oh, I have to go, I think my friends are calling, say bye to…" She pretended to wave to one of her friends, who stood looking in the opposite direction.

"Daniel?" Jessica added.

Lucy smiled clumsily, nodded, and promptly left.

"A gin and tonic for the love of my life," Robbie said, handing Jessica a small glass of liquid. Looking at Samantha, he added, "And for my dear friend, a cosmopolitan."

"Cocktails?" Jessica said, looking at Samantha, who smiled broadly and started to enjoy her drink.

"Where's Lucy?" Daniel hesitantly asked.

"Her friends were calling, apparently," Jessica said and shrugged.

"Yes, apparently," Samantha added with a chuckle. "Sorry, I don't think it was meant to be."

No," Daniel said, relieved but also a little despondent that at forty, he still hadn't settled down, hadn't found the woman of his dreams.

"A table!" Robbie said suddenly as he raced over to a tall round table and made his claim by placing his drink on it. They all followed over and found their place.

"So, how is everyone?" Daniel asked and placed his two drinks on the table.

"Jasper!" Robbie sighed. "This promotion that he's chasing is really doing my head in."

"Don't be so mean. You know he's desperate," Jessica said.

"Yeah, I know, I do feel for the guy, but still," he said.

"Oh, very caring," Jessica scolded.

"He has a point," Daniel jumped to Robbie's aid. "Asking him to work late all the time is a bit much."

"True, but I feel sorry for him. I mean, his wife is such a bitch," Samantha piped in.

"I agree," Robbie said. "Look, I don't mind helping out, but every night for the last month he's asked me to stay late." He groaned. "And I never get to see my very understanding girlfriend," he strategically added.

Jessica smiled sweetly at Robbie. "You make a good point. You're lucky I am so understanding."

"Well, don't be," he said. "I don't want to be there."

"Well, you said it's all done now, so after next week, I should have you home?" Jessica placed her hand on Robbie's cheek.

"Yeah, hopefully," Robbie added.

"My understanding isn't bottomless, you know," she added.

Robbie leaned over and kissed her. "Glad to hear it."

Samantha rolled her eyes. "So," she said, turning to Daniel, "how's the book coming along?"

"Yeah, good, thanks," Daniel lied.

"Okay," Samantha said suspiciously. "The last time we spoke about it, you said the same, with equally no elaboration."

"Yeah," he paused, "it's good." He emptied one of the glasses in front of him.

"What's wrong?" Jessica added.

"Oh." He let out a slow breath. "I feel like I'm stuck in a rut. It's like I'm going around in circles." He started on the second glass. "I've hit a point where all my ideas feel uninspired, or worse, just stupid."

"Probably because you ARE in a rut, my friend," Robbie said. "When was the last time you met someone who inspired you, when you just connected, when someone just made you feel good?"

"Thanks, I feel so much better now," Daniel said sarcastically, rolled his eyes, and finished his drink.

"I mean, you need to put yourself out there, be available, mate," Robbie said, trying to be encouraging.

"I am. I spoke to Lucy," Daniel said defensively.

"Okay, I bet she approached you." Robbie paused, looking judgingly at Daniel.

"Fine, she approached me," he admitted and shrugged dismissively.

"Then you tend to lose interest almost instantly," Robbie added.

"It's true," Samantha agreed. Jessica nodded.

"Yeah, I guess you're right. I just feel there is more out there, and I'm waiting, I guess." Daniel sighed as he thought of his recurring dream.

"Well, don't wait too long. Forty now," Robbie added, and Jessica discreetly thumped him on his arm.

"It's your birthday, you're forty," Samantha said, "and I think that's worth celebrating." She smiled and rubbed Daniel's arm. "The night is young, and so are you!" she added.

"True," echoed Robbie, who raised his glass. "A toast to the young, handsome, and lovely birthday boy!" They all raised their glasses, and the next moment, they were emptied.

Jessica looked around the room with a smile.

"Well, I think we should make the most of this life while it lasts. No more talk of work, Jasper, or age. Tonight is Danny's birthday, so who's going to the bar?"

The music suddenly changed to something a little more to Jessica's taste. She took Robbie by the hand and pulled him towards the dance floor.

"The usual for me, please," she said to Samantha as they left.

"I'll go get the drinks then," Samantha sighed.

Daniel got up to go too. "Stay here, or we'll lose the table," she said before walking to the bar.

Daniel sat there and looked around the room. He paused at his friends on the dance floor and thought how happy they looked together. Robbie squeezed Jessica's bum; Daniel chuckled and shook his head. He scanned the sea of faces, each meaningless to him, just background noise. As he had done for many years, he was looking for her. He wasn't even sure anymore if she was real or just his imagination desperately trying to fill the empty space in him. However, hope kept her alive, or perhaps somewhere deep down, he just knew that she was out there.

Daniel's attention was drawn to a woman who walked across his field of view, and for a moment, he felt a cold shiver run down his spine. He looked around frantically as the bland sea of faces blocked his view. It can't be, he thought, overwhelmed with disbelief and denial. He scanned the room again, and then his eyes locked on her: his mother, exactly as he remembered her in old photos when she was young.

His heart started pounding hard in his chest, and he felt frozen, unable to move. His mother stood perfectly motionless, her gaze unflinching, and she appeared almost translucent. She smiled kindly at him before pointing to a group of people standing on the other side of the dance floor. He heard a voice whisper around him; it felt soothing, and he was overcome with an irresistible urge to look at where she was pointing. He briefly tore his gaze away for only a second, and when he looked back, she had vanished. He scanned the room again, but she had gone. Daniel looked over to where she was pointing, and a group of women stood there chatting. One looked familiar: it was Lucy, and he sighed.

Samantha returned with a tray of drinks, stealing Daniel's attention away. "I bought doubles for everyone." She smiled but suddenly noticed Daniel's confused expression. "You feeling okay?" she asked, concern growing in her tone.

Daniel was as white as a sheet, and he was shaking.

"You look like you've seen a ghost," Samantha said, rubbing his arm.

"I–" Daniel stuttered, "I thought." His words drowned in the music.

"What's wrong?" she said, now holding his hand.

"I know this will sound impossible." He paused and took a deep breath. "But I thought I saw my mother."

"That's impossible," she said, concerned.

"I know it couldn't be her." His voice softened as he stared blankly, lost in a distant memory. "Whoever that was, she looked like my mother when she was young." He paused. "You know, that old photo I have of her."

"The one with your dad? I think they were standing on a hilltop," Samantha said.

"Yeah, that's the one," he sighed.

Samantha smiled reassuringly but didn't know what to say.

Robbie and Jessica returned from the dance floor. "Drinks, cool. Thanks, Sam," Robbie said.

"What's up?" Jessica asked, noticing the solemn atmosphere.

Daniel suddenly snapped out of his mood. "Drink!" he shouted. "It's my bloody birthday!" He desperately wanted to avoid the fast-approaching melancholy.

"Now we're talking!" Robbie said with a broad grin.

Jessica bought the next round, then Robbie followed suit, and then Samantha. They refused to let Daniel buy anything, not even a bag of crisps. The night continued like this, and as the evening went on, an alcohol-fuelled happiness stole away Daniel's melancholy. The music was pumping loudly, and the smell of sweat, perfumes, and body heat radiated from everyone around. The drinks were flowing, and their laughter added to the atmosphere that filled the room. Everyone quickly forgot their worries.

His friends were up once again, dancing and laughing, but despite their attempts to pull

Daniel with them, he chose to stay at the table. As he stood there, he watched them and smiled warmly. Something always held him back, whether it was a feeling of awkwardness or self-doubt, he never found the courage, happy to sit on the sidelines. The mysterious woman he saw earlier crept back into his thoughts as he stood there. Who was she? As he thought, he remembered that she was pointing to a group of people standing in the corner. He stood up and looked over again, but the group she pointed to had now gone. He turned away, disappointed that he didn't go over earlier. Was she pointing to Lucy? That made no sense. Was Lucy with someone he was meant to see or meet?

"I wonder who was over there," he muttered, feeling very drunk. "Well, Daniel, yet again, you think and don't act," he said, berating himself.

He stood at the table and pondered his life choices, considering how he ended up alone. He knew he had friends who would do anything for him, but he felt an emptiness inside that no amount of alcohol would dampen.

"Hey." He felt a tap on his shoulder.

Daniel turned and stared, unable to speak. His heart fluttered, his mouth dried, his pupils dilated, and all he could do was smile.

"Are you okay?" she asked. Daniel nodded but was still unable to speak.

She smiled kindly. "Oh, that's good. You looked a little sad, I just wanted to..." She paused. "Well, you're okay."

As Daniel watched her walk away, the dense fog of emptiness that had surrounded him for so long suddenly evaporated. In its place was a blissful warmth that spread through his heart like a flame burning from within. All his loneliness was forgotten as he felt himself rise to incredible heights that he never thought possible. He was helplessly captivated by her and felt a need to know who she was. Somehow, she felt familiar. His mind whirled as he desperately tried to remember where he had seen her before.

Robbie suddenly slapped Daniel on his back. "You okay?"

Daniel spun around to see his friend, who stood there with his usual optimistic grin, but it was like Daniel had been hexed. All he could see was her, like a ghost of a memory that obscured his vision. He hopelessly wanted to keep her in his mind.

"Danny? Snap out of it." He slapped his cheeks gently.

"Sorry, what?" It was like he had just awoken from a spell. "Yeah, yeah, just very drunk, mate." He smiled guardedly.

Samantha and Jessica came back over to the table, their voices ringing with laughter as they shared a private joke. Samantha's cheeks were flushed from her encounter with a rather persistent, intoxicated admirer.

"It's crazy out there," Samantha said, giggling. She noticed Daniel's odd expression. "I wish you would dance."

"You will never meet anyone standing here," Jessica added, looking around for her drink.

"I'm good, honestly," Daniel said, still trying to gather his thoughts.

"We all look like pratts up there, but no one cares," Robbie agreed with Samantha's sentiment.

"Speak for yourself," Jessica added.

Robbie chuckled. "My round, I think," he said

and went to the bar.

"I'll give you a hand," Daniel said gingerly, following closely behind, hoping to see that woman again.

He scanned the club frantically, searching for a trace of her, but she was nowhere to be found. He was unsure whether it was the alcohol or some spell that had been cast, but confusion clouded his thoughts. He felt like reality was slipping away. He shook his head, trying to clear his mind.

Then he felt himself being pulled to the bar. "I think you've drank too much." Robbie paused and smiled wickedly. "Or not enough."

Robbie glanced at the bar staff, who were all busy with other customers. He sighed and turned back to Daniel. "I think this will take a while, mate."

Daniel wasn't paying much attention; he nodded indifferently as he looked about for the woman who had captivated him. He was certain that he knew her, but it was like the memory was just out of sight. Damn this alcohol, he thought. His recurring dream slipped into his mind, and for a moment he wondered if it was her.

Robbie looked back over to Jessica and shrugged, indicating that it may be a while before the drinks would be coming. Jessica rolled her eyes, and impatience quickly got the better of her; she locked arms with Samantha and pulled her off to dance, leaving their table unguarded, which another group quickly claimed. Robbie and Daniel stood silently, each lost in their thoughts, staring blankly at the other people in the club.

"I was thinking about a documentary I watched recently," Robbie's thoughts spilt out into conversation. He noticed that Daniel wasn't listening, so he gave him a sharp prod. "You listening? I watched this documentary the other day."

"Sorry, mate." Daniel's attention turned to Robbie; he squinted, trying to unblur his vision.

"Democracy is over, my friend," Robbie said, slightly slurring his words.

Daniel looked at Robbie, confused. "What are you on about?"

Robbie sighed heavily before he spoke. "It's all a fraud and the vote doesn't count for anything."

"We just had an election and I believe we all had a vote." Daniel paused and wobbled slightly. "Someone won, I forget his name." His memory went blank, and he grabbed the bar for support.

Robbie sniggered and leant in conspiratorially. "Did we really have a say?" He tapped his nose and winked. "What choice did we really have? They all drive to the same goal." He stepped back, looking at Daniel for a response. None came, so he continued, "Control, it's all about control, my friend."

"Yeah, politicians are pretty crappy people." He stumbled as a man bumped into him, who apologised with a smirk. "Did you see that?" Daniel said, feeling quite offended.

The girl he was with looked at Daniel apologetically as she tried to keep the guy she was with from falling over.

"Yeah, just another idiot," Robbie said, looking back to the bar staff.

"Ah, screw it." Daniel shrugged and took a deep breath, trying to clear his mind.

"Think about it." Robbie lowered his voice. "Every government that gets in becomes more draconian, taking more of our freedoms. Remember, my friend, freedom is yours and cannot be given. If it is given, it can be taken." He paused as one of the bar staff passed him and served the person standing next to him. "Which means, we are not free!"

"Yeah, well, to be honest, it's best to get on with your own life. The rest can sort itself out," Daniel said. "No point worrying about stuff I can do nothing about."

"That's rather defeatist of you," Robbie said, surprised.

"Nah, not really. As you said, we aren't free, and we have little choice. So, is there any point in even trying anymore?" Daniel paused as one of the bar staff passed him to serve the person standing on their other side.

"Of course there is. Life is amazing. You just need to find the right person, that's all," Robbie said, bursting with enthusiasm. "That's where your defeatist attitude is coming from, mate."

"The right person?" Daniel said, feeling deflated. "Do you really believe there is someone out there? For me, I mean."

"I don't doubt it, just have to trust in fate," Robbie said encouragingly.

"Perhaps." Daniel steadied himself. "I know I am drunk," he wobbled slightly, "but seeing you and Jess together, it is just beautiful."

"She's great," Robbie beamed.

"I envy you guys. I am so happy for you both, but I really envy you guys."

A young girl behind the bar wearing a red cap and a club t-shirt stopped before Daniel. She stared at him, waiting for a response. "What can I get you?" she said unenthusiastically when none came. The endless sea of desperate faces gaping at her had started taking its toll on this young girl's spirit. However, the club paid well, and she had her degree loan to pay off.

"You're not buying anything tonight, Danny." Robbie leant in and stole the bartender's attention. He then ordered the drinks.

Daniel rested a hand on his friend's shoulder and wavered ominously. "I know I may be a little drunk, but you're like a brother to me." He looked at his friend. "I love you, dude."

"Love you too, you soppy git," Robbie said and put an arm around his friend.

"Hello again," came a soft voice that Daniel

recognised and hoped wasn't just a fantasy. "May I get to the bar? Sorry, I didn't mean to interrupt. You guys are clearly having a moment," she said with a giggle.

Daniel was struck speechless, like a shy boy meeting a beautiful girl for the first time. Her sweet aroma was intoxicating, her lips soft and inviting, glinting a vibrant cherry hue, and her voice delicate and soothing as a gentle summer breeze. Her bright blue eyes were as captivating and mysterious as a sea stretching endlessly into the unknown. Her hair, as dark as a moonless night sky, cascaded over her delicate shoulders like a gentle waterfall, glimmering with flecks of starlight. He was enraptured by her beauty, lost in a dream that he never wanted to be woken from.

Robbie noticed Daniel's mesmerised expression and grinned broadly. He gave a slight nod in the direction of the young woman, gesturing for Daniel to talk to her. However, Daniel stood rooted to his spot, staring at her, unable to find the words and oblivious to Robbie's encouragement.

Robbie stepped in. "Hello." He smiled politely. "My young, intoxicated, silent friend here was just swearing his undying love." He grinned mischievously. "Of course, I love this handsome, witty, and charming man too. However," he raised a finger, gesturing for her to wait a moment, swayed a little, then continued, "my better half is over there on the dance floor." He pointed to Jessica. "That beautiful woman in red." He emphasised the word *woman*.

She strained to look. "Oh yes, she is very pretty." Then, turning to Daniel, her gaze lingered as she smiled. "So tell me, where is your beautiful woman?" she said, overemphasising the word woman, light-heartedly mimicking Robbie.

Daniel felt the sound of her voice resonate through his being. It was like they were connected, which was beyond all logic or reason. He struggled to find the words to articulate what he was feeling; he stood there obmutescent.

"Daniel," Robbie jumped in, rescuing his friend, resting his hand on Daniel's shoulder. "This fine specimen of a man is Daniel."

"I'm Aya. It's nice to meet you, Daniel," she said playfully, then looked Daniel up and down, "you fine specimen of a man." She smiled warmly.

As Daniel gazed at her, a curious sense of familiarity washed over him, as though they were two pieces of an old puzzle that were finally reunited. He couldn't explain it, but somehow he knew her. They stood in perfect stillness, their eyes locked in a deep embrace. An unseen connection was somehow reignited, a hidden but familiar link transcending words.

"He's forty today," Robbie's words rang like thunder, shaking them from their trance and dragging them back to reality.

Aya smiled curiously at Daniel, who gave a hint of a smile but remained silent.

"So," she said softly, "it's your birthday?"

He grimaced at being reminded and managed to say, "Yeah," and sighed.

"Well, don't feel too bad. Birthdays are not all bad," she said kindly. "It's my birthday too."

Hearing Aya speak calmed him. "Well then, not all birthdays are bad," he said, smiling.

"No," she replied, looking deep into his eyes, "not bad at all."

"Drinks?" Lucy's voice was laced with irritation as she abruptly interrupted their conversation. Her voice was like a sharp razor, cutting through the tender moment between Aya and Daniel. She stood with her arms crossed, her gaze fixed on Aya while pointedly avoiding looking at Daniel.

"Sorry," Aya said to Daniel, then, giving Lucy a brief look of recognition, she turned her back on them and leant on the bar. Lucy lingered for a moment, then left to return to her friends.

Robbie gave Daniel a look of approval. He pulled him close and whispered encouragingly, "She is lovely, and she likes you."

Robbie gently nudged Daniel to the bar with a friendly pat on the back. "Good luck, mate," he said, leaving him to find Jessica and Samantha with drinks in hand.

Daniel leant on the bar next to her. "Hello, Aya," he spoke softly.

She turned, their gaze locked, and then she smiled warmly. "Hello, Daniel."

They were interrupted by the bartender asking Aya what she wanted to order.

"I better get those drinks," she smiled apologetically.

"Sorry, of course." He moved back to give her space, but she gently grabbed his arm. She leaned forward on the bar and ordered her drinks.

"Aya, can I buy you a drink?" He felt the alcohol lose its grip as his mind cleared, and all he could see was her. She smiled and gestured to the drinks sitting on the tray.

"Let me give these to my friends. Otherwise, Lucy will end us both." She laughed. "I'll be back in five."

Daniel watched Aya as she walked over to her friends. He was transfixed, absorbing every movement. Her exotic gait was perfection as she moved with the graceful fluidity of an angel.

...

Her friends were bursting with curiosity, as inquisitive smiles spread over their faces.

"He's kinda cute." Joanne sighed dreamily, looking in the direction where Aya had just come from, catching Daniel's eye. His face flushed red when he spotted her looking his way, and he quickly glanced down at his drink.

Aya giggled. "There's something about him. I can't quite put my finger on it."

Lucy rolled her eyes and huffed in indignation. "You don't even know him." She reached for her drink. "Personally, I thought he was a bit odd," she added coldly.

The other girls looked at each other, raised their eyebrows, and exchanged smirks. Aya ignored Lucy's comment and handed out the drinks. "Well, I liked him. He was, well, I…" she stammered to find the words.

"Exactly!" Lucy said. "He was odd."

Their conversation was distracted by a group of young men who started to dance near them, clearly trying to be noticed. The girls looked mischievously at each other and giggled. One of the men, a tall and ruggedly handsome man with short blond hair and piercing eyes, cast Joanne a seductive smile, which caused her to blush slightly. Dropping her gaze coyly, she reached for her drink and took a sip, hoping to calm down her racing heart. But when she looked back up at him, he was still staring at her intently and gave her a mischievous grin. She shyly grinned back, much to the amusement of her friends.

"Why do the boys all flock to you?" Lucy asked, her voice tinged with envy.

Joanne felt her cheeks redden and tried to act nonchalant as she shrugged and shook her head in response.

"Joanne is lovely, that's why men love her," Rebecca said, jumping to her friend's rescue.

"Well, I think you should take the chance whilst you can," Leanne added, only half in the conversation. She was looking over at one of the other men dancing, a tall guy with short hazelnut hair, but what caught her attention was his excessively tight jeans.

Lucy's agitation grew. "Look at them, they look like, well, oh, why bother!" She turned her back on them.

Rebecca put her arm around Lucy. "Tony may have been a jerk," she said, trying to comfort her friend, "but there are plenty of good guys out there."

Lucy sighed heavily and took a long, slow drink, emptying her glass. From the corner of her eye, Lucy saw someone walking towards them. She turned to see a good-looking young man with a cute smile standing beside her. Lucy felt flushed, and her face showed it.

"Hi," he said softly, his voice barely audible over the music. "I just wondered if you'd like to dance?" A twinge of nerves echoed in his voice.

Lucy looked stunned at the sudden attention, then at her friends, who all nodded in approval. "Yes," she said, "thanks." A broad smile grew across her lips.

"You have a lovely smile," he added, then took her hand and led her to the dance floor. The tempo slowed, and they pulled in close. Lucy blushed as they danced to a slow rhythm. Her friends watched silently as she relaxed, enjoying the attention, and as for Tony, he quickly slipped from her mind.

Aya looked over to Daniel and smiled knowingly, "I'll see you all in a bit if that's okay," she said softly.

Leanne, Rebecca, and Joanne looked over at Daniel and all giggled. "We will see you later," Joanne said. "He is cute," she whispered.

"Go on, we'll meet up with you later," Leanne

added. "Who's up for a dance?"

....

Aya made her way back, feeling Daniel's gaze following her. When she looked up, his piercing eyes conveyed an unspoken admiration. His gentle smile warmed Aya's heart, and she felt as if time stood still. She teasingly smiled back.

"Hello, you," she said softly.

"Hello, you," he replied.

Robbie, Jessica, and Samantha beamed joyfully as they watched Daniel and Aya from the edge of the dance floor. Robbie's explanation of their behaviour filled Jessica and Samantha with a sense of intrigue and happiness for their friend. They couldn't contain their excitement for Daniel's newfound interest. They walked over, grinning widely, bursting with curiosity and questions.

"Hey!" Robbie said, smiling at them both.

"These are my friends, Jessica and Samantha, and you met Robbie earlier." Daniel gestured to his friends, who smiled in greeting. "This is Aya," he added.

"Aya, nice to meet you," Jessica said, brimming with curiosity.

"It is nice to meet you," Samantha added warmly.

Robbie looked at Daniel, shook his head, and patted his friend on the back. "You're lost, my dear, dear friend." He laughed.

Jessica and Samantha encircled Aya, while Robbie pulled Daniel to a safe distance, away from the coming interrogation. His friends knew him well and saw that he was utterly enamoured with Aya. They had never seen him act this way.

"C'mon, mate, let's leave them to it." Robbie put his arm around his friend, and they walked over to the edge of the dance floor.

"I'll see you in a bit?" Daniel said to Aya. She smiled, looking slightly apprehensive.

Daniel was awed by her beauty and the intense bond that seemed to rise between them with each passing moment. He felt an unearthly pull to her, a powerful call from his soul. He knew in his heart that she was the woman from his dreams, that he had finally found her, that she was real.

"What do you think they're saying?" Daniel asked Robbie whilst looking back over his shoulder.

Robbie shrugged. "Don't worry about it. It's in the hands of the gods now." He laughed dismissively.

"I like her, y'know," Daniel quietly said to Robbie, transfixed on his inquisitive friends orbiting Aya.

"I know, mate, and don't worry, you know them. They won't say anything bad."

"Yeah, I know, but…" His words trailed into silence.

"You two had quite the connection there, two peas in a pod! I've never seen you so gobsmacked." Robbie chuckled. "You must have been utterly bewitched!"

"She looks so familiar, like I've seen her before," Daniel mused as he watched them chat. "It's almost like I know her."

"Perhaps you've seen her about and just don't remember," Robbie offered.

"Yeah, I guess that could be it, but… I don't know. It feels like something more than that."

He trailed off as he thought of fate playing a part.

Robbie chuckled while taking a swig of his drink. "Thinking about that fate stuff again? I can tell, because your face squishes up like you're in pain," he jested.

Daniel rolled his eyes. "Yeah, that fate stuff. I think…" He paused. "No, I feel we were meant to meet, here and now."

"Heavy." Robbie sighed and downed the rest of his drink. "I don't know, Danny, maybe there is such a thing as fate, someone pulling all our strings, who knows?" He shrugged. "When we met Jess all those years back, was that fate or coincidence? I mean, that could have gone either way. I couldn't stand her, remember?"

"Yeah, she was a royal pain in the ass!" Daniel laughed, fondly remembering when they had first met her.

"Yeah, I remember it like it was yesterday. Jess came storming up to us and said…" Robbie paused for a moment, trying to recall her words. "Something like, you children are too young to be playing with fire! I swear she stamped her feet." He nearly spilt his drink as he let out a boisterous laugh. "Then she stood her ground, to be fair to her, and gave us the toughest look I have ever seen!"

"Oh God," Daniel chuckled, "she really was something else. She was a year younger than us too."

Robbie cocked an eyebrow at him curiously. "So why did you ask her to stay?"

Daniel thought briefly before replying, "I don't know. I thought that she would tell on us, I guess. I had to say something." He shrugged.

Robbie thought for a moment. "That's right! You told her we needed someone responsible to watch the fire." He erupted into laughter again, shaking his head and marvelling at the genius of Daniel's idea.

"Yeah, and she lapped it up." Daniel spasmed with laughter. He shook his head. "Please, stop, stop!"

"You were a genius, my friend!" Robbie added, and patted Daniel on the back.

They reminisced fondly, chuckling at the memories of their childhood antics. They randomly erupted in breathless fits of laughter as they remembered their exploits and misadventures. Despite the passing years, their friendship remained as strong as the day they met.

"We had our base camp there. Remember, every spare moment we had, we would be there." Robbie was lost in happy thoughts.

"Yeah, until I fell out of that old tree and broke my bloody arm, and we were banned from the woods by my Nan," Daniel added, remembering the pain, and rubbed his arm.

"True, true." Robbie looked at his empty glass. "But that didn't stop us!" He laughed.

"Yeah, Sam wasn't too pleased with us. She was almost as bad as Jess at times!" Daniel shook his head.

"Nah, little Jess, there was no stopping that one!" They burst into laughter again. They calmed and drifted into happy memories. "I guess me meeting her all those years later in college, was, well…" He paused for a moment. "So you think it was all fate?" Robbie said calmly.

"It just seems right." Daniel gulped the last of his drink. His gaze became distant and thoughtful. "Do you ever feel like there is something more, something beyond what we see in front of us?" He paused as though he drifted somewhere else. "Like there is something waiting for us, you know, when it all ends?"

Robbie shook his head. "Come back to me, mate. All this drinking has gone to your head."

"It's like a thin veil which covers the world, hiding what lies beneath." His voice now sounded distant, as vague memories of moments in his life drifted back to him. "I was never sure if any of it was ever real."

"Time to wake up." Robbie shook his friend gently, a look of unease spread over his face.

Daniel snapped out of his daze and smiled apologetically at Robbie, then turned his gaze towards Aya.

"What you should really be thinking about is her," Robbie said softly, a hopeful note in his voice that went unnoticed by Daniel. "Whether it's fate or coincidence, the way she looked at you with such… Are there even words?" he exclaimed. "She likes you."

Daniel's smile grew wider, radiating warmth. "Yes, she does," he whispered.

….

Samantha gestured to Daniel and Robbie, laughing by the dance floor. "Aw bless, the children are enjoying themselves," she said in a playful tone.

Jessica laughed, and Aya grinned as all three gazed over momentarily.

"Aya, so what do you do?" Jessica quizzically inquired.

"Well, I trained as a horticulturist," Aya answered.

"Oh, that sounds, err... Well, I have no idea what that is." Jessica blushed slightly.

"Well, I primarily offer advice to farmers on sustainable agriculture, things like how best to grow crops in poor conditions. I spent most of my career in Southern Africa, which was amazing, such a beautiful place." A hint of sorrow flickered behind her eyes.

"Wow, sounds better than the nine-to-five we have to endure," Jessica said, and Samantha nodded in agreement.

Aya smiled fondly. "Some of the most amazing people I've ever known were in Africa. They inspired me and pushed me to achieve things that I thought were impossible. But sadly, some were also taken away too soon. It's bittersweet," she said, with sadness now echoing from her words.

They chatted for some time about Aya's life in Africa, the villages she visited, and the people she lived with. They were fascinated by her life there and the stories that she shared.

"Your time there sounds like it comes straight from a book, an autobiography written by some avid explorer. *My Time in Africa*," Jessica said in awe.

"I think it would be a boring book," Aya laughed at the idea.

Jessica protested, "Well, I would love to read it."

"Anyway, what I would like to know, after Africa, what brought you to Wales?" Samantha quizzed.

"I have family here," Aya answered and glanced over to Daniel, which didn't go unnoticed by Samantha. "I'm visiting my grandparents."

The subject then quickly changed. "So, Daniel," Samantha said, and gave Jessica a sly grin. Aya shifted uncomfortably and took a sip of her drink.

"We don't mean to pry," Samantha said reassuringly, "but watching you two together was so lovely."

Jessica beamed. "I have never seen Danny look at anyone like that before."

"No, it's okay," Aya said. "Daniel is," she paused and looked over at him again, "well, he is…" Her cheeks betrayed a slight blush. Daniel turned at that moment, and their eyes locked. A flicker of a smile trembled on her lips. "Sweet," she whispered.

"He certainly is," Samantha said, offering a friendly smile.

Aya laughed, bringing her attention back to Jessica and Samantha. "So, how long have you guys known each other?"

"Forever, I think," Samantha complained in jest.

"It's been years," Jessica said. "We knew each other since we were kids." She looked up in thought. "I remember when I met the boys. They were building a camp out in the woods. We were young, eleven or twelve perhaps."

She looked over to Robbie and smiled as she watched him and Daniel talking.

"I like the colour of your lipstick," Samantha said.

"Thanks," Aya answered. "It's retro red, apparently. I bought it online."

Jessica interrupted, "Thirteen, it was his thirteenth birthday."

"That's right, I brought cake," Samantha laughed fondly.

"Anyway," Jessica continued, "they were trying to burn the woods down, I swear. So…"

"So, you told them to behave and that you should supervise," interjected Samantha.

"Thank you, Sam." They all laughed. "To think, if I didn't, my life may have been very different now."

"I guess that's fate," Samantha added with a grin.

"Yes, fate," Aya said, barely a whisper, looking at Daniel.

…

Daniel noticed that they were all laughing about something.

"That's it," Daniel said. "Paranoia has the better of me!"

Daniel gave his empty glass to Robbie. "Could you get me another JD, mate?" He walked over to Jessica, Samantha, and Aya, followed by Robbie, who went straight to the bar and waved to the bar staff.

"Don't worry, we only told her your deepest, darkest secrets," Samantha said in jest.

"It's been very interesting, eye opening," Aya said with a playful smile drawn across her lips. "Daniel, oh, the secrets!" she mocked jokingly, but her expression was one of reassurance.

Daniel smiled, his face slightly reddened. He badly feigned a nonchalant attitude, which his friends quickly saw through. Robbie returned to Daniel's relief.

"So, what were you guys laughing about?" Jessica moved the attention from Daniel onto Robbie.

"Well… This and that." He stumbled his words slightly. "But mainly about how lucky I am, my dearest." He laughed, which earned him a suspicious look.

Daniel's attention was fixed on Aya; he could only see her. His breath drew in sharply as he was overwhelmed with a feeling of an intense connection. His heart thumped in his chest, and his skin tingled like electricity pulsed through his veins.

Suddenly, he needed to be alone with her. "Would you like to dance?" The air went silent around him, and he took in a deep breath. "With me?"

Daniel's friends stood motionless, speechless, stunned, and shocked at what Daniel had just said. He had never danced in all the years they had known him, no matter the occasion or who asked. It would have been fair to say that it was a universal truth, a fixed rule woven into the fabric of creation: simply put, Daniel Halton does not dance.

"Is this the end of time?" Robbie said in shock. "Since when do you dance?" He asked what they were all thinking.

Daniel, seemingly oblivious to the world around him, held out his hand. She placed her hand in his, sending warmth through her body, causing a rosy hue to paint across her cheeks. She looked into his eyes, and as he tightened his grip slightly, she smiled lovingly.

Robbie raised his glass to his friend in admiration and hope, and he muttered a prayer to whatever god was listening: *Please don't let him fall on his ass.*

As Daniel stumbled towards the loud music and flashing lights of the dance floor, a feeling of dread crept up; he felt his heart pound in his chest. He tried to shake off his fear and took a deep breath, but it was useless, he was too terrified. His steps suddenly dragged, and he paused, muttering to himself, "What am I doing here?" as he smiled, trying to hide his growing anxiety.

Aya looked at him, and her warm smile offered a quiet reassurance. She squeezed his hand as though she could sense his anticipation, and all fear evaporated. They stepped out onto that dance floor, the fast-paced music suddenly stopped, and a slow rhythm started to play. Fate, Daniel thought, and smiled nervously. He took her in his arms, as he had seen so many others do on the many occasions he had sat on the sidelines. She laid her head on his shoulder, and somehow, all the fear and worry he had felt seemed so foolish now.

He felt the warmth of her body and the rhythm of her heart beating softly. They slowly moved together to the gentle melody, swaying in perfect practised harmony as though they had done this a million times before. He pulled her tight towards him and held her firm. She looked up at him, and as their eyes met, everything was as it was meant to be. He saw the same look of pure bliss on her face that was flowing through his entire being. He inhaled deeply and willingly drowned in the intoxicating fragrance of her skin, which now enveloped him.

As they glided together, he felt a deep connection to her that extended far beyond the physical. He felt he could sense her thoughts, feel her emotions, and share her joy. The two of them moved as if in a dream, their bodies perfectly in sync. The moment was perfect: the music, the room, the lights, the way she looked at him. He thought she must have been an angel who had come down to earth just to be with him. As he held her, the room faded away from his awareness, his focus solely on her at that moment.

This is it, he thought, *the moment I have been searching for.*

"I'm lost," Daniel whispered. "I don't understand what is happening."

A soft smile graced her lips. "You're not lost." She was like the sun: warm and bright, and even at its lowest, it was the most beautiful thing in the world.

Daniel closed his eyes and let out a sigh. *Is this love?* he thought, confused, suddenly trying to rationalise the moment. *This is what I have been waiting for*, he told himself, and even though she didn't say anything, he just knew that she felt the same.

"How is this possible?" he whispered. "I feel like I have just awoken from a dream into a dream. Are you real?"

"Daniel, do you believe in fate?" Aya asked softly.

"I believe in you," Daniel whispered, a slight tremble in his voice.

He leaned back, looked deeply into her eyes, and released all remnants of self-control, losing himself entirely to her. Slowly, their lips touched for the first time, but it felt familiar. The universe slowed, and time stood still as though suspended in that moment. Daniel realised that his life had always been grey, but now colour flooded back in, the emptiness that had tormented him vanished, and for the first time, he felt alive.

Their kiss gently lingered, refusing to part, as their hearts beat in unison to a perfect rhythm as though they were one. Aya closed her eyes, wanting to memorise every detail, and she collapsed into his arms, submitting completely to him. He held her close, not wanting to let go for fear that this was just another dream and he would once again awake to an empty room, but he could feel the warmth of her breath on his lips, the beating of her heart, and the touch of her skin.

Their lips slowly moved away and their gaze locked, neither wanting to lose sight of the other. The world spun and a sweet-smelling warm breeze caressed them as though they were no longer in the club but standing far away on some distant hilltop.

"Can you feel that?" Daniel asked softly.

"Yes," she whispered.

They paused in perfect symmetry, clinging to the moment for as long as they could. The club fell away, swept by a summer's breeze, and for the shortest of times, they stood together on a hilltop. They turned to watch a distant orange sun slowly fall behind the world's edge.

"Is this real? Am I dreaming?" Daniel asked.

"If it is a dream, then I never want to leave," Aya said tenderly.

Daniel never thought it was possible to be so completely happy and content, to feel so full of light. All self-doubt had been driven away, and nothing else mattered. He knew that it was meant to be, and all his searching had finally ended. He was intoxicated, but it wasn't the drink; it was Aya. There had only ever been Aya.

The scene faded, and the club returned. Then, as quick as it started, they were thrown back to the present moment. The music rushed back but was now unwelcome. The noises of people's voices poured in, and the lights flashed annoyingly around them, but their eyes remained locked.

"There's something about you," Aya whispered. "I…" Her voice faded. She put her hand to his cheek. "Daniel," she whispered.

The slow song that had started their journey ended, now replaced with loud pumping sounds that blasted from the amps around the room.

They were jolted from their trance. "Time to go, I think," she said abruptly but kindly.

They walked from the dance floor to the captivated audience of Samantha, Jessica, and Robbie.

"You were ages. That song seemed never to end. It's gone midnight," Robbie said, a little irritated.

"Gone midnight?" Daniel replied, a little confused. "How?" he probed.

Before anything else could be said, a rather happy-looking Lucy appeared out of nowhere. Surprisingly, she acknowledged Daniel and looked at Aya, gesturing that they had to go.

"She seems in a happier mood," Daniel said.

"I think it may have something to do with that guy over there." Aya pointed to a group of guys hanging around her friends.

"Sorry, looks like I have to go." She leaned over the bar and grabbed a pen. "Here's my number, call me." She kissed Daniel. "Call me soon," she added, then waved a brief farewell to everyone and left with her friends.

"Well, happy birthday, mate," Robbie said. "She looks like a right catch." He grinned mischievously.

"Yes, she does," Jessica followed up, looking suspiciously at Robbie from the corner of her eye.

"You two seem to get along great. Is that love in the air?" Samantha mocked kindly and laughed.

"Must be fate," Robbie mocked in jest.

"Alright, alright, let it go. Obviously, she's amazing, and of course I'm going to see her again!" Daniel grinned with an exuberant expression. "What am I saying? She's awesome!" he shouted out happily and downed the drink that was handed to him. "Happy birthday!"

His friends looked at each other and laughed, mirroring Daniel's excitement.

"Who wants to dance?" Daniel said enthusiastically. "I wish to make a fool of myself, and I really don't care!"

Samantha and Jessica didn't miss the

opportunity to take Daniel to the dance floor and kindly allowed him to fulfil his wish. Robbie eagerly filmed the moment, for posterity's sake and historical value, he concluded.

The drinks flowed, and Daniel emptied glass after glass as an array of different beverages kept coming. His head spun, lost in a haze of intoxication and sublime happiness. His friends were caught up in Daniel's wake, dragged along by his exuberance. He danced, only to leave the floor to empty another glass, but all too soon, the music ended, the lights came on, and the sea of once happy smiling faces were tired and hazy.

Robbie grabbed Daniel as he wobbled, the adrenaline that had fuelled the evening beginning to wane. Jessica and Samantha pushed through the crowd to join the long queue to the cloakroom. Robbie and Daniel waited for them near the exit.

Daniel was now uncomfortably drunk. He slurred his speech and lost his ability to walk in a straight line, but tonight, the universe smiled at him, and he felt like the luckiest man alive.

"She is sooo beautiful," Daniel said, babbling,

"and I...I...love her!" He looked down and mumbled, "I do bloody love her, dude."

"Yes, mate, she was lovely, and you love her... Now just hold onto my arm or you'll be flat on your ass." Robbie struggled to keep Daniel from falling.

They stumbled from the club with Jessica and Samantha following behind, arm in arm.

"Where's the taxi rank?" said Robbie.

"I don't know. Can we call for one?" Jessica quickly added.

"No chance," Samantha said.

"You should have booked," Jessica said to Robbie.

"No, you should have booked," Robbie retorted, almost dropping Daniel.

"Guys!" Samantha scolded them both.

"I love you all," Daniel added as Robbie lost his grip and Daniel fell over.

"Over there," Samantha said, pointing to the taxi rank.

They helped Daniel up and walked over,

joining the queue of agitated people, all now just wanting to go home. They stood together, fatigue and melancholy setting in, except Daniel, who had a big grin.

"Oi!" A voice came from behind Daniel, and he felt a shove on his back. Daniel stumbled slightly and turned around to see a rather angry, clearly very drunk, stocky-looking man standing in front of him.

"You spilt my drink earlier, and I think you owe me something!" He slurred his words as he swayed about, barely able to stand. Daniel noticed a short girl standing behind him, pulling at his arm and telling him to leave it.

Now, Daniel had no recollection of the event. However, it was possible that he did, in fact, bump into not just him but several people at some point during the night's festivities. He raised his hands in the universal sign of peace and lowered his head slightly.

"Good sir," Daniel said in his best voice, however equally slurred. "My good sir, I meant ye no harm, as to do so would not be a joyous event, and I would be sad," Daniel pulled down the side of his mouth and made a sad face.

"Oh God, he's doing the sad face emoji,"

Samantha said with a groan.

Unfortunately, his aggressor did not see the humorous side of this and stepped forward to swing at the intoxicated Daniel. Like the heroes of old, Robbie, Jessica, and Samantha instantly stepped in.

"You touch him and..." Samantha didn't need to finish her sentence. He looked over at Robbie, who was no small guy, and Jessica, whose looks could kill at twenty paces, and stopped in his tracks.

"Whatever, I can't be bothered, but you're lucky I don't..." His sentence didn't end because, at that point, he stumbled away and fell flat on his backside.

"I think, good sir, we are done here!" Daniel took a bow just as Jessica grabbed him by the arm and dragged him into the taxi.

They pulled up outside Daniel's flat. Robbie got out and helped him to the front door.

"We will see you tomorrow, mate," he said, kissing his friend on the cheek and laughing.

"Get off." Daniel pushed him away, then called out, "Love you, man," as Robbie walked away. He looked at Jessica and Samantha, who watched him from the back seat of the cab, and blew them a kiss. "I love all of you!" They laughed and blew a kiss back.

Robbie stopped before getting into the cab. "You sure you're gonna be okay?"

Daniel waved him away and bowed. "I am more than okay. However, I feel I must pee pee now, so fare ye well."

Robbie smiled and sat in the taxi. It pulled away, and Daniel watched as the taxi drove down the road and out of site. He fumbled about looking for his keys, slurred several curses, and made a racket that could wake the dead... Well, at least the living who were sleeping. He groped around, searching for the lock. After bouts of confusion and frustration, he finally managed to open the door and fall in. He edged his way to the bottom of the stairs leading to his apartment.

Daniel looked up at the looming assent that towered forebodingly before him and sighed heavily. He lifted one foot and carefully placed it on the bottom step. As he clung tight to the rail, he heaved himself up. He paused, enjoying the sense of achievement, and looked to the next step he planned to conquer. Again, he lifted his other foot, and with deliberate movement, he lowered it onto the next step and heaved himself up again. A broad grin stretched across his face. *I got this*, he thought, now awash with confidence. He kept going, step after step, finally reaching the top of the first flight, but fortune did not smile upon him. He slipped and fell backwards, rolling down the staircase and smashing his head on the steps as he went. He landed in the hallway with a loud thump and a painful groan.

He opened his eyes and was met with the most beautiful sight. A lush grassy field spread out before him, so vivid it could only be a dream. The sky shimmered in an orange hue as the sun began to rise, painting the landscape in hues of blue and purple. He could see trees swaying gracefully in the distance, their branches billowing like a slow-motion symphony. In every direction, he saw droplets of white and yellow flowers dancing among the blades of grass. As he listened more closely, a gentle melody filled the air around him, as if each instrument were slowly coming alive, adding more complexity to the song as they breathed life into being. With every note played, vibrant plants sprung up from the ground: red roses embraced morning glory vines, while daisies reached out towards clusters of lavender petals, creating a breathtaking array of flora.

He looked down at his hands, and they started to glow with whiffs of colourful mist that whirled about them. He started to make shapes in the air, and then, as by magic, the shapes took familiar forms and came alive: cats, dogs, rabbits, and all other kinds of animals. He started to mould creatures that he had never seen before, born of imagination, and they, too, sprung to life, all radiating from him, like a conductor but orchestrating creation itself. Daniel was filled with such joy and acceptance of this place, he fell back into the soft grass, laughing out loud. He started to sing loudly as he was filled with a burst of energy.

"You're not supposed to be here." A kindly yet stern voice stole his attention, breaking the serenity of the moment.

Daniel turned to see who was talking but couldn't see anyone.

"This is all wrong, and you're early or late. I forget which way round it goes." The voice paused. "Are you staying? No, no, no, of course not, you can't stay."

Daniel tried to speak; however, no words

would come to him. He suddenly felt odd, as though he belonged there and didn't simultaneously.

"Now go. I will be seeing you soon enough," the kind voice said.

"Danny, wake up," he heard a soft voice carried on the breeze.

Suddenly, the field was gone, and it was dark. Daniel felt a warm hand brush his cheek. I know that feeling, he thought. He painfully opened his eyes, and the blurred image resolved into Aya.

"Aya?" Daniel croaked.

"It's okay. Are you stalking me?" she said, trying to hide her worry.

Mr. Kapoor was standing by her, shaking his head in disappointment. He looked concerned and was clearly frustrated that Daniel had come home in such a poor state.

"Let me help you up, son," said Mr. Kapoor. He leant down and picked him off the floor. "I'll get you to your flat."

"Thanks," Daniel groaned quietly, feeling rather sorry for himself.

"What's Aya doing here?" Daniel asked, trying to hide the pain he was feeling all over his body.

"She's my granddaughter and is staying with us for a few weeks. Now stop talking and focus on your walking, please," he said sternly.

I guess fate can be cruel too, Daniel thought to himself as he looked apologetically at Aya. She smiled lovingly back at him and watched as her grandfather helped him navigate the staircase to his flat.

Daniel looked back at her, feeling embarrassed and foolish, and mouthed, "I'm so sorry." She laughed and offered a merciful smile to counter his embarrassment.

"Goodnight, Daniel, sleep well," she whispered softly.

CHAPTER 5

A Flip of a Coin
Trust in fate; what more can we do?

When Daniel awoke the following day, he felt like he had turned to stone: he struggled to move, and every small effort felt laborious. His body ached all over, caused by the fall from the previous night. The impact had left bruises all over his body and a dull ache in his bones. With a significant effort, he managed to pull himself into a sitting position. His head throbbed with an intense ringing in his ears. He looked around his bedroom, his vision still blurry. He tried to recall what had transpired the night before, but his memory was foggy and indistinct. As he thought, fractured images flashed before him, which only amplified the feeling of nausea.

Daniel remembered falling down the stairs the night before and looking into Aya's eyes. He cringed in disbelief, felt engulfed in self-pity, shuddered, and sighed in regret. He slowly and painfully swung his feet off the bed to meet the hard, cold floor. With a painstaking effort, Daniel shakily heaved himself up; it felt like a thousand lead weights had burdened him. He slowly shuffled towards his dressing gown hanging on the rear of his bedroom door, each movement making him wince in soreness.

"Never again," he croaked, his throat dry.

The world appeared dull and irritatingly noisy; every sound thundered about him, echoing throughout his head. Daniel squinted towards the window, and the sun shined in, filling the room with a warm yet unwelcome light. He turned away and groaned loudly.

The next moment, Daniel frantically sprinted off to the bathroom, forgetting all his aches and pains. He spent what felt like an eternity being reacquainted with the decisions he made from the previous night's jovialities. He wretched and heaved until, finally, the demons had been exorcised and some semblance of normalcy had returned to him. He staggered to his feet and unintentionally decided to test the durability of his skull against the bathroom cupboard. The cupboard won, and he swayed as the bathroom spun in a kaleidoscope of colours. He dropped to his knees, then collapsed onto the floor in a heap and lay there, unwilling or unable to move, lamenting his life's choices.

He awoke a few hours later, and to his surprise, he was feeling a little better, though the newly acquired bruise was very much prevalent. He stripped and crawled to the shower half in a daze; the warm water cascaded over him, soothing his sore body and dulling the pain.

Slowly, he began to remember last night's events and hung his head in shame at his foolishness. He thought of Aya, her perfect smile and soft voice, and for the first time that morning, he felt a pang of happiness. *I can't be all bad if she likes me.*

Daniel had formulated a cure to counter the inevitable effects caused by a heavy night of excessive alcohol abuse. He had stumbled upon the wonderous healing effects after waking up on a park bench one cold morning and stumbling into a trucker's cafe: the tried and tested, ever-reliable fry-up.

This was his surefire method of easing all those nasty adverse effects that a hangover brought, the only path to recovery that ever worked for him. He suddenly yearned for the sizzling sound of bacon on the pan, the aroma of freshly brewed coffee, and the sight of a perfectly cooked golden egg. The mere thought of this hearty cure was enough to make his mouth water and his stomach grumble in anticipation. The only question that plagued his mind was whether he should cook or go to the café. The Greasy Gas was not the most pleasant name, but the food was sublime. However, the mere thought of having to dress up and step out into the bustling streets, with all the chaos of traffic and people, filled him with a sense of despair and hopelessness. The decision was clear. Still, if he cooked in his present state, there was a possibility that he would end up being carried out of his flat over the shoulder of a fireman. He didn't think Mr. Kapoor would take too kindly to that. *Fate*, he thought, *I will leave it to fate.*

"Where is that coin?" he mumbled while looking for his lucky coin.

During his youth, his grandmother gifted him a coin that featured a divine image of an angel and a "Yes" inscription on one side. In contrast, the other side portrayed a demonic figure and a "No." In moments of doubt, he would turn to this simple coin for direction, convinced that the whims of fate would point him in the right direction.

"So, tell me, fate, shall I go to the café?" He flipped the coin high into the air, caught it in one hand, placed it on the back of the other hand, and looked to see fate's decision. It was an emphatic "No," much to Daniel's relief. He didn't want to face the world just yet, and having to talk to people who often frequent the café was not high on his list. With a sigh of relief, he made his way to the kitchen.

He stumbled into the kitchen and groaned, feeling wretched from the night before, looked around, his mind blank, then a rumble from his stomach. *I need food.*

With a well-practised motion, he started to work on his beloved cure: a sweet black coffee, followed by eggs, beans, bacon, sausage, hash browns, and the obligatory slice of freshly cut white bread, still warm from the oven. Unfortunately, the latter was not available, so toasted just out-of-date bread would have to suffice.

With a steaming cup of coffee and a glass of carton-ready orange juice placed neatly by his side, he carefully arranged his breakfast on the table. The sight of the array of mouth-watering delights before him was almost too much to bear, and he couldn't resist taking a moment to admire the perfect creation that lay before him. However, the feeling of admiration was soon overshadowed by a rumble in his stomach that reminded him of his hunger. Without further hesitation, he quickly devoured the meal. After he finished, he sat on his sofa, leaned back, and rubbed his satisfied stomach, feeling content and full. He sipped his coffee, and as the warmth and aroma enveloped him, his eyes began to feel heavy. Soon, he drifted off to sleep, feeling utterly relaxed and content.

Daniel found himself engulfed in a deluge of memories that cascaded over him, each more vivid than the last. They swirled around him like a tempest, bringing up images of people and places from long ago that he thought he had forgotten. He recalled being held in the warm and loving embrace of someone dear to him, transfixed on her kind and loving blue eyes. The next moment, he was back in his high school classroom, daydreaming about his French lesson and his secret infatuation with Miss Lambert, his French teacher. Then, he remembered fishing with his father and triumphantly landing a colossal carp, with his father rushing over to congratulate him.

Memory after memory filled his thoughts. He felt like he was on an emotional rollercoaster that twisted high and dipped low until it all abruptly stopped at Aya, the beautiful woman who shimmered before him like a mirage. He thought that he heard her call his name, her voice a soft and gentle whisper.

He felt stuck between his memories and the present, the lines between them blurring until he couldn't tell them apart. Eventually, all the memories faded away, and the world Daniel knew vanished like a forgotten dream, leaving him with a sense of nostalgia for something that he couldn't remember.

Daniel was awoken by a soft breeze tickling his face. He stretched out, opened his eyes, and was greeted by a warm orange sun hanging softly in a sea-blue sky. As he gazed, the colours started to dance and play in the sky, creating a stunning display of multicoloured hues that stretched out as far as the eye could see. He was in awe of the view before him and felt grateful for the opportunity to see it.

He felt a tickle on his neck and realised he was lying on the grass. However, he didn't feel surprised and smiled to himself with contentment. He stretched out again, not wanting to move, gazing at the stunning display and noticing how it softly pulsed with an unseen rhythm. The place felt incredibly alive, like it embodied life itself. Daniel struggled to find the right words to describe this beautiful place, fearing any description would fall short of its true beauty. He surrendered himself to the gentle rhythm, letting it carry him.

As he lay there, he was embraced by a captivating melody that danced and swirled around him. He couldn't help but feel moved by this perfect song. The clouds had now changed shape and formed many different animals, which sprung to life and playfully danced to the melody's rhythm, creating a magical display. Far off beyond the sky, he caught sight of bright, shimmering stars gracefully gliding across the sky; they seemed to be watching from high above. At that moment, he was overcome with an overwhelming sense of joy and contentment; he felt inexplicable vitality. It was as if it had awakened a new life within him, and he couldn't help but be entranced by this sensation.

He closed his eyes and drifted off to sleep.

He was abruptly awoken from a serene dream of basking on a secluded beach, relishing the soothing sound of the waves crashing on the shore. A faint whistle caught his attention, but he initially tried to ignore it and return to his tranquil dream. The whistle persisted, growing louder and more insistent. Daniel felt a growing irritation and shifted to his elbows, scanning his surroundings for the source of the interruption. Unfortunately, he couldn't discern anything from his current position, so he reluctantly sat up. The peace was now overshadowed by mild irritation, uneasiness, and growing apprehension as the source of the whistling grew closer.

As quick as it had begun, the whistling ended, and Daniel was startled by an unusual and unsettling voice that appeared to be emanating from every direction. It was like music, nothing like Daniel had ever heard before. Its tone was loud and clear, but he couldn't understand its meaning. The sounds weaved about, forming strange images in his mind, and as he listened, the tones changed, becoming increasingly multi-toned and intricate. He found himself in a situation where a response seemed to be expected; however, he struggled to come up with anything to say. His mind felt utterly empty, devoid of any ideas or thoughts, and he found an inability to speak.

A small orb of light popped out of nowhere and hovered in front of him. Slowly, with each passing second, it grew in size and intensity. The light quickly became blinding, causing Daniel to raise a hand to shield his eyes instinctively, yet the warmth of the light radiated an aura that felt both welcoming and friendly. It tingled against his skin, and he could feel a power pulsating through the air.

The light dimmed as Daniel looked up, and a low humming sound resonated from it as it began to change before his eyes. A soft glow now radiated out and began to shimmer as it swirled and twisted, taking on new shapes and forms with each passing moment.

The light dissipated, revealing an aged gentleman, his head shaking and his words unintelligible. Clad in long white hair, a beard, a pointed hat, and a long white robe, he presented an appearance that could only be likened to a traditional wizard, the type Daniel used to read about when he was a child.

The man stepped forward and stared intently at him, still shaking his head and looking very put out. He leaned down as though he was trying to figure something out, the elderly man's eyes holding Daniel's gaze. He stood up straight and, with a little effort, removed his pointed hat and scratched his head. Then he spoke again, slower, but Daniel could understand his words this time.

"What on earth are you doing here, my boy?" He spoke in a deep, kind, yet stern voice.

Daniel remained silent, realising he did not know where he was.

"What on earth are you doing here?" he said again, sounding even more stern and perhaps a little less kind.

The man appeared bewildered at Daniel's presence and sighed heavily.

"I'll ask again," he said. "Well, what on earth do you think you are doing?" He paused, expecting an answer. "Cat's got your tongue?" He didn't look amused.

Daniel was about to say something but suddenly realised that he didn't know how he got there. He just shrugged and gave a half-smile.

The man looked displeased; his thick white

eyebrows furrowed over his eyes. "Young man, you are not supposed to be here yet. You have arrived much too early," he scolded.

Daniel felt peculiar as he listened to the elderly man's words. He suddenly noticed that the man hadn't moved his mouth as he spoke. The words seemed to form in Daniel's mind as the letters blended together and took on new shapes, yet he understood their meaning without effort.

"Early?" Daniel said out loud, wanting to hear his own voice.

The man shook his head again, then a broad smile stretched across his old, wrinkled face. Daniel felt instant joy wash over him, and he began to laugh.

"The old ways, I almost forgot," he said, but this time, he spoke the words so Daniel could hear them. "Yes, early," he continued, his words now bright and clear.

"Who are you?" Daniel asked, but looking at the wizard, he reminded him of the man from the coffee shop, his father's old friend.

The elderly man looked down at himself and seemed to examine his appearance. He ran his long, bony fingers through his hair and beard, then brushed down his bright white robe adorned with bright silvery pentagrams.

He pondered momentarily. "Apparently, I appear to be a wizard," he said in surprise. "I've always loved your worlds." He chuckled. "And where is my staff, Daniel?" he said inquisitively.

"Staff?" Daniel said. "I don't know, sorry."

"Oh, you really are here way too early," the man said, letting out a long sigh.

As the wizard asked Daniel about the need for a staff, an image of a long, ornate wooden staff appeared in Daniel's mind. The next moment, a long wooden staff crowned with a large red ruby materialised in the man's hand. Daniel was a little shocked at the event, but in a way, he expected it.

"Ah, that's better. Now I am a proper wizard. Thank you, Daniel."

Daniel paused, stared at the wizard, and deduced that he must be dreaming. He smiled broadly. *If this is a dream, well, it's a pleasant one*, he thought.

"It's beautiful here," Daniel said, looking around.

Tall, swaying sapphire grass stretched out in every direction, dotted with splashes of indescribable colour, like painted flowers on a canvas. The scene was tinted by the golden glow that flowed from the sun, and a warm breeze rustled through the trees whose branches reached high up into the sky, carrying vibrant leaves that came alive in the sunlight. The air tasted sweet and brought a sense of perfect calmness. This is perfection, Daniel thought. He took a deep breath and held it, not wanting to let the moment diminish in any way.

"Yes, it is perfect here, but perfect is all it could be." The wizard chuckled, seeming to read Daniel's thoughts. "Yes, this is a lovely place, but you shouldn't be here." He reached down and pulled Daniel to his feet. "It's not your time yet." The wizard's voice had softened slightly, teasing a caring attitude peeking out from behind his seriousness.

His words suddenly struck true. Daniel knew that though he wanted to be here, something was not as it should be, something was very wrong. In an instant, he knew exactly what the wizard was thinking, he knew his thoughts and mind. He suddenly understood completely, and without any doubt, he knew the kind intent behind the wizard's words. Daniel thought it was a peculiar feeling to know instantly someone's thoughts. Still, in this place, it felt as natural as breathing. He smiled quietly and simply accepted it.

"Walk with me," the wizard said, mirroring Daniel's smile.

He started to walk away, and Daniel followed. As they walked, he looked around. It was indeed a fantastic place. In the distance, he saw stone castles, their towers standing tall, surrounded by sprawling green forests. Birds playfully swooped low in the blue sky, then soared up, hovering on the updrafts. Animals that he did not recognise leapt about in the tall grass. Suddenly, Daniel stopped agape. He pointed and looked at his companion. The wizard stopped when he noticed that Daniel had stopped.

Looking to where Daniel was pointing, he laughed and said, "Well well," and continued walking almost indifferently.

"It's a..." Daniel exclaimed in shock and awe.

"Yes, I believe it is," the wizard said nonchalantly and continued moving ahead.

"But it's a dragon!" Then a loud, thunderous

roar echoed out over the land. "How is that possible?" Daniel asked whilst still trying to believe what he had seen.

"Oh, anything is possible here, but you know that," the wizard spoke with such certainty, yet Daniel felt overwhelmed by the fantastical world he had woken up in.

"Don't worry, it will all be clear when it is meant to be clear," the wizard said as he strolled ahead.

"It feels overwhelming," Daniel said. His imagination burst to life, and his mind flooded with all sorts of different images, like a whirlwind, and he struggled to understand it all. He felt inundated with the plethora of information he was being exposed to; it was impossible to grasp any meaning.

The wizard seemed to sense Daniel's puzzlement. "Don't worry. When you've fully arrived, it will all be clear. You're too early, that's all. Now let's get you home," he said. His sternness had now faded away, leaving a kind and understanding manner.

Daniel looked at his companion. The wizard looked calm and collected, his long white hair moving with the breeze. His eyes closed, and his face relaxed. He raised his staff, and the long grass parted before them, revealing a vague outline of a track that meandered as far as Daniel could see. It moved and swayed, twisting and turning in a snake-like fashion as Daniel watched, eventually settling down and transforming into a cobbled pathway.

Tall and leafy trees lined the path, their branches reaching out to brush against each other, forming a canopy over them. Shafts of coloured light broke through the lush green rooftop overhead, creating beams casting down to the ground below.

The trees were giant and looked old, though they had just sprung up from the ground. Their trunks were twisted into odd shapes, their bark was dark in colour and formed deep ridges that ran up their entire length, and it looked like they had been there for hundreds or thousands of years. Daniel heard water trickling and splashing; he thought there may be a small stream not far from where they were.

"Yes, that will do," the wizard said and started along the path.

Daniel looked at his companion as he joyfully walked ahead; he seemed almost perfunctory to what had just happened. The wizard raised his hand, beckoning Daniel to follow.

As they walked, blooms of tiny flowers sprung out of the ground in between the cobblestones making up the path. The flowers glistened with colour the likes of which Daniel had never seen before, both in vividness and beauty. They seemed to be alive and bowed to them as they walked, and as Daniel smiled, the plants grew brighter and more magnificent, as though they reacted to his joy.

Daniel and the wizard walked in silence for some time. Then, a thought occurred to him. "How do you know my name?" he asked, turning to his companion.

"Oh, we all know each other here and there. We all come here and there to rest and reflect occasionally when the time is right." The wizard paused and smiled cheekily. "If there even is such a thing."

"Rest? Reflect? What is this place?" He had an overwhelming need to find answers to the many burning questions that now echoed in his head; he felt like a geyser that was ready to erupt.

"Daniel, I suppose you could call this place

heaven, paradise, oneness, the here and now." He paused and chuckled. "Perhaps even the quantum singularity? If that makes more sense to you." He paused. "However, they would all be wrong, shrouded in limitation and perception."

Daniel just looked blankly. The wizard shrugged and continued, "This is the place where you are meant to be, where we are all meant to be when we are meant to be here." He paused. "Not before, my dear boy." A glimmer of that sternness returned and flickered in his eyes.

"But how do you know my name?"

"Well, I know everyone. How can I not?" He smiled broadly. "But that doesn't answer your question."

Daniel laughed; it was the most natural thing in this world to do.

The wizard appeared undisturbed as the cobbled path gave way to a narrow, barely visible grassy track. It soon changed direction and veered down a bank, where it met the sound of rushing water. Their path now turned to follow a stream that meandered through the landscape for as far as Daniel could see.

The water looked clear and inviting. "Can we stop a while?" Daniel asked, wanting to spend some time in such a beautiful spot.

"Surely you can't be tired?" the wizard asked, looking perplexed.

"No, but this place is overwhelming, and I just want to breathe it all in. It feels like a perfect dream, and I know I will eventually wake up, but I just want to linger a little longer."

"Well, this is such a beautiful spot. It would be a shame to pass it by," the wizard agreed and sat down beside the stream. He then removed his shoes and socks and carefully placed them neatly on the ground near where he sat. He playfully dangled his feet over the edge into the gently moving water as he hummed softly.

Daniel couldn't help but follow his example. He removed his shoes and socks, sat on the ground next to him, and placed his feet into the cool flowing stream. A gentle spray brushed his face as he fixated on the mesmerising flow of the bubbling water. His mind wandered far away, carried by some invisible current; he lay back and closed his eyes, succumbing to the moment.

Without warning, a sudden sensation of plummeting through the earth and hurtling backwards overtook him. In an instant, he slipped out of his own world and into an endless expanse of alternate possible realities. Some were strikingly distinct from his own, a bewildering array of unfamiliar landscapes and alien creatures. Others were eerily similar yet subtly askew, as if existing within a parallel universe. He traversed through time and space, watching the emergence and demise of stars. He witnessed the genesis and obliteration of everything that has existed and will ever exist.

A wave of dizziness washed over him, causing his vision to blur and twist around him in a whirlpool of colour and shape. The sensation intensified, causing his head to throb in pain. The chaos paused momentarily, and he found himself standing on the edge of a swirling vortex of colour and light. He lingered, swaying precariously on the brink of this whirling tunnel, before an inexplicable force tugged at him with an almost magnetic pull. It was impossible to resist its power, and he was quickly drawn in, whisked away by an unseen current. He fell tumbling about, knocked from side to side; he had lost all sense of direction. The walls became blacker and blacker; all light faded until Daniel could no longer see the tunnel. He plunged further into this unknown until nothing was left except blackness.

Daniel crashed onto the hard ground with a sudden jolt, the impact producing a sharp, resounding pain that resonated through his body. As he gradually came to, he found himself lying in the centre of a desolate and barren room, utterly devoid of any signs of life. The sole object in the room was a towering structure situated at the far end which emitted a faint, diffused light that sullenly illuminated the area around it. The structure was shrouded in a pitch-black silky cloth that hung down to the floor, completely obscuring its features. Its rippled fabric crawled along the ground like it was groping to find where Daniel lay.

As Daniel rose to his feet, a chill swept over him, leaving him feeling isolated and desolate. This was an unfamiliar sensation, a stark contrast to the feeling he had experienced by the stream. An inexplicable force seemed to be directing him towards the object, and he could hear a voice in his mind whispering, beckoning him closer. Though hesitant, he obeyed the command and began to move towards the source of the sound. With each step he took, anxiety and fear grew. He tried to resist, but as hard as he tried, he was compelled to listen and obey.

Finally, he reached the object. It appeared to have grown in stature, somehow more menacing and ominous. The shimmering black sheet hung motionless as though it had been holding its breath in anticipation of Daniel's arrival.

Daniel's hands trembled as he reached to touch the cloth draped over the sinister object. After a moment of hesitation, he pulled the fabric away, and it fell quickly to the ground. It revealed a tall, dark mirror, its frame shrouded in dark and unusual carvings. The carvings depicted scenes of torture, suffering, and death, each detail etched with a haunting precision that sent chills down Daniel's spine. The unsettling images seemed to come to life around the mirror, beckoning him closer and closer. He stared at his reflection, and he couldn't help but feel a sense of unease wash over him. It looked different, it didn't mimic his movements. Instead, it stood there watching. Daniel was terrified and stumbled back; his reflection smiled, raised its arms, and stepped forward.

He heard a soft voice, barely a whisper, "Daniel…" Its words echoed around the room, resonating off the cold walls.

"Who is this?" Daniel asked hesitantly.

A chorus of voices radiated from the mirror. They spoke gently, almost as if talking to a child.

"You are safe here," it hissed, "there's no need to be afraid. Step closer and embrace who you are."

Daniel shakily placed one foot in front of the other and edged closer, but something inside made him hesitate, and he stopped.

"I will show you the secrets of the world." Its voice was cold and hollow. "I will show you the hidden truths about yourself."

Daniel found a strength inside, a light that shone through the fear and bleakness. "No," he whispered. "No!" he said again with conviction.

As Daniel stood before the mirror, studying his reflection, he was taken aback to see that his features had transformed into a black stone. In an instant, the mirror shattered into countless shards and fell from its frame, crashing to the floor like a waterfall crashing on the rocks below. It washed out, causing him to quickly move backwards.

He looked up at the empty frame; a dense black mist had now appeared where the glass once stood. As he stared into this bleak void, the outline of a person emerged from its shadow. His heart lifted with hope as Aya appeared.

As Daniel smiled and extended his hand towards her, another figure appeared. Robbie. The two of them stood still, gazing into each other's eyes. Daniel withdrew his hand, sensing that something was amiss.

Robbie suddenly grabbed at Aya, but Aya didn't fight or struggle. She pulled him close, and they kissed with a fiery passion that burned brightly against the blackness of the emptiness. Their lips met in a violent collision that sent shock waves of horror through Daniel's body. He ripped at her clothes, tearing them off in shreds, and she tore desperately at his, throwing them onto the ground. Their naked bodies pressed hard against one another as Robbie's hands roughly ravished her, fondling and groping, leaving bruises and scratches in his wake. She moaned with pleasure as her nail ripped into his flesh, drawing droplets of blood that trickled down his back. His hands viciously pushed between her thighs, and she screamed as she flung her head back.

"Stop!" Daniel cried out and fell to his knees. "No more, please," he whimpered.

Robbie pushed her to the ground, and she lay there, willing to accept him. Robbie rolled onto her, pushing her legs apart and forcing himself inside her. She screamed, wrapping her legs around him, moaning feverishly.

"I love you," she moaned loudly, her eyes locked onto his. "I love you, Robbie!" Their lips moved together slowly, exploring the soft flesh of one another's mouths.

Daniel felt his heart fracture, his mind lost in a sea of pain and hatred. *How could they do this?*

Daniel knelt there sobbing, his hands over his face. He couldn't watch any longer. The sound of their passion and pure lust filled the space around him; their groans and moans of pleasure were pure torture.

"No!" Daniel shouted, desperate as he was

overcome with anger.

A burning hatred ignited in him, and he leapt to his feet and ran at the horrific scene, now bursting with pure malice. As he rushed towards them, he screamed out, cursing their very existence, but suddenly, an invisible force lashed out, throwing him back to the other side of the room. He crashed to the ground, sharp spikes of pain adding to his torment.

"No, no," he sobbed.

Suddenly, all went silent, and the torment that had driven him to the edge of despair had ceased, leaving an eerie calm lingering in the air. Daniel painfully edged to his feet. The room was now bright white, and the ominous frame that was once his tormentor had gone. In its place was a bed, sitting alone, not far from where Daniel was now standing. He paused and stared, wondering what horrors he would meet next.

As the thought of the bed entered his mind, he suddenly found himself standing near it. The sudden change of position startled him, and he stumbled back. He noticed that in his hand, he held a small revolver. He stared at the gun, curious how it had come into his possession. He had no recollection of ever finding a weapon. It had a plume of black smoke wisping calmly from the end of the metallic barrel. An eerie sense of ease washed over him as the wisp danced about and faded.

As he approached the bed, he noticed two figures lying motionless beneath a pristine cotton sheet, their bodies outlined by its fabric. He was confused by what he saw, but his eyes widened as two tiny red spots appeared; they stood out as an insult, blemishing the sea of white. Then, like streams trickling down a mountainside, crimson lines meandered down the still figures trickling off the bed and splashing to the floor. Daniel stood frozen at what was unfolding before him. With a shaky hand, he mustered the courage to pull back the sheet.

Suddenly, without warning, a hand firmly grasped Daniel's shoulder and forcefully pulled him away from the horrific scene. The next moment, he realised he was back by the peaceful stream, just as before. The wizard continued to hum his tune, and Daniel's feet remained submerged in the cool, refreshing water. Daniel's companion stopped his hum. "I think it's about time to get you home." A distinct echo of concern hung on his tone.

Daniel wiped his face with the back of his hand and noticed that it felt sticky, as though he had been sweating. His eyes felt sore, and his body ached. He was overcome by a sense of deep sadness and cried like all the hurt in the world was his burden alone to carry.

"Why did they do that? I trusted them." Daniel felt sick at the thought.

"That never happened, Daniel. It wants you to be sad. It feeds off your misery. That is its purpose." He rested his hand on Daniel's shoulder. "Trust me, your friends are true." The wizard smiled kindly. "Now, go sit in the stream, and it will all feel so much better."

Daniel didn't even think to question as he followed the instruction and stepped into the cool stream. The water gently rushed over his feet, and he started to feel a little lighter.

"Now sit," his companion said.

As if controlled by a puppeteer, he lowered himself into the water, which rose up in a cool embrace, submerging Daniel in the flowing current. The water rushed over his body, carrying away his tears, massaging his aches, and soothing his sadness. A sudden wave of exhilaration burst from him, and he leapt up in the air out of the water, shouting aloud with laughter. He started splashing around like a young child playing in a puddle. Daniel's laughter was contagious, and the wizard burst out laughing at the frivolous site in front of him.

"That's much better," he said, and like a father calling in his child, "Daniel, time to come out now."

Daniel didn't argue. He smiled and laughed, climbed out, and sat back on the bank, feeling awake and refreshed.

"We have been here long enough; it is time we moved on." He stood up and brushed himself down, put on his socks and shoes, placed his hat back on his head, and reached for his staff, which he leaned on. "Up, up now." He smiled at Daniel, then turned and walked away. "No more time to waste; you have been here far too long."

He raised his staff high in the air, and as he did, the trees parted. Daniel could see a clearing ahead of them, and in the centre sat a small cabin. The path was now straight and true. "The quickest way now is the best," he said.

...

They reached the cabin easily and quickly, only pausing when the wizard was startled by a sound he did not recognise. He then muttered incoherently to Daniel and hurried on. The cabin appeared to be very old and heavily weathered. It was covered in carvings of ornate symbols clearly depicting animals, plants, and other signs that Daniel did not recognise. It was painted in bright colours that seemed to move and dance over the house, creating the illusion the cabin was moving.

"We are here," the wizard said triumphantly, pointing Daniel to the door. "You must enter of your own volition. I cannot help here."

Daniel went to the door and paused, turning back to his companion.

The wizard smiled reassuringly. "This place isn't for me, just you. Now go in, and I will see you when…" He seemed to slip away in thought. "Well, when indeed."

"Who are you?" Daniel hastily called out.

"I am a just dream within a dream." He laughed as he shimmered brightly for a brief moment, and then he was gone.

Daniel turned to the door and reached for the

handle. As he touched it, the world around him warped away, and in an instant, he was standing inside the cabin. He looked about; it felt familiar to him, as though he had been there before, or perhaps it reminded him of something that he couldn't quite remember. He saw a small table and three stools resting near the fireplace and decided to sit for a moment and consider what he should do next. He pulled out a chair that was partially tucked under the table and sat down.

A soft, warm glow radiated from the fire, which warmed him and made the old cabin feel welcoming. The fire crackled and danced in the hearth, sending flickering shadows across the rough-hewn logs that made up the cabin walls. Above the gentle flames sat a black kettle, its contents bubbling and simmering as it hung over the heat. The scent of woodsmoke filled the air, creating a cosy atmosphere that enveloped the small space. It was as if the old cabin itself was alive, its heart beating with the energy of the fire.

"Would you like tea?" a voice gently asked.

Daniel turned to see a woman walk from an ornate door on the far side of the room. She looked ancient, and her face was cracked with age. She hobbled as she walked to the fireplace, almost struggling to place one foot in front of the other. However, as Daniel watched, he was shocked to see she was no longer old when she reached the kettle. She had transformed into a young woman in her mid-thirties.

"That's better." She had a soothing, kind tone.

She placed three cups on the small round wooden table, which rocked slightly under their weight. The aroma of a sweet drink filled the air as the steam escaped from the kettle. After wrapping a cloth around the handle, she walked towards the table and poured the liquid into the cups.

"Would you like tea?" she repeated with a kind smile.

"Yes, please," he answered, feeling very welcomed.

She slid the cup towards him and said, "I'm sure you have many questions. Some may be pertinent, some not so much, and some you might already have the answer to without even realising it."

Daniel wrapped both hands around his cup, feeling the warmth. "I'm not sure where to begin," he confessed.

"Perhaps we should start by trusting in patience and accepting that when you are meant to know, you will know," she said with calm reassurance.

Daniel stared down at the liquid in his cup, watching the motionless surface. He envisioned it as a vast lake reaching out, touching the horizon, upon which a small boat held him in this peaceful solitude. He felt a longing to disappear into this infinite silence, to let go of everything and drift to wherever it chose to take him. But, in the hidden shadows of his mind, he sensed a painful memory that wanted to be heard.

"I know what lurks in the shadows," she said. "I sense your pain, but the places you dream of will not protect you."

"How can you know my pain when I don't understand it myself?" Daniel snapped, instantly regretting his tone but holding back an apology.

"As soon as you entered here, the light touched you. It illuminated the shadows that hide your pain, exposing truths," she said softly.

She sat beside him and rested her hand on his, but Daniel moved his hand away and turned his head. "I know who you are," he said. "I knew you as soon as I saw you."

Sadness spread across her face, and it was now her pain that was being exposed. "I never wanted to go when I did," she said. Daniel looked up to see small pools of water glisten in her eyes. "Leaving was the hardest thing I ever had to endure." She paused. "But know this: there was no other way. We have always been connected, Daniel. I never left."

"Somehow, I knew. I have always felt you near," Daniel said sombrely. "But…" He sighed heavily, and his words faded.

She smiled and wiped away her tears, then threw her arms around him. "Welcome home, son."

Daniel heard footsteps approach from behind. Then a hand rested on his shoulder and squeezed. A man sat on the other stool and took the third cup but didn't drink.

"It's good to see you again," his father said.

"Dad?" Daniel said in disbelief.

The man smiled. "Of course."

Daniel's mind raced with a million questions,

each one pushing out the last. He struggled to focus, but finally, one emerged, the most obvious yet the least important. "Where am I?"

His father sighed. "It will not be the answer you want," he said.

"I need to know what is happening. Am I dead?" Daniel said, desperately wanting a straight answer.

"When you are meant to know, you will not need to ask," his father said.

Daniel furrowed his brow in confusion as he tried to make sense of his words. He wanted clarity, but the answers seemed only to elude him further. "Why is it so hard to explain to me what is happening?"

His mother knelt before Daniel and said softly, "This is where we are meant to be," but her voice was sorrowful. He sensed something was lurking unsaid, as though she was hiding something. She stood up. "I would like to show you something." She paused and grinned briefly. "Before you go. It might help," she added.

As she spoke, the cabin walls vanished, revealing a large open clearing that was surrounded along its edge by tall, ancient trees. Their branches interlocked and encircled them, like an impenetrable wall. The day had ended, and night had fallen; the sky was clear and filled with bright stars that danced about as he watched. Daniel was awestruck as they darted across the sky, leaving a vivid kaleidoscope of colour in their wake.

The ground was covered in a soft, vibrant carpet of grass, which swayed to give the appearance of a wave slowly caressing a shoreline. A sweet fragrance hit him, reminding him of all the smells of home and happy childhood memories. A gentle sound rose up, caressing the air with a sweet melody. It resonated throughout the clearing, penetrating everything. Daniel felt it throughout his being and was captivated by the rhythm. To his astonishment, the notes materialised, forming waves of colour that whizzed past him and spun in the air around where he stood. He turned to his parents, who stood smiling at Daniel's disbelief.

In the clearing, he saw children playing, talking, dancing, and singing. The peaceful atmosphere seemed to engulf them. They ran about laughing and joking together in carefree abandonment, entirely immersed in their frivolity and without a care in the world.

"They're all kids," Daniel said, suddenly noticing that there were no adults.

"Age is..." his father answered. "Age is whatever you want it to be."

"They play as children because it's fun," his mum added, laughing while watching two kids playing catch.

As Daniel watched, his eyes widened, and a sudden burst of youthful joy overwhelmed him. He saw a group of carefree children running through the grass. Their happiness was contagious, and Daniel burst out laughing. Suddenly, he felt an urge to join them, a need to shed his adult worries and frolic in the grass without a care in the world. His mind was filled with whimsical thoughts, yearning to be freed and embrace his childhood once more.

"Not just yet," his father said, gently holding Daniel's arm as he was about to run.

Daniel paused like he was standing between two worlds. He wanted to go and play, but somehow he knew he couldn't.

"It's not your time," his mother said. "If you went out there, you would be unable to return, and you have a different path to follow."

A young woman stood on the edge of the tree line, away from the children. She stared directly at Daniel, ignoring the playful scene in the clearing. Though she appeared some way off in the distance, he could see her in perfect clarity; he felt as though he could easily reach out a hand and touch her.

Her hair was long and black, falling perfectly past her shoulders onto the ground. It was of such darkness that no light reflected from it. Instead, it seemed to suck in all the light that dared try to offer illumination. Her skin looked pale, almost deathly white, yet it glowed with bright radiance, appearing soft and tender without a single blemish, sitting in such stark contrast against the blackness of her hair.

Her eyes were the colour of sapphire, sparkling a deep blue and peering out from below long eyelashes. As he stared into them, they held no warmth in their beauty but were cutting and stark. Yet he was drawn to them; they were alluring and carnal. Her full, blood-red lips held no smile, yet appeared soft and inviting. She wore a plain white robe made of a silky material that was so fine and delicate it revealed every perfect contour of her frame.

As Daniel stared, the childish thoughts just moments before fell away and were replaced with a growing desire to meet her lips with his. His heart started to pound as though he had fallen willingly into her spell. A yearning welled up inside him, and he wanted to lose all control, to collapse into her, to lose himself. She shrouded all his memories, but he no longer cared to remember; his focus was purely on her. She beckoned to him and he heard her voice, soft and alluring. Daniel had to go to her, he belonged to her, but his father, sensing Daniel's emotions, gently placed his hand on his shoulder.

"You cannot go there. She stands at the doorway to Shadow," he said sternly, but there was concern in his voice.

Daniel turned to his father but did not see him. His eyes were glazed; all he could see and hear was her. He felt absorbed by her, and he did not care.

"To fall into Shadow would be to fall into eternal bliss," Daniel uttered in a trance-like state.

His mother and father gave a glance of concern to one another, instantly knowing each other's thoughts; they knew what stood there beckoning their son. In the next instance, Daniel held the cup of still liquid, and again he stared, but this time, all he saw was Shadow. He looked up to his father for reassurance, who smiled and nodded encouragingly.

"Okay, son, drink, and I will take you to her," his father said, knowing that this was Daniel's only way out. "It'll be alright, son. Now drink."

Daniel turned from his father and now saw the strange woman running towards him; his heart soared as he saw her quickly approaching.

"Drink," his mother said.

As Daniel drank the liquid, a sudden shrill came from the tree line; its voice sent shivers down his spine. The liquid quickly took effect, the mist that shrouded his mind lifted, and slowly, the truth was revealed. Her beauty instantly dissolved, and the illusion that hid her was gone. Daniel gasped in horror at what he saw.

Her black hair was no longer smooth but

now looked razor-sharp, ominously sprawling high up into the air. Her skin was cracked and covered in black veins that spread across her. Her lips were no longer tender but now twisted and vulgar. But what horrified Daniel most was her coal-black eyes, now revealing an eternal emptiness.

"Go!" his father shouted and pushed Daniel back.

Daniel fell backwards, thrown far from the world occupied by his parents, away from healing streams, endless lush green fields, tall majestic trees, and wizards. His body lost all sense of gravity and was thrust into the vastness of time and space. Dazzling lights danced and twirled around him like a display of shooting stars. They intertwined, weaving an intricate web resembling complex pathways that seemed to stretch on for eternity. The brilliance was almost blinding, causing him to squint and shield his eyes. Like a trapped fly, Daniel fell into the shimmering web, and his body tingled with an indescribable sensation. As soon as he was ensnared, he felt every strand of the web, every connection that bound them all together. At that moment, he felt like he was a part of the web, his limbs intertwined and stretched out, following every pathway.

His mind expanded, his senses sharpened, and with a sudden clarity, he knew the fate of every being. Then he saw a glimmer of truth. His voice echoed as he said, "There are three." The vibrations from his words seemed to pulse through the strands, sending ripples throughout the entire structure.

The rumbling vibrations pulsated throughout the web, radiating outwards along the lines fading into infinity. The reverberations steadily grew in intensity. The web shook violently, and the space around him burst with energy. It was like standing on the edge of an earthquake, waiting for the inevitable eruption.

Then suddenly he was thrown free. He thought that this would be his final end. Silence descended, and he felt himself drift into an empty dark void. He closed his eyes, ready to fade away and accept his fate, when suddenly a voice cut through the silence.

"Daniel, wake up!" a familiar voice cut through the silence.

A sudden flash of light and a glowing orb appeared, pushing back the darkness that had enveloped him. Daniel's eyes widened with hope as he lunged forward, stretching out his hands and grasping it from the abyss. With each passing second, the orb grew brighter and hotter until his fingertips were scorched black by its searing heat. Yet he refused to let go, somehow knowing that he had to hold on tight. The orb burst into flame, and Daniel went to scream out, but suddenly, he found himself back in his apartment, sweating profusely, his heart racing. The pain was almost unbearable, and he clutched his chest, falling onto his side, then all went black.

"Daniel, wake up!" He felt a cool hand resting on his forehead.

He opened his eyes to a slither; the image before him was hazy. He could make out the silhouette of a woman. She had a soft glow around her. As she came into focus, the fogginess fell away, and he was captured by warm blue eyes looking lovingly at him, the familiar blue eyes of Aya.

"What happened?" Daniel croaked in a husky voice. His mouth felt as dry as the Sahara.

"I found you here, not moving." Aya was holding back tears born of fear. "You had me scared."

"I..." Daniel said with a low wheeze. "I don't know, I was drinking a coffee, I think." He felt confused and uncertain. He rubbed his head and tried to get up, but Aya gently pushed him back.

"Sit," she demanded, "you look terrible."

"It's good to see you too," Daniel said faintly, trying to smile. "But what are you doing here?"

"I came up to see how you were doing. Your door was open, and I called in, but there was no answer. I was worried, especially after your trip down the stairs."

She was worried about me, Daniel thought, briefly forgetting about the pain in his chest. However, a sharp stabbing reminded him, and he winced.

"I saw you on the couch, I was going to leave, but you didn't look right. I've been trying to wake you." She looked concerningly at him. "I was worried."

Like the cavalry late for a rumble, in burst two paramedics.

"We had a call," one said, trying to catch his breath, whilst the other looked around for the emergency.

"Oh yeah." Aya awkwardly grinned. "I called an ambulance." *Sorry*, she mouthed.

Fifteen minutes later, the very understanding paramedics were gone. Daniel had been warned about the dangers of excessive drinking. He felt very foolish, especially as his shame was being exposed in full site of Aya.

"Do you want a coffee?" Daniel asked, now feeling much better.

She nodded. "Yes, please, that would be nice, but I'll make it. You sit. Don't you move a muscle!" she demanded. She went to the kitchen and started looking for the cups.

"Second cupboard over, coffee is on the side, milk in the fridge," Daniel called over.

"Thanks."

"I'm sorry," Daniel said, "I must have looked like a right mess."

"Do you take sugar?" Aya said.

"No thanks."

"Oh, and don't be silly. I'm just relieved that you're okay."

Aya returned from the kitchen with two warm

mugs of coffee. She placed the drinks on the trunk and sat next to Daniel. She felt relieved and angry, simultaneously wanting to slap and hug him. Instead, she sat there quietly. She reached over and held Daniel's hand, avoiding eye contact for fear of crying.

"I could get used to this," Daniel said, a grin forming.

"I bet you could." Aya chuckled.

Daniel sat back and sighed heavily. He turned and looked out the window at the blue sky. A vague expression drew across his face.

"You look deep in thought," she said, concerned.

"I know this sounds weird, but something happened." He paused. "I remember, well, it's hard to put into words," Daniel said, eyes fixed on a small wispy cloud.

"You mean when you were out cold?" Aya said, looking curiously at him.

Daniel breathed deeply and let out a long mournful sigh. "It's like I was in a trance, and I was somewhere else. It felt so real." He turned to Aya. "And then I heard you calling me to wake up. Odd, I know." His voice was now almost a whisper.

Aya remained quiet, but the expression on her face said more than any words could have.

Daniel shifted uncomfortably. "I'm young, healthy, and in my prime," he demanded, "and there's no need to look at me like that. Honestly, I am fine."

"You need to look after yourself," she said, looking stern, but her expression quickly eased into a smile. She brushed Daniel's cheek with her hand. "And don't scare me like that again," she added, her soft touch suddenly becoming a playful slap.

"Ouch!" Daniel complained and rubbed his cheek.

They sat there silently for a moment. Then, they both burst out laughing.

"Okay, Okay." Daniel raised his hands in defeat. "I take your point." He had to concede to Aya's glare.

She looked content with his submission and offered a smile as compensation.

"Anyway, I was thinking," she said brightly, now changing the subject, "maybe we should go out again." She paused and thought for a moment. "Perhaps when you are feeling better?"

"What do you mean?" Daniel asked. "I'm fine." He reiterated his earlier point.

"Well," she said, appearing to be in thought, "perhaps it would be a good idea to keep an eye on you."

"That's a great idea, a perfect idea. I would like your eyes on me," Daniel said cheekily.

Aya giggled. "Well, I could manage that. I was thinking perhaps a movie?"

"Cool, what film?"

"They're showing *The Bridge* at the Electric," Aya said.

"Cool, probably my favourite film," Daniel replied, feeling the need to please her. He had heard of the film but had never gotten around to seeing it.

"Awesome, it blows my mind that stuff, life and death." She pondered for a moment. "Some people find it morbid, but I don't know, it just fascinates me. You probably will think me weird."

"Funny you should say that. Yes I do, I think you very odd." He feigned fright.

"You're heading for another slap if you don't behave." Her cheeks slightly reddened.

Daniel laughed. "No, I'm sorry. I agree, I agree, it is a fascinating subject."

"Oh, you tease!" Aya snapped and slapped his arm.

Daniel pretended to be in pain. "You would hit a dying man," he joked.

"Not funny."

"Sorry," he said in submission, realising probably not the best jest due to what had just happened.

"Well, anyway," she said, moving the conversation on, "I can't believe you love that film."

Daniel shrugged, hoping that he wouldn't be quizzed.

"Okay," Aya said, "your favourite band?"

"Fidler," Daniel answered truthfully this time.

"Me too!" she said excitedly.

"Favourite food?" Daniel asked.

"Freshly fried chips with mayonnaise."

"No way!" Daniel said in genuine surprise.

"Favourite TV show?" she replied.

Daniel thought. "Ahh, you got me there. I don't watch TV."

"Neither do I! It was a trick question," she said, laughing.

"This is so weird. I mean, I feel that I know you."

"Yeah, I know. The first time I saw you…" Daniel trailed off. "What happened the other night."

"Yeah, I know. I have never felt that way before."

"Neither have I, I…"

"We are acting like school kids having their first crush." She laughed and took Daniel's hand. "Whatever it was, it felt like it was meant to be."

She got up to go. Daniel watched her as she walked to the front door. She paused and turned to him.

"I'll be over later with the DVD, say about seven?" Aya said.

"I thought we were going out?"

"Well, I think it probably would be better to have a night in, if you don't mind me coming over and spending alone time with you. I mean, just me and you, alone in your flat." She smiled seductively

Daniel was speechless, but his broad, childish grin said a thousand words.

"I haven't seen that film," he blurted out, feeling a need to confess his white lie.

Aya paused and smiled. "I know," she said.

…

Daniel had jumped up as soon as she had left and started to consider preparations for the night. He wanted it to be perfect. He rummaged through his cupboards, looking for something to cook. His eyes darted over the various tins and packets, desperately looking for inspiration, but none could be found. Daniel quickly concluded that he was not prepared for such a momentous occasion. He wanted the evening to go flawlessly, so he promptly chucked on whatever clothes he could find, left his apartment, and headed for the local supermarket. As he walked down the road, he came to the realisation that he was, in fact, a terrible cook.

"Sam," he muttered to himself.

Samantha was the best cook he knew. She won a cooking competition once; granted, she was only fifteen at the time. Still, Daniel had always remembered sneaking a taste of her apple and blueberry tart. Since then, he had boasted that it was the best thing he'd ever tasted.

Daniel stood outside the supermarket and realised that his best course of action was to head home and call the one person who could save the day, or evening at the very least. He called Samantha and, in his most pitiful voice, asked for help. However, before she would offer any advice, she spent the first thirty minutes probing Daniel about his newly found romance.

Once she was satisfied, she offered some great ideas, none of which he would be able to cook. So she offered to come over early and prepare everything. All Daniel would have to do was heat everything up and serve.

Seven came, and there was a knock at the door. Daniel jumped up, and Aya stood there holding a DVD and a bag.

"Snacks for later," she said, referring to the bag. "Hello." She smiled and stood there expectantly.

"Sorry, where are my manners? Please come in." Daniel beckoned her in.

Aya walked in, brushing past Daniel. As she passed, he breathed in deeply. She was intoxicating. She was wearing a little black dress that looked like it had been sprayed on. It clung to every curve of her body and stopped just short of her knees. Her hair was bunched high atop her head, exposing her slender neck. As she moved past Daniel, he watched her every movement, entranced. Aya looked back at him and smiled.

"Coming?" she said.

Daniel stumbled over his words and unwillingly snapped from the trance. He thought she was more perfect than before. *How am I so lucky?*

She entered the front room and noticed a laid

table, a candle burning in the middle, and a lone rose sitting in a glass.

"You didn't have to go to such trouble. Looks lovely," Aya said.

"No trouble for you, I wanted to. Sorry, I know this is a bit cliché," Daniel said.

"No, no, it's perfect." She walked over to Daniel and kissed him softly on his cheek.

Daniel's heart raced, and he blushed just a little, but enough for Aya to notice.

"Would you like to eat?" Daniel said, now trying to take control of his senses.

"Sounds wonderful."

They sat down for what turned out to be a very successful meal. Samantha had outdone herself. The meal was impressive, starting with razor clams with spring onions and almonds, followed by mussels with chorizo, beans, and cavolo nero, and finished with raspberry s'mores.

"What can I say? That was fantastic," Aya said, impressed with what Daniel had served.

"Well, thank you," Daniel said.

"Honestly, this was great. How did you put all this together?" she asked.

"Oh, you know the chef rarely reveals their secrets," Daniel lied terribly

"Oh really?" Aya said with growing suspicion. "So, a chef rarely reveals their secret?" She chuckled. "They usually write a book." She laughed, sipped her wine, and eyed Daniel from over the brim.

"Well..." Daniel leaned back and took a drink from his wine glass. "Well, you start by..." He paused, looking for the words. "Well, by..."

"Yes, please go on. I am intrigued." Aya narrowed her eyes.

"Oh, okay, you start by calling a good friend who is an awesome cook." Daniel looked away and blushed.

Aya laughed aloud. "Well, the food is awesome, and, well, who was the chef?"

"Sam." Daniel smiled and shrugged.

"Well, Sam is an excellent cook, but..." she smiled and took Daniel's hand, "the company is better than the excellent food."

He blushed even more, and Aya smiled

lovingly. They left the table, made themselves comfortable on the couch, and laid out all the snacks, though neither felt they could eat another thing. He put the DVD in the player and sat back on the couch. Aya moved over to him, waiting for him to raise his arm; she snuggled in tight and sighed in contentment.

…

"Fading memories," Daniel said quietly, barely a whisper. "Where were we?"

Aya's gaze seemed lost in this place; she didn't notice his words.

"It smells good here."

"It does," she replied, and let out a small sigh.

"I love the smell of these sweet flowers."

"Where do you think we are?"

"I don't know, but it feels like we belong here."

"Together."

"Together."

"Is this a dream?"

"I don't know. It feels real."

"It feels right."

"It feels right."

"Wake up, Daniel. It's not your time just yet."

...

CHAPTER 6

Providence
Life is an endless journey, never knowing where it may lead.

Samaira was born in the small village of Mawlynnong in Meghalaya, India. The village was a beautiful, idyllic place, with green hills and blue waters that reflected the sky, where children ran around playing and laughing while their mothers cooked on open fires and their fathers tended to the farm animals.

The townspeople were happy people; they needed nothing but each other. They lived off the land in an environment so pure it could be described as a second Eden. It wasn't always an easy life, but it was a happy one.

Samaira was born with star-bright blue eyes, which were so unusual that the villagers considered it a sign of her being spiritually gifted. They even called her "God's little gift." It was a unique occurrence, as no one in the village had ever seen such an eye colour before, or at least not in living memory.

When she was born, it was said that the sun shone so brightly that it lit every corner of the village and cast a soft, warm light that pushed away all shadow, and that when she came into the world, she brought a feeling of joy to all about her. However, she did not smile nor make a sound. As she grew, her bright blue eyes intently watched all the world evolve around her. She watched people come into her young life and leave, yet no matter how people tried, Samaira still made no sound. There was a hint of sadness hidden behind her young eyes, as though there was a longing for someone who was not there, and she was waiting for them to return to complete her. It was on her sixth birthday, sitting with her mother by a stream in the early morning sun, when Samaira spoke for the first time.

"I am broken," Samaira said to her mother. "I feel empty." Her voice sounded lonely.

Her mother was shocked and heartbroken to hear such sad words, but though she tried, she could do nothing to help her child, and Samaira fell into silence once again. However, an event was soon to take place that would change Samaira's life forever.

Samaira walked home from school and found herself lost in thought. She daydreamed about a young boy with bright blue eyes who was familiar to her in a way she did not understand. She only ever smiled when she thought of him, but her heart sank, and her smile faded when she awoke from the dream.

Suddenly, she heard a commotion from farther down her path, just out of sight as the road veered off to the left.

She cautiously approached the bend in the road. Suddenly, a small, skinny boy sprung out of nowhere and collided with her. They both fell in a heap on the ground as Samaira's school books flew into the air, and their contents fluttered down all around them.

"Sorry, sorry," said the panicked little boy whilst he struggled to scramble up to his feet and catch his breath. He turned to run, which would have left Samaira to her fate, but something caused him to hesitate.

He slowly turned to her, stretched out his hand, and smiled broadly.

"Let me help you," he spoke with a kind voice.

"Thank you," Samaira said, smiling coyly, accepting the help. Looking around, she sighed. "My books are…" She stopped, looking at him curiously. "Your eyes, they're—" But before she could finish her sentence, the little skinny boy's pursuers had caught up. They seized the little boy, pushing Samaira out of the way and back onto the ground. She landed with a thud.

One of the boys in the group, taller and with a face marked by his tough street life, grabbed the little boy by his shirt, lifting him off the ground. The taller boy loomed over the little boy, casting a menacing shadow that seemed to stretch out. The atmosphere grew colder; even the sunlight was pushed back, fading into a dim haze.

He struggled to break free from the iron-like grip that held him.

His frustration and fear were palpable until a sudden flicker of movement caught his eye. Turning his head, he caught sight of Samaira, which seemed to fill him with a sense of hope and strength.

He suddenly turned to his captor, whose face was twisted with anger and hatred, and punched with all his might. However, his little hand made an insignificant impact and buckled on the big boy's chest.

The bullies laughed in well-practised unison, jeered, pointed, and hurled abuse at the little boy, and he was thrown to the ground next to Samaira. They sat there staring up at their aggressors like two lambs surrounded by hungry wolves. The menacing shadows of their persecutors cast over them like a dark storm, promising ruin and despair.

Unexpectedly, Samaira stood up and showed no fear, which shocked the bullies, who stepped back but continued their verbal assault, which now included Samaira.

Samaira looked down at the little boy and held out her hand, smiling reassuringly.

"Take my hand," she said warmly. He did, and she pulled him to his feet.

"What's your name?" she asked, ignoring the taunts in the background.

"Aisim," he replied, wiping away a tear he had tried to hide from her.

The larger boy in the group did not like being ignored. He stepped forward with the intent to bring about more harm. His shadow seemed to grow taller and darken, blotting out what little sunlight there was. Something unexpected happened: Samaira and Aisim found courage in one another that they did not realise existed until that moment. Their bright blue eyes shone out, filled with determination and resolve. They turned to their attackers in perfect unison and stepped towards them.

"Back off!" one of the bullies sneered, but a growing fear filled the air, and it did not radiate from either Samaira or Aisim.

The two took another step, not a word said, still hand in hand, and stood there, now a pillar of strength. A faint warm glow radiated from them. The shadows that had encompassed them seemed to shrink back in trepidation at the growing light that shone from them.

Two of the bullies ran off in shock at what they saw, leaving only the taller boy who had grabbed Aisim. He stood there determined not to be scared off, steadfast in his resolve. As the two young children approached him, he stumbled back and fell to the ground. Now fear started to take its grip; he held up his hand to protect himself from the imagined threat to come. The shadow that had cast such a doom was now gone, and the sunlight streamed in and brought light and warmth.

Aisim showed no aggression or violence. He appeared calm and wanted no revenge. He stood over the now cowering boy on the ground, held out his hand in friendship, and smiled kindly.

The bully was overcome with shame as he took Aisim's hand and was helped up.

"It's okay," Aisim said with forgiveness in his voice. "What is your name?"

"Advay," the boy answered, bowing his head in disgrace.

Aisim smiled, nodded, and turned away.

As Advay stood there, he watched Samaira and Aisim walk away hand in hand. A realisation was cast over him, a self-reflection of his actions, and Advay was forever changed from that moment.

Fate had made its plan for Samaira and Aisim,

and despite hardships and sorrow, they were where they were meant to be.

Samaira turned to Aisim and smiled.

...

Aisim had recently moved to Mawlynnong from another village, several miles away, to live with his Aunt Aashritha.

Many years previously, his father and mother had tragically died in a house fire when he was only two. After the tragedy, his uncle had been there to raise him with loving care. He tried his best to provide little Aisim with a stable family environment.

However, Aisim was haunted by the events of the night that took his parents all those years earlier, which caused him to become reckless and mischievous.

When Aisim approached his sixth birthday, his uncle was taken ill, and it was decided that it would be best for little Aisim to live with his aunt.

Aisim never spoke about the event that had thrown his life into such turmoil and chaos. He only once confided in Samaira; however, he only ever said how his father had pushed him out of their burning home. He then went back in to find his mother, but neither returned. There would be times in later years when Aisim would have night terrors reliving that night. He would see a shadow, not a fire, engulfing his former home. Then the shadow would turn to find him, to finish what it had started. However, Samaira would always know how to cast light into those dark thoughts. Eventually, the shadow faded with Samaira's radiance and never returned.

When Samaira and Aisin were of age, they were married and found their place in the village. Samaira spent much of her time helping others. She studied medicine and eventually completed a medical course. She discovered that she had a natural healing talent. People would come to her from other nearby villages for help; she never asked for any payment, but people would gladly give what they had.

Aisim found his talent lay in spiritualism. He helped people, much like Samaira; however, he would heal the soul. Often, he would talk with the villagers about what lay beyond what was seen around us. Somehow, he could see beyond the horizon, beyond what others saw. He had an uncanny ability to see into people's hearts and thoughts and helped them to overcome personal struggles. The Kapoors were soon renowned for their healing talents; between Samaira and Aisim, they were one, healers of body and soul.

They had five children, first twin boys and later three girls. When the two boys were born, they were both strong and healthy.

The birth had been painless and quick for Samaira, and the boys were born within an hour. Samaira was spared any discomfort. It was as though she had been carried far away to a place of peace and calmness.

Samaira felt overwhelmed with joy as she held her twin boys for the first time. She gazed into their bright blue eyes, and they gazed back at her, echoing her love. A gentle breeze swept by, carrying the sweet scent of lilies into the room.

Samaira was entranced and spoke softly. She looked down at one of the boys and said, "Divit," then turned to the other and said, "Ehsaan."

They smiled as they fixed their gazes on their mother, yet refrained from making any noise. The room was filled with a soothing ambience that emanated from all around them, providing a sense of safety and comfort.

Samaira was filled with an immense feeling of peace, and it brought tears of happiness to her eyes. Aisim looked on with a newfound understanding, and he went to Samaira's side and kissed her tenderly.

When the boys were three years old, Divit contracted tuberculosis. After several weeks of struggle, he lost his battle for life and passed away. Ehsaan's health quickly deteriorated soon afterwards, and he fell into a trance-like state, as though his soul had left his body, leaving only a shell behind.

No matter how his parents tried to help him, he did not respond, and to their dismay, they could not help their son, but could only watch as he grew weaker each day.

Aisin woke up to a soft, cool breeze which caressed his face. He looked over at Samaira, who was sound asleep next to Ehsaan, and saw a smile on her face as she was lost in a happy dream.

Aisim pulled the cover over Samaira and sat next to his son. He brushed the hair from Ehsaan's face, closed his eyes, and prayed for his son's recovery.

After some time, he stood up and turned to see that though his son lay next to Samaira, he also stood at the end of his bed, Divit standing beside him.

The two boys smiled at their father, then faded away, leaving two orbs of light. They started to move about and then danced around each other, spinning faster and faster, getting brighter, until the whole room was filled with light. Then in the next second, they vanished.

Aisim paused for a moment and sighed heavily, for he knew that Ehsaan had left. He then turned to Samaira and lovingly woke her, breaking the news gently.

The loss of their sons was incredibly difficult for them. Despite having helped numerous others, they could not prevent a tragedy from befalling their own children. As a result, they came to believe that their boys, Divit and Ehsaan, were not meant to remain in this world and that their passing was meant to be. There was a comfort in this understanding and the thought that they would all be reunited when the time was right.

Soon after this, they had the three girls. First came Assia, who grew to have long brown hair which matched her deep hazel eyes. A little later, Melinia, who looked a lot like her sister, but a little taller. Lastly, the most inquisitive of their children was Ayaissa, who did not resemble her sisters. Instead, she was shorter than them, had bright blue eyes similar to her parents and long dark hair. Her aspirations towards life were also very different.

Assia and Melinia shared the same desires in life, to simply have a family and find a husband who would provide for their children. They pictured moving to a city, or at the very least one of the larger towns, the type of house they would love to own, the schools their children would attend, and the holidays they would take. With childish vigour, they often spent hours planning their weddings and crafting their ideal lives.

Ayaissa was not interested in any of the things her sisters craved. She, instead, had always loved learning and discovering new facts about the world rather than thinking about a husband or children. Her ambition was to travel and explore. She would spend her days daydreaming about leaving the village, imagining herself in faraway places, and meeting new people. Exploration was her drive.

Her unwavering curiosity and adventurous spirit often led her to explore the surrounding countryside, where she was usually found turning over rocks to see what lay beneath, exploring old caves, and daydreaming about the life she would one day find. She carried a small green notebook with her, where she wrote her thoughts and the discoveries that she had come across. She would imagine herself as a great adventurer, traversing some unknown plain in some faraway land, ready to embrace whatever fate threw at her.

Ayaissa had shown none of her parents' gifts and only seemed to share their unusual bright blue eye colour, which disappointed some in the village. However, one day, while on her way home from school, she chanced upon an injured bird. One of its wings was outstretched and twisted, and as it hopped along, it dragged it along the ground. When the bird saw Ayaissa, it stopped its struggle and looked curiously up at her.

"Hello, little bird," Ayaissa said with a smile. The bird chirped.

Ayaissa reached down and gently scooped the bird up in her hands.

She moved her mouth close to the bird and whispered softly, "Fly now, little one, and find your way home."

Her hands started to glow warmly, and the bird suddenly spread its wings and flew. She stood there for a long moment as she watched it fly high into the sky, singing its song as it faded into the distance and out of sight. Ayaissa felt suddenly exhausted and yawned, barely being able to keep her eyes open.

Upon returning home, she shared with her parents the events that had occurred, how she wanted the bird to fly and be healed, and the warm sensation she felt rising up from inside. It was then that her parents realised that she had inherited their gift.

"You have the gift," Samaira said to Ayaissa, who sat exhausted on a chair with her head and arms sprawled over the kitchen table.

Ayaissa answered with a yawn.

"I wondered if it would show itself," her father added.

"I'm so tired," Ayaissa complained.

"You gave a little of yourself to heal that bird," Samaira said and brought over a hot, sweet cup of tea. "Drink this. It will help."

Ayaissa drew herself up, carefully sipped the hot drink, and sighed contentedly.

"Drink up, then bed," her father said.

Ayaissa rolled her eyes. "I'm not tired," she yawned.

Word of this quickly spread throughout the village, causing people to view Ayaissa in a new light and expect great things from her. However, she did not desire the newfound attention and simply wished to travel, and her focus remained unchanged. She wanted to leave, and she knew her destiny lay elsewhere.

Samaira tried to teach Ayaissa what she had been taught, how to control her gift and use it safely. However, Ayaissa's mind drifted to those faraway places. Her parents hoped that she would find her place in the village as they had, but they eventually had to accept that, at some point, she would leave.

Over the course of time, Ayaissa discovered a remarkable talent for cultivating plants. Through the simple act of placing her hands on the soil, she found that she possessed the ability to breathe life into the earth. It was as though she shared an intuitive connection with the natural world, and the environment willingly responded to her every touch. Ayaissa enjoyed her newly discovered gift; whenever she could, she would use it. Her garden soon became a popular spot for people to visit. It bloomed with many different types of flowers, tall leafy plants, and lush green shrubs. The aroma that filled the air was sweet and filled people with a sense of youthful vigour.

Ayaissa followed in her parents' footsteps and dedicated her spare time to helping others. She spread her understanding of the natural world to those who asked and helped many farmers who would come to her for advice.

By the time Ayaissa had left school, she was well respected, and the rumour of the girl who could talk to Mother Earth had spread far and wide. She was no stranger to demanding work and found employment at local farms, shops, and wherever else she could earn a little money. Although she cherished her community and the kindness she found there, she experienced a persistent desire to venture out and discover new horizons. This inner longing haunted her, as though fate was urging her to leave, to go where she was meant to be.

Ayaissa found herself caught in a recurring dream that she couldn't shake. Each time she fell into a deep sleep, she was transported to a serene land of lush green fields. In this dream, she always held hands with a young girl with striking sapphire blue eyes and raven black hair that cascaded down her back in gentle waves. They stood side by side and watched the breathtaking display of the sun's final moments of the day explode in a cascade of vibrant colours. Ayaissa couldn't help but notice that a lone figure always stood in the distance. He seemed to be admiring the same view, but as the sun slowly sank beyond the horizon, the man vanished from sight like a fleeting mirage. She couldn't explain why she kept having this dream, but she found herself looking forward to it each night.

"What does my dream mean?" Ayaissa finally asked her father.

"You will know when the time is right," her father answered.

"When the time is right?" Ayaissa said impatiently.

"Patience, Ayaissa," Samaira said. "All will be made clear when the time is right."

"Don't be too quick to wish time away, little Ayaissa. Before you know it, you will be old and grey like us," her father added with a kind smile.

"Patience is not found in youth, but born of age and understanding," her mother muttered, then shook her head and chuckled.

The years did eventually pass, and it was time for Ayaissa to leave as she had planned. Once all the necessary preparations were complete, she took a deep breath and bid her beloved village a bittersweet farewell. It was finally time to set her carefully crafted plans into motion, which she had been tirelessly working on for what felt like a lifetime. Excitement and nervousness swirled within her as she ventured into the unknown, determined to see her dreams come true.

"Take this," Samaira said.

Ayaissa held out her hand, and Samaira placed a sapphire blue pendant on a silver chain in her palm.

"This has been in the family for as long as it has been told." Samaira closed Ayaissa's hand around the pendant. "Keep it safe, and it will keep you safe." She placed her hand on Ayaissa's cheek. "I will pray for you, precious one."

"I'll be fine," Ayaissa said, wrapped the silver chain around her neck, and hugged her mother.

"Remember, you have your uncle's address in your bag," Samaira said. "Don't lose it."

"Please look after yourself," her father added and hugged her again.

Assia gave her a long purple and gold scarf. "This will keep you warm on your travels, little sister," she said, and hugged her tightly.

Melinia, with tears running down her cheeks, gave her a silver ring. "Wear this and remember me," she said, squeezing Ayaissa tightly.

Leaving her family and friends was difficult, but she felt a mysterious force drawing her towards a faraway destination. She knew she had little choice but to follow destiny's call.

...

Ayaissa first moved to Mumbai, where she lived with relatives. She soon found work and saved every spare rupee she could. She always remembered her parents and sent money back home, though Samaira would always tell her not to. Eventually she had enough money to buy a plane ticket to Istanbul, where she found casual work, and the cycle continued: she saved, sent money home, and travelled.

Leaving Istanbul, she hitched to Bulgaria, then Romania, flying to Italy, crossing France, and finally crossing the English Channel to Dover, UK. This journey took her a year, and it was a year that transformed her. She was no longer simply a girl from a small village in India, but she had grown, and the world had opened her eyes.

She witnessed hardships—not the same that she had felt in her life, but more severe, amplified by a feeling of isolation. She saw the brutality of war, conflicts, people's inhumane behaviour towards each other, and the deprivation caused by extreme poverty. She came across locations where the wealthy ignored the poor, where abundance existed but was not given to those most in need. She encountered the worst of humanity, but also discovered glimpses of hope, witnessing love and kindness in the bleakest of situations. She met people with nothing to spare, yet they shared what little they had and helped others in need. Her journey transformed her in unexpected ways, opening her eyes to a world torn between Light and Shadow.

Ayaissa developed a remarkable gift of empathy, which helped her to establish deep connections with others and even to comprehend their innermost feelings. Wherever she went, she brought people closer together and, at times, even helped people resolve long-standing conflicts. As she journeyed, news of her remarkable talents spread out before her; people from all walks of life sought her guidance, and she willingly extended her compassion and understanding. When she finally arrived on the shores of England, she matured into a strong, patient, and wise young woman, far removed from the young girl who had left her village a year earlier.

Ayaissa made her way across from Dover to Cardiff, finally ending her journey at her Uncle Ras's home. He owned a small apartment block consisting of three flats. The ground floor was where Ras lived, the first floor Mrs. Joan Bennet, and the top-floor flat had been empty for some time after the last tenant left to be married in Scotland to his childhood sweetheart.

He had only ever seen her as a baby, and he was overjoyed to finally meet his niece; this lifted his spirits and inquisitive nature. She spent the first day updating her uncle on all the latest news from the village, and he sat listening intently, offering new questions as the conversation continued. When his curiosity was finally sated, he showed her where she would live while staying with him.

Uncle Ras set her up in the top-floor flat, where he knew she would be safe and he could keep a watchful eye on her, feeling a sense of responsibility and adopting the role of her parents. He never had children; his wife died many years back, and he lived alone. He would spend his days pottering about and tending to a small garden at the rear of the property, where he grew many different plants with various levels of success. However, as he discovered, with the help of Ayaissa his garden blossomed into a beautiful oasis of life and colour.

Joan would often check up on Uncle Ras and

keep him company, spending countless hours talking about the many years that had passed in their lives. They would exchange stories over a bottle of wine until the early morning hours.

Ayaissa settled in and found life easy. Unlike the struggles she had to endure in her past, everything seemed to fall into place for her. Soon she found work on a local farm, putting her talents to great use. She quickly made new friends and was much liked by those she interacted with. Joan and Ayaissa became good friends and often talked about their travels. Ayaissa would sit listening intently to the many stories Joan told.

Ayaissa felt that she had arrived at the place she was meant to be and was happy.

...

It was a sunny day in June. There was not a cloud in the sky, and the sunlight gleamed, bringing life and vibrance to all it touched.

Brynn sat alone on an old wooden bench in the park. He was lost in thought as he stared out onto the tranquil stillness of the pond stretching before him. Enticed by the shimmering sunlight on the smooth surface, he drifted off into a daydream, remembering a dream that he often had. Where he stood on a hill, and all around him was lush green grass swaying in an unseen warm breeze. The scent in the air was sweet and invigorating. The sun was setting in this place, and as it hit the horizon, it exploded in an array of vivid colours, but just at that moment, he noticed two people standing far off in the distance. As he turned towards them, the sun slowly set, and they would fade out of sight.

He was awoken by the sound of children playing in the playground behind him. They were shouting for their father to push them higher on the swings.

Brynn stretched, finished the last few bites of his sandwich, and casually threw what remained into the pond. The water rippled out as the scraps hit the surface with a small splash, breaking the calm. His gaze lingered as he watched two ducks squabble over the bobbing leftovers, their loud quacks echoing through the serene surroundings.

"Now, now, there's no need to fight," he said to the ducks, who responded with loud quacks.

Brynn sighed, shook his head, and then laughed. "Oh, so you think it's funny to argue with me?" Again, the ducks responded with several louder quacks.

He threw his last few scraps. "I'm afraid that's all I have today."

The ducks looked at him suspiciously and

quacked a little louder.

"I wouldn't lie to you guys," Brynn added, opening his bag to show that it was empty of any food.

Brynn heard a soft giggle coming from behind him. He turned around to see a young woman standing by the trunk of an old willow tree. She seemed to be watching him intently. He noticed her pretty smile and smiled warmly back at her. She came over and sat down next to him on the bench.

"Those ducks don't seem to enjoy your conversation," she said, trying to keep a straight face.

"Yes they do. We chat for hours," he said, feigning seriousness.

"Oh, I see, so what do they say during these long conversations?"

"Oh, mainly quack, followed by a quack, ending with a rather surprising and unexpected quack." He made the sound of a duck.

She laughed, no longer being able to contain herself.

"Has anyone told you that you have a wonderful smile?" Brynn said, gazing at her.

"Possibly," she answered and smiled.

"Well, you do. I would say that you have a perfect smile. In fact, if there was a smiling competition, I know you would gain the first prize," Brynn said with casual confidence.

She laughed again. "Well, thank you. I'm Ayaissa."

"Now, a beautiful name to go with your beautiful smile. I'm Brynn. It is a pleasure to meet you."

"And a pleasure to meet you too, Brynn." She chuckled. "Do you visit your ducks often?"

"Daily. You see that black and white one, she's Jamima, and that one is Stephanie." The ducks paid little attention now that the food had all gone. "Oh, and way over there is Lianne. You have to watch her, she can get a little frisky. I think it's the heat," he joked.

"Hello, Jamima, Stephanie, and Lianne." Ayaissa waved to the ducks.

They quacked loudly as they swam away. "They said hello," Brynn added.

Ayaissa stretched out and leaned back onto the bench. Her slim summer dress draped loosely, revealing her slender curves. Brynn tried not to look.

"It's so peaceful here. You chose a nice spot," she said.

"I come here to think, contemplate," Brynn

said as he turned his gaze back to the water.

"And talk to your ducks too." She smiled

"Of course," he answered. "I know a perfect place for lunch, and the food is fantastic. You hungry?" Brynn asked, hoping to spend more time with this girl that intrigued him.

"I could be," she answered, looking at Brynn with an air of familiarity.

Brynn stood up and patiently waited for Ayaissa to join him. As she sat there, she stared at him momentarily, feeling a growing sense of familiarity towards him. There was something about him that she couldn't quite comprehend.

"Do I have something on my top?" He laughed and brushed himself down.

"No," she said with a smile and stood up, wrapping her arm around his. "Let's go get that food."

...

They met every day at the same time in the park on that old weathered wooden bench. Jamima and Stephanie would often join them and squabble over the floating scraps until Lianne would invade and break up any quarrels.

They talked about their hopes and dreams, the past and the future. Ayaissa felt an instant bond with Brynn that she had never felt before with anyone else. It was as though fate had decided at the dawn of time that she should meet Brynn on that sunny day.

Uncle Ras was slightly more cautious about Ayaissa dating and often grilled Brynn about his motivations. An uncomfortable Brynn would sit there and politely dull Uncle Ras's suspicions. Ayaissa laughed during these events. She knew Uncle Ras was looking out for her and meant no harm. Over time, Uncle Ras came to like Brynn. The grilling changed into Uncle Ras talking about his life, how he met his wife and ended up owning an old house in Cardiff, which he had converted into three apartments many years previously.

Ayaissa found her ideal partner in Brynn, who not only made her happy but also grounded her and gave her stability in life. As time passed, their love grew stronger, leading Brynn to propose when Ayaissa turned twenty-five, and she happily accepted. Their wedding was an intimate gathering of close friends and family, and though it was wonderful to be reunited with loved ones, saying goodbye was just as hard as it was when she left her village five years prior.

They started their life together in the flat on the top floor. It was perfect for their needs, and Uncle Ras was happy for Ayaissa to be close as he had grown fond of her company.

Ayaissa found her calling when she started working at a nearby animal rescue farm. As soon as she stepped inside, she knew she was in her element. Her natural abilities with animals shone through as she quickly excelled at her responsibilities. Every day, she felt a sense of fulfilment and purpose as she used her gift to help heal injured creatures that came through the doors. She soon turned her talent into a profession and studied to be a veterinary nurse. Brynn was a talented software developer, but struggled to find full-time employment in Cardiff despite his best efforts. He eventually ended up freelancing for a few companies, but work was sporadic, and the pay was often poor. Finally, he had to look further afield, which led to him having to spend weeks away from home.

Life was good, though Brynn's work was often a talking point. Ayaissa missed him when he was away. She felt like she once did when living back in India, a feeling that something was missing. This time, she knew what it was: Brynn. His luck eventually changed when he found work with MicroTac, an IT company based in London. He was offered a full-time position that played to his talents, the money was good, and the company would even help with the move and supply accommodation. Brynn was both excited and anxious, and as he sat on the train on his way home, he wondered how he would break this bittersweet news to Ayaissa.

"Ayaissa, I'm back," Brynn called out as he entered their apartment.

Ayaissa ran out of the bedroom, leapt into the air, and wrapped herself around him, pushing him back against the corridor wall.

"I've missed you," she said, giving him a long slow kiss. "I didn't expect you back until this evening."

"I left early," he said to her, his arms holding tight to her waist.

"Well, I'm glad you're home." She gave him another kiss. "Do you want a drink?"

"Yeah, I could murder a coffee," Brynn said.

He let her go with a final kiss. She smiled and whispered, "I'm so glad you're home."

Ayaissa went off to the kitchen and started preparing some fresh coffee. Brynn went to the front room and paced up and down. Eventually he stood by the window and watched the people below.

"I have good and maybe bad news." He paused and waited to see if she responded. "I've been offered a job," Brynn called out hesitantly.

"Oh, must you work away again? I do miss you when you're not here." She sighed.

"Well, it's different this time." He paused. "You would be coming with me."

Ayaissa smiled and thought about it. "I'll have to see if I can get the time off work."

"No," he said and walked over to her. "I have been offered a permanent position." He paused and waited to see her response.

"Oh, I see." She brought two coffees over to the coffee table in the front room and sat down. Brynn followed her.

"I know it's a lot to take in, but what do you think?" he asked.

"I don't know," Ayaissa said. She blew across the hot coffee in her cup, creating a slight ripple on the surface. "Tell me about this opportunity."

Brynn leapt at the chance. "It's a hell of an opportunity for me," he said, spilling with excitement. "I will be managing a team of developers working on some real ultramodern projects. The money is good; in fact, it's perfect. They will give us a flat, with the choice to buy it later, and they will even cover the cost of the move."

"Sounds great," she said, but with a slight sigh in her voice.

"Oh, and no more away from home." He held her hand. "We don't have to make a decision today, and if you say no, it'll be no."

"I'll have to leave my job," she said quietly.

"Plus, Uncle Ras, should we leave him?"

"I know it is a difficult decision, but we have a chance to—"

"To?" she interrupted. "Aren't we happy here?"

Brynn didn't answer, but instead continued. "Oh, and I have been looking into work for you too." He handed her a list of veterinarians in the area where they would live. "We won't be in the heart of London, but on the outskirts, there are parks and plenty of places to walk our dog?"

"Dog?" Ayaissa said. "You've never wanted a dog."

"Yeah, let's get a dog," Brynn said.

"Brynn, you are nothing if not prepared. Well, where are we to live then?"

"So, are you saying yes?" he said hesitantly, unsure what to expect.

"Of course, I always love an adventure," she said and smiled. "We'd better start preparing, and give me that list of vets."

Brynn almost exploded with excitement and relief.

"Let's go out tonight and celebrate our new adventure," Ayaissa said. She leaned forward and kissed him. "You can't fight fate," she whispered.

She got up and walked to the bedroom; Brynn watched in awe of her beauty as she slipped out of view.

"Well, are you coming?" she called out.

...

"One final push," said the midwife. "C'mon, I know you can do it."

"I am, I am!" screamed Ayaissa. She pushed with all her might. Her face went red and sweaty as she panted. She had been fighting to deliver the child for nearly ten hours. And though every time the midwife said they were almost there, it felt like this baby would never make an appearance.

"It'll be okay," Brynn said. Ayaissa glared at him in response. If looks could kill, there would have been one less life in the world.

Ayaissa screamed out, eyes wide open as she pushed with all her might. Everything she had to give, she gave in that moment.

"It's a girl!" cried the midwife, then silence.

The room suddenly went cold, and the lights dimmed as a shadow grew. The air felt thick as fog and smelled of blood. Ayaissa's eyes widened as she saw a shadowy figure take form and loom over her baby. Brynn stared in shock and horror at the little bundle lying limp in the midwife's arms. He felt helpless. Ayaissa screamed in desperation, and pain rushed through her. Brynn took her in his arms to try to comfort her, but there was nothing that could be said or done. The midwife desperately tried to revive the newborn, but nothing. Minutes passed, but it felt like time had stood still, frozen at that moment.

Then, the words they dreaded most: "I am so sorry," the midwife said in a broken, solemn voice.

"No, this can't be, this can't be!" cried Ayaissa. Brynn's tears were rolling down his cheeks as he held her hand.

"Give me my baby," demanded Ayaissa, resolute in her resolve.

The midwife hesitated at first but saw a fire in Ayaissa's eyes.

All of a sudden, the midwife was overwhelmed with sadness, and tears began to flow down her face. She slowly went to Ayaissa's side and carefully handed the little baby to her. She cradled her little girl and rocked her to a throw; tears streamed down her cheeks. Brynn stroked the little girl's head but was overwhelmed with grief and fell to his knees. Ayaissa kissed her on her forehead, and then she leaned in close.

"Come back to me," she whispered, then closed her eyes and repeated, "come back to me."

As the ominous shadow crept across the walls, it cast a sinister veil over the room, leaving only a faint shimmer of light. The once hopeful atmosphere now turned cold and desolate, as if all life had been sucked out of the air. Brynn stood up, his heart thumping in his chest, and looked at Ayaissa, who remained still and muttered to herself. The shadow loomed over her and the baby, like a predator capturing its prey. The room fell silent, not even the outside traffic could be heard. Brynn felt frozen, and his breath created a mist as it drifted out in front of him. Suddenly, Ayaissa's eyes burst open and radiated a brilliant blue light that shone like stars in the night. Something hidden screeched as it was struck with the light that radiated from Ayaissa and shrunk away.

"A life for a life. A soul for a soul," she said forcefully and with a burning determination, staring at the shadowy figure that lingered in the dark corners. The lights in the room flickered and buzzed; Brynn fell back and slammed against the wall.

"I offer myself freely," she shouted out with conviction.

Ayaissa's whole body glowed brightly. The midwife fled the room in blind terror. Ayaissa started to shake violently, but she held onto her baby.

"You shall not have her!" she screamed, her voice no longer recognisable.

There was a bright flash, and all the lights exploded in the room.

Then silence.

The room was filled with a quiet calm that made Brynn's skin prickle. He swallowed hard, his throat dry as dust. There were no sounds; he heard not a breath or movement anywhere. The only signs of life came from the small wispy shapes that floated out through the shattered windows.

Then there was a cry. It was a new cry, unheard before in the world, the tears of a baby.

Brynn stood up, shaken by that sound and the sight of the tiny figures moving slowly in Ayaissa's arms. The baby looked so delicate and fragile as it looked up at her mother.

Ayaissa lay there exhausted. She opened her eyes and saw the shadow disappear. She smiled in relief, and her eyes fell heavy once again. "Brynn?" she whispered.

Brynn, trembling, answered gently, "I'm here." He leaned in and kissed Ayaissa, who lay limp as though all her strength had been taken from her.

"I'll take her now," Brynn said softly. "You've done enough. It's time to rest."

Brynn reached for the little bundle and gently lifted his daughter. Ayaissa lay lifeless and exhausted; she had given everything and more to save her daughter.

She turned her head and smiled. "Meet your daddy," she said in a weak, trembling voice.

"She is perfect like her mum," he said with a tear in his eye. "Aya," he said, looking to Ayaissa.

Ayaissa looked up at her baby and whispered, "Hello, Aya." She reached over and gently touched her hand.

Little baby Aya smiled and burped.

...

Samaira woke up in the middle of the night, fearful; she instinctively knew her daughter was hurting. Aisim was already up and looked concerned.

"Aisim, we must go to her," Samaira said, distressed.

"Yes, I feel it too," Aisim answered.

"I had hoped that she would be spared," Samaira said.

Aisim said nothing but gazed into a dark

corner of the room.

"Will it ever end?" Samaira sighed heavily. "What more does it want from us?"

Aisim put his arm around Samaira. "It wants what it has always wanted. This will never change."

The sun rose in the morning sky, casting its warm light across the village, indicating the start of another day. Samaira and Aisim were already awake and quickly made their way to the local store, where the only public phone was kept. They expected a call from Ayaissa. Not long after they had arrived, the phone rang, but it was Brynn.

He didn't say what had happened during the birth; in truth, Brynn didn't understand himself. He conveyed that Ayaissa was well, and baby Aya was a healthy girl. They felt relieved but concerned, knowing that Brynn wasn't being entirely truthful about the events that took place during the birth. Brynn promised Ayaissa would call as soon as she felt better.

The next day, true to his promise, Ayaissa called her parents, and they spoke at length. However, she held back details, not wanting to distress them. Instinctively, her parents knew something significant had occurred during the birth that would bring lasting consequences to her future. Samaira and Aisim decided to leave their home as soon as possible. They knew they had to be with their daughter and Aya.

Assia and Melinia had found the life they had longed for. They were happily married and had moved several miles away to a larger town. Aisim sent word to their daughters that they would be leaving to see Ayaissa and were unsure when they would be back.

Leaving was difficult. They knew they may not be returning for a long while, if at all. It was only a hope that they would ever see Assia and Melinia again. They did not know what fate had in store for them, they just knew that the pull of destiny beckoned them to be at Ayaissa's side.

It was a tearful departure, saying goodbye to their daughters, but they clung to hope and trusted in fate, believing they must walk the road set out for them. Arrangements were made, and they soon landed at Gatwick Airport. Brynn nervously waited for them. He had arrived three hours early, not wanting to be late.

"I've heard a lot about you since the wedding," Samaira said in well-spoken English to Brynn.

"Hopefully only good." He smiled clumsily.

Aisim smiled. "We don't bite."

Brynn shuffled nervously.

"Unless we are hungry," Samaira added, looking sternly at Brynn, who gulped and went a little pale. "That was a joke," she added, smiling warmly.

"It's okay, son," Aisim said, resting his hand on Brynn's shoulder. Brynn suddenly laughed and instantly relaxed.

Samaira grinned. "Good, now please take us to our daughter."

The journey was uneventful, stopping only once for some food, and the conversation was easy. When they arrived, Samaira and Aisim found Ayaissa sitting in the front room of the flat, cradling baby Aya. They immediately rushed over to their daughter and smothered her and baby Aya in a warm, affectionate embrace.

"We missed you," her father said. "It has been a lifetime since the wedding."

"Let's look at our little Aya." Samaira took Aya in her arms and stared into her deep blue eyes as though she were searching for something. "Hello, little one." She kissed her on her forehead.

She turned to Ayaissa. "We must talk." She handed Aya to Aisim, who walked out of the room, beckoning Brynn to follow.

"Brynn, will you show me little Aya's room?" Aisim asked. Brynn looked over at Ayaissa, who reassured him.

"Of course. Sorry, it's a bit of a mess at the moment. I forgot to put the clothes away." Brynn squirmed, leading Aisim to Aya's room.

Once they had left, Samaira looked thoughtfully at Ayaissa.

"We felt your pain. What happened?" Samaira asked.

Ayaissa hesitated and gathered her thoughts. "All I know is I just wanted to save my baby." She paused, looking into the corner of the room. "And I saw something."

"Go on," Samaira said softly, holding Ayaissa's hand.

"A shadow. I felt it. It was cold and empty and wanted Aya." Tears welled in her eyes as she stared blankly. "It was like we were both pulling at her, it was…" She turned away, put her hands over her face, and started to cry. "I felt like I was going mad," she whispered.

"You are not going mad," Samaira said. "It has haunted us for many years. It is shadow, emptiness, nothingness." She paused in thought for a long moment. "It is all that life is not, and it wants…" Her words faded.

"Wants? What could it want from me? Why Aya?" demanded Ayaissa.

"I do not fully know. Your father sees further

with these matters, but he believes it is trying to stop something that has been destined to happen. Still, he knows not what that is." Samaira stood up and walked to the window. "It's funny how people are so unaware," she said, her words barely audible. "We can sometimes sense what others cannot see. Have you not felt this before?" Samaira asked, not turning her gaze from the street below.

Ayaissa thought for a moment. "Yes, when I was travelling, wherever I found pain, I felt the presence of something else."

"You must trust in your gift. It will guide you. I know that we are always being led to where we are meant to be," Samaira said, smiling reassuringly at Ayaissa. "Where there is shadow, there is always light. Remember that, especially when the shadow is darkest."

They remained silent for some time, neither finding the right words, lost in thought about what hid just out of sight.

Ayaissa broke the stillness. "I just knew I had to stop it from taking her, and something came over me. I felt something inside me explode."

Samaira stood there and watched Ayaissa staring blankly as she relived the moments in her mind.

"I give it freely," Ayaissa mumbled.

"Our family has an ability," Samaira said, catching her attention. "Remember when you healed that broken bird's wing?"

Ayaissa looked at Samaira and nodded.

"We can give some of our lifeforce to heal others, but it takes from us. What is gained is lost," she said gravely. "The love you felt in your heart for Aya brought it out of you." She sat next to Ayaissa. "When Aya was lost, it was your lifeforce that brought her back."

"Brynn said that I shouted out in a language he did not understand. It was like a dream, or more like a nightmare that I was lost in." Ayaissa breathed in deeply and let out a long heavy sigh.

"Yes, my dear Ayaissa." Samaira looked away, seemingly to some distant memory. "What you freely offered has been taken from you, your lifeforce." Her voice was full of grief.

"Yes, I know, and I would change nothing," she said resolutely. "How long do I have? Will I see my baby grow up?"

"Who can really say? It could be months, years," Samaira said, holding Ayaissa's hands in hers. "Live what time you have; enjoy little Aya and your handsome Brynn." She smiled.

Brynn walked back in with Aisim and baby Aya. Seeing her baby instantly lifted the feeling of doom.

"There's your handsome young man," Samaira said, smiling broadly.

Brynn blushed slightly and looked around. Aisim chuckled.

"So, what shall we do for dinner?" Samaira asked.

...

Samaira and Aisim stayed in London for a further two months and helped with baby Aya wherever they could. The evenings were full of happy memories, as they all shared stories of their younger days, and about their hopes for the future. However, soon their time together came to an end, and it was time for Aisim and Samaira to leave. After bidding farewell, they travelled to Cardiff to see Uncle Ras. They stayed with him for about a year, often returning to visit Ayaissa, Brynn, and Aya. Samaira and Aisim developed a deep bond with Aya, sensing something unique and intriguing about her that was not at once discernible. They watched in anticipation and anxiously waited to see what only time could reveal.

They often wrote to Assia and Melinia, who also planned to visit as soon as possible. They deeply missed their home and daughters, but knew they had to remain. They felt they were caught in the period of calm just before the crushing storm. There was an eerie sense of foreboding lingering that Aisim particularly felt.

Their wait ended when Aya was one year old. Ayaissa began to have nightmares. She saw a shadowy figure standing in a dark corner of her room at night. Initially, it was vague, barely visible, but as she stared, it would take form. The air would start to feel damp and chill. It would stand there and appear to watch quietly. The atmosphere would darken, and it felt like all happiness bled from the room. She was overcome with a feeling of grief, like the day Aya was born and the shadow had tried to steal her baby. Then the shadowy figure would start to approach Ayaissa, slowly, relentlessly, ignoring her screams. It loomed over her as it came, smothering her in darkness and fear. Ayaissa would scream for the shadow to leave her baby alone as though it whispered evil things to her in the darkness.

Eventually, it would disperse, fading away when the morning light crept into the room. Ayaissa was exhausted after these events, barely being able to leave her bed. Brynn tried to reassure her, but whatever he tried did not help. He turned to Samaira and Aisim for help, the only people he believed understood what was happening. The shadow continued to return every night, draining Ayaissa of her life. It had formed a bond with her, a link that grew stronger as she grew weaker and weaker.

Samaira, Aisim, and Uncle Ras decided that they had to end Ayaissa's torment before it was too late. They had to break this dark attachment that the shadow had formed with her; it was time to face this menace. The flat was not the right place to confront what haunted Ayaissa; Uncle Ras knew a place away from people where they would not be disturbed.

It took an hour to drive from Uncle Ras's apartment to their journey's end. He pulled off the main road and headed down an overgrown track, the car struggling to handle the many potholes. The trees grew thicker and denser as they went on. Soon, the dense patchwork of leaves rejected the sunlight and left a soft haze illuminating their way. They stopped the car, deciding that it would be better to walk the rest of the way.

They left the car and headed into the dark woods, following an overgrown path. It twisted and wound around the trees as it led them higher and up a small hillside. Eventually, they broke through a tree line and entered a small clearing in the centre of the woods. They were surrounded by tall ancient trees on all sides, which made it feel like they were watching them and judging their actions. It was now late afternoon, and the sun was low enough to cast a long shadow over them, chilling the air.

Aisim walked to the centre and ran his hand

over the ground. "Here will do," he said.

They all stopped, placed a blanket on the ground, sat in a circle facing one another, and held hands. Aisim looked at Samaira, who smiled lovingly. Aisim returned her warmth.

"I call all the spirits of this place to guide us to our destination, take us where we need to be," Aisim called out. He repeated this several times.

The wind rustled through the trees, and they started to sway back and forth as if they disapproved of what they were observing. Aisim's voice grew louder as he spoke. The air tingled with electricity as his words echoed, bouncing from tree to tree, and they answered with a hiss from their leaves. Everyone could feel themselves vibrating with energy, causing the hairs on their arms to stand up. An unnatural darkness fell over them, like a cover concealing them from any remaining light.

"I call forth the shadow that haunts." A frigid biting wind blew over them. "It's here," Aisim said flatly.

Suddenly, a shadowy figure appeared behind Samaira and screamed, "Ozul!"

It approached them, but the energy Aisim generated repelled it back, and it gave a low hiss when it realised it could not get close.

"Why do you haunt Ayaissa?" Aisim asked in a commanding tone. "Tell me now!"

The figure shook its head. "You can't help her! There is only Ozul!"

"Why do you haunt her?"

"She has freely given herself!" It hissed coldly. "You have no authority."

"You have no authority here!" Uncle Ras said sternly, but the creature laughed.

"What is Ozul?" Aisim demanded.

The figure started to laugh again. "Everything! Nothing! Without! Within!" It seemed to dissipate and reappear. "You can never understand, you are finite, you will all end, then there will be only Ozul." Its last words echoed about them like a swarm of locusts on a path of destruction.

"Why Ayaissa?" Aisim said in a commanding voice.

The shadow-like being laughed again, but more cruelly. "That doesn't matter! She will follow and give herself freely. She will become nothing! It will end! All must be undone so that eternity finds its end."

"What will end?" Uncle Ras asked.

"With your help." The figure laughed with pure malice in its voice. "With little Aya's help!" it croaked.

"Enough!" Aisim shouted. "It is this that will end now!"

"In the midst of darkness, a glimmer of light still shines. Life persists, shadows flee. Love endures and overcomes all. Peace prevails as shadow fails." Samaira roared with such power that the shadow appeared to fade slightly.

"How can we banish it?" Uncle Ras said desperately. "If it's connected to Ayaissa, how can we separate them?"

"We must sever the connection," Aisim replied.

"But how?" Uncle Ras said, fearful for his niece.

"We need to drive it away, back to the darkness, back to whatever sent it forth."

"How? Can you even do this?" Uncle Ras was now overwhelmed by doubt and despair.

Aisim noticed a dark shadow hung over Uncle Ras. The shadowy figure laughed ominously and whispered, "He's mine."

"Of course, I am Aisim," he said, now realising that only one course of action was left to him.

Aisim broke the circle and stood up and faced the shadow. He looked back at Samaira and smiled sadly. She understood and looked proudly at him.

Uncle Ras knew precisely what his brother was about to do. He jumped up, pushed his brother aside, leapt into the shadowy figure, and vanished.

"Ahh, a soul for a soul!" Its cold laugh echoed throughout the clearing.

"No!" cried Aisim.

"I accept your offering." The shadow laughed at Aisim, then it disappeared in a flash, and the dark veil retreated.

"He's gone." Aisim fell to his knees and wept for his brother.

Samaira went over to Aisim and helped him to his feet.

"We shall find him, not leave him in shadow, but we can do nothing now. We must return and recover our strength."

...

After Uncle Ras passed away, his brother Aisim inherited everything. It took some time and investigation to sort things out, but eventually they moved into the ground-floor flat and took over the duties of landlord. Fortunately, Mrs. Bennet was always available to provide assistance when needed. Sadly, the top-floor flat remained vacant for many years, despite numerous advertisements and low rent offers. Over time, the flat deteriorated and needed extensive repairs.

One day, a young man stumbled upon the "Top-floor flat available to let" sign. He found it to be in the perfect location with reasonable rent, and for some reason, he had a good feeling about it.

CHAPTER 7

Aya
Whom do you see when you look in the mirror?

Aya was awoken by the morning light shining through a small opening in her tent. She raised her hand, casting a shadow over her eyes as she squinted and rolled over. A moment later, she heard voices outside, and with a groan she sat up, looking around for her clothes. She hadn't slept well; the night had proven to be hot and uncomfortable. She grabbed a flask filled with tepid water, which lifted her mood.

Aya worked for a charity called the Creation Foundation. The organisation introduced sustainable agriculture techniques to farmers in developing countries. The basic principle was to increase yields and to share the excess in poverty-stricken areas. She was exceptionally qualified for her position. She had spent many years at the University of

London studying for an agriculture degree, specialising in cultivating plants. The legacy that had passed down to her nourished and nurtured her skills, and it was clear to those around her that she was gifted.

The camp where she was staying on this occasion was situated on the outskirts of Davedi, a village in the southern Sahara area.

…

Aya's gift was clear from an early age. She had a natural connection to living things, especially plant-life, which she had inherited from her mother, and it flowed through her veins like a hidden river. Despite her father's desire for her to follow a more conventional career path, Aya remained committed to her passion for plants. She discovered solace in nature and felt most at ease when surrounded by the greenery she cherished deeply.

"It is through struggle that we grow and learn," her mother would say to her encouragingly. "The essence of life is a gift that must be cherished, nurtured, and protected. It is this essence that connects us all."

As time passed, her father grew to appreciate

the happiness that Aya's profession brought her and was proud of the person that she had become.

Though kind and supportive, her father had his beliefs in a different place, believing that what he could see and touch was all there was. He was now choosing to rationalise away the events that took place during Aya's birth. He believed that when you died, you died, and he didn't feel the need to explore any more profound meanings.

Death did not worry him. "What's the point in being afraid of the inevitable?" he used to say, shrugging his shoulders and burying his head back into the paper. "All that matters is the here and now, and the rest will sort itself out."

At first glance, Ayaissa and Brynn may have seemed like an unlikely pair, but as the old saying goes, opposites attract. However, a more correct statement might be that opposites find balance. Their meeting may have seemed like chance, a roll of the cosmic dice, but their tale was born long before the formation of the first star, long before the first atom collapsed into matter, and long before time and space exploded into a reality. Their story was written with the first thought, the seed that blossomed and grew, with roots that ran deep and branches that touched everything. Aya was the realisation of the idea, a stunning blossom on the tree of life.

...

Aya reached for her clothes, which were loosely piled in one corner of the limited space in her tent, exactly where she had thrown them the night before. With well-practised moves, she strategically slipped into them and crawled out of the small opening. She stood outside her tent for a long moment, breathing in the fresh air and enjoying the cooler morning sun. Aya shaded her eyes and gazed up at the clear, blue sky; there wasn't a single cloud in sight.

"It looks like it's going to be a perfect day," she mumbled quietly.

Aya stood for a moment and looked back at some of the older homes that lined the edge of the village. She watched as the sun slowly crept across the rooftops. The golden morning light chased away the shadows that skulked into the cracks, hiding from the sun's gaze. The appearance of people leaving their homes marked the beginning of another day in the village. The silence that hung moments before was now overlaid with the bustling noise of daily life.

The village, though small, felt alive, and the community was welcoming. Aya enjoyed her time there and couldn't imagine ever wanting to leave.

She felt a sense of peace. She was frozen in anticipation, like the moment just before the plunge where everything hung still, waiting for that next decisive step. She breathed in deep and closed her eyes, and her senses swelled. A soft breeze brushed past her ear, and suddenly, a whisper caught her attention. "Makena."

Aya's eyes snapped open, and her gaze was captured by a young girl standing at the edge of the village. Their eyes locked, both looking curiously at the other. Aya felt that the girl looked familiar, a memory just out of recollection. She smiled at the girl, but her expression did not appear to change. Aya thought that perhaps she saw a trace of a smile quivering on the girl's lips.

The girl raised her arms, beckoning Aya to come to her. Aya stepped forward as though commanded by some silent impulse.

"Aya!" Abruptly, a voice rang behind her from

somewhere in the camp. She turned away briefly, but when she looked back, the girl was gone. She stared for a moment, then shrugged off the growing feeling of fear fluttering in her stomach.

Aya made her way into the centre of the camp to the designated food storage area, which consisted of a small tent, home to several sealed containers of food and drink. Placed outside and slightly to the left were several plastic tables tied together to form one extended eating area. Lined on either side were blue plastic chairs, which everyone in the camp had complained about at least once. A canopy of thin white cotton sheets fluttered overhead, which offered some welcome shade from the hot sun. Aya approached the tent and signed out her morning rations, which consisted of one bottle of cool water from the only fridge on the site and a fruit and oat bar: healthy, but it tasted a little like soggy cardboard, or so she imagined, not knowing precisely what soggy cardboard actually tasted like.

Some of her workmates were already up, chatting about various assignments but mostly complaining about the hot, sticky night they had all endured. Aya waved a general morning greeting aimed at whoever happened to notice her and sat down at the end of the long table, wanting to avoid getting embroiled in their conversation.

"The bloody weather!" Jake complained loudly and finished the rest of his drink. "It's starting to get on my nerves!" he said with a growing irritation haunting his voice.

Harri, Longsy, Fynch, and Jake all grunted in agreement.

"I know," added Harri, shaking his head. "Last night, I hardly got any sleep." Sweat ran down his rosy face and splashed onto the table; he quickly mopped his head with a well-used handkerchief.

Harri was in his late fifties, a man of a large build, some would say well-rounded; it was always a mystery to Aya why he would choose to work in a climate that clearly was his enemy. What more confused her was why he left his well-paid job as a manager of a well-known high street bank, giving up his comforts to travel halfway across the world to be an underpaid and overworked driver. She concluded it was either a mid-life crisis or he was running away from a crime syndicate for embezzling millions. In truth, Harri had always lived a "normal" life. He woke up, went to work, came home, and did precisely the same for thirty years—until the day he sat on the tube and noticed some bold black writing scribbled on the window behind him:

WANT SOME FUN?

GET THE GOOD SHIT!

07823894612

He paused and looked at that telephone number for what must have felt like an eternity until something snapped in him. That day, he got very high, walked into the area manager's office, laughed uncontrollably, and passed out. The bank was very understanding and eventually wished him all the best as they pushed him out of the door.

Jake looked hard at Harri, who now waved his arms around, trying to scare away an insect that buzzed around his head, clearly attracted by his excessive sweat. "Don't get me started on those bloody bugs!" Jake said, and promptly swatted the annoyance, much to Harri's relief.

Harri slumped in his chair and looked longingly at the fridge. "Yeah," he said with a sigh, knowing he had already had his morning rations, "I lost count of the number of times I was bitten last night."

Again, a general grunt in agreeance from those sitting around them. Silence fell upon the group, who now sat with heads hung low. A shadow seemed to creep over them, pushing away any joy the morning sun might have brought.

Aya rolled her eyes. "It's a lovely morning," she broke the silence. "Now, now, children. If you carry on like this, you won't be allowed to stay up past your bedtime again." She tried to lighten the depressing mood.

Fynch looked up. "Aya," he said glumly, letting out a long, drawn-out sigh, "forever the optimist."

"Look at this place. It's so alive!" Aya said with a broad smile stretched across her face. "Just look," she whispered.

Suddenly, a cool breeze brushed over them, carrying a sweet aroma. Harri smiled as though someone had whispered the punchline to a joke. Then he giggled like he was once again a small child without a care in the world, finally erupting into a wholesome laugh. The others looked at him, but Harri's newfound joy was contagious, and they all laughed. Aya smiled as she watched her friends, took a bite of the cardboard bar, and winced as she swallowed. They felt their moods and spirits rise like a curtain had been opened, letting in a new morning's sunlight.

Jake breathed in deeply. "You know, it's not so bad here." The stress of moments earlier had bled away.

"Exactly," Aya whispered.

As if lifted by the gentle breeze, all their troubles and annoyances that hung so heavy on them moments before faded. They silently stared at the vast landscape that stretched seemingly forever as though it was the first time they had noticed the beauty surrounding them. Their thoughts drifted far away to old, happy memories of family and friends. Each sat with a warm smile etched across their face.

"Now," Aya interrupted the peace, "what do you grumpy old men have planned for today?"

Jake chuckled. "Who are you calling old?"

"Okay, well-used?" she playfully replied.

"I'm not grumpy, am I?" mumbled Harri, but nobody heard him.

"Come on, get out of here," Jake joked. "You're going to be late…again."

"Yikes," she said, looking at her watch, then quickly waved goodbye and hurried over to the Operations tent.

Operations consisted of a large tent positioned at the edge of the camp. The tent was once beige but now bleached by the sun and looked rather shabby. It had a large opening covered only by a thin canvas that flapped back and forth with the breeze.

Inside the tent, it always felt cool, thanks to a solar-powered air cooler, which often was a topic of heated conversation in the camp, especially on sweltering days. Positioned in the centre was a large operations table. Unlike the canteen table, this was made of stainless steel and very robust. It was always covered with various maps. The maps were constantly updated, as they offered a lifeline to resources, information about the terrain, and the locations of all the villages in the region. More tables were on the left of the tent, home to communication equipment and laptops. At the rear were stacked boxes of files. To any outsider, this would look like chaos, a disorganised mess. In fact, it was a well-oiled machine, perfectly tuned to their work.

People busied about, focussed on their work. They were divided into teams, each having its own lead operator. Simon's team examined the most recent data gathered by the field agents, Jan's team focused on developing strategies, and Kevin's team planned where to send the field agents. Lastly, Richard's team initiated contact and discussed agricultural techniques and how the organisation could offer assistance. Aya was a member of Richard's team, which suited her well.

No one seemed to notice Aya, so she sat down and ate the rest of her breakfast. John and some of the other field agents were already there.

"Morning," John said, noticing Aya and nodding his head.

Aya grinned and waved whilst swallowing her last mouthful of food.

"Ah, Aya, morning," Richard said, looking up from a series of maps sprawled on a table before him. "I need you to see a local farmer." He paused, shuffling through some papers. "Ah yes, I believe his name is Bolajii. You'll find him in Umtata, not too far from here." His focus returned to the maps.

Richard had been running the project for the last three months, after Oswald Jeyson, otherwise referred to as Oggy, was taken ill and left the project to return home to Scotland. Oggy was highly relaxed in his manner, hence the appearance of disorganisation and chaos, which Richard unfortunately inherited. Richard was very formal compared to Oggy and hated the mess left behind. He had started to organise the place, taking on the task enthusiastically, but eventually, the long, sticky nights, insect bites, and relentless heat were all too much, and he learned to cope with Oggy's legacy.

"I thought I was due some leave?" Aya said, feeling a little irritated.

Richard pretended not to hear Aya's complaint.

"Richard?" Aya said louder. "I was due some leave."

He looked up and smiled awkwardly. "I know, but we have two teams off, and I can't afford to lose my best field agent now, can I?" He sounded a little more stressed than usual.

"Okay, okay, as you asked so nicely," Aya said with just a hint of sarcasm. John chuckled, which earned him a stern glance from Richard. "When do we leave?" Aya added.

"Today," John said, shrugging his shoulder after seeing Aya's expression.

"Today?" she said, raising her voice.

"Yes, I'm afraid so. However, it should only be a quick visit," Richard said, not looking up from a map he appeared to be studying with significant interest.

"How far?" Aya sighed.

"Three hundred miles," John answered, laughing and shaking his head.

"Oh, for—" Aya said, about to cuss.

"Oh, and you'll have Kofi with you," Richard jumped in before Aya could finish her sentence,

Despite the absence of luxuries in the camp, Aya found it manageable. However, she had just spent the last month away on a tough assignment and had to live in very harsh conditions whilst away. She hoped for and was due some much-needed time off. All the field agents found the physical and mental strain of living in such an environment and dealing with the constant daily challenges very taxing, so some time away to recharge was necessary for maintaining a healthy mental state. Aya was looking forward to a well-earned break. However, it would have to wait until this assignment was over.

Aya and John left Operations, mentally preparing themselves for the long journey ahead. John had worked with Aya for many years, and they had spent much time together. John was in his mid-fifties and was well-travelled or well-worn, as he would often say. He had been hired by the organisation to act primarily as a driver and to support the team in any way that was needed. He had served in the British army and was no stranger to dangerous situations, and those skills had shown themselves to be useful on more than one occasion.

Aya thanked the September morning weather. It was warm, but a pleasant breeze offered relief from the heat. She had been to this region last year in June, and that was a scorching month: the temperature hit 44 degrees Celsius, and during monsoon season, it was both hot and humid.

"I'll meet you at the jeep," Aya said. "I just need to collect my things for the journey."

"See you by the jeep. Be quick, please; it's a long drive," John added.

Aya rolled her eyes and went off to her tent. After a short while, she went across camp to meet John and Kofi. Aya sat in the passenger's seat of the jeep. Kofi sat in the back; he would act as interpreter. They all took a moment to check that they had what was needed for the trip. Kofi started to rummage through a rucksack that rested on his lap as though he was looking for something in particular.

"Let's go!" John said, possibly feigning enthusiasm.

"Wait, please," Kofi said abruptly.

"You okay?" Aya asked.

Kofi pulled out a photo, smiled, and sat back.

"We can go now," he said, sounding calmer. "Sorry."

It was 7 a.m., the sun was climbing in the sky, and a quiet whisper of a breeze brushed over them. Aya took a deep breath and let out a long, drawn-out sigh as she settled back into her seat. They left the camp behind and headed onto an open road barely visible to Aya. John was used to the area and saw what she could not. They drove out into what looked like nowhere. She looked out across the vastness that spread in every direction, offering a freedom that could not be found anywhere else.

It was a dry land spotted with sporadic lines of lush plants. Some stood tall with thick stems that bowed slightly under the weight of their large green and red leaves, whilst others were small, fragile, flower-like, and adorned with beautiful petals. This menagerie of greenery must have been following some underground water supply, stretching out like long tendrils forever searching for that life-giving water.

They travelled for several hours without incident. Aya stared out into the beautiful land, lost deep in thought, being gently rocked as the jeep bumped about. She considered the endless challenges here, yet life endured, it always found a way.

They passed a pack of African wild dogs, just lazing in the morning sun; one or two leisurely looked up at the jeep's passing, creating a dust cloud in its wake, but saw nothing of interest, yawned, and laid back down. A herd of antelope moved slowly to some unknown, well-travelled destination. She wondered what life must look like to them, whether they were worried or had any stresses or concerns, apart from whether they would be eaten that day.

"It's beautiful out here," she said to no one in particular.

"Yes, it is," Kofi replied.

John grunted but said nothing, too busy focusing on the road.

"My ancestors have lived here since the world began," Kofi added.

Since the world began, Aya thought. *When was that? Perhaps it's now, and we are the first to see this wonder. Or maybe we are the last.* That last thought made her a little sad, that one day this will end. She sighed.

"Life never ends," Kofi smiled.

She turned and looked at Kofi, slightly confused. He smiled reassuringly.

Around the early afternoon, they reached their destination. As they entered the village, Aya saw several red, round clay-brick houses with straw roofs no more than six metres in width. They were set about in a large semi-circle. The locals busied with their well-practised routines, and a few oxen and chickens who appeared oblivious to their arrival wandered about. They stopped and were first greeted by three scruffy-looking dogs, who ran over to them, wagging their tails and barking with excitement, possibly hoping for a treat. Aya chucked what was left of her breakfast bar, which she found loosely wrapped and half-melted in her jacket pocket. The dogs sniffed at it, then indignantly walked away.

Kofi got out to ask a couple elderly women if they could help. They sat on a long wooden bench outside one of the houses. They appeared to be in a heated debate over a garment one of the women was holding, oblivious to Kofi standing there. He coughed, then coughed again a little louder. They stopped and looked curiously at him. He asked if they knew where to find Bolajii. He was the farmer Aya had been tasked with contacting. They initially seemed confused by his inquiry, but after a few questions back and forth, they pointed to a large house that sat away from the others at the end of the village.

Aya and John left the vehicle, and they all made their way to the house pointed out by the women, who had now lost interest in them and returned to their heated conversation. It was at least three times larger than the other houses in the village, though of the same design.

Just as they approached the house, a tall, slim, elderly man stepped out and was slightly taken aback to see strangers in the village. He smiled politely, greeted them, and asked why they were there. Kofi and Bolajii spoke for several minutes, but despite the initial warm greeting, Bolajii appeared hesitant. Eventually, an accord was struck, and Kofi turned to Aya and John for formal introductions.

"Bolajii, meet John," Kofi said. Bolajii greeted him warmly. "And Aya."

Aya stood just behind John, and as she stepped out to greet Bolajii, he looked startled. She felt slightly awkward as Bolajii stared momentarily, but he smiled broadly, easing any tension.

"That was odd," whispered Aya to John as Bolajii turned away. John nodded and shrugged but looked suspiciously at their new host.

It turned out that not only was Bolajii a

farmer, but also the village's doctor and lawmaker and was seen as the local wise man. He was the one who would coordinate all work being carried out, resolve any issues, and even perform marriages. Though the village had no leader, Bolajii was well respected, and his words were always heeded.

They were invited to come inside the house. Upon entering, Bolajii led them to a spacious room the village used to discuss local matters. The seating was arranged in two semi-circles around the edges, with a well-used fire pit in the centre. An opening in the roof above the fire allowed for ventilation and offered an opening for the afternoon light to creep through, casting long shadows across the room.

Aya looked around and was amazed at the artwork that decorated the walls. All sorts of scenes were displayed, some portraying daily life in the village and others depicting great warriors battling in some ancient rite. There was one painting that especially caught her eye: it was an image of a young girl. Aya stepped towards it. She thought for a moment that the girl in the painting looked like the young girl she saw earlier in the morning.

"Makena," Bolajii said, closely watching Aya's

interest.

Feeling Bolajii's stare, Aya suddenly felt uncomfortable and quickly looked away.

Once seated, they were given food and water, which they welcomed after their long journey. Aya gathered her thoughts and focussed on the task at hand. It was a productive conversation. Aya knew her job and knew it well. She had a natural charm and, even through a translator, could confidently explain the goal of the organisation and the importance of having the support of the local people.

When their team first approached a new village, gaining trust became crucial. The locals were often sceptical of outsiders, making persuading farmers to share their crops with neighbouring villages challenging. Negotiation was the key, but it wasn't always easy. Many of the farmers she met used traditional farming methods passed down through generations, so offering more modern techniques wasn't always enough. Moreover, there were often rivalries between the villages and usually a long history of conflict, which meant Aya had to be cautious. Nonetheless, her empathetic nature enabled her to connect with others and succeed where others would have failed.

Bolajii, however, readily accepted Aya's proposal without any objections, which made Aya feel slightly uneasy and suspicious of Bolajii's true motives.

On several occasions during their conversation, Bolajji called Aya "Makena," but quickly corrected himself and apologised, then continued with what he was saying. She noticed that he sometimes stared at her but would remain transfixed instead of looking away when she turned to catch his gaze. This made her feel uncomfortable. There was something familiar about Bolajii, but she could not quite put her finger on it, like a word teetering on the tip of the tongue. Hidden behind his dark eyes, Aya sensed a hidden sadness that hinted at a past loss or hardship.

Several hours had passed since their arrival, and the evening had arrived. John had hoped to return to camp before nightfall and spent the last hour hinting to Aya for them to leave. However, despite his trying, he knew her well enough to know that she went only when she was ready.

Aya eventually politely explained that they had to go, and they thanked Bolajii for his kind hospitality. Bolajii led them outside and walked with them to the jeep. Whilst they walked, he spoke with Kofi; often, Aya heard her name being referenced and the word Makena. John noticed it too, and told Aya not to worry. Bolajii kept glancing at Aya, quickly looking away this time when she caught his stare. She was beginning to wish she hadn't taken this assignment; though their time there had been positive and welcoming, she felt something wasn't right.

They soon reached their vehicle, said farewells, and found their seats. Bolajii stood by Aya and smiled at her. However, there was a sadness in his eyes that he could not hide this time. He spoke to her, though she did not understand. She smiled but did not respond. She looked to Kofi for support, but he was rummaging through a backpack and not paying any attention to their interaction. Bolajii smiled back, lingered for the briefest of moments, then turned away and headed back to the house where they had come from; he did not look back.

"Oh hell, what's wrong with this?" John muttered, revealing a growing irritation.

Aya looked over to John for some reassurance, but there was just fatigue and frustration oozing from him. He got out, popped the bonnet, and had a look to see if he could find the cause of the engine not starting. After about half an hour of tinkering and cursing, it became clear that they were going nowhere.

"Any idea what could be wrong with it?" Aya asked.

"No, it's turning over but not starting. Perhaps the spark plugs, not sure. We'll have to radio it in."

Aya picked up the CB mic and radioed, "Base camp, this is Jeep 12. Come in, over." The radio crackled loudly, and she repeated, "Base camp, this is Jeep 12. Come in, over."

"Base camp here, over," answered a well-practised response.

"Our jeep will not start. Requesting instruction, over," Aya replied.

"Received. Please wait. Over."

They all sat waiting for the response. At this point, people gathered around them to see what was happening. Bolajii came walking over and exchanged some words with Kofi.

"Bolajii said we are welcome to stay here if

there are any problems," Kofi said.

"Thank him for his kindness," Aya said, gesturing to Kofi to translate.

Bolajii smiled and beckoned to some women. They talked briefly with him and then hurried off to a nearby house.

"Jeep 12, come in, over," a voice came across the radio.

Aya picked up the mic and replied, "Jeep 12 here, over."

"We have some bad news. All jeeps are out. We will not be able to get a pickup for five days. Will this be an issue? Over."

John and Aya looked at one another and sighed.

"We have been welcomed to stay here," Kofi added. "I believe Bolajii is excited at the prospect."

Aya half-smiled uncomfortably and nodded. "Base camp, this is Jeep 12. That will not be a problem. We are safe and have a place to stay. Over."

"Okay, that's good news. If we can get a pickup earlier, we will send. Please check in every ten hours, over."

"Okay, over."

"Enjoy your stay. Base camp, over and out."

John had already taken their emergency kit to the house he was beckoned to. Aya leaned back against the jeep and took a deep breath.

"This is a good place. You have nothing to fear here," Kofi said reassuringly.

"I know." Aya paused. "What were you and Bolajii talking about? I heard my name being said."

"Oh, nothing to worry about," Kofi said, smiling, avoiding Aya's inquiry.

As they walked to the house, Aya fell deep in thought. She felt Kofi's response was aloof at best, a lie at worst, which only fuelled her suspicions.

When they entered the house, Bolajii was already there and greeted them excitedly. It was a simple space with three narrow beds along each wall. It was decorated similarly to the house where they had sat earlier. However, it felt less grand and more personal to whoever lived there. They had kindly draped netting over the beds to give some relief from the night bugs and offer a little privacy.

"After unpacking, please come see me. I will have some food for you all. You are my guests," he said with a broad smile; Kofi promptly translated. Bolajii paused before leaving the tent and glanced at Aya. He looked at her as though they knew each other, though this was their first meeting.

It did not take long to settle in and unpack what little they had brought with them, and they left to see Bolajii, though John just wanted to go to bed after the long day.

"Kofi?" Aya said, looking at him. "What's going on?"

Kofi avoided eye contact and pretended to be looking for something in his backpack.

"Kofi! This isn't funny, what's going on?" she demanded, starting to feel angry.

Kofi looked up at her, his eyes watering. "You know that picture I carry with me? It is of my daughter. She left this world long ago, and to see her again," he paused, "I would give anything."

Aya went to pursue the issue with Kofi, but

John held her arm and shook his head.

"Now isn't the time," John said in a fatherly manner.

When they arrived at the house, they entered and were beckoned to sit as before. The group was offered more food and water and was again welcomed by an enthusiastic Bolajii.

"*Jy is welkom om hier te bly,*" Bolajii said.

"You're welcome to stay here," Kofi added.

"Thank you, Bolajii, you are very kind," Aya replied.

"*U slegte geluk is ons geluk.*" He smiled. "*Binnekort vier ons my dogter se huwelik,*" he said with excitement.

"His daughter will soon be married." Kofi smiled and nodded to Bolajii, who couldn't hold his excitement.

"*Jy sal vir die true bly.*" Bolajii gestured to Aya and John as though eagerly awaiting their response.

"We have been invited to the wedding," Kofi added.

"Oh," Aya said, surprised at the invitation.

"Thank you," added John with a nod. "When is it?"

Both Aya and John looked at Kofi for the answer.

"*Wanneer is dit?*" Kofi said, turning to Bolajii

"*Twee dae tyd*," came the response.

"Two days," Kofi said, turning to Aya and John.

"I guess we're going to a wedding," John mumbled.

"We would love to be his guests. We're honoured." Aya placed her hand on her chest and lowered her head slightly.

No translation was needed; Bolajii smiled and laughed, clapping his hands. Everyone around them laughed and was clearly happy at the news that they were staying for a while. Aya wondered why they were so pleased with this news. She guessed that they did not get to spend time with outsiders very often. They spent some time there meeting Bolajii's family, who all welcomed Aya as you would an old friend or a family member you hadn't seen in a long time. The evening came to an end, and everyone bid their goodbyes. Aya felt more at ease with her current situation, but a nagging feeling persisted that something wasn't quite right.

Aya didn't return to the house. Instead, she sat alone at the edge of the village, lost in thought. She noticed that she was mindlessly fingering the blue sapphire pendant her mother had given her when she was younger.

"This kept me safe, and it will keep you safe now. Keep it close to your heart, precious one," Aya's mother had said when she first gave her the pendant.

This brought a smile and a feeling of sadness as she thought about her mother and father so incredibly far away and how she missed them. Kofi noticed her sitting alone and walked over to her.

"May I sit with you?"

"Yes, the company would be nice. Have you seen John?"

Kofi thought briefly. "I saw him last enjoying a little cannabis with a group of young men. I don't think he understood what they were saying, but he was giggling a lot."

Aya chuckled. "And I thought he was tired. Well, we're here for a while, so best to fit in, I guess," she said, shrugging her shoulders.

Kofi sat down next to her. "You seem to be here, yet your thoughts are far away."

Aya stared out into the night sky. "How many do you think are out there?"

Kofi looked up thoughtfully. "Who knows, only God would know such things."

"Do you really think there is a God watching us here and now?" Aya said almost in a whisper.

"I like to believe that there is. I believe He made us, all of us. He made the beautiful, the ugly, the good, and the bad. I like to believe that He has a plan for us all," Kofi said. His words seemed to fill him with contentment.

"You mean fate?" asked Aya.

"Yes… Fate." He paused. "That is a good word." Kofi smiled. "I believe He has given each of us a destiny. He has given us this beautiful playground to play in; He is kind, patient and generous." Kofi's heart seemed warmed by the idea that he had a purpose. "But don't anger Him. I think He can sometimes tell us off too." He laughed aloud.

"I'll bear that in mind." Aya laughed. "It does

make you wonder."

They were silent and deep in contemplation, taking in the sight of the tiny lights piercing through the night sky that enveloped the world. The countless possibilities shining down, the unknowable in all its beauty, hinting at its existence. A bright light shot across the night sky, leaving a long, sparkling tail in its wake.

"Will it last?" Aya broke the silence.

"Only He knows," Kofi said. "We are not to know His mind. One day perhaps I will be able to ask Him." He grinned and remained transfixed on the endless night sky. "And perhaps he will look kindly on me."

"Kofi, why did Bolajii call me Makena earlier?"

Kofi paused and reached for the photo that he had earlier. "This is my daughter, Lesedi." He stared lovingly at the girl in the picture. "I will see her one day; I know this to be true."

"She is very pretty," Aya said softly.

"Yes," Kofi said with sadness. "Bolajii had a daughter. She has also left this world, but you reminded him of her."

Aya thought about this for a moment. "Makena?"

Kofi nodded.

"He doesn't seem to realise I am not her," Aya said.

Kofi remained silent.

"Kofi?" Aya said, concerned.

"Aya." He paused momentarily. "He believes that you are her."

"Bolajii is in mourning, I understand, but I am not her," Aya said. "And I'm worried that he doesn't realise this."

Kofi held his daughter's picture in his hands. He couldn't help but feel overwhelmed with emotion. He stared at her image, taking in every detail, from the curve of her smile to the sparkle in her eyes. A single tear escaped his eye and landed softly on the photograph, a poignant reminder of his love for his little girl.

Aya placed her hand gently on Kofi's shoulder. He inhaled deeply and released a long, sad sigh. "Thank you," he murmured.

Aya's smile radiated warmth and eased Kofi's pain. "May I ask how she passed?"

"It happened a while back. She..." His voice trailed off. "The pain is still too near."

"I understand," she said softly. "Kofi," he turned to her, "am I going to be safe here?"

"Bolajii will not harm you, this I know," Kofi said without hesitation. This eased Aya's worries a little.

She left Kofi to his thoughts and looked back at the infinite expanse that spread above her. "Makena," she whispered.

...

The following day, they were awoken by a cockerel screeching at the top of its voice. Aya sat up and noticed that Kofi had already left the tent. There was a commotion outside; loud, panicked voices filled the air, and some women cried out, sounding deeply stressed.

"John, you up?" Aya said.

"Yeah, I hear it," came the reply.

They left the tent and were greeted by people rushing about, with a large group gathered near the house. Kofi was talking to a few men and pointing in various directions.

"Hallo," came a young voice. They turned to

find Bolajii with a young boy by his side.

Aya and John smiled and greeted them. Bolajii looked panicked and quickly spoke to the young boy briefly.

"Bolajii say hello. He, err, say, boy went from the village," the young boy spoke in broken English. "Gone, lost. Need to find." He pointed to the large group of people gathered. It was now clear to them that this was a search party.

"Is there anything we can do?" John asked.

The boy turned to Bolajii, and words went back and forth again.

"Err, yes, if...er... Go...help look." The boy pointed to where Kofi was standing.

John and Aya were about to go off when the boy grabbed Aya's arm. "Wait, please," he said.

John stopped and looked at Aya for a sign of what she wanted to do. "I'll be fine. Quick, go and check back with me later. Take care, John."

John nodded and ran over to Kofi. Bolajii walked off, and the boy holding Aya's arm beckoned her to follow. She followed them to the communal house and went in.

There was a vastly different environment to

when she was there last time. Candles now lined the edge of the seating area, and incense smouldered. The air was filled with the fragrance of lavender, and swirling wisps of unusual, coloured smoke danced around the heat emitted from the candles.

Bolajii beckoned Aya and gestured to take a seat.

"Makena," he said and knelt before her. He took her hand and whispered strange words that penetrated her thoughts, creating visions of a childhood she did not recognise. She felt faint as she breathed in the scented air around her.

"Makena. *Jy is lank gelede geneem, nou is jy terug,*" Bolajji said.

Aya started to sway and fell to her side. Bolajii caught her and laid her down in the centre of the room. As Aya lay there, Bolajii knelt by her and started to chant words that she did not initially understand, but as she listened, she felt all resistance slip away, and at that moment, she understood his words.

"Makena, my daughter. You were taken long ago. Now come back and speak to me as you once did," Bolajii said in a chant-like fashion.

Aya answered, but it was not her voice that she heard. "Baba, I have missed you."

"I have been looking for you, but—" Bolajii's words were cut short.

Aya suddenly let out a piercing scream, which caused Bolajii to stumble backwards and fall to the ground. A bright white light burst out of her chest and soared into the air, spiralling around the room before descending and intensifying, hovering just a few feet from the floor.

A young girl's form began to take shape from the light, appearing to float like an angel sent on a divine mission from Heaven. She radiated warmth and love, and her glowing aura lit the room.

All that gazed upon her felt any feelings of sadness replaced with unconditional love and happiness. Bolajii cried tears of joy and clasped his hands together as in prayer.

Aya narrowly opened her eyes and briefly saw the light all around her, but the room was a blur, and she could not make any sense of what was happening. The world around her appeared fluid, nothing was solid. As she stared, her vision moved away, beyond the walls. She felt like her body was limiting her, and she shed it like clothes falling to the ground. She felt she had vast wings that allowed her to soar high into the sky and see everywhere. She knew everything there was to know. She saw her father sitting in his front room at his desk working and saw her grandparents sleeping in their bed. She was whisked away to India and flew through the town where her mother once lived as a young girl, then a second later, she was flying through the streets of Cardiff to a small pub where she watched her friends drinking and laughing.

Then everything stopped. She was standing in front of a man she had never seen before. He turned to her and smiled. Her heart raced with excitement. She felt an indescribable connection to this person; she felt whole. She reached out to him, and he to her. Suddenly, she sensed something was wrong as a cold chill washed over them.

He looked at her, concerned. "Go!" he shouted, pushing her away. A dark shadow enveloped him, and he was gone. Aya tried to stay, to help, but she was thrown back and pulled from the scene.

She drifted through time and space; she saw

the universe unravel, all of matter undoing, until everything collapsed to a single point, then nothing. She hung there, motionless, waiting expectantly, staring into the empty nothing.

In a blink, she was thrown forward. There was a blinding flash, and everything instantly came into being. It appeared as a blank canvas waiting for an artist's creation to come to life. Aya saw images form in her mind, like a story being born, words forming, images taking shape. She felt like she was reading a book, and as the words formed, they sprung from her consciousness and burst into creation, erupting all around her into reality.

Aya watched as time and space unfurled before her. She saw the sun appear, planets form, life burst into existence, and complexity grow. The next moment, she saw the earth eaten by a dying star as it grew and exploded, devouring all it once gave birth to. Further still, her mind raced; she saw lights go out one by one as the stars died and the universe grew cold until there was just a vast eternal emptiness, then the universe evaporated into nothingness and was gone once more to linger as a potential waiting for its rebirth.

Everything began and ended in emptiness,

Aya thought. Then she heard it speak to her, the eternal Shadow, deformed and twisted, devoid of life of all that is good. It spoke in a sound that was an affront to creation itself. It clawed at Aya with every vile sound. She was filled with pain and hurt. She was reminded of all the loss in her life, all the pain that she had felt. She was confronted with images of torture and horror as she saw those she loved ripped apart, screaming in agony, begging her for help. Aya tried to scream out, but in the nothingness, she had no voice.

A light formed in the darkness around her. It radiated from her, burning away the nothingness, bringing everything. It glowed bright, warm, and inviting. She felt comfort and began to cry as the light held and cradled her.

"It is okay now, my little Aya, but you can't stay here." The voice soothed and washed away all the evil thoughts that had invaded Aya's mind.

"I don't want to go," Aya said, feeling awash with love.

"We will see each other again, my little one. Now go, they are waiting," the voice said with a kindness that Aya felt pure joy and giggled like she was a child once more.

"I don't understand," Aya whispered.

Aya was thrown back to the present moment.

"My brother is in danger, Baba. You must be quick," Makena said with urgency.

"Where is he?" Bolajii asked.

She smiled and looked at Aya. "She knows. She will show you."

Bolajii's son, she thought, and instantly hovered over Labaan. He was clinging to a branch high up in a tree. He looked pale and was injured; his leg had a big cut along its length, and blood ran down the tree trunk and soaked the ground below. An African leopard circled the tree, and the scent of Labaan's blood had driven it into a frenzy. It tried to climb up, but Labaan stabbed it with a broken spear. However, he was frail, and it was only a matter of time before he would lose his struggle.

Makena smiled at her father and beckoned him farewell. As she faded, she spoke, "We will see each other again, Baba."

Makena slowly faded until only a radiant, glowing orb floated where she once stood. The orb shot up into the air and swooshed around the room, extinguishing the candles as it flew past them. It rose sharply and shot back into Aya. She screamed as the light hit her and writhed about on the floor, lashing out violently. But then, just as abruptly, she stopped and sat up calmly. Everyone in the room watched her closely. She looked back and beamed.

Bolajii spoke first as he called out for a translator. Aya stopped him. "I understand now," she whispered. He looked shocked. Aya grinned. "It will be okay," she said kindly. "Labaan is by the lake, at the narrowest point. Where you taught Makena to fish."

Bolajii smiled and said, "Thank you." Aya now understood his words and responded in a language that she did not recognise but instinctively knew. He gently knelt before her and took her hand, tears in his eyes.

"Go," she whispered, "he needs you."

He rushed from the house, calling for help as he left. Aya left the house moments later to see Bolajii and a few armed villagers running towards Labaan's location. Aya felt a sudden panic and quickly followed them; she knew something terrible was about to happen. The villagers moved swiftly, and soon she fell behind. Suddenly she heard a cry and lots of shouting; she followed in the direction of the noise. When she had arrived, the leopard was lying dead, stabbed many times. Panic and fear were in the air, and she intuitively knew something dreadful had happened. It had been a short but brutal fight. The leopard had wounded several people before they were able to kill it.

Bolajii knelt next to the body of someone lying on the ground; she thought it was his son. His hands were pressed hard against the abdomen of the person in front of him as he tried to close an open wound, but blood gushed out from between his fingers and she watched as life drained away.

Bolajii gestured to where the others stood around another person who had been injured.

"Please, go help," Bolajii said to Aya.

A young man lay on the ground. The leopard had torn away the flesh down his left leg, leaving strips of flesh hanging from his thigh bone. Several people desperately tried to hold his leg together, and the young man cried out in pain as he begged for help.

Aya slowly approached, and as she moved,

she felt herself becoming lost in thought. Her mind became clear, and the chaos around her began to subside. With each step she took, she felt a sense of calm wash over her until she walked completely silently, like she was floating above the ground.

A white aura radiated from her. She seemed to shimmer like a new star born into the universe. Aya felt part of her had faded to some distant place, accessing some ancient knowledge.

The villagers all went silent as she approached, and they slowly moved back, clearing the way.

She knelt in front of the man lying on the ground. Aya paused and looked around, surrounded by a haze of whirling colours. The forest faded away, as did her companions, and all that was left was the man lying there helplessly looking at her. Their eyes locked, the man smiled, and his pain vanished.

Aya felt a heaviness weigh on her heart, and then a dreadful hissing sound caught her attention from behind. She turned around and was met with an indescribable emptiness that seemed to have erased all signs of life, light, hope, love, and peace. It was as if everything had been pushed out of existence. From the void emerged a shadow that spread like a virus, infecting all about it. It had no texture or clear form, but it was clearly visible against the luminous light of this place.

"You have no right," it hissed. A voice echoed out from within the blackness, pained and cruel. "You have no right. He is mine!"

A Shadow lunged forward and encompassed Aya where she knelt. In the darkness, visions of death and despair filled her mind. She was shown suffering and anguish, mutilation and disfigurement, hatred and violence.

Aya felt a profound despair welling up inside her. *So much pain*, she thought. As she collapsed into the despair, the Shadow closed in tighter, slowly suffocating her, removing all hope. She fell from the warmth of the light onto a cold emptiness, each moment chipping at her humanity. Unseen hands clawed at her as she tumbled through the darkness; they tore at her clothes and at her very soul. Naked, she fell deeper and deeper into the void, lost to all she once knew, lost to all she was and had hoped to be. Seconds seemed like minutes, minutes like hours, hours like years. When will this torment end, she thought as her mind was lost to confusion and misery.

Suddenly, just when all hope was lost, Aya remembered her mother's gift. She groped for it and found it where it always hung around her neck. She grabbed the blue pendant and instantly felt warmth return to her body. She closed her eyes and thought of her mother, father, grandparents, and friends. She remembered all those she cared for and all those who cared for her. Then she caught a glimpse of *him* once more—the man she felt an inexplicable connection with, a stranger who wasn't really a stranger. In that moment, she felt empowered as a newfound strength flowed through her.

In a flash, a blue light exploded from Aya. A wretched scream surrounded her, and she was thrown back to the young man's side. The Shadow was gone, and she was once again surrounded by pure light. Aya was filled with the purest of love; her eyes sprung open and burned with the brightest blue. She knew exactly what to do.

With practised movements of her hands, she drew symbols in the air that glowed brightly and then faded away as she completed each complex pattern. Aya clasped her hands and closed her eyes. The light dimmed slightly, like a veil had fallen over them.

"Life is taken. Life is freely given," she whispered.

A white fire burned from her eyes and leapt into the man lying on the ground. His body glowed, slightly at first, but soon brighter and brighter until it burst into a bright blue flame.

She placed her hands on the wound. "Life is taken. Life is freely given," she chanted.

A white mist began to flow from her, down her arms to the man before her. As it touched him, he closed his eyes and appeared to fall into a calming sleep.

"Life is taken. Life is freely given," Aya said again and again.

The man's wound closed like some invisible stitching pulled the skin back together.

"Life is taken. Life is freely given," Aya said one last time.

Aya watched as the wound closed and left no scar or mark, as though no injury had ever existed. The world around her slowly came back into focus. She again saw the forest floor, the tall trees, and the sky above. She heard the sounds of birds and animals all around, hiding in the trees. She felt a cool breeze welcoming her back. The same people stood around her as before, but she noticed that the young man was gone, and instead, a small child was sleeping soundly in front of her.

Suddenly, Aya felt a wave of weakness wash over her, as if all the energy had been removed from her body. She collapsed onto the ground and lost consciousness.

…

Aya painfully opened her eyes and found herself in a beautifully decorated room. She was lying on a large, soft bed. Bolajii was sitting by her, waiting for her to wake.

"Makena, you are awake." He paused. "Sorry, Aya," he corrected himself.

"What happened?" she croaked in a dry voice.

"You do not remember?"

Aya gently shook her head.

"You saved Labaan, my son."

"I remember a man lying on the ground, a boy…" She trailed off, staring into a hazy memory.

"I was with my brother who—" Bolajii paused,

and a pained expression crawled across his face. "You went to my son, but he is no man just yet, still a foolish boy." He shook his head in worry. "What do you remember?"

Aya said nothing and started to cry. Bolajii rested his hand on her forehead and spoke in a whisper that he had said a thousand times before. "Sleep now, my precious one, sleep till the morning light brings a new hope." And she fell into a deep sleep.

CHAPTER 8

The Adventures of the Fantastic Mrs. Bennet
Friends will be friends.

"Good morning, Daniel! How is our expectant mother doing today?" Joan asked in her usual warm greeting.

"I'm good, thanks, Joan," Daniel replied, tired and half asleep.

"I'm glad you are doing well." She laughed. "But Aya? Is she okay?"

"Sorry, I didn't get much sleep," he yawned. "She's got a few cramps, not feeling the best today so she's resting."

"Don't worry, I'm sure she will be fine," Joan said reassuringly.

"Yeah, I know." He sighed. "But, well, I can't help but worry," Daniel said, sounding concerned.

Joan smiled. "I know it's tough right now, but

you two will get through this. It'll be okay."

Daniel grinned gratefully at her kind words.

Joan stared nostalgically as thoughts from her past were ignited. "Sometimes life can be difficult," she sighed.

"Everything okay?" Daniel inquired, noticing a hint of heartache inch onto her expression.

"Yes, I'm okay." A sad smile flickered on her lips. "Come sit with me." She sat down on the top step and patted the floor next to her. "You know, sometimes life can be kind, but sometimes unpredictably cruel. But it is that struggle that keeps us going."

Her expression altered and became stony. "I am old, tired, and I have seen too much and lost too much."

"You're not old," Daniel said, trying to lift Joan's sudden mood.

"Thank you, dear." She laughed, knowing it to be a kind lie.

"I was thinking about an old friend, a very dear old friend."

...

Work was Joan's life, and it would take her to places worldwide. However, when she found time to relax, she loved Sicily. The culture, the people, and the rich long history of the land always brought her back. There was one place she always stayed whenever she visited Sicily: a small quiet town called Sutera, which lay some eighty miles north of Palermo. She had friends who owned a small townhouse there and offered it to Joan whenever she wanted.

She had bumped into her old friend Jimmy whilst in Palermo and invited him to stay with her. He was happy to take her up on the offer; the thought of spending some time relaxing and perhaps doing a little writing appealed to him greatly.

The road that led to Sutera was dusty, long, and winding. Joan knew that the road could be treacherous if one wasn't familiar with it, but she had driven this route many times before. As they drove, she was reminded how beautiful and peaceful Sicily could be. The air was clear, and the sky was a brilliant blue. The rolling hills, punctuated with rocky outcrops, seemed to go on forever. The countryside was blanketed with wheat, maize, and wildflowers, and the villages they passed by were quaint and picturesque.

As they crested a small hill, she noticed, in the distance, a mountain appearing on the horizon. It jutted out of the land in stark contrast to the sea of flat fields surrounding it. Built around the mountain was the town of Sutera.

Joan stopped the car, and they got out.

"That is an awe-inspiring view," Jimmy said, taking out his camera.

"Yes, it is." Joan breathed deeply, feeling invigorated by the fresh, warm air.

Joan watched the mountain grow large on the horizon as she approached, mesmerised by its beauty. She felt awestruck by the sight of the familiar village: the homes with their terracotta roofs reflecting the hot sun, the buildings a jumble of shapes and speckles of white and brown that matched the rocky landscape, the stone church towering on the top of the mountain casting its gaze over the land, and the numerous snake-like winding roads stretching away for miles. As they approached their destination, Joan felt a warm sensation of being home again and couldn't help but smile in contentment.

They entered the outskirts of Sutera, and the long dusty road slid away behind them. The path ahead was in stark contrast to the journey that had taken them there. They were now confronted with an old, cracked, cobblestone road which quickly steepened.

The road grew narrower with every metre they travelled, the little white houses standing on either side, shoulder to shoulder with their heat-cracked walls, slowly eroding what little space was left.

They pushed past the town's edge and into the cobbled centre of town. Locals bustled about, some walking, some on bicycles, and the occasional donkey laden with goods added to the cheerful cacophony of life found in a small Sicilian town. Everywhere Joan looked, she saw signs of a vibrant and bustling culture.

The heart of Sutera was its central square. Joan found a charming piazza with a fountain and a clock tower at its centre. The shops and restaurants around the square were packed with people. The air was alive with the sounds of voices and music and the smells of fresh focaccia and roasted coffee beans. Joan took a deep breath and smiled. This was the place she had been longing for.

At the far corner of the square, Joan spotted a small café. They decided to go there for a cup of coffee and a bite to eat. After ordering, they found a table outside and sat down to take in the sights and sounds of the square. Joan watched as the locals went about their daily lives, greeting each other with warm smiles, and she smiled back at them.

"Ahh, this is the life." Jimmy sighed contentedly, sat back in his chair, and sipped his coffee.

"That's the truth," Joan agreed. "So, what have you been up to? It's been about six months since I've seen you."

Jimmy looked lost in thought as he scowled his memory. "Has it really been that long? I last saw you on that Island." He smiled broadly. "What was the name?" His voice drifted off.

"Yiaros," Joan answered.

Jimmy laughed. "Right, Yiaros, when you fell overboard into the sea."

"I was pushed!" Joan protested with a laugh. "But thanks for jumping in after me."

"Hey, someone had to make sure you didn't have all the fun," Jimmy replied with a grin.

"Much appreciated," she said warmly before handing Jimmy a cake. "Here, enjoy your buccellato, it's on me."

They sat there quietly, enjoying the moment. Suddenly, their peace was broken.

"Joan!" a voice called out across the piazza.

Jimmy tapped Joan and pointed. "I think someone's calling you."

Joan looked to where Jimmy was pointing and saw a woman barrelling towards them, pushing through the crowd. As she got closer, Joan recognised her.

She was around the same age as Joan, in her early thirties; however, she was a few inches shorter, her long black hair was intricately woven into a braid that hung down over her right shoulder, and she had dark chestnut-brown eyes and high cheekbones that gave her a slightly exotic look. Jimmy thought that she looked very striking.

"Lorrettsa!" Joan said, running over to meet her and embracing one another. "How have you been?"

"It is so good to see you!" Lorrettsa said, slightly strained, not answering the question.

Joan could see a look of deep concern in her friend's face. The two stood back from one another, but Lorrettsa held Joan's hand as if she could not bear to let go.

"It's good to see you too," Joan said, leading Lorrettsa back to the table. "This is my friend Jimmy. Jimmy, this is my very good friend Lorrettsa."

Jimmy stood up and gave a curt nod in greeting. "Nice to meet you, Lorrettsa."

After sitting down, Joan noticed that her friend seemed ill at ease.

"I thought you were away in America?" Joan asked.

Lorrettsa looked even more anxious now as she hesitated before answering. "I had to come back."

"Is everything okay?" asked Jimmy with a concerned tone.

Lorrettsa put on a fake smile and turned to

Joan, looking for confirmation that she could speak freely.

"You can trust Jimmy with your life," Joan said reassuringly.

Unable to hold back her emotions any longer, Lorrettsa began to cry. Joan moved closer and hugged her friend tightly to calm her down.

"What's wrong?" Joan said softly.

"I had to return because my brother, Antonio, is missing," Lorrettsa said frantically.

"Missing?" Joan asked.

Jimmy added, "When did he go missing?"

"It was five days ago." She started to cry again, and Joan tried to console her friend. "He was home as usual, he went to bed like any other day." She paused, and the colour drained from her face. "But in the morning, he was gone," Lorrettsa said, staring blankly as though she was in shock.

Lorrettsa explained she had spent every moment looking for her brother, searching the streets, talking to his friends and the authorities.

"Haven't the police helped in any way?" Jimmy asked.

Lorrettsa's face changed from sadness into anger. "They are useless! No help at all, just excuses." Her eyes were wide with panic. "I am scared that he might be…" She was unable to finish her sentence.

"That's not good," Jimmy added under his breath.

"Will you help?" Lorrettsa asked, looking hopefully at Joan.

"Of course we will," Joan answered. "We'll do everything we can to find your brother."

"Thank you so much." Lorrettsa smiled. A small glimmer of hope echoed in her eyes. "Please come to my home later perhaps?" Suddenly, all expression drained from her face. "I'm sorry, I must go."

"We will see you later at your house." Joan gave a saddened smile.

Lorrettsa thanked them both again and ran off down a side street.

Jimmy turned to Joan. "Well, our relaxing break may turn out not to be so relaxing after all." He finished his coffee and put it down on the table.

"That was odd," Joan said, feeling puzzled.

"What do you mean? She's bound to be a little off, her brother is missing."

"I understand, but there was something she wasn't telling us. Plus, why tell us to come over later? Why not now?" Joan said. "No, something is not right."

"True. Well, nothing we can do right now. I guess we'll find out more later."

"Let's go back to the digs," Joan said, leaving the table. Jimmy got up and followed, grabbing his backpack.

...

The sky was filled with an eerie indigo and silver shimmer, which faded into a soft black as the night began to take its hold, and the streetlights offered little illumination as compensation. They made their way into the quiet, empty street where they would find Lorrettsa's house at the end of a short row.

Jimmy noticed a man hobbled in a darkened alcove across the street, his silhouette barely visible in the fading light. When Jimmy looked at the man, he withdrew, allowing the dark shadow to envelop him, appearing to evaporate into emptiness. Jimmy turned to Joan, but her expression was lost in concern for her friend.

When they got to Lorrettsa's house, all the lights were off. They knocked several times, but there was no response. The house appeared to be empty.

"Lorrettsa?" Joan called out, and knocked on the door again with more force. "Are you there? It's me."

"No one's home," Jimmy said.

"This gets even stranger," Joan added. "She said that she would be in."

Jimmy stared incredulously at Joan as she went to a side gate and tried the handle. "What are you doing?" he asked.

"It's locked," Joan replied before trying to climb over the gate. "Well? You going to help me or stand there staring?"

Jimmy heaved an exasperated sigh before coming over to give her a hand. She clambered over the top, and her fall was broken as she landed in some old rubbish bags on the other side.

"Yuck!" Joan complained.

"You okay?" Jimmy asked, concerned.

"Just a minute."

She unlocked the gate and let Jimmy in, and they inched around to the back of the house.

Peering through the window, they were horrified by what they saw: a body lying motionless on the floor in the dark.

"Quick!" Joan shouted, motioning for him to kick in the door. The door broke from its hinges and fell to the ground.

They rushed into the room to find Lorrettsa sprawled out on the floor. Joan checked for a pulse and found one; it appeared she was only unconscious. Jimmy picked her up in his arms and laid her on the sofa.

Joan removed a vial of smelling salts from her bag and waved it under Lorrettsa's nose. Her eyes flew open, but they were coal-black. In shock, Joan and Jimmy stepped back. Lorrettsa lay perfectly still, staring up at the ceiling.

Suddenly, she spoke, but in a voice that was not hers. "Ozul," she said, her voice a cracked hiss.

"Lights! Quick!" Joan said, panicked.

Jimmy dashed to the switch, flicked it on, and flooded the room with brightness. Lorrettsa screamed and sat up, her mouth open unnaturally wide, and she vomited out a thick black liquid. The air filled with the smell of sulphur.

She fell back onto the couch, coughing and gasping for breath.

Joan looked at Jimmy, both lost for words and frozen, not knowing what to do. Then Joan jumped into action, rolled Lorrettsa onto her side, and lowered her head slightly off the sofa. More of the vile substance splashed onto the floor.

Jimmy went over and slowly raised one of

Lorrettsa's eyelids. Her chestnut-brown eyes had returned, and he sighed in relief. Once her breathing had returned to normal, Joan laid her back down and took a moment to process the events.

"I... I..." Joan stuttered, looking for the words to describe what had just happened. "What on earth was that?"

Jimmy shook his head in confusion. "It was like something from a horror movie!"

"What did she say? Ozul?" As she spoke, an icy chill filled the room. It lingered for a moment and seemed to hiss the word *Ozul*.

Joan and Jimmy looked at each other in consternation.

Jimmy shivered and grabbed her arm. "Never say that word again! Something isn't right here."

The two stood in strained silence as they contemplated their next move.

"Should we call someone?" Jimmy eventually said, breaking the eerie quiet that had descended around them.

"Call who? She already told us authorities weren't interested," Joan replied, but she still couldn't take her eyes off Lorrettsa.

"I don't know, a doctor perhaps?"

Joan scoffed sceptically. "And tell them what, exactly? That our friend appears to be possessed and is spewing satanic puke!"

Jimmy sighed heavily and looked away. "Okay, okay. We can't leave her here like this."

"No, we cannot," she said indignantly. "Let's get her upstairs and into bed. Well, she can't go up like this. I'll go get some towels." She went off to the kitchen and came back with a bowl of water and some towels.

After cleaning up as much of the mysterious substance as possible, they carried Lorrettsa into her bedroom and laid her down. Exhaustion crept over them both as they silently watched their friend sleep. Lorrettsa looked deathly grey, and her breathing was shallow but unhindered.

Joan suddenly awoke to the realisation that Lorrettsa's parents were not there. "So where are they?" she said aloud with a mix of worry and confusion.

"Who?" Jimmy looked confused and tired.

"Her parents. Rosalina and Giovani." Panic was now pushing back the fatigue.

Jimmy looked at Joan and opened his mouth to speak, then closed it again as if he were contemplating something deeply. After a few moments, he just shook his head and said, "What a night," and rubbed the back of his neck.

"Where the hell are they?" Joan said, sounding concerned.

"Stay here with Lorrettsa, and I'll see if I can find anything that may explain this nightmare."

Joan sat in an armchair near Lorrettsa's bed and tried to make sense of what had happened, feeling more confused and overwhelmed by the minute. The word *Ozul* echoed through her mind. She shivered and sunk deeper into the chair, looking for some warmth.

Jimmy left Joan and wandered from one room to the next. He noticed that there were no signs of the general clutter that a lived-in house would have. The place was immaculate. The beds were neatly made, the mirrors were polished to perfection, jewellery hung motionless on their stands, perfume bottles looked unused, and the hairbrushes had not even a strand of hair entwined in their bristles. He checked downstairs, and again, apart from the stain left behind by the black liquid and the broken back door, everything was perfect... Just too perfect. The cups in the cabinets were stacked, each set on top of the other and placed with immaculate accuracy. The dishes were placed in their rightful homes with precision. Nothing, not even dust or cobwebs, appeared on any surface.

"It doesn't add up," Jimmy muttered to himself. "Either everyone in this house spends their days cleaning and tidying or..." He paused. "Or what, exactly?" He placed his palms over his face and groaned loudly.

Jimmy returned to Joan, feeling none the wiser after his search.

"Something isn't right here," Jimmy said, explaining what he had seen.

"I know," Joan answered.

"I think we need to leave. I just have a feeling," Jimmy said, now sounding worried.

"Look, we can't move Lorrettsa. We'll have to wait until the morning."

"I know," Jimmy admitted. "But I have this feeling like…"

"Like something bad is about to happen!" Joan finished his sentence.

"Yeah." Jimmy nodded. " I know this sounds weird, but I feel like I'm being drained of any joy."

"I know, I feel it too," Joan said, trying to hide her concern. "Anyway, we better try and get some rest. Hopefully the morning will bring us some answers."

"Sleep?" Jimmy laughed. "Here?" He rummaged through drawers and eventually found some spare blankets.

"Here you go," Jimmy said, covering Joan with one of the blankets he had found.

"Thank you." Joan smiled, pulled the cover over herself, and tried to find some rest. Jimmy made himself comfortable on the floor next to her, and after rolling about, he eventually fell into a cramped, uneasy sleep.

Joan awoke in the middle of the night to a strange, eerie light hovering above Lorrettsa's bed.

"Look," Joan whispered, trying to wake Jimmy, thumping him. He didn't wake, just turned over, groaning.

As Joan stared, she could see it was a small round glowing orb, encompassed in a hazy mist-like glow. The orb floated down to Lorrettsa and hovered just by her forehead. A beam of bright light shot from it, making Joan jump. She stood up to rush to Lorrettsa, but something stopped her. The room felt warm, and as she looked at her friend, she could see the colour returning to her face, and her breathing returned to normal.

The glowing orb moved towards Joan, hovering just inches away before floating through the door. All Joan could do was stare with a mix of fear and fascination. Without thinking, she finally followed, tracking the light as it entered one of the bedrooms.

The room initially looked like a model home, the way Jimmy had described it.

The wooden floor gleamed in the light of the orb as it hovered in the centre of the room.

The orb pulsated, sending a stream of light out in every direction, finding every corner and purging every shadow. The orb shone brighter and brighter, evaporating any hint of darkness. Joan smelled flowers and felt a warm breeze brush across her, filling her with happiness and peace. When the light faded away, it was as though a veil had been lifted. The room was no longer immaculate; it was mayhem. There were clothes all over the place, the bed was broken with covers ripped, and the furniture looked like it had been mangled and mutilated as it lay fractured about the room. The floor was covered in splintered shards of glass, the remnants of shattered bottles of perfume and makeup, as if a terrible disaster had occurred.

The glowing orb went from room to room, drawing Joan along. As it made its way through each space, the light seemed to clear away a layer of mystery and showed reality for what it was, as though it was purifying the house, unveiling the truth that had been hidden from sight. Every room revealed the same desolation, the same destruction and turmoil.

As the orb went downstairs, it revealed a truth

that Joan didn't want to accept. Lorrettsa's parents lay motionless on the floor. Stunned, she rushed over to check for signs of life, but there were none. The orb continued onwards, but Joan stayed behind, instead rushing off to get Jimmy.

Jimmy was in tow when she returned, and the orb had disappeared. The house was a wreck, yet the atmosphere seemed to be changed for the better. Even if joy still eluded them, a lingering beautiful fragrance in the air and a lingering warmth brought them a little comfort.

"We have no choice, we'll have to call the police," Jimmy declared.

"I know. Could you call them, please? I need to think," Joan said, leaving the room in deep thought.

The police arrived about three hours after Jimmy had made several repeated calls. The local police station was closed, so his call was diverted to a station in another town, several miles away, who could not help, diverting him to another station in a larger town. They were eventually put in contact with a constable who lived in Mussomeli, who, prior to receiving the call, was soundly asleep, happily dreaming of a pasta dish that his Nonna used to make for him when he was a child, a dream that he was not happy to be awoken from.

The constable was in a bad mood when he

arrived at the scene, but his temper dissipated upon being faced with the tragedy found in the house.

Realising the seriousness of the situation, he made a call, and within thirty minutes, there were another five officers in the house. However, the police officers who arrived paid little attention to Lorrettsa's parents, but instead searched the house. They also ignored the constable who had arrived first on the scene. They had a quiet word with him and pushed him to one side, where he stood looking uncomfortable.

After about an hour, they appeared not to find what they were looking for. An unmarked van pulled up outside of the house, and Lorrettsa's parents were placed inside. They went to take Lorrettsa too, but Joan and Jimmy stood defiantly in their way. It wasn't until the constable stood up that they said they would come back later when Lorrettsa was up.

As quickly as they had arrived, they left, and Joan, Jimmy, and the constable stood silently in the room.

The constable looked distressed; he wouldn't make eye contact with anyone before quietly muttering, "Sorry," and walking away.

"What just happened?" Jimmy said in delayed confusion.

"We need to move Lorrettsa out of here," Joan

said fearfully.

Ominous noises drifted from the room upstairs.

"Mama? Papa?" a voice called.

Joan and Jimmy bolted up the stairs to find Lorrettsa standing outside her parents' bedroom.

"I remember now," she said softly. "I did this." Her eyes were staring into the room, unblinking.

"There's no way you could have done any of this," Jimmy said with a nervous laugh.

"Come back to bed," Joan said delicately and led Lorrettsa back to her bed.

Despite Joan's efforts to console her, nothing would stop the flood of emotion that poured from Lorrettsa. She couldn't keep it all bottled up any longer, and the tears spilt down her cheeks as she wailed uncontrollably.

Eventually, Joan asked the one question whose answer she feared the most.

Taking hold of Lorrettsa's hand, she asked in a trembling voice, "What happened here?"

"I did this," Lorrettsa answered, looking broken, her eyes empty, her face revealing the stress that she had been under.

"What do you mean you did this?" Jimmy said, sitting on the edge of the bed.

Lorrettsa took a deep, shaky breath and began to speak.

"My mama had called me when I was away. She didn't say why, but said I had to return home. I guess she didn't want to worry me." She paused and took a deep, calming breath, held it for a moment, then let it out. "I soon found out that my brother had been taken. My parents were panicked. We heard rumours, only silly rumours of children going missing. I didn't want to believe it, it couldn't be true…" She trailed off. "But it is all true."

They sat quietly, hanging on Lorrettsa's last words, realising the ramifications.

"Go on," Joan said, breaking the silence.

"They say it's a cult as old as life itself, a shadow, a myth." Lorrettsa looked away. "A myth," she whispered.

"Okay, if this cult exists, then why take Antonio?" Jimmy said, listening intently.

Lorrettsa stared blankly into empty space. "I do not know why," she whispered softly, "but I have felt why." Tears rolled down her cheeks. "I felt the hatred, the cold emptiness, the madness, the desire to kill!" she shouted out.

"It's okay, it's okay," Joan whispered.

"Is it? Are you so sure?" Lorrettsa screamed in Joan's face, hatred in her eyes. Then suddenly, her expression dropped into misery. "Sorry, sorry." She squeezed Joan's hand as though it was a silent cry for help.

"I searched for Antonio when I got home. Somehow, they knew. They came to the house, they spoke words that I did not understand." She started to raise her voice. "Then I felt it... It consumed me. It whispered to me. It hurt me."

Lorrettsa let go of Joan's hand and ran for the window. Jimmy leapt up and tackled Lorrettsa to the ground. She lashed at him, scratching and punching. Joan was now also trying to restrain Lorrettsa.

"Let me go!" she screamed. "Let me go!"

Jimmy held on tight, trying to avoid the onslaught.

"Don't you understand? I killed my...my..." She screamed out in pain and then suddenly went limp.

Jimmy cautiously looked up. "I think she passed out."

"She's in shock, severe trauma," Joan said. "I've seen this before."

"We need a doctor, a hospital. This is more than we can cope with," Jimmy said, panting for breath.

"Okay, I know someone who may be able to help," Joan said.

"Good. Let's get her there before she wakes."

...

They left Sutera and went to the nearby town of Mussomeli, where Joan knew someone who she hoped would be able to help Lorrettsa. Julie Linderman specialised in mental trauma and worked as a clinical psychotherapist specialising in post-traumatic stress disorder, serving in the British Armed Forces. She was often sent to military bases all over the world to offer counselling for those military personnel suffering from trauma. It was on one of those trips that she experienced armed conflict firsthand when the base that she was assigned to was attacked, causing her to take a life. That trauma stayed with her and drove her into severe depression. She was eventually discharged, retired, and moved to the small town of Mussomeli, a place far removed from the busy London city she grew up in. This brought her peace and calm, and her life had been that way until Joan and Jimmy had shown up.

It was no easy feat convincing Julie to help. She had left that life behind her, a place filled with death and trauma, and had found a new, peaceful life.

They told Julie about the events of the night, and to their surprise, she had heard the rumours of a secret cult. She, of course, put it all down to hearsay. However, Joan's story did spark a curiosity in her. Julie agreed to help and promised to do her best to look after Lorrettsa. Joan said that she would call whenever she could to see how Lorrettsa was doing.

Once Joan was satisfied that Lorrettsa would be safe, she and Jimmy headed back to Sutera, where they would start their investigation. They spoke with families who had reported a missing child, and they soon found that children had disappeared from small towns throughout the region for years, but the local authorities had never followed up on any of the reported missing children. Their search led them from Sutera to neighbouring towns, each family telling the same story, and a pattern soon emerged. Only three children ever went missing at a time, all thirteen-year-old boys, and they went missing every seven years.

"That does sound like a culty thing to do," Jimmy said.

"Yes, I only hope we can find them before it's too late," Joan replied.

They were led from town to town, whisper after whisper leading to dead ends. After searching for three days, they felt desperate and lost. They had been told stories, rumours of a secret cult that worshipped an evil, but nothing concrete.

They stopped at a roadside cafe high on the outskirts of a small coastal village, deciding to reevaluate what they knew, which was truly little. Night had fallen fast, and a cold mist had covered the roads, making driving exceedingly difficult.

Jimmy brought over two coffees and placed them on the table.

"Lovely, thanks," Joan said, tired but thankful for the temporary rest.

Jimmy took a map out of his backpack and laid it open on the table. It was covered in notes and crosses documenting their journey.

"This is hopeless," he said with a heavy sigh. "They could be anywhere. They may have even left the country."

"No, we'll find Lorrettsa's brother and the rest of them. I made a promise," Joan said defiantly.

"Yeah, a promise that you may not be able to keep," Jimmy said, instantly regretting his words.

"Look, we're both tired. It's been a long couple days, and the stories we've heard are heartbreaking." Joan stared into the black liquid floating in her cup, bringing back unwelcome memories.

"Okay, so what do we know so far?" Jimmy said. "A cult, missing children, and some sort of ritual perhaps."

Joan sat in silence for a while. Jimmy sat back, exploring the map.

"I haven't been completely honest with you, Jimmy, and for that, I'm sorry."

Jimmy raised his head, looking at Joan expectantly.

"You must understand that I didn't know, but I started to have my suspicions as we went on, and I couldn't be sure until now."

"Go on, I'm all ears." Jimmy sat back, folded his arms, and looked intently at Joan.

"I believe this is the Kovom Order," Joan proclaimed.

Joan had first heard of the Kovom Order as a rumour that she'd initially ignored. However, time and time again, it would rear its head as though always watching from the shadows. It was always elusive but, in some way, always there, influencing politics and cultures. This had sparked Joan's interest, and for many years, she had dedicated her time to following leads, but each led to a dead end. Until, by chance or fate, she acquired a small manuscript that spoke of a monk living in seclusion, having a vision, nothing too unusual. But this monk spoke about a battle between two deities locked in conflict, one seeking balance, the other seeking unification, or at least that's what the manuscript depicted. He was instructed to form a group that would be tasked with guiding humanity away from what he said was the Great Union and to create a group that would be dedicated to this task, the Kovom Order.

Joan pulled a manuscript from her backpack and unrolled it over the map. "Somewhere on this manuscript is the answer. I am sure that these disappearances are connected to this," she said, looking it over.

Jimmy shook his head. "Why didn't you say earlier?"

"I wasn't sure that there was anything to say. I didn't want to complicate things further. If I was wrong, we would be chasing a shadow," Joan said apologetically.

"So why now?" Jimmy said, trying to stay calm.

Joan stood up and walked to the edge of the road. She pointed out to the sea. Jimmy followed her finger and saw a storm far out at sea.

"It's crappy weather, yeah," Jimmy said, unimpressed.

"No, look again. The weather is clear everywhere else, just a storm in that one spot. Doesn't strike you as odd?" Joan pressed her point. "Read the translation on the manuscript."

Jimmy picked up the manuscript and read the translation, mumbling the words under his breath.

Joan spoke, "*When light surrounds, and Shadow is trapped, it will hide deep in the ground. Shadow will remain in the midst of a raging storm where the truth is false. You will know and see where the shadow thrives amidst death. This is nowhere, where time stops, life ends, and Shadow falls.*"

They both stood there looking at the strange phenomena teasing them, daring them to investigate what lay beyond the storm's edge.

"I see your point. Where are we anyway?" Jimmy said, looking back at the map.

"We are nowhere," Joan replied in a calm, quiet voice.

"That town doesn't exist on the map," Jimmy said.

"I think we were meant to find this place," Joan said, trying to find a little hope.

"Just dumb luck, nothing more," Jimmy said.

"Perhaps." She shrugged. "Or perhaps there is

something that is nudging us where we need to be."

"Nice thought. Perhaps if they could clear that storm for us, that would be great," Jimmy said with a touch of sarcasm hinted in his tone.

Joan laughed. "Come on, let's go see what we can find."

Porto Dei Morti—Port of the Dead—was situated on the west coast of Sicily. It was a small seaside port only known to locals of the area and quite isolated from the tourist routes.

They arrived at the small town just before midnight. Everything was closed as they drove through the streets to the harbour.

"Looks like another night sleeping in the car," Jimmy muttered. Joan shrugged.

"We need to find a boat," Joan said, almost excitedly.

"Do you have a death wish?" came the response.

"Nope, but we do have a lead, and we are going out to sea. This can't wait," Joan said with renewed determination.

They parked the car, gathered their backpacks, and walked along the harbour, hoping to find someone who would be able to help.

"Over there!" Joan pointed to a light on the edge of the pier. "Looks like someone may be about after all."

They made their way to the end of the pier, where they were confronted by a strange-looking old man who was short, hunched, had a long grey scruffy beard, and wore tattered clothes. His face was weathered and bore the marks of old deep scars, and his toothless grin made Jimmy grimace. He was wearing blackened glasses, obscuring his eyes.

Joan was undeterred by his appearance and asked if he knew where they could rent a boat. The old man looked out to sea and chuckled. He said something in a language that neither of them understood and pointed to a dilapidated small wooden motorboat that creaked loudly as it rocked up and down with the waves.

"Will that even start?" Jimmy looked doubtfully at the boat. "I think it's seen better days."

"Look," Joan said, pointing to an old, weathered dinghy tied to the side of the boat.

"Is that meant to make me feel better?" Jimmy said, shaking his head.

The old man then uttered something they both could understand: "*Isola dei Santi*."

"Island of Saints," Joan muttered, and without

THE FINAL JOURNEY

a second thought—and to Jimmy's dismay—she said to the old man, "We'll take it. How much?"

The old man smiled grotesquely and walked away, muttering something to himself. They watched him for a moment as he turned a corner and was out of sight.

"Come on." Joan rushed over to the boat and clambered in. Jimmy reluctantly followed. The whole experience left him feeling uneasy. The man looked strange, and those glasses... What was he was hiding?

...

The waves fought harshly against the small wooden boat as it rocked back and forth on the darkening sea. The wind blew, and the rain beat down heavily, causing the boat to sway violently. The two of them had hastily thrown on their yellow raincoats, trying in vain to find some protection from the harsh weather. Jimmy gazed out at the deep, dark ocean and felt a chill. There was something about it that made him feel uneasy, and he wished he hadn't agreed to come along. As he shivered, Joan appeared beside him. She smiled at him reassuringly and shouted over the roar of the wind and rain, "It's alright, Jimmy. I know what I'm doing!" He looked at her doubtfully but nodded his head.

As they pushed farther into the storm, the sea grew more violent, and the boat groaned loudly under the strain. They both clung to the steering wheel, fighting to keep the boat on course. The wind howled, drowning out the sound of their voices. The sea showed its anger at their presence as its black waters lashed at the sides of the boat, trying to claim them. The waves thrashed and pounded around them as they desperately raced for shore. All around, the sea swelled with a dark, menacing force, creating mountains of tumultuous water that seemed to have eyes and follow their every move. The only thing visible in all directions was an endless expanse of black liquid alive with rage, bearing down on them like a ravenous beast looking for its next kill.

Somehow, the boat kept going up and over the waves and crashing hard down and into the troughs. Suddenly, Joan screamed as she was thrown across the deck, but Jimmy lunged forward and grabbed her. He pulled her close and held her tight. A huge wave loomed up out of nowhere, bigger than any other wave they had encountered. It crashed over them like a freight train, smashing the boat's windows in the small cabin, destroying what little shelter it offered. Joan and Jimmy were thrown to the floor and knocked unconscious, but somehow the little boat still punched through the waves, holding its course.

Joan opened her eyes and found that the boat was bobbing joyfully just offshore. The rain had stopped, but the sky was filled with a menacing blanket of grey fog blocking out any starlight. Jimmy lay beside her and groaned loudly. She was relieved to hear his voice. She stood up and looked around. The storm seemed to be circling the island as though it had retreated to a safe distance, not daring to approach. Joan wondered if it was meant to keep people out or perhaps keep something in; the thought filled her with dread. The island looming ahead of her seemed both beckoning and a warning all at once.

Isola dei Santi was a desolate and unforgiving place. Its craggy rocks jutted up from the sand like broken charcoal teeth. Sparse, withered trees clung to the land like skeletal hands, motionless in the oppressive air. The island appeared devoid of any life; nothing more than dead roots and brittle branches remained, and a thick mist hung low across the land, creating a haunting glow.

"I guess this is why no one ever comes here," she said, unsure if Jimmy was listening. He answered with a louder groan.

She helped him to his feet.

"You're okay," she said, looking him over.

"I think this is what death feels like," Jimmy croaked.

Joan, however, looked stubborn in her resolve and gestured to him to help lower the dinghy into the water. As they stepped out onto the blackened sand, they were greeted by an eerie silence. No waves lapping or birds chirping, nothing but an oppressive stillness that seemed to swallow up their presence. A chill wind suddenly swept through, carrying a mist that swirled around them like malicious tendrils trying to grab at them. The mist obscured any hint of visibility, which would make progress slow. As they shivered in the frigid air, they felt as though they had stepped into a world where all hope was lost. Despair and misery washed over them, taking away what little hope they had found in beating the storm. Joan motioned for them to keep moving. They headed inland, following a long-abandoned path, not really knowing what they were looking for or what to expect from this place.

The two of them stumbled through the murky darkness, their feet dragging with the weight of an oppressive silence that weighed heavily on them, and with each step, they felt an aching dread welling up, expecting some horror to snatch them and drag them to their doom. The mist seemed to drain the life from them, sapping their energy and bringing about a deep hunger and thirst. Searching desperately for some respite, they cautiously scanned their surroundings in vain, praying for a solitary sign of life yet finding nothing but despair.

"It's dead here." Jimmy's voice was harsh against the silent backdrop.

Joan nodded, daring not to speak.

The island was relentless, which made the going difficult, but Joan was used to harsh environments, and though tired and drained, she pushed ahead with relative ease. She paused every now and then and pulled out the manuscript from her backpack, then scoured the surroundings, looking for landmarks. Once satisfied, she beckoned Jimmy to follow.

They left the path some time ago and now trudged through the rocky terrain, their feet dragging and their muscles aching. Joan pushed ahead, and desperation fuelled her forward despite the obstacles, and Jimmy followed, tired and lost in thought. She paused when she thought she recognised a landmark described in the manuscript, scanning the land with intense concentration, searching for something amid the jumble of rocks and boulders. When a glint of recognition appeared in her eyes, she beckoned Jimmy to follow before pushing on with renewed vigour.

They pushed past exhaustion and kept going, refusing to accept defeat despite the island's attempt to hinder them.

They came across something that stopped them in their tracks. It was a small, crumbling stone hut, barely standing, its roof caved in, its walls covered in dry, dead moss. Joan looked at it with invigorated interest, her eyes gleaming with anticipation.

"This is it," she said, her voice low but brimming with excitement. "I'm sure this is what the manuscript talks of. This is the place where it all started."

Jimmy looked at her incredulously. "This? This is what you've been searching for? A derelict building?"

Joan was deaf to Jimmy's complaint, now driven by a deep anger and curiosity. She pushed through the splintered wooden door, which creaked and whined at her touch. The building was as decrepit inside as it was outside. The mist cast a dull glow which crept around the room, dimly illuminating the fractured remanence of long-forgotten memories that lay scattered about, abandoned now, much like all hope in this place. She stepped over broken furniture and debris as a single-mindedness overcame her. A roar in her head drowned out the voice of reason calling for caution, her only mission being to find out what lay hidden within these four walls. For that moment, nothing else mattered. She had lost herself to desire, to want, to a craving that had to be sated. The need to find the secrets that may be hidden here was all that now existed.

Joan started pushing furniture aside, which broke upon her touch. She pushed aside the dirt and rubble that hid the floor, searching for something that she might recognise as a clue. She stopped and took out the manuscript again, scouring the translation. "Here it reads: *Santioni Araria, touched by Shadow, truth's whisper, the seed where knowledge flourished. His words cast Shadow over Light; his words strip back the blinding burning Light, and that is when it will be revealed to you, only in Shadow, only in death's loving embrace.*"

"Santioni Araria?" Jimmy inquired. "You think this was his home?"

"It has to be here," she muttered. "Yes, this is the place, he lived here. This is where it all started!"

"So, what are we looking for?" Jimmy replied.

Joan stopped what she was doing and sat back on an old table which wobbled under her weight. "To be honest, I don't know. Something, anything that may still be, a clue." Her voice lowered as her enthusiasm bled away. "Anything," she whispered.

Jimmy sighed and walked over to the hearth. "Well, when anything is hidden in stories, it is always behind a secret panel behind the fireplace." He chuckled complacently.

As he moved, a rotten floorboard creaked beneath his weight, quickly followed by a loud crack. It gave way under his foot; his heart raced as he stumbled forward, instinctively lashing out as he managed to grab a half-fallen beam which had hung precariously balanced for many years. The beam easily shifted under Jimmy's force and gave out a loud groan as it snapped and fell with a thunderous crash. The sound reverberated through the room before fading away into an eerie stillness. Jimmy was pulled back just in time and lay panting heavily on the ground, looking up at Joan.

"Be careful!" Joan scolded.

Out of the corner of Joan's eye, she noticed something under the fallen roof. Her attention was now fixed on a small, wooden chest.

She approached it with care, now heeding the voice of caution.

"Help me with this." She motioned Jimmy over.

They carefully pulled the chest out into the centre of the room. It looked old and weathered by time. Any colour had long faded, leaving the wood looking frail and dull. They sat and looked at the little chest resting on the floor, both silent in anticipation.

"Would you like the honours?" Joan said.

Jimmy ripped the lid off with a sudden jerk, and the old hinges screamed in protest. A chill ran down their spines as an icy gust of wind whistled through the ruins of the hut. It echoed for a moment as it shifted old papers and spun like a vortex in the middle of what was left of the room, then faded away, leaving only a feeling of emptiness.

Joan thought she heard a whisper: *Ozul*. This was a word that filled her with a sense of bitter sadness, a memory that she had tried to bury, which now had returned to haunt her.

She leaned forward and peered into the box. A look of pure wonderment and apprehension crossed her face.

The box held a small, leather-bound book. Joan slowly reached in and took it out gently, fearing that it might crumble away in her hand.

She began carefully opening the cover, and it held a series of yellowing parchments. The inked writing, now barely visible, was written in a language that she didn't recognise. Some of the parchments had now been lost to age and crumbled when exposed to the chilly air. Joan carefully closed the book, placed it back in the box, and closed the lid.

"I believe these are the words of Santioni Araria," she said, holding the chest close to her. "We have found where the Kovom Order was born. Finally, I will have answers."

Jimmy looked sceptically at Joan and asked, "Do you really think this will help us locate the missing children?"

Joan's face flushed with embarrassment; she had almost forgotten why they were there in the first place. Looking up into his eyes, she replied, "I believe that if we can figure out who these people are, this will lead us right to those kids." She paused. "I can't promise anything, but this is all we have."

Jimmy looked at her, and he couldn't deny her honesty. "Okay, you're right. This *is* all we have, so what's next?"

"Well, I can't read it," she sighed. "We need to find someone who can."

"Sounds like a plan, but let's not stay here too long. This place gives me the creeps," Jimmy replied, now standing by the door, ready to leave. "Any ideas where we can get this translated?"

"Actually, yes." Joan smiled. She emptied some of the contents from her backpack onto the floor and made room for the small box.

As they slowly made their way back to the boat, Jimmy couldn't shake the feeling that they were being watched. The empty stillness of the island seemed to press in on him, making the hairs on the back of his neck stand up.

"Why do you think it's so quiet here?" he asked quietly.

"The manuscript speaks of a place where a

Shadow appeared one night and spoke with Santioni. When he stepped out of his hut the next morning, the island was dead, and the seas raged around it," she answered, equally quietly.

"Was there no one else here?"

"Yes, there was…well, before the vision. The next morning, all had gone, and only this mist remained," Joan said, looking around, feeling unwelcome.

"I wish I never asked," Jimmy muttered.

As they pushed off from the shore and began to head back to the old boat, Jimmy felt relieved. He couldn't wait to get back to the mainland, away from the draining mist. But Joan was lost in thought; she sat staring out into the dark waters, her fingers caressing the box, feeling every contour. There was something in those pages, something important, and she felt drawn to it like a moth to fire.

As they began their journey back to the mainland, the ocean's waves had calmed down, as if the storm wanted them to leave with their prize. The sea was now tranquil, and the black water lay still, only gently rocking the boat as it chugged along. There were no signs of the fierce winds that had lashed out just hours before. Despite this calmness, Jimmy felt on edge. The feeling of being watched had only grown stronger throughout their journey, and he couldn't shake the sense of impending danger.

They finally reached the harbour, and Jimmy was relieved to be back on solid ground. The early morning sun was now casting its light over the small seaside port. The welcome warmth offered a stark contrast to the overcast grey sky found on the island. This filled them with renewed hope.

Jimmy turned back to the island. "Look!" he said as he pointed in disbelief.

"How is that even possible?" Joan said, intrigued.

Jagged bolts of lightning flashed, and thunderous cracks reverberated through the air in the distance. The storm that had temporarily relented as they departed the island had now returned with a vengeance, unleashing a new fury upon the ocean and sky, encircling the island as before.

"It's like someone threw a switch! I'm done with this place," Jimmy said, a shiver running down his spine. "Let's get the hell out of here!"

Joan promptly agreed.

After they had securely moored the boat, they walked back along the pier, but they quickly noticed that the entire dock was deserted. Joan looked around, her brow furrowed in suspicion. "I have a bad feeling," she muttered to herself as they made their way back to the car.

Though the sun had woken, the atmosphere around them appeared to thicken with an ominous presence. They stepped down a narrow cobblestone street. As they walked, the sound of their footsteps echoed off the houses that lined their path, emphasising the unusual silence.

"Listen," Joan whispered.

"I don't hear a thing," Jimmy said quietly.

"Don't you think that's odd?" she asked. " It's early morning in a seaside town, where is everyone?"

"Oh, I see your point."

A looming dark silhouette rose from the ground, like inky fingers stretching skyward. It blotted out the sun and plunged the street into shadow.

Jimmy turned to Joan. "I have a really bad feeling."

"Exactly my thoughts." Joan gave a nervous smile.

Suddenly, a figure materialised in front of them, like some cursed entity from the depths of hell, standing before them with menacing intent. He was short and heavily built, his clothing tattered and frayed. His face was twisted and contorted like he had experienced a thousand years of pain and torture. His black eyes were deep pools of emptiness, radiating an icy cold aura that paralysed them as he slowly advanced.

The man's voice was low and menacing, each word reverberating off the walls that lined the street. "Hand over the box! Now!" He brandished a long, ornate silver knife, which he raised threateningly in front of him.

Joan's eyes widened in fear, her breaths coming out in shallow gasps as she clutched the backpack closer to her chest. "I don't know what you're talking about," she stammered, trying desperately to play ignorant.

"This will be your last chance." He spat out his words, his face now transformed into a mask of pure loathing. He took a step forward, and Jimmy stepped in front, blocking Joan from view.

"We don't want any trouble. We're just a couple of tourists who rented a boat." His words seemed to trail away amidst the silence that followed.

But the assailant stood almost motionless. The tension in the air was thick with the anticipation of what was about to follow. Silver glints of light flashed off the blade as it swayed back and forth in the dim streetlight.

Suddenly, the man exploded forward with a

rage-filled roar, thrusting his knife out for Jimmy's heart. Instinctively, Jimmy dove out of the way just in time, snatching hold of the man's wrist as he flew past.

Terror raced through Jimmy's veins like electricity, and he felt death breathing down his neck. He and the attacker tussled until Jimmy was shoved back. His aggressor jumped again; this time, the blow from Jimmy hit the man square in the jaw, causing a rotten tooth to fly out of his mouth and bounce along the ground. As the man stumbled backwards, Jimmy didn't let up and threw another punch, landing it on the side of his face and sending him crashing into a wall. The man shook his head, then sprang at Jimmy with renewed fury. They both crashed to the ground. Joan watched in horror as they lay motionless, a pool of red forming around them.

"Jimmy?" Joan said, a growing concern now in her voice.

The attacker moved, and Joan held her breath, but then he fell back, rolling off Jimmy, who was lying there panting on the ground.

"That hurt," Jimmy groaned.

Joan steadied herself against a house. Her breath was heavy and she felt overwhelmed by the relief that washed over her. She helped Jimmy up, but there was no time to rest. They heard more footsteps and voices coming.

They raced through the empty street, their feet pounding hard against the cobbled ground, their hearts thundering in their chests as they gasped for air. They careened around every corner, weaving frantically between alleyways and buildings to lose their pursuers. With sweat dripping down their faces and lungs burning, they refused to stop until they were sure they had escaped.

"We can't stay here," Jimmy said.

"No," replied Joan.

"We need to get back to the car."

"Probably being watched," Joan said.

"You said you knew someone who could translate the manuscript?" Jimmy asked.

"Yes, they helped with the first translation. However, they're a long way off now in Palermo, and I don't think we will be able to reach them," she said, desperately looking for a solution.

They pushed farther along cobbled streets, blind to their destination but hoping that something would reveal itself. A sudden turn down a dark alley revealed a cluster of ramshackle houses, far older and smaller than those on the main street.

"Come inside!" a voice beckoned from behind a slightly open door.

Without hesitation, desperate now for help, they entered the house, not knowing what awaited them inside. The room was bare aside from a bed jammed against one wall and an old, decrepit set of drawers against the other. Above the drawers hung a tarnished wooden-framed photo of a young child; the glass that covered it looked like someone had punched it violently, and the broken glass had faint splashes of red along its splinters. Hanging above it was an image of Christ on the cross; however, Christ's face had been disfigured. A faint scent of smoke and mildew floated through the dreary darkness. The candle flames glowed weakly all around, unable to disperse the fog that seemed to hug everything in sight. Shadowy figures lurked along the walls, making ghostly shapes as they moved across whatever they touched.

A woman sat on a stool, cloaked in a shadowy darkness, her face barely lit by the dim light cast from the candles. She was etched with wrinkles, her skin grey and thin, and her hair hung white and straw-like over her shoulders. She did not look up as they approached.

"What do you want here?" she asked gruffly in broken English.

Joan looked at Jimmy, who shook his head. Joan held back the full truth. "We were being chased by muggers, I think."

The old lady cackled hoarsely. "Liar!" she

screeched, causing them to step away in shock. "You've been to Isola dei Santi." She got excited at the name and shrilled with delight.

Joan answered cautiously, "But how would you know?"

The old woman's eyes widened. "You have the words?" she said, leaning forward, licking her lips, and sniffing the air.

"We have nothing!" Jimmy said forcefully. "Come on, Joan, let's go."

"No," the old woman's voice softened slightly, "please stay for a while."

They paused for a moment and turned from the entrance.

Joan sighed. "Yes, we have it," she admitted, desperate for help. Jimmy looked at her opposingly, not happy that she had divulged that information.

"You are unwise to admit this," the old woman said, her expression now full of sadness.

"I have little choice," Joan asserted.

"There is always a choice, my dear." She coughed violently, covering her mouth with a tatty cloth.

"Look." Jimmy gestured discreetly to Joan, pointing to the cloth. It was splattered with small, dark spots of what looked like blood.

"Perhaps I can help them?" the old woman said softly as she stared at a dark corner of the room, her eyes gleaming with a sorrowful intensity. Then her tone betrayed a deep sadness. "I will not listen anymore." She started to weep quietly. It was as though she was having a conversation with some unseen force hiding in the shadows.

Suddenly, her voice changed sharply, grew in ferocity, and dripped with contempt as she spat, "I won't." She sneered angrily. "You can't make me!"

The woman fell into silence and covered her face with both hands. "Then again," she whispered, "perhaps I will." She looked up, her expression now gentle. "Please, can you give me his words?"

She stretched out her trembling hands, every wrinkle on her skin betraying a long, hard life. With some reluctance, Joan pulled the box from her backpack and placed it in the old woman's hands, who quickly snatched it.

With some effort, she placed the box on the table next to her and opened it. To Jimmy's surprise, it opened without a sound. She hesitated for a moment, then reached in and removed the book from its resting place. She lightly laid the book on the table next to the old box. She opened it, and her heart sank as she was confronted with the damaged pages.

"No, no, this won't do. His words must be

heard," she said with surprising calm. She began to delicately flip through the pages, muttering to herself.

"This text is written in an ancient tongue," she said, her voice shaky and weighted down with sadness. "His words must be read; they must be known." Tears formed in her eyes as her breath caught in her throat. "What is broken must be made anew."

She looked at Joan, her face showing a struggle between kindness and hatred. She said with a strained voice, "I must help you." She picked up the book, carefully placed it back in its box, and returned it to Joan.

"Find Arrino." She spoke as though she struggled to hold onto her sanity. She reached into her pocket and revealed a silver coin. "You must give this to him; he will know what it means."

She scribbled down an address on a scrap of paper, wrapped the coin in it, and held it out. As Joan reached down, the old woman grabbed her hand and quickly placed the bundle firmly in it. Her grip lingered for a moment as she looked deep into Joan's eyes, a wave of sadness and pain breaking through her expression as she spoke again. "I am sorry."

The old woman released her grip, and Joan stepped away, placing the coin and address into her pocket. The old woman glared at each of Joan's movements, her scowl deepening with every moment that passed. Joan and Jimmy moved to leave, but their steps faltered at the sound of the old woman's melodic voice. She sat there quietly, humming softly under her breath, before she began to speak.

"The shadow shall come, and soon all will be none. For shadow will consume all, and Light will fade away. Ozul, oh Ozul, swallow us whole."

As she chanted, shadows curled around the room like tendrils, enveloping everything in darkness. Joan and Jimmy were shocked to see that her eyes were pure black. They hesitated only for a moment before bolting for the exit.

"Ozul!" Her mouth opened wider than humanly possible, and her voice bellowed over them like an erupting volcano. She let out a loud shrill that echoed throughout the room like a tornado, knocking Joan and Jimmy to the ground. The room warped around them, extending outwards in an ever-widening black abyss as the light faded away. All that they could see was a slither of light betraying the exit.

"Run!" Joan cried out as they clambered to their feet, smashed through the door, and tumbled onto the street below. They looked back in horror. The old woman hovered by the open door, her face distorted with rage.

"Ozul!" she screeched as the shadow swallowed her. Her screams echoed out of the darkness, invading the daylight.

Jimmy and Joan scrambled desperately to their feet, fear propelling them forward through the streets until they felt far enough away. Breathless, Jimmy spoke first.

"What the fuck was that?" he said with a quavering voice, looking at her with wide-eyed panic.

Joan could only shake her head in disbelief. "I have no idea, but whatever this is, it is happening, and we have to end it!"

She drew out the address from her backpack, breathing heavily. "We have our lead."

"That could be a trap, or another one of whatever that fuck that was!" he said, heavily panting.

"I know! I know! But it's all we have." She grasped his arm. "Please, let's find this Arrino."

...

They came to the address the woman had given them, a rundown-looking house on the outskirts of town. As they knocked on the door, their hearts pounding, they heard a gruff voice from inside.

"Who is it?" bellowed a deep, menacing voice.

"We are looking for Arrino," Joan replied.

An angry response followed quickly. "There is no one with that name here, now fuck off!"

Joan was undaunted. "We must speak with him!" she demanded.

"Open up!" Jimmy banged hard on the door.

The door creaked open, and the barrel of a shotgun slipped out.

"I said leave now!"

Jimmy backed away and pulled Joan with him. She stopped, took out the coin, and held it in front of her. A moment of tense silence filled the air until the shotgun was lowered and the door swung open.

An intimidating figure of an old man filled the entirety of the doorway, his wiry frame towering over them. His scruffy grey beard and piercing blue eyes held an air of authority as he watched them with intimidating scrutiny.

He snatched the coin from her and clutched it tightly in his fist. His eyes narrowed, piercing like daggers into hers as he spoke with a deep growl. "If you have this, then Bianza is lost." His voice filled with a pang of deep sadness. "She is doomed to suffer and bleed forever."

The air around them seemed to freeze as he uttered a barely audible prayer. His eyes then flew open, fierce and bright, and he said in a voice sharpened with icy venom, "So, you have it?"

They felt a palpable dread as his piercing gaze searched their faces.

"We have the book," Joan eventually admitted. "We were told that you could help, or at least we hope that you can." She removed the box from her backpack. "We need answers desperately, and time is running out."

The man's face contorted with a blend of apprehension and shock as he looked upon the plain wooden box Joan held in her hands. He directed his gaze up to her, then to Jimmy, before announcing in a sarcastic tone, "The Book of Words!" With a lamenting shake of his head, he gestured for them to enter his house.

The room that they were led to was full of what appeared to them as research. Papers were strewn about on every surface, many with scribbles of strange symbols and obscure writings. Two of the walls were lined from floor to ceiling with bookshelves heavily ladened with dusty old books and ancient tomes. The man gestured for them to sit at a small table in the corner; he stood a few metres away.

"I can help you read the manuscript that hides in that box," he said, each word teasing an alternative motive. "But I need to know why you want to do this." He snarled suspiciously.

"How can we be sure that we can trust you?" Joan replied, echoing Jimmy's thoughts.

Arrino laughed. "Well," he looked Joan straight in the eye, "you can't."

Their gaze locked, and Joan tried desperately to read Arrino's expression, which proved impossible.

"I have other things that I could be doing, so you know where the door is." He turned and walked away.

"Wait!" Joan called out, and Arrino stopped and turned his head. "Okay." She took a deep breath. "We believe that what the Kovom Order is doing is linked to a series of disappearances. We think that if we can decipher these writings, we might be able to figure out what they're up to and put an end to their sinister plan."

"Disappearances, yes." He sighed heavily.

The man scanned their faces carefully before gesturing to the box. Joan opened it. This time, it creaked and groaned loudly. She removed the book and gently handed it to Arrino.

The man's eyes burned with intensity as he laid the book down on the desk slowly, almost reverently. He then opened a cupboard and pulled out an aged bottle of whisky along with three glasses, which clinked against each other as he placed them on the table. He filled each glass to the brim and placed them in front of his uninvited guests. "Here, drink." His voice was dark and dangerous. Both Joan and Jimmy reluctantly drained their glasses while Arrino watched them carefully, his eyes never leaving them.

"You will need the courage. You have no idea what guards the secrets hidden in those pages."

"That's true, but we are starting to see," Jimmy said, reliving their experience in the small house earlier that day.

Arrino laughed mockingly. "You haven't a clue, son." His eyes twinkled with malicious delight. "The door that you are about to open can never be closed." His ominous warning lingered in their minds, and Jimmy poured himself another drink.

"You need to understand that the Kovom Order is not a game. It's a force to be reckoned with and an enemy that you do not want to notice you. Should you pursue this, you're throwing yourselves directly into Satan's den, risking your lives and your very souls. Heed my warning: the Devil will come for you if you continue down this path." A cold chill spread through the room with his words, leaving a feeling of dread lingering in the air.

"Get comfortable," Arrino said coldly as an ominous grin drew across his face.

Arrino sat at his desk with a glass and a bottle and assiduously worked his way through the manuscript.

"Will it take long?" Jimmy asked, as he shuffled about on a chair.

"The pages were brittle, the ink faded in most places, and the text was written in an ancient tongue that few can read anymore. So, what do you think?" Arrino replied, his voice full of sarcasm.

It was slow, tedious work, and the damage to the manuscript made the deciphering incomplete. It was difficult to understand many of the meanings that were written, and it took him all night to decipher just one page. His fingers ached, and he felt withered and tired.

"Here," he said, waking Joan up from an uncomfortable sleep and handing her the page that he had deciphered.

"I'm going to get some sleep. I'll try again in a few hours." He left the room, and she heard a door slam in another part of the house.

She jolted Jimmy awake and read the notes to him in hushed murmurs.

"It says that this language was a primal form of Sumerian, used by a cult devoted to Ozul, the God of Shadow and Death." She stopped abruptly and read on in silence before continuing. "It tells of a vision Santioni Araria had after going through an inner turmoil—a plague cloaked the island, killing both people and animals with no cure. He prayed desperately but to no avail. The notes then go on to describe how he cursed God in anger and had another vision, something about balance and an evil attempting to disrupt humanity, with Ozul's name mentioned again. The details are too hazy to make out the whole story, but he was visited by Ozul, who granted him knowledge beyond his comprehension. He was taken to the edge of existence and shown Arakumani, whatever that means. When he woke up the next day, the island was deserted, and he realised what his purpose was."

Jimmy let out a long breath. "Wow, that's a lot to take in."

"I know, but after all we have seen, is it so far-fetched? I've always believed that there was more than this." She paused. "But I never thought… I mean, God of Shadows?"

"Well, this doesn't get us any closer, and we've lost another day." Jimmy sounded disheartened.

"Let's find some food and wait for Arrino to translate another page. What other choice do we have? We can't risk going outside and bumping into our friends, you know, the ones who wanted to cut us open."

After a few minutes of opening doors, they stumbled across the kitchen where Joan managed to scrounge up some bread and cheese, and Jimmy discovered a bottle of red wine; simple food, but it was welcomed. They then settled down for the long wait.

Joan pored over papers and books, driven by her insatiable curiosity, while Jimmy drifted off to sleep. The hours passed slowly, but eventually a door opened in another part of the house, and Arrino entered the room, barely giving them a glance, and sat back at his desk.

He paused and reached for his glass. Seeing that it was empty, he beckoned to Jimmy to fetch more from a cupboard that he pointed to. Jimmy obliged and poured Arrino another drink. A flicker of a smile tremored on his lips in gratitude, and he drank deeply, emptying his glass. Jimmy quickly filled it.

"Thank you, son," Arrino said.

Arrino spent the day painstakingly studying the second page, his heart sinking at the sight of its fragmentation. Portions of the text were fractured beyond recognition, but he used knowledge gleaned from earlier research to assemble the jigsaw puzzle of words and sentences. Eventually, his efforts paid off, as he uncovered a terrible truth so dark and horrific that it chilled him to the bone.

Suddenly, Arrino said out aloud, breaking

the silence in the room, "He was shown a ritual, a task that must be carried out every seven years. This contains information about a ritual. It's called the Blood Moon Ceremony, and it requires the sacrifice of three innocent lives."

"We have to stop them," Joan said, her voice shaking in disbelief.

Arrino nodded gravely. "You must understand, this won't be easy. The Kovom Order is powerful and dangerous, but what lies behind them is far worse." He glanced over to an old photograph on a side table. "I am the last," he whispered.

"It appears that there is only one place where it can be held, where it all started: Isola dei Santi."

"I need a drink," Jimmy said, poured himself a large whisky, and emptied the glass.

Arrino looked closely at the manuscript and made a few more notes.

"The ritual is marked by the passing of Comet Ozullini. As it nears our moon, its tail causes an unusual astronomical phenomenon: it causes the moon to appear blood red, but it is only visible from one location on earth, Isola dei Santi." He wrote something in a worn notebook. "And it appears that we have only three days."

"Comet Ozullini?" Jimmy inquired. "I've never heard of it."

"Not unexpected. As I mentioned earlier, they are an influential group who keep much of this information hidden. They control news outlets and TV channels and even infiltrate governments."

Silence fell as they contemplated the significance of his words.

"Who are you really?" Joan suddenly asked Arrino.

Jimmy stopped what he was doing and looked at him.

Arrino remained silent.

...

The hours dragged by, growing increasingly unbearable with each passing moment, and they were no closer to agreeing on a strategy as every idea felt like suicide, which only added to the unbearable tension and frustration that now hung in the air.

Eventually, they came to the realisation that they had only one choice: they would need to discreetly hire a boat and make their way along the coast at night, approaching the island from the opposite side. They hoped that the storm would supply some secrecy to their approach. Arrino said that he knew someone who would be able to lend them a boat that would get them there.

They left for Isola dei Santi early in the morning of the day that the ritual was going to take place.

The sea was a relentless enemy this time around, beating down on the boat like a hammer. The vessel creaked and moaned under its own weight, and with every wave, it drew closer to collapse. Torrents of rain poured down out of the black sky, drowning Jimmy's vision in a curtain of water. Joan held tight to her backpack and the box within, pressed tight inside the small, cramped cabin, whilst Arrino held the wheel, keeping the boat on course.

The boat pitched and bobbed up and down and side to side with each gust of wind. Jimmy struggled to keep balance; he desperately reached for the railing, but it was slick with rain and he was unable to secure any kind of grip. The waves tipped the boat precariously from this side to that, threatening to topple it over entirely.

Suddenly, a great swell of water lifted itself from the depths and crashed into their vessel, catapulting Jimmy overboard. Joan's heart nearly stopped as she desperately scanned for any sign of him, instantly forgetting about her own safety, but he had vanished without a trace.

Arrino tied the wheel securely and grabbed Joan, pulling her back to the cabin and pushing her firmly onto the ground.

"He's gone!" Arrino shouted out.

"No, we have to go back!" Joan fought to get up, but Arrino's firm grip held her tight.

"He's gone, girl!" he said in a softer tone.

She lay there stunned by the sudden emptiness, but the boat surged on relentlessly against the raging swells. The harsh waves pounded the hull, yet still, the vessel held firmly in its course, pushing ever further into the unknown depths of despair.

Arrino gritted his teeth in determination as he grabbed the wheel. His muscles ached and strained as he pushed the boat past its limits, desperate to break the storm and make it to shore.

As the sea grew calm once more, Joan couldn't help but feel defeated. The grey mist that surrounded them was oppressive, every breath a struggle. She could feel Jimmy's absence like a weight on her chest, and it only made the guilt she felt for dragging him into this nightmare even more intense.

A glimmer of hope echoed in her as she remembered Jimmy's words. *You can't run from the crap life throws at you, so just fling more crap back at it.* She laughed to herself.

Now was not the time to mourn, she thought; even her tears were taken from her by the relentless rain.

Arrino lowered a dinghy into the water. It had seen better days: the fabric was worn and tatty, and it was covered in patches and barely holding any air. When it hit the water, it sat low, barely afloat. It bobbed in the gentle surf that rolled in, but with each wave that nudged this little boat, it threatened to sink.

There were two oars, each tied to either side of the worn-out boat; they were splintered and cracked, but firmly held together with tightly bound knotted rope.

He placed some basic supplies in the boat and then climbed in. The dinghy sunk lower under the strain.

"You coming?" Arrino sounded almost indifferent as he looked intently at Joan.

Joan, with some effort, stood up and gazed at the storm's edge. She wiped the tears from her face, and with a heavy heart, she uttered a final farewell. "Goodbye, old friend."

They landed on the bleak, cold shoreline. The ominous grey mist was there waiting to greet them.

"We need to head inland," Arrino said. Joan did not respond.

"There is a high point about a mile in," he added.

Joan suddenly wondered how he would know this as distrust grew inside of her.

The journey inland was more difficult this time; it was colder, and visibility was poorer. The cold bit hard and crept deep into their bones, making every footstep painful.

As they pressed forward, they were haunted by strange, unearthly sounds echoing out from the mist that fed into their imagination. Joan had to fight back panic and shivered at the thought of what dark things and nightmares lay beyond, just out of sight. She looked to Arrino for companionship. However, he looked unmoved by this place, almost indifferent. The mist seemed more hostile this time to Joan, as though it had been awoken for some nefarious purpose or simply to hinder them in their goal.

Suddenly, she heard an eerie moan come from amongst the dead trees to her right. She stopped and stared wide-eyed into the thick mist. Her heartbeat stuttered inside her chest, and a shudder ran up her back. Then a hand grabbed her arm, and she almost screamed out in a panic.

"Do you want to stay here? If not, keep walking." Arrino offered no comfort in his tone. It almost sounded like hatred was welling up from some deep, hidden place within him.

They walked quietly, which was only matched by the deathly silence of the island. The oppressive weight of sorrow for Jimmy's loss and the emptiness and desolation of the island weighed on her like an anchor, dragging her down to cold depths that she never believed could have existed. Her soul felt broken, split by a pain so deep that it threatened to consume her until her last breath. The island seemed to thrive on her pain; the mist danced about her and mocked her grief.

As she watched Arrino, he moved with such conviction and certainty, never stopping to look for landmarks or ponder a direction. Every turn, every path taken, appeared well-known to him. She had a feeling of dread that Arrino could not be trusted, and the realisation that she was alone with him in this desolate place terrified her.

She noticed a change in his mannerisms and general tone as soon as they had broken through the storm. He seemed angrier than usual, more detached, even less human.

When they finally arrived, Joan felt as if a thousand years had passed. She ached to her core, drained of all emotion and strength, and even the will to live had left her. Nothing made sense anymore. Time and space seemed to stretch out, contorting the natural laws like a defiant insult to the very fabric of creation. Though night had fallen, there was no starlight to be seen, just the endless greyness obscuring all natural light.

"Now we wait." He sat down at a vantage point. He opened his backpack, pulled out two blankets, and threw one over to Joan. "I suggest you get comfortable."

He took a bottle of whisky from his bag and took a long swig, then offered it to Joan, who shook her head.

"More for me," he grunted and turned his back to her.

Joan tried desperately to stay awake, but she was overcome by sheer exhaustion and fell into an uneasy sleep. She was abruptly awoken by a painful jab to her shoulder.

"We must head inland. I think I know where this will all happen," Arrino said.

Joan took a moment to come around. "What? How do you know?" she said, rubbing her bruised shoulder.

Arrino looked at her with pure contempt. "I know because I know!" He sounded irritated at Joan's question. "I saw their torches in the distance." He unsuccessfully tried to hide the growing cruelty in his voice.

"But how? This fog is thick," Joan pressed,

overwhelmed by a feeling of suspicion.

Arrino didn't answer but simply packed his bag, snatching the blanket from Joan. "Inland!" he demanded, his voice laced with anger.

Joan felt uneasy. She felt alone and vulnerable having to trust this man whom she did not know, but she had little choice. *There are always choices*, the old lady's words echoed around her. Joan decided that she would make a choice, and at her first opportunity, she would lose Arrino and take her chances.

She kept going, but now watched Arrino closely, scrutinising his every move. However, he was relentless in his resolve to reach his destination, and she soon felt she was being dragged along in his wake.

Fatigue pressed hard on her. Though her body begged for just a few moments of respite, the thought of stopping, even for a second, terrified her. She was worried that if she rested here, this place would never let her go.

The terrain was unpredictable, from wet, muddy paths to dry, dusty fields. Arrino remained unrelenting and carried on, driven by some veiled objective that Joan could not fathom whether it was for good or bad.

The ground grew sharp and rocky and cut into her feet, which caused her to wince with every step. The trees that lined their path were broken and lifeless, their bare branches like thorny fingers reaching out menacingly. The air grew thick with the suffocating silence, an oppressive stillness that seeped into each step they took. Nothing moved in this oppressive wasteland except for them, as if time had stopped long ago and only a ghostly echo remained, like an infinite abyss of bleakness and despair. She found herself longing for the eerie groans that plagued them earlier; anything was better than the dark emptiness that now surrounded them. She even found herself grateful not to be alone. Every so often, she glimpsed a decrepit old house, a silent reminder of a life lost long ago.

They entered a long-abandoned village. The crumbling old houses and broken windows looked like tortured graves, concealing now only ghosts from a forgotten past. The silence in the air was oppressive and heavy, carrying a lingering sorrow from years of abandonment. Every step they took echoed around the empty, desolate streets, threatening to awaken an unseen evil.

Arrino suddenly stopped in his tracks, a looming sense of dread settling in the air like thick smoke around him. Fear and dread coursed through Joan's veins as she heard him utter her name.

"We are here, Joan," he said in a chillingly calm and malicious tone.

Fearing the worst, she took a step back only to be confronted by his growing anger.

"Why are you so frightened?" he angrily demanded.

Joan frantically searched for an escape, her heart pounding painfully in her chest.

"Ozul is here with us now." A sinister smirk was plastered across his face.

Arrino smiled repulsively, and a black tar-like substance oozed from his mouth. In a single fluid motion, he lunged at Joan, his hands outstretched like talons, ready to tear her apart. But she was faster; thrusting her head forward, she connected with Arrino's nose in a sickening crunch, and he stumbled backwards.

"I guess you can feel pain!" she spat through gritted teeth as her clenched fist swung forward, smashing into Arrino's jaw with a crack.

He fell backwards onto the ground. Joan didn't wait and took the opportunity to run. However, she didn't get far before he swung out with an arm that seemed to stretch beyond normal limits, striking her with enough force to pick her up and send her crashing down onto the hard ground.

With lightening movement, he stood over Joan, his face no longer human but twisted and contorted, a caricature of what he once was.

He clenched his fist and reared his arm back, ready to attack, but then something stopped him. His mouth twisted in anguish as a single tear rolled down his cheek. All the rage was replaced with despair, and he murmured brokenly, "Ozul cannot be beaten."

Arrino's scream pierced the night, and his body wracked with unbearable pain as a stake burst from his chest. Thick rivers of blood gushed from his mouth and ran down his chin, staining his clothes with a thick black tar. His rib cage split open in a mangled explosion of flesh and bone, and he crashed to the ground with eyes still wide open in shock.

A familiar hand reached down for Joan.

"Let me help you up," Jimmy said with a smile.

Joan moved away from him. "This is a trick. It can't be you!" she said in disbelief.

Jimmy knelt and smiled reassuringly. "All me, I'm afraid."

Joan flung her arms around him, pushing him to the ground. "But how? I thought..."

"It was weird. I was drowning, you know, the works, life flashing before me, imminent death, when I smelt lilies and I saw a light, more like an orb of light, just hovering in front of me. I felt kinda lighter, and as it moved, I followed it to shore. Then it kept buzzing around me like that fly that just won't get the hint, so I said, 'What do you want?' and it beckoned me to follow it, leading me to you." He paused and put his arms around her. "Then I saw you being attacked, grabbed the first thing that I thought looked like it could do some damage, and, well, you know the rest."

Joan whispered, "Thank God you're alive."

Their eyes locked as though they were trying to read one another's thoughts. An unspoken connection drew them together as though they were one soul separated by two bodies. Joan inched closer and closer until her breath became shallow, and her heart pounded. His warm breath caressed her lips, almost daring for their mouths to meet.

Suddenly, they heard a noise shattering the silence. Not too far away, they heard approaching footsteps and the chanting of strange words which echoed in the night air.

They scrambled to their feet, ran for a nearby dilapidated building, and hid. Joan noticed that the skeletal bones of a family who once lived here lay across the floor, a bleak reminder of its unsettling past.

"Rest in peace," she whispered.

The noise grew louder, and they could see a dim flickering of torchlight reflecting on the old stone walls.

"Arrino!" Joan said, panicked.

"Too late to move him," Jimmy replied.

"No, look." She pointed to where Arrino had been killed, but his body was gone.

"That can't be good." Jimmy shook his head.

"Oh," Joan said, pulling Jimmy down.

The black hooded figures crept forward, dragging their feet against the ground in a sinister disciplined march. Each measured step reverberated off the cobblestone ground and stone walls like a deafening drumbeat, filling the air with dread and portent. They slowly advanced until their ominous silhouettes stood just metres away from Joan and Jimmy's hiding place. They sat still, daring not even to breathe. The sinister procession moved past them, oblivious to their presence.

Joan and Jimmy slunk low and followed at a cautious distance. The eerie sensation in the air grew thicker as they approached an uncovered clearing where twenty black-robed figures stood in utter silence, surrounding a central earthen stone. An otherworldly fog moved between them, emitting a cloying stench of incense and death that brought on a feeling of nausea.

"Look!" Jimmy said, pointing up to the sky.

Suddenly, the clouds parted with a deafening roar, revealing a massive blood-red moon that pulsed threateningly in the sky like an open wound, casting an eerie reddish glow over everything below it. As if awakened by a grotesque imitation of creation, the trees around them began to snap and sway unnaturally, their branches thrashing like whips in the now-howling wind. The air grew bitterly cold, as though any hint of life had to be extinguished, as though something dark and sinister was stirring deep within the Earth itself.

In the middle of the stone formation appeared a man wearing a robe that stood out blood-red in the moonlight. He bore a grotesque golden mask, which looked like a human face that had been contorted through agonising pain. He carried a long staff in one hand that was crowned with a silver blade that hummed ominously as he raised it skyward.

Dark shadows encircled him as three cowled figures wearing pure white robes stepped from the shadows. They held up fluttering candles that illuminated the scene. Many black-robed figures lined the perimeter and chanted loudly, their sacred incantation filling the air. Their hideous voices reverberated throughout the island, which reacted to their ancient words like a sinister spell, slowly revealing its cruel intent.

THE FINAL JOURNEY

They watched, frozen in fear, as the four figures stood around a stone slab altar where a body was lying motionlessly, draped under a white sheet. The black-robed figures that surrounded the four chanted louder and louder, then suddenly fell silent. Joan and Jimmy felt the anticipation hanging in the air, a morbid curiosity now holding their gaze.

The red-robed figure appeared to mutter some words, then revealed a long silver dagger. He raised it high above his head, gripping the long knife that glinted in the moon's light. With one swift motion, the blade slashed through the air and plunged into the silent figure lying there, who screamed out before falling deathly silent as a pool of crimson spread from underneath the white sheet and ran down the sides of the stone.

"No... We're too late!" Jimmy gasped, his throat closing up in horror at what he saw.

The other three figures dropped to their knees and stretched their arms outwards, palms facing up towards the moon. A new low, menacing chant began slowly but gained in speed and volume as it was now joined by howls coming from the mist all around. The red-robed figure now moved slowly to the three, chanting with the others. He paused and looked down at the three who now knelt before him, and with one clean sweep of the blade he sliced across their wrists in quick succession, an errant rain of scarlet droplets spilling to the ground beneath them.

"Ozul! My life I give freely!" they all cried out.

Then he drew the knife along his own throat. A thin red line appeared following the blade as it cut into his flesh. A rush of warm blood poured from the wound and over his hand, pooling beneath him. He wobbled and fell to his knees, struggling to utter his final words. "Ozul."

Then all fell still.

The black-robed figures now moved silently, their faces shrouded in shadow. They moved with an eerie precision as they arranged the lifeless bodies in a macabre display. Each body was carefully positioned so that their feet met at the base of the altar, and their arms were placed above their heads in a ghastly imitation of a cross, with the altar serving as its central point.

"No!" Joan screeched, her stomach heaving with dread.

Jimmy jabbed his finger toward two cloaked figures who were standing at the edge of the clearing.

"We can't let this insanity happen again," he snarled.

They rushed forward, each step bringing them closer to their quarry. Jimmy passed

Joan a hand-sized rock, and she felt its surprising weight in her palm. Her lips curled into a feral grin as she tightened her grip on the weapon.

"Let's finish this," she spat out as fear was replaced with determined anger.

As they approached, they saw two other white-robed figures standing there.

"The other children," Jimmy said.

"Antonio," Joan dared not to hope.

They moved in unison, their aim perfect as they launched the stones that found their mark, crashing into the heads of the two black-clad figures. The robed men crumpled to the ground, out cold.

Joan and Jimmy scrambled towards the white-robed children, who stood motionless, seeming not to notice the commotion.

Jimmy knelt in front of one of the children and pulled back his white hood. It was Antonio, but to their horror, his eyes were pure black with an unworldly power radiating from them. Their arms rose, a wave of dread sweeping over Joan and Jimmy as they heard a sound like no other, like a hundred voices chanting at once. The others in the ritual stopped their chanting as though they were being summoned. They moved in unison, sprinting forward towards them at an impossible speed.

"Run, now," Jimmy said, dragging Joan along.

"Antonio!" Joan cried out and tried to grab him, but the second child, with ease, stepped forward and pushed Joan and Jimmy to the ground.

They scrambled to their feet and ran for their lives into the grey, cold mist, closely followed by black-hooded figures. They had no idea if they were going the right way. All they knew was they had to keep moving. Minutes bled into hours, and exhaustion was upon them. Their pursuers were relentless, driven by some hidden evil force craving their blood.

They ran blindly, stumbling over rocks, clambering through vast muddy fields, cut and bruised, but they were determined not to die in this place.

They stumbled into an abandoned village where they hoped they would be able to catch some rest. Their gasps for breath echoed in the silence as they frantically ran down a street. They suddenly stopped when a hooded figure stepped from the shadows and blocked their path. Quickly changing direction, they turned onto another street, only to be blocked by a menacing figure again. Panic began to set in as they realised that another figure stepped from the shadows with every step they took. This happened over and over, and they felt like they were being toyed with.

As if fate were playing an evil game, their frantic running led them to the heart of the village, the town square. They paused desperately, looking for a way out, but soon realised they were surrounded and had no escape.

"This is it, I guess," Jimmy said, reaching for Joan's hand.

Joan looked up at Jimmy and smiled. "If this is the end, I couldn't think of anyone else whose side I would rather be by."

The figures swarmed forward with ferocious intensity, expecting to make quick work of their prey, but Joan and Jimmy had some fight left in them yet. They fought back with everything they had but were outnumbered and outmatched. Joan threw punches and kicks that staggered the attackers, but they kept coming. Jimmy stood shoulder-to-shoulder with her, delivering blow after punishing blow, yet still the enemy advanced.

"What is it with these guys?!" Jimmy said, panting heavily as he ducked beneath a swing that sailed over his head, then quickly retaliated with an uppercut to the man's jaw, sending him backwards.

"Possessed?" Joan groaned.

Jimmy was then jumped by three of the attackers, who pushed him away from Joan's side. She screamed out and went to go to

Jimmy's aid, but a fist flew through the air and caught her on the side of her head, and she fell backwards to the floor in searing pain. A robed figure raised a knife, and it came down, but plunged into Jimmy's back as he jumped in front of Joan to protect her, then collapsed in a heap.

A shadow crept around Joan and Jimmy as the evil robed figures advanced, seemingly undefeatable. Despair spread like a fog through the desolate landscape as all seemed lost. But then, a shimmering orb of light appeared from nowhere and blocked their attackers' path. The air around them crackled with energy as a blinding white light erupted from the orb, piercing the figures and causing them to writhe in pain. Joan watched in awe and terror as the powerful light ripped through their enemies like it was cleaving through shadow itself. They let out sickening screams before falling silent.

Gripping Jimmy tight, she closed her eyes and waited for whatever would come next, but only silence followed.

She gasped in horror as she slowly opened her eyes and saw that the square was empty of all but them. There was no sign of their attackers anywhere to be seen.

She looked back at Jimmy, who was lying in her arms. "Jimmy! Don't you dare die on me," she said with tears in her eyes.

Jimmy smiled. "I'll be fine." Then his eyes closed, and he fell quiet.

...

"You just can't stop a story there!" Daniel exclaimed. "I mean, who ends a story there?" He paused, waiting for Joan to fill in the gap.

She laughed. "Thank you for listening."

Daniel pressed for an answer. "Yeah, yeah." He smiled and dismissed her words, eagerly wanting an answer. "So what happened to Jimmy?"

Noticing the time, Joan said, "Oh, doesn't time fly. I really have to go. I've already gone on for long enough." She stood up and strolled down the stairs towards the front door. "I'm meeting a dear old friend, and I don't want to keep him waiting."

Daniel stood there looking at Joan as she walked away. "I bet it's Jimmy you're going to see," he called out, hoping for an answer that would settle his curiosity. "It is, I bet!" he persisted.

Joan replied with a mischievous grin. "I'll tell him you said hi." She waved as she closed the door behind her.

...

"There you are," Jimmy said. "You do like

keeping me waiting."

Joan smiled and took a seat opposite Jimmy. He called over the waitress and ordered a coffee for Joan.

"Stop your moaning," Joan said and gave a playful grin. "How have you been?"

"Good," he said and sipped his coffee. "I have it."

"Show me," Joan said eagerly.

Jimmy leaned down, reached into his backpack, and retrieved a rolled-up parchment that had been tucked away out of sight. A look of trepidation spread across his face as he slowly handed it to Joan, who took it eagerly. She gently unfurled it and laid it out on the table. Her eyes scanned its surface, taking in every crease and tear. It was heavily damaged, however there was enough of the ancient text legible to make her shiver.

The parchment spoke of ancient secrets and powerful magic, whispered by the gods themselves. Goosebumps prickled her skin as she traced her finger over the faded words, feeling a sense of destiny unravelling before her very eyes.

"Fate," she whispered, and breathed out a

heavy sigh.

"Well?" Jimmy said impatiently. "Is it him?"

Joan hesitated, not wanting to believe what she had read. "Yes, it is him," she finally said. Hearing her own words somehow solidified the truth.

She turned from the fragmented words that lay hauntingly before her and stared out the café's window. They both remained silent as each contemplated the gravity of the situation.

"What should we do?" Jimmy finally said.

Joan turned back and smiled. "We must do whatever we can to keep Daniel safe."

CHAPTER 9

Miozu
When Shadow finally falls.

Aya spent several days in bed recovering from the events of the night before. Bolajii's wife, Nala, visited her while she was recovering. Nala treated Aya as a mother would treat her ill child, with patience, love, and endless kindness.

All thoughts of the upcoming wedding were replaced with mourning for the loss of Bolajii's brother, Ayan. The funeral ceremony lasted for several days. Ayan was bathed and perfumed with herbs and special oils. He was then wrapped in a burial shroud and placed in the communal meeting space, where people could pay their respects and grieve the loss.

When the final day of mourning came, Bolajii's brother was placed on a funeral pyre. The pyre was approximately six feet tall and consisted of a basic design composed of a large wooden frame and a bed of woven straw. The structure was decorated with various figurines of gods and wooden plaques which had been intricately carved with ancient symbols depicting nature.

As Bolajii approached his brother, he began to sing a sorrowful melody. He held a lit torch in one hand, and in the other he carried herbs that he scattered on the ground as he walked. His voice echoed through the air, powerful yet broken. Those around him remained silent with heads bowed in respect.

Bolajii stood just a few feet from the pyre as he sang the last words, and his voice fell silent. This marked the final end of Ayan's life on Earth, and the lighting of the pyre marked the beginning of his journey back home. The flames took hold and burst with a vibrant energy that consumed all it touched. The smoke quickly rose into the sky, carried by a gentle breeze.

Everyone gazed upwards and watched the smoke drift higher and higher. It swirled and twisted with the wind, forming different shapes as though alive. It weaved mischievously, then suddenly swooped low and shot into the clouds. It was like a playful child dancing freely for the first time.

Bolajii watched and smiled as he imagined Ayan's spirit freed from the anchors binding him to this world.

"You are free, my little brother, truly free," Bolajii said as a tear rolled down his cheek. He raised his hands skyward. "Ayan!" he cried out.

...

John had radioed in a little later than scheduled. He thought it best to not mention all that had happened. In truth, he wouldn't know where to begin. However, he did explain about the leopard and Aya's fall into illness. They were concerned to hear that she had been in bed since her ordeal and now wanted her to return to base camp as soon as possible.

Richard decided to arrange for an emergency medic to check on Aya, just to be safe, he reasoned, and John agreed. Luckily, a doctor was visiting a nearby village, so they arranged for him to see her later in the day. Upon arrival, Doctor James Hazwell—or Haz, as most people called him—was taken to see Aya.

Nala made it very clear that she was displeased by his arrival and informed Haz that Aya was resting, did not require his help, and promptly ushered him from the room. Nevertheless, when Nala left on an errand, Haz took the opportunity to evaluate Aya's health. Upon examination, he could see no physical injury. If it weren't for her slightly palish skin colour, she would have the appearance of a woman in peaceful sleep.

"Aya," Haz said, trying to wake her gently.

Aya just responded with a yawn and rolled over. After some thought, he reluctantly had to agree with Nala's assessment that rest was all she needed and promptly left, wanting to avoid meeting Nala's stern glare.

John told him that Aya had been awake for short periods and had eaten and drank a bit. However, she quickly fell back into a deep sleep, grumbling that she felt drained. Haz asked John to keep him updated, and if there were no improvement in a couple days, he would return and arrange for her to be flown out.

After Richard had spoken with Haz at length, he told John they had as much time as needed for Aya to fully recuperate and to only return when it was safe for her to be moved. As per protocol, John promised to update the base camp every ten hours on their situation. However, he did ask that a replacement vehicle be sent as soon as possible. He intended to leave as soon as Aya felt well enough to travel.

Aya awoke in a room that she did not recognise. It was small and looked like a child's room. The walls were painted in a warm, sun-kissed yellow and rich, earthy browns. Drawings fixed to the wall looked like they were created by a young hand. The room's furniture was minimal yet functional. At the foot of the bed was a wooden chest, doubling as a table that may have been used as a child's drawing desk. To her left was a wooden table, which was covered in a traditionally dyed earthy green fabric that draped down to the floor. The cloth was delicately stitched with images depicting age-old stories passed down from parent to child for generations. A tall Maasai doll dressed in red with beaded jewellery was perched on top of the table, and placed next to it was a small bowl of water with some scented herbs floating on the top, filling the room with a sweet fragrance. A weathered drum stood tall in one corner of the room, next to a few simple but beautiful shakers made from gourds. In the opposite corner was a woven reed basket filled with many handcrafted toys.

"You are looking much better, Makena. How are you feeling?" Nala said, entering the room and feeling Aya's head.

Aya looked curiously at her but instinctively recognised her as though some distant memory had awakened.

"I am," she instinctively said, reaching for Nala's hand. "I'm okay, only tired."

"Well, tell me." She paused and sighed. "Do you remember?"

Aya smiled kindly. "Yes, I remember it all." She hesitated and looked around. "How long have I been here?"

"Four days," Nala replied, adjusting her covers.

Four days? Had it really been that long? Aya thought. "How is Labaan?"

"He is alive, thanks to you. He acts as though nothing ever happened." Nala shook her head. "He is a foolish boy who probably hasn't learnt his lesson."

Labaan ran into the room, stopped, and stared at Aya.

"What are you doing here?" Nala said sternly.

"It's okay," Aya said. "Hello, Labaan."

"Hello," Labaan said quietly, his stare fixed on her.

"Oh, go, go, go outside." Nala rolled her eyes and shooed Labaan from the room. "I will be back once I find something for him to do." She turned to her son. "Something that will keep you out of trouble." She left the room, dragging a reluctant Labaan with her.

Aya smiled, lay back down, and fell into a deep sleep.

...

The village had been discussing Aya since the events of that night. They believed her arrival was a sign from Efanu, the deity of light and life. According to the villagers, everything had a deity that governed its existence, whether it was to bring good or harm. In their belief, Efanu represented light, while Miozu represented shadow, and both were considered to have a role in creation; both were respected and paid homage to.

Bolajii possessed the gift of communicating with spirits who haunt the fringes of the material world. He was known as a Mist Walker, someone who could peer into the spirit realm. He had been warned that Aya's arrival would awaken Miozu, a deity who brought death. Bolajii was convinced that Aya had become entangled in an invisible battle between light and shadow; however, he did not understand why. He asked Efanu for answers, but the god remained unusually silent.

He sat at the end of Makena's bed and looked at Aya sleeping and wondered what role Aya had to play in the god's cosmic games.

Bolajii decided to meditate on the situation, allowing his mind to explore his memories and perhaps open up possibilities that he had not considered. His thoughts drifted back to his youth, when his gifts were noticed by Miozu and he was led to the Kovom Order. His mind drifted through their teachings, as though he was being guided by an unseen current, and he recalled how he learned that the gods appear in many forms, with many names. *We are all pawns, whether of Light or Shadow*, he thought.

He drifted further, seeing the Great Union. "This must be stopped," he muttered.

"The Great Union is a deception, it brings pain

and sorrow. We must find the one who will bring it about, and deliver him to Ozul, to Shadow. That is our task," Bolajji said, though it was not his voice, but a memory that spoke through him.

His mind drifted further, to when he was recruited by the organisation. He was shown haunting images of the horrors that he had committed in the name of Ozul. Bolajii sighed heavily at the recollection; it was a burden that he carried and a torment that was his penance.

"I see you," a hiss filled his mind. "You turned from me to a lie."

Bolajii remained calm and unmoved by the presence that had revealed itself, allowing the dream to lead him.

"You will return and see the truth." A cold wind rushed about him, but Bolajii remained still.

His thoughts moved away from the Shadow as he remembered the vision that was bestowed on him, that saved him from the darkness. He remembered his escape and how he spent many years wandering, avoiding the Kovom Order, eventually finding a home in the village of Umata.

Then Efanu spoke to him. "The Great Union has always been, will always be; it is the ultimate sacrifice, the ultimate gift. Aya must find her way."

Bolajji opened his eyes and looked across to Aya. "Find peace, little one," he said.

...

There were times in Aya's past when she felt like she was walking in a hazy dream, as though all the world was hidden behind a thin veil. She felt detached, separate, as though she didn't belong. She knew that something was missing, something was amiss.

While she slept, Makena's memories inundated her mind with faces that were unknown yet strangely recognizable. The lines between Makena's world and Aya's blurred as the memories intertwined. Aya felt moments of utter confusion and pure clarity as she tried to understand it all. She experienced a sense of liberation, as if a barrier had been lifted. She felt unrestricted and gained a deeper understanding of herself.

Aya woke up in the middle of the night, feeling refreshed after a long sleep. She was clear-headed and had discovered a newfound inner strength. She felt eager to stretch her legs and move around again. She clumsily got to her feet, wobbled, and sat back on the bed. *I can do this*, she thought, and tried again. As she rose for the second time, she felt a little better and managed to carefully walk over to the door using whatever she could find as support.

Aya left the room and found that she was standing on a small landing. There was only one other door at the end of a short corridor. She thought that must be Bolajii and Nala's room. She quietly went downstairs, not wanting to wake them.

The stairs led to a darkened room, dimly lit by the glowing embers from a once-bright fire. Shadows subtly skulked about, dancing at the edge of the fading light. A large armchair was placed just in front of the hearth, and she made her way over and collapsed into it. The dying fire still gave off enough heat, warming and welcoming her. She sunk into the chair, which felt like a comforting hug. Aya thought it wasn't so bad here and released a happy sigh of contentment. She noticed books stacked neatly on the shelves, and her imagination took hold, wondering if they held long-hidden secrets or even answers to her many questions. Her thoughts turned to the past days and the adventure she'd been through since arriving.

Arriving? she thought to herself. Had she ever really left?

"Makena," she whispered, and the embers seemed to glow a little brighter at hearing that name.

She stared into the light of the last flickering flame, clinging to remain.

…

Aya was woken by Nala the following day, and didn't seem surprised to see her. Nala smiled, said her morning greetings, offered her some food, and then left the house to go on some errands. Aya had things to do too. She decided that John should return to base camp without her. She had unfinished business, and she needed answers.

After a lengthy discussion, many reassurances, and much convincing, John and Kofi reluctantly agreed to return to base camp without her. Still, John insisted that Aya check in with Haz daily via radio and update him on her health. He also promised to come back for her no later than two weeks.

Aya said goodbye to her friends and returned to Bolajii and Nala's house. She felt at home, or at least part of her did. She had a terrible internal conflict, as though two personalities were pulling at her physical being. She knew who she was, but on some deeper level, she felt Makena's presence loitering, skimming the outskirts of her awareness, watching, waiting, and wanting to return to her family.

Aya had been trying to get answers from Bolajii for days, but whenever she brought up the events of that night, he would deflect and say that everything would be revealed when the time was right. Although this didn't satisfy her need to understand what was happening to her, she eventually found comfort in her surroundings. It was as though she was back home, and that brought her a sense of peace.

On the fifth night after her friends had left, Aya was awoken in the middle of the night. She was shocked to see a faint, ethereal glow hovering at the foot of her bed. It cast a soft, eerie light across the room. Makena's translucent form took shape. She hung suspended between realms, looking solemnly at Aya as though she had one last message to bring her.

"Makena?" Aya said, her voice almost a whisper.

Makena said nothing; she just hovered there, staring at Aya.

"Why are you here?" Aya asked, her voice now trembling.

"I have come to warn you," Makena said in a ghostly whisper. "It seeks to harm you."

Aya felt cold at hearing these words. She shivered and pulled her covers tight around her.

"It comes for us, Aya. You are part of the ending, as I was part of the beginning." Makena's words trailed away, like mist blown away by a soft breeze.

"I don't understand," Aya said, dreading what may come next.

"You must find him. We must be whole again. We must—" A sudden icy breeze swept through the room, extinguishing her presence like a candle in the wind. "We must become whole..." Makena's last words lingered in the air for a moment, and then she was gone.

As the room grew darker and colder, Aya found herself unable to move. She felt frozen in this darkness, suffocated by an overwhelming and deathly silence. The world around her faded, and her vision blurred. It was like a shroud had slowly descended over the land, extinguishing all light and life. Aya felt utterly alone in this black void, consumed by a profound sense of emptiness and sadness that can only be felt in the embrace of death.

Aya was overcome with a sense of fear and impending doom. She felt a deep foreboding, like an unseen calamity was coming for her. She could almost sense icy cold hands clawing in the darkness, desperate to take her.

"You!" a cruel voice screeched at her, filled with unimaginable rage.

Frigid tentacle-like fingers groped at her, stumbling to find their mark. Aya screamed and struggled to find some escape, trying desperately to free herself from the unseen force slowly encircling her. Suddenly, an iron-like grip closed around her arm; magic or fear made it impossible for Aya to move. She continued struggling as hard as she could, adrenaline coursing through her veins and breath heaving in and out of her bated lungs. She fought wildly against the invisible bonds that held her but was helpless as a leaf on the wind.

A terrible, cracked voice cursed and blasphemed in an inhuman rage. It screamed profanities at Aya and sounded like it was coming from all around, echoing off the walls and filling her with terror. She struggled against her bonds as hard as possible, but despite her newfound inner strength, she felt powerless to escape this nightmare.

Shadow had her frozen in its chilling grasp, and there was nothing that she could do. Aya felt her neck and chest crushed by an invisible weight, choking and squeezing the air out of her lungs. This hidden terror pushed her down, smothering her beneath the covers, and with each breathless gasp for air, she felt hope being choked away.

As Aya took that last breath, time seemed to stand still. Her mind filled with the image of the stranger she was so drawn to.

She heard him once again. "Run!" he shouted.

"Daniel," she whispered with a sudden realisation.

Aya felt a surge of strength course through her, and in a blind panic, she pushed herself free from her attacker. She fell from her bed to the floor, gasping for breath. Aya staggered to her feet and stumbled as she ran blindly, desperate to find the door. A sudden blast of icy wind halted her escape. It hit her with full force and knocked her off balance, causing her to fall backwards. She screamed in agony as sharp gusts cut into her skin like knives. She was violently lifted off the ground and thrown across the room, slamming hard against a wall, and she fell unconscious onto the floor.

The door burst open at that moment, and Bolajii rushed into the room, his long coat flying out behind him. He held outstretched in front of himself an amulet that glowed brightly with a fiery intensity as he ran towards Aya. The charm pierced the darkness, causing it to flee from light. The grotesque voice rang out once again.

Bolajii suddenly stood still, surprised by the sudden movement of a shadow shooting towards him at high speed. Before he could react, the Shadow engulfed him and knocked his amulet from his hand. It threw him into the air, cruelly smashing his body into the ceiling. As he fell, it grabbed him mid-air and slammed him hard into the solid ground. His bones cracked under the force, and he coughed up blood. Bolajii's limp body was then tossed back towards the door.

Bolajii was not ready to accept defeat, and he staggered painfully to his feet, his head spinning. He closed his eyes and clasped his hands in front of his chest.

"*Amma Efanu, cianu erra ool.*" As he spoke these strange words, a light radiated out around him. There was a shriek of immense pain as the darkness reeled back away from the glow. Then suddenly, a whirling vortex formed between Aya and Bolajii. He saw her lying on the ground and panting hard.

"Aya!" Bolajii said sternly. "Get up now and come to me."

Hearing Bolajii's voice, Aya found a new strength, as though she had been infused with some ancient magic. She stood as commanded, as though compelled to obey.

The Shadow condensed into a thick blackness, and the silhouette of someone stepped forward, but it was no ordinary figure. Aya screamed in terror as she realized that it looked just like her, but its bones were twisted and broken. It was grotesque. This hideous insult to all that was good stood between her and Bolajii. The creature laughed at her; it was a chilling sound, like metal scraping against metal. The creature grinned cruelly, its teeth black and empty sockets for eyes. Aya pressed herself tight to the wall but was unable to look away. The figure stepped forward. Aya's heart pounded in her chest, and she felt death was upon her.

"*Amma Efanu, C anu zoo Aya!*" Bolajii's words rang out, and a bolt of light shot from his hands, striking the monstrous figure in the back. It stumbled forward, turned abruptly to look at Bolajii, and cursed violently.

The creature opened its mouth and it seemed to stretch almost to the ground, like a doorway was opening to another realm. It let out a scream of incomprehensible words. Then Bolajii vanished, consumed in a black swirling cloud, disappearing from Aya's sight. She heard him shout out in a language that she did not understand. She heard a thud and furniture breaking violently, and then Bolajii's voice suddenly fell silent.

The creature slowly turned back to Aya; it wore a malicious, twisted grin across its decaying features. It began moving towards her, deliberate and thick with malice. Bones creaked and cracked with each step. Terror-stricken, Aya gasped for breath. She tried to crawl away from the advancing horror, but with Bolajii gone, she felt defeated by grief. The creature, filled with cruel intent, made gurgling sounds as though it mockingly laughed at her pain.

Suddenly, a ball of brilliant white light materialized in front of Aya and Makena appeared. She grabbed the creature and pushed it away from Aya.

"Run!" Makena cried out. "You must run!"

Aya watched as Makena's light and the creature's darkness tried to obliterate the other in a frenzy of fighting. It was a battle that could have lasted eternities, but Aya knew that if the creature won, it would mean the end of Makena's existence. The creature was relentless, and she could feel its anger and hatred for Makena. To her dismay, she saw Makena's light flicker and grow dim, and with that, she felt her own lifeforce waning. She was suddenly struck by the realisation that her bond with Makena was unbreakable; if Makena disappeared, so would she. She couldn't let the darkness consume them both. It had to be stopped. She had to find a way.

Aya stood to her feet and rushed to Makena's aid, but there was an eruption of energy that knocked Aya backwards onto the ground.

Aya opened her eyes, and to her surprise, she stood in a sprawling field that seemed to stretch out endlessly before her. The sky was a perfect blue, and a warm golden sun shone its light down. The land was covered in a vibrant green grass that swayed gently with the wind. In the distance, she could see majestic mountains towering over the landscape. She felt as if she was standing on top of the world. She was at peace with herself and her surroundings, and she let out a long sigh as she looked up to the heavens and smiled. The horror of the earlier moment faded from memory; all that existed was the here and now.

"My dear little Aya, how I have missed you."

A familiar voice appeared beside her, and Aya turned to see her mother standing there.

Aya stood silently, shocked to see her mother. She tried to speak but could not find the words.

"Remember my gift to you. It will protect you always," her mother whispered. "I will always love you."

The next moment, she was standing back in the room. There was a sudden scream, and Makena's shining glow vanished, and she was gone but not yet lost. The dark creature turned to Aya, its hideous grin stitched across its face.

Clasped in Aya's hand was her mother's amulet. Instinctively and without hesitation, she held the amulet towards the evil before her. Without words needing to be spoken and without incantation or taught knowledge, the amulet started to glow. It started as a dim pulse, like a heartbeat coming to life. It seemed to possess a will of its own. Its surface burned with an intense energy that grew stronger with each pulse, filling the room with an otherworldly aura. As it made contact with the darkness, a hissing sound was heard, and the cleansing scent of lavender filled the air.

Then, a powerful force surged forward from the amulet, enveloping the creature. The light was blindingly bright and seemed fuelled by a source that lay beyond the physical world.

It instantly destroyed the creature's form, causing it to writhe and make terrifying sounds, but Aya remained steadfast in her resolve. She held onto the amulet tightly, feeling its power course through her as the light grew even brighter, vanquishing the darkness as if it were a disease being purged from the room.

Aya thought of her mother, her father, her friends, and Bolajii. She was filled with a feeling of love. Finally, she thought of Makena. Suddenly, a blinding light burst into the room. It shone brighter than all the stars in the night sky, and from it came an explosion that emanated a destructive blast of energy that ripped through the remaining darkness. The windows blew out, and furniture was thrown across the room, shattering against the walls. A final grotesque sound howled like a dying beast's last effort to cling to life.

Then all went silent, and the room was back as it was. Only fading wisps of a grey mist lingered, but they dispersed in the breeze from the broken window.

Aya slumped on the floor, feeling drained. She had never felt such power before. It both intrigued and frightened her. She stared at the amulet and couldn't help but wonder what other secrets it held. For now, she was content knowing that she was safe and that the darkness that had threatened her was gone.

Her voice echoed weakly as she called out Bolajii's name, realising that he had disappeared what felt like days ago. As her heart began to race with panic, she mustered the strength to raise her voice. "Bolajii!" she called out.

In a moment of relief, a hand appeared in front of her. Looking up, she saw him standing there, his presence reassuring. With gentle care, he helped her up. They slowly worked to fix the overturned bed and sat down as exhaustion finally took hold.

"Bolajii, what is happening?" Aya spoke in a frail voice.

"That was Miozu." He sounded beaten and depleted.

"Miozu? I remember seeing that before. When I was by Labaan when he was hurt."

"It is emptiness. It is the nothingness that exists when the light fades," Bolajii said and winced a little.

"Why is it here?" Aya asked, struggling to remain awake.

"I cannot say, Aya, but…" He slumped forward and winced in pain. Blood trickled from the side of his body and pooled on the bed. Aya then saw blood oozing out from between his fingers.

"You're hurt!" she said, panicked, and scrambled to her feet. "I must get help!"

"No!" Bolajii said forcibly. Then the harshness eased in his voice. "Sit, please," he said in a whisper. "I do not have much time left."

Aya sat, tears rolling off her cheeks as she looked desperately around the room for help, but none was to be found.

"Where did you get such an amulet?" Bolajii asked, pointing to her blue amulet.

"My mother gave it to me when I was young," Aya said, now overwhelmed with sadness.

"Where is she now?" His voice was barely audible.

Aya looked down. "She is…" Her words faded.

"I understand," Bolajii said, taking her hand. "Life is a gift that we cannot hold onto for long. It is borrowed and must be returned." He paused momentarily, looking at Aya's amulet. "That is a wonderful gift she gave you. Treasure it always."

Bolajii slid to a more comfortable position and wrapped a sheet around himself like he was cold. Aya helped, and he smiled in appreciation.

"I'll do my best to explain." He took a pipe from his coat pocket. "Ah, good. This one made it," he said with relief as he painfully reached for tobacco and placed a small amount into his pipe. He tried to grab some matches but winced in pain. Aya offered to help and lit his pipe for him. Bolajii took a deep draw from the pipe, savouring the sweet aroma. The smoke alleviated his pain as he exhaled, and he looked much more relaxed. He smiled contently and closed his eyes.

"You know, I found this pipe when I was young," he quietly said as he drifted away to some distant memory. "It was just lying in the road, waiting for me." He chuckled as he remembered a happier time, then coughed up a little blood.

Bolajii took another long draw from his pipe and sighed. Again, the smoke flew up into the air and lingered for a moment. He opened his eyes, which appeared to be clouded and glazed over. However, they gleamed softly as he continued staring at the wall opposite him. It was obvious to Aya that he wasn't really looking at anything in the room, but was actually seeing something far away, a place beyond reach known only to him.

It was as if the presence he normally exuded had been completely drained, leaving nothing but an echo of himself on his face. But there was something familiar beneath his empty gaze, a whisper of what made him who he used to be. Bolajii looked like someone whose lifeforce had been sucked out from under them and left in an icy wasteland. He spoke as though he were no longer present with Aya, but elsewhere, in some other land.

"We are more than what you see in the mirror, which is just a skin we wear. It is something we do, not what we are." Bolajii slowly drew from his pipe, more out of habit than a conscious decision. As he let out his breath, the smoke swirled softly around him. His voice became monotone and hollow. "We are more than this…this illusion, this that holds all meaning yet offers only lies." His voice faded to a whisper. "The Light shines beyond the Shadow. The Shadow swallows all Light. For one to be, the other must remain. But all must be one, one must be all, the beautiful union…" He paused. "The Great Union."

Bolajii looked at Aya with glazed eyes and smiled. "You and Makena are aspects of spirit, separate but one. You exist as part of spirit, yet exist separately."

He drew deeply from his pipe and blew out grey smoke. Aya watched the smoke hang in the air around him; it appeared alive and moved in a graceful swirling motion.

Bolajii continued, his voice weakening with every word. "Life is a gift that is given by Efanu, who grants us life, and is taken by Miozu, who grants us death." He sighed heavily. "I do not know how Miozu has been able to create, it is not its purpose, something has contaminated the cycle." He paused, lost in thought.

"I don't understand," Aya said, crying.

"Neither do I." Bolajii coughed again. He looked at Aya and smiled warmly. "Makena was my daughter. Who she was, who she is, still lives in spirit. Aya, you, too, are part of that spirit, both you and Makena. That which makes you will endure for as long as spirit endures." He coughed and clutched his wound.

"You must find him," he spoke softly, barely audible. "The one who will be looking for you." He coughed again, blood splattering over his hand. "You must complete your journey."

Bolajii smiled.

"We are drops in the ocean, we are leaves on a tree, we are a grain of sand in the wide endless desert."

"Bolajii, I must get help, please," Aya pleaded with tears in her eyes.

"I must sleep now. I do not think I will wake again," Bolajii said, looking out the window into the darkness beyond. He closed his eyes. "Makena?" he whispered, and let out a final breath.

Bolajii was gone.

Nala suddenly rushed into the room followed by several of the villagers.

THE FINAL JOURNEY

"Where have you been?" Aya cried out, tears blurring her vision.

Nala saw Bolajii slumped over on the bed, his lifeblood spilling out onto the floor. Aya sat beside him and held his hand tightly, not wanting to accept that he was gone. Aya sobbed heavily. She felt lost, as though her own father had passed.

Nala went to Aya's side and took her hand. "Come, child." She helped her to her feet and embraced her as a mother would comfort their child. "I heard an explosion, and then we were here within minutes," Nala said softly, looking at Bolajii's lifeless body.

Aya looked at Nala, confused. Had it only been minutes? It felt like hours had passed.

Nala approached Bolajii, sat beside him, and held his hand. Then she leaned in and whispered something in his ear. Aya thought she saw Bolajii smile briefly.

They wrapped Bolajii's body in a cloth and moved him to the communal hall. Nala stayed with Aya, but they did not speak. They left Makena's room and sat together silently in Nala's room. Aya rested her head on Nala's lap as she stroked Aya's hair.

Nala began to sing a lullaby she had once sung for Makena; her voice was gentle and rhythmic, and it soothed Aya's sadness and pain. Aya lay there thinking about the loss she had felt throughout her life. As Nala's melody continued, it filled her mind with warmth, and she drifted away to the stranger she had seen in her dreams. Daniel, she thought. When Nala had finished her song, Aya was soundly asleep.

...

Aya awoke in her bed and abruptly sat up. She was shocked to see that she was in Makena's room. The room appeared undamaged: the windows weren't broken, the furniture sat as before, and even Makena's toys were in a basket in the corner. She looked about the room and tried to remember what it looked like before she slept. Was it the same? Aya felt awash with confusion. Then, a sudden hope rose inside her.

"Bolajii!" she said aloud.

She sprang out of bed and dashed downstairs. To her surprise, she found John sitting with Kofi, eating breakfast.

"What are you doing here?" Aya said in astonishment.

John and Kofi both leapt from their chairs and rushed over to her.

"You're up!" John said in sheer surprise. "Thank God!" He gave her a bear-like hug.

"Yes, it is good to see you are up and about. You

THE FINAL JOURNEY

are looking well," Kofi added, smiling broadly.

"I'm good," she answered, still confused. She pulled away from John, walked over to the table, and sat down. The others joined her.

"Has anyone seen Bolajii?" Aya asked, trying to ignore the look of wonderment on her companions' faces. Her friends looked solemnly at each other.

"Don't you remember?" John said, sounding concerned.

Aya began to feel sick as the realisation that it was all real started to dawn on her. "Don't play games. Where is Bolajii?"

"He's…" John paused, "dead, Aya." He looked thoughtfully at her, judging with concern every micro-expression on her face.

Aya suddenly stood up and knocked back her chair. Her heart raced.

"It wasn't a dream," she said to herself.

Kofi stood up in time to catch Aya as her strength gave way and she collapsed. He sat her down in the chair by the hearth.

John knelt by her. "Aya, he died a week ago. We returned and found that you could not be woken from sleep. Nala said that you must rest." He sounded angry. "We had no idea what she was doing. They wouldn't let us move you or call in a doctor. God only knows how you haven't died from lack of food or water!" He calmed and looked at her. "You look surprisingly well." Confusion echoed in his voice as he studied her.

"They set his spirit free as they did his brother's," Kofi said. "His body is no more, Aya. He is gone."

"I want to go home," Aya said. "I just want to go home."

...

Aya's heart pounded with anticipation as she finally arrived back at her grandparents' house. The familiar scent of spices and warm tea welcomed her as soon as they opened the door. Without hesitation, she rushed to them and fell into their comforting embrace. Their arms wrapped around her like a warm blanket, providing a sense of safety and comfort that she had been longing for.

"You are home, Aya," Samaira said reassuringly, as though she instinctively knew that Aya had been suffering. "It'll be okay now."

"Welcome home," Aisim said warmly. "You are safe here."

They went into the front room and sat down. Aya slumped into an oversized pillowed chair and sunk into a pool of divine comfort. She let out a sigh, and all the worries of the world left her.

Samaira went into the kitchen and started making some tea. Aisim sat down by Aya.

"We know," he simply said. "Bolajii was a great man."

Aya raised her head. "How?"

"We have a lot to tell you, Aya, but now is not the time. You must rest, clear your mind, and put down the heavy burden that you now carry."

Aya lay her head back down and started to cry. Tears flooded from her like a dam had broken, and all her pain rushed from her. She felt suffocated by the weight of her grief, like the weight of the world bore down on her. She collapsed, buried her face into a cushion, and cried out in anguish. She screamed, emptying herself of all the agony and sorrow that had consumed her for far too long.

Aya cried until there were no more tears. She cried until the pain dulled into a distant ache and she was utterly exhausted. When she finally raised her head, Samaira and Aisim sat, patiently waiting.

Samaira smiled kindly. "That better? You look a little lighter now." She poured some tea into a cup and handed it to Aya. "Drink this, you will feel better."

Aya took a small brown cup from her grandmother, and as she moved the cup to her lips, she was hit by the warmth radiating from the liquid, and the sweet smell of lavender soothed her. She drank, and as the warm liquid moved down her body, all the hurt, misery, and sorrow evaporated.

For the first time in what felt like a lifetime, Aya smiled.

...

Several months passed. Aya did not return to work, but decided to take a much welcomed break. She buried herself in research, trying to decipher Bolajii's last words to her, trying to understand.

As time passed, she slowly drifted from the world that Bolajii had awoken in her, which now seemed so far away. She was happy to finally be back on what she felt was solid ground, a well-trodden, known path. She started to find her old life again, saw her friends, and soon pushed what she had experienced to the back of her mind.

Then, one day, she saw a young man walk down the stairs from the flat upstairs, though he did not see her.

"Who is that?" she asked her granddad.

"Oh, a young man who moved in upstairs into our old place. Daniel."

"Daniel," Aya whispered.

...

Destiny touches the very fabric of our life, winding through a divine tapestry whose intricate woven threads lead us along our path.

Like streams meandering down a mountainside eventually to meet a vast awaiting ocean, each stone slightly altering its projection. We, too, by the obstacles we meet, traverse our fate. With each challenge, we have brief moments of choice that lead to consequences shaping our journey.

Then the veil of mortality descends on us like a mist, and we are left with the realisation that life was but a fleeting moment. Unsolved riddles permeate our mind as we contemplate our place in this cosmic drama and wonder if we really had any choice. Could we truly alter our destiny, or had the outcome already been decided?

...

PART 2

CHAPTER 10

Not Just Another Day
Letting go is the hardest part of any journey.

"Daniel, wake up!" Her voice was an echo whispering on a distant breeze, and as he strained to listen, he felt her warm breath caress his cheek. He turned to her, but like wisps of smoke, she faded in the midnight air.

A pale, warm light from an unseen sun filtered into the room. Daniel's eyes opened to a squint. He stretched out a kink in his neck and moaned out a loud yawn. *It's the start of another day*, he thought as he lay on his bed and looked up at the ceiling. The steady rhythm of rustling leaves and chirping birds filled the early morning quiet. He leaned back into the soft pillows and closed his eyes. As he lay on his bed in those first waking moments, he tried to remember his dream from the night before. Only fragments remained: flashes of images of her walking along a green hilltop, just out of reach. He chased after her, but as he reached out, she faded in a shadowy mist.

The dream slipped from Daniel's mind, despite desperately trying to cling to her image there in that perfect place. He felt like he hung half in the dream world and half in this; he longed to be back in that perfect dream with her. A tear rolled down his cheek. He slowly wiped it with his hand and took a deep breath. He looked at the tear on his finger, then rubbed his thumb over it, feeling the wetness run down his hand. His thoughts lingered on her, the woman he so desperately wanted to hold onto and simultaneously wanted to forget. He felt a sharp pain in his heart and winced. *Why did she have to go?* he thought. *Why am I still here?*

The harder he tried to remember that perfect time, the quicker it faded from memory, and soon any remaining fragments left his mind, leaving a feeling of hollowness. He had tried to forget, to block out a deep pain that tormented him, and it was now only in dreams that he dared to think about her.

He rubbed his eyes and lay there, unmoving, staring into the room, wishing he had never awoken. Time lost all meaning as he watched the sun peek through the gap in the curtain, casting golden beams across the room. Dust particles shimmered and danced in the morning light like tiny stars twinkling in a night's sky. He felt like he was teetering at the edge of a chasm, staring into the endless abyss, wondering whether to jump. *Perhaps I will find her in the depths, the eternal void; all I have to do is jump*, he thought solemnly.

The world rushed in like a tsunami colliding with a coastline. The sounds of people outside busying about their daily lives exploded into the room, voices competing with the sound of the morning traffic, and even the faint echoes of birds singing to one another with melodious repetition scratched his mind. Something was different today, he thought. He felt odd, as though he was disconnected.

The outside world seemed strange and foreign. Daniel's senses ruptured as he was thrown into a duality; part of the world felt obnoxious and invading, yet simultaneously distant, as though he had been removed from it and was watching from a faraway place. He struggled to find any reason to move, to get out of bed and play the game for another day. He lay there, lifeless, just staring into the empty space that she left. Still, he wasn't always like this, but since that moment, the juncture that changed everything and took all meaning from him, he had been dying a little each day.

Daniel lay still, listening to the growing symphony of sound just outside the walls of his apartment, wondering about the countless lives repeating their daily activities, round and round they went. It's all a never-ending cycle; he frowned at the thought.

"Are we doomed to repeat the same life? Will this insanity ever end?" he muttered scornfully. His words hung in the air, searching for a home.

He lay motionless, barely able to move; confusion welled inside him, erupting into a fountain of uncertainty. On the one hand, there was warmth in his heart, a love for her, while on the other, a deep and ever-growing anger that burned inside. His mind crept into the beckoning darkness, wanting to hide from the light shining brightly, exposing his pain. For the briefest moment, he hated everyone around him with an intensity that ripped at the good. He couldn't shake the loathing and despair that had started to take over, yet he knew it would not be what she would have wanted; but she was gone, and he was alone in the eternal hollowness that was left.

"How could they carry on? When she was..." Daniel said to those outside. His words trailed away to a distant memory as he drifted back to her, to what was and should have been, and overwhelming sadness and regret consumed him.

"I hate this world," Daniel said, speaking through gritted teeth, spitting out his words. The noise outside seemed to grow a little louder as he spoke.

"I hate you all!" His words were fuelled with spite and anger. "Why can't you all just go away?!"

Daniel was consumed with self-loathing and guilt for not saving her. However, he knew on one level there was nothing that he could have done to change anything. Still, his thoughts raced, playing through scenario after scenario, each as fictional as the last. *There must have been something I could have done*, his thoughts repeated in a deafening madness. He turned his back to the world outside, lost in a sea of hopelessness. He felt a vengefulness welling inside him, a growing disdain for life and the life he once cherished and loved.

The world knocked hard at his mind, thumping, wanting to break in, and no matter how he tried, he could not shut it out. Life would not be silenced so easily, and it was determined that its voice would be heard. Daniel's emotions swirled: irritation into anger, anger into irritation, focus into chaos, confusion into helplessness. He just wanted to be left alone, to sink into his misery and the memory of what once was. However, the more he tried to cut out the world outside, the more it seemed to want to be noticed, to be known, and to be heard. He tried to ignore this cruel awakening, this devious invader. Still, it grabbed his attention with grotesque force, ripping him from his thoughts of her into a swirling mess. The more his resentment and anger grew, the louder this invader seemed to press upon him.

Daniel desperately clamped his hands hard over his ears, closing his eyes tight, and the noise outside slightly dulled into a muffled moan. However, he did not find any escape. A rhythmic sound, seemingly emanating from a far-off place, washed over him. At first, it was just the remnants of an echo of a strange melody, like a tiny ripple on the ocean, barely noticeable. Whether morbid curiosity or intrigue, it ensnared his attention, and he could not turn from it. Daniel listened and was engulfed by the fragments of a beautiful tune. Its hypnotic tempo resonated throughout his mind like it was sent to soothe his pain.

As the sound slowly enveloped him, its song became clear and distinct. Daniel could only tumble into its tune as though he had lost all control, carried like a leaf on the wind.

"I have come to you," a sudden captivating, melodious voice sang to Daniel. "I understand your pain, your suffering."

Daniel started to cry, overwhelmed by the feeling of love and compassion around him.

"I will free you," it whispered kindly. "Simply say yes…" Its song trailed away.

For a brief moment, Daniel needed to believe that somewhere, there was still hope, that somehow someone could save him from the abyss where he lingered.

He closed his eyes and whispered, "Yes."

A pain instantly exploded in his chest, as though his heart had fractured into a thousand pieces. The once sweet melody suddenly corrupted and crackled into a screeching, twisted sound. Daniel screamed out in pain, begging for it to stop. He watched helplessly as it invaded his mind, searching for his deepest desires, exposing every dark place within him, revealing hidden secrets and his deepest heinous appetites.

He now heard many cold and harsh voices filling him with guilt. Laughing at his weaknesses and his shameful thoughts. Tormenting him and begging him to jump into the blackness of the chasm.

"Why?!" Daniel screamed. "You said you would save me," he sobbed as his tormentors laughed wickedly.

"Shhhh, I will save you," a voice mocked cruelly. "Now sleep," it hissed.

A slumberous sound caressed Daniel's mind into submission, unable to fight the call of the Shadow, and he fell into darkness.

...

Daniel was no longer lying on his bed in his room, but standing in a vast meadow. It appeared to extend as far as he could see in every direction. However, in stark contrast to his dreams of lush green fields, the land about him appeared eroded and vanquished.

The ground beneath his feet was dusty and hard. It was covered with the remnants of once abundant life now wilted and lying deathly silent, left as a reminder that in this place, there is only death to be found. There appeared to be a scattering of flora but they offered no sweet scent or vibrant colour; they were dull and spewed a rotting smell that appeared as a swirling, tainted mist. A blanket of necrotic plant life suddenly erupted from the ground around him, responding to Daniel's arrival. Long blades of greyish spines reached up, sharp as broken glass. They cut at Daniel as though their only purpose was to bring agony to any traveller who may have stumbled upon this barren place. The only sound was the rustle of the blades as the wind snaked through the landscape, fuelled by the cold, frozen air that swirled about.

There were no living trees, no life, no colour, only decaying tangled corpses, a dark reflection of what was once living. In the distance, an eerie red glow crept ominously, like an animal that lurked in the shadows, waiting to pounce.

The vast expanse of a sterile black canopy overhead served as an imposing companion to the bleak landscape Daniel had awoken to. In some ways, he felt this place reflected his inner self, a visualisation of his pain and suffering. However, there were still a few stars desperately pushing through the veil. Their pure beams of light acted as hope's champion and appeared to dance and twirl like children playing in a park on a sunny day. They radiated shafts of pure light and energy. Where they touched the ground, life began anew as tiny wisps of green shoots appeared and stretched skywards towards their warmth. Each star, pinpricks of silver against the darkness, was a guiding light, giving direction and purpose to those who dared to hope and dream in this foreboding place. They invaded the bleak landscape, delivering a diffused, soft, lustrous light. A sense of wonderment flowed through the air, and Daniel felt like the entire universe was alive. He felt like everything that had ever existed or would ever exist was here in this moment, and he was the sole witness to this show of cosmic majesty. He could only be humbled as he dared to gaze upon the spectacle. The beauty and grace of the starlight could only inspire hope even in the most despondent heart. The stars seemed to whisper to him, offering a guiding light in his darkest hour, wanting to show him that there was so much more than the empty world he had wandered into.

This world was not ready to let Daniel go; hope could not be tolerated here. A thick, dense fog swelled around him, and the starlight faded, as did the life that lived for only a brief moment, now withered, returned to dust, along with any hope it brought with it.

A cold chill gripped him, and he wrapped his arms around himself. A vague memory of comfort and warmth pressed against his mind, a feeling now alien to him since he had arrived here.

Daniel heard voices coming from deep within the fog. As he stared, he could see shadowy figures watching him. He called out, but no answer; they remained unmoved. He felt a growing fear as these "Watchers" started to move towards him. Daniel started to run, stumbling through the sharp, lifeless landscape. He tripped, fell crashing to the ground, and was pierced in the leg by a sharp blade-like plant. He screamed in pain. Daniel turned to look at his pursuers, but they had vanished. He struggled to grasp what was even real anymore. Was this just another nightmare?

"You are here because you are lost," came a voice from within the fog.

Daniel looked about and saw a Watcher standing only a few metres from him where the fog thickened.

"You are here, as we are here." It paused. "We are all lost."

"Who are you?" Daniel called out.

"The lost, the forsaken, and those who strayed too far from the light into shadow all end up here," the figure said. "To wander in this ravenous fog which consumes any memory of happiness, home, family, and love. It takes who you are and contorts it, deforming those here, turning them into twisted monsters, desperate creatures, to live a nightmarish twilight existence, never to escape their suffering."

"I don't know how I got here," Daniel said.

"We never do," it answered in a hollow voice.

"How do I leave?" Daniel asked, fearing the answer.

The Watcher gave a hollow laugh. "I am a Watcher. I see the monsters, I see the torment, I see no escape." It laughed cruelly now.

"Liar!" Daniel cried out in anger.

The Watcher laughed, then abruptly stopped, standing motionless, just observing him.

Daniel limped away, looking over his shoulder, but the Watcher remained still, eventually vanishing in the fog. He shivered uncontrollably, realising that he may be lost here for eternity.

The fog around him retreated suddenly, but no starlight returned; instead, it revealed an otherworldly scene. A pack of grotesque creatures lurked on either side of him. They resembled humans, but their eyes were fathomless and black, their hair ragged and wild. Their bodies warped with bent spines that forced them to crawl on all fours like loping beasts. At the sight of Daniel, their malicious grins exposed razor-like teeth and slithering forked tongues.

Daniel's heart raced as he tried desperately to run away. His injured leg caused him to stumble and limp in agony, but no matter how hard he tried, they kept following, herding him ever onward like a lamb to the slaughter. Their growls seemed to get closer, then suddenly fade, as though they were tormenting or playing with their next meal. His heart raced as he gasped for breath, but little could be found in the thick fog. Still, he pushed on further, past the pain, past the need to rest. Whenever he turned, a creature would scream and lunge at him, forcing Daniel to change direction. This happened time and time again. It became clear that they were taking him somewhere, and he had no choice but to obey.

He toiled until his strength faded. He could take no more, and he fell to his knees, expecting certain death, but to his surprise, the creatures retreated into the fog.

Daniel could only stare in puzzlement at what lay ahead in the distance. Thick swirling smoke rose high and met with the overhead foreboding canopy. This threatening haze extended slowly, slithering out with snake-like tendrils, following some unseen path; then, soundlessly, it fell like a tidal wave crashing against a shoreline. Daniel then realised that it was the source of the fog that had enveloped him.

Out of the thick smoke, a spectral figure appeared. The hazy wisps around the shape coalesced into the figure of a tall soldier wearing a ripped military uniform drenched in dried blood. Its uniform appeared to be an amalgamation of many eras throughout human history. It wore many medals won for glory and valour in the line of duty. Still, they were not shiny and golden, instead tarnished and covered with a thick black tar-like substance oozing from the nails that held them in place. The medals were there not to celebrate but to mock, a bleak reminder of the irony of war. Its face merged and twisted in on itself. It morphed into people from many cultures, showing no defined features, yet each clearly expressing anger and rage. It was the personification of human lust for war.

Its gaze was like two bottomless wells of darkness that filled Daniel with terror. A guttural roar blasted out from his mouth, piercing his eardrums with a searing pain. The soldier drew out a giant sword that burned with a ghostly silver hue. An eerie stillness blanketed the scene, the calm before an approaching storm. Then it pointed its fiery blade at Daniel and charged forward. A thunderous noise shook the air as he howled his battle cry. The land trembled under his pounding feet as each step collided with the dead earth, resonating a dreadful sound. An army of faceless skeletal soldiers marched out of the fog behind his charge. It was a legion of death, a gloomy reminder of the fate that awaits beyond life's boundary. They beat down on cracked and broken drums fused to their crumbling bones. With every pounding on their ghostly drums, they moved closer, their beats becoming more and more deafening, until their thunderous sound suffocated every space with its torment.

Daniel tried to flee but made little progress. His wound had split open, and blood ran down his leg, spilling onto the ground. He heard a slurping sound; looking down, he saw the earth absorb his life's blood, desperately drinking it. Not even a stain was left. The ground started to rise, burying his foot, trying to pull him in. Daniel pulled hard, screaming in pain, and surged forward. He struggled to move, wincing with each step, but instinctively he knew he had to leave and did not belong there.

Daniel fought on, the once hard ground now soft, and each step felt like he was wading through tar. His strength felt drained as he panted heavily. He finally collapsed but, refusing defeat, dragged himself along the ground, fearing that if he stopped even for a second, the earth would swallow him whole.

The deathly brigade advanced with relentless momentum, filling his thoughts with a paralysing fear. The horror consumed every corner of Daniel's being as the soldiers of death surrounded him. He could go no further. The thumping of the drums besieged his mind, encircling him with images of torment, revealing painful memories from his past. Daniel stumbled, eyes transfixed on his aggressors; the booming noise erupted into a chorus of shouts like a roar from an angry beast.

Daniel lay on the ground, eyes closed and covering his ears. The earth started to pull him down gently. A sense of acceptance of his fate sent him into a surreal calm. *Perhaps this is the final escape.*

"Daniel!" a soft, familiar voice called out.

"Aya?" Daniel was filled with renewed energy and pulled himself free, and he struggled to his feet, looking around for her.

A monstrous laugh reverberated, and he was at once confronted by the tall soldier, his sword pointing directly at Daniel. The soldier then raised his sword above his head, and it exploded into a dark, reddish flame.

"For country, honour, death, for shadow," it croaked. Then, he turned the sword on himself and plunged it through his chest. A grotesque sound erupted from the soldier. He burst into flames, wailed in misery, and then, in a flash, only glowing embers remained. The skeletal drummers stopped their beating and bowed their heads.

Suddenly, the ashes started to rise, spinning around, and a wind started to howl as it grew in size and power. Daniel felt himself being pulled in, but the earth had grabbed him, either to aid or not wanting to lose its coming feast; he was held fast. The skeletal soldiers surrounding Daniel were raised and sucked into the vortex of destruction. He watched as they spun around, bones cracking and grinding into dust. Then, abruptly, a shadow snapped around the soldiers like a giant mouth, consuming what they were, leaving only Shadow.

Daniel screamed in blind panic as the Shadow lunged at him, lifting him off the ground and carrying him high into the blackness overhead. He struggled for air as his lungs filled with a poisonous toxin; he coughed violently, trying to expel the venom that was eating him alive.

The beast's bile struck Daniel with a pure, wicked intent. He felt like his heart had been ripped open, and his innermost self was exposed for the beast to devour. Daniel's soul cried out in agony as the malignant force invaded every inch of his being. It devoured him, ripping through his essence like barbed wire and tearing at his flesh like it was paper. The hatred that flooded out from the beast was unrelenting. Its malice had been crafted purely to hurt Daniel, to make him suffer in the most personal way. As it tore through him, it devoured any hope, and all it left was misery and anguish. Any memory of joy or pleasure that he had once known was incinerated, leaving nothing but an endless abyss of torment and pain. It was a presence so powerful and malevolent that he felt helpless, unable to stop it from robbing him of any shred of who he was. The anguish pulsating within him seemed to go on for eternity, as if he had been thrown into an endless hell from which there could be no escape.

He was thrown down, and as he tumbled, he cried out, begging for help, for a respite from the nightmare, but no one answered his call. He hit the ground hard and lay there unable to move, his bones broken, as a crimson flow flooded from him, absorbed by the desperate earth. Through teary eyes, he was confronted with vile images of mutilation and death; life was distorted and warped, and all the while, the beast laughed.

Daniel's broken body was gently raised from the ground. The Shadow held him softly, soothing his sadness and cradling him like a mother holding her baby for the first time.

"I can end your suffering," hissed an empty voice. "Just reach out, and I will save you."

Daniel cried out as a stabbing pain pierced his heart; he felt like his chest had burst. With a trembling hand, he slowly outstretched his arm, reaching into the blackness holding him.

The air around Daniel crackled with electricity; a searing, white-hot light erupted, piercing through the Shadow. It illuminated the darkness like the birth of a star exploding into life. The light momentarily burned his eyes, and he shielded himself from its brilliance. The Shadow dropped Daniel, and he hit the ground, coughing up blood. A piercing, soul-rending shriek filled the air, sending a shudder of fright through Daniel's body. Its venomous voice hissed, full of hatred, as though it had been born out of a pit of spitefulness and rage as it spat vile obscenities.

"Leave!" it commanded in a wicked hiss, its words turning Daniel's blood to ice. "You do not belong here!"

The Shadow swooped towards the light, but it burst with a bright, luminous colour, like an exploding firework. The Shadow was pushed back, writhing in anger and frustration.

"The cycle will end!" it screeched as it retreated into the fog like a wounded animal.

The light ripped through the darkness like a sword, banishing the shadows that had held Daniel's mind captive. He felt a surge of energy, the pain instantly dissipated, and the suffering that had trapped him lifted.

"Danny," a kind voice said, "let me take you home."

He saw a glowing orb of light hovering over him through blurred vision. Then, a figure of a young girl emerged from its radiance. Her hand seemed to glow as she extended it towards him with an inevitability he could not ignore. He lifted his hand to meet hers, and she gently pulled him to his feet.

In the next instant, Daniel was back in his room, bent over the side of his bed, clutching his stomach, and black vile poured from his mouth all over the floor. He coughed and gasped for air. He fell back onto his bed, the world spinning. He started to cry, overwhelmed with a deep sadness.

"Get a grip," he said, scolding himself. "Get a fucking grip!"

He leaned over the side of his bed again, and a thick dark tar hit the floor. He fell back, emptied of the poison that had infested him.

"It was just a dream," he said, not believing his own words. "It was just a dream."

Tears flooded his pillow, and he screamed out until nothing was left in him and he was exhausted. He lay gasping for breath, staring blankly at the ceiling.

Then silence fell, and he lost consciousness.

"Wake up!"

Daniel abruptly sat up as though following an order, startled. His eyes scanned the room, looking for anything that may be different. The room was as it always was, and only the sounds of the world outside could be heard. He rubbed his eyes; it was all just a horrible dream, he thought and sighed heavily.

Daniel stared into the empty space in his room and waited, hoping for a sign that would give him a reason to continue. He did this now every morning, and he had always found his reasons, but today was not just another day. Sitting there contemplating his life choices, he felt rather than heard a scratching coming from behind the wall opposite him.

He stared curiously, then distinctly heard a scraping sound. Holding his breath, he listened quietly, slightly turning his ear towards the sound. It felt like a welcome distraction from the horrors of the dream he had endured. As he listened, he could almost hear a muffled growl, angrily cursing behind the wall. Daniel's eyes widened as he recognised that sound.

"It wasn't a dream," he gasped. "It has come back for me." He whimpered as he stared, frozen in terror. The scraping became louder, as though it was trying to claw its way in. *It's not real*, Daniel thought, taking a deep breath, trying to calm his nerves. Suddenly, there was a thunderous thud from behind the wall, and Daniel's heart raced.

"Let me in!" it screamed. The noise exploded, the scratching now hammering, pounding at the walls, *boom, boom, boom*, echoing around. It was unbearable and caused the room to shudder and shake.

"Not again, please, not again!" Daniel cried out.

The walls started to tremble uncontrollably. There was a loud crack as they splintered, sending chunks of brick raining down like a hailstorm. The bed shook wildly as if alive, and Daniel was thrown forcefully to the floor. The room began writhing and twisting, pressing in on him, contracting like a giant fist, squeezing all air from his lungs. He gasped for breath as the pain increased, then the room grew dark, and the Shadow loomed over him again.

"I can save you, Daniel. I can give you what you want. Just reach out and give yourself to Shadow," it spoke with a cold, heartless tone. "She can be yours once more."

Daniel could feel himself being squeezed and struggled to take even one breath. Dread and trepidation now overwhelmed him. The pounding at the walls was accompanied by a howling, piercing gale that forced itself into every corner of the room, smashing all in its wake. A twisted noise erupted, shrieking with a burst of deafening laughter, shouting incomprehensibly. Daniel clasped his hands to his ears so tightly that it caused him pain; he couldn't take any more.

"Stop!" Daniel shouted with rage, anger, and hurt. "Stop!"

Everything instantly fell still, and an eerie silence filled the air. Dust slowly floated to the ground, and the smashed furniture hung motionless. Daniel gradually lowered his hands. He could breathe again, and a sweet fragrance caught his attention. There she was, looking at him, a shining light cleansing the world of darkness. She smiled, but there was sadness in her blue eyes.

"I know what happens now," Daniel said, trembling. "I remember."

Daniel tried to stand but stumbled backwards onto his bed. His heart thumped hard in his tightened chest, the hurt was unbearable, and the air thinned around him. He grabbed at his chest in a vain attempt to stop the inevitable, and the room spun, and then it all went dark.

"Aya!"

…

Daniel stood in his kitchen with a cup of coffee in one hand and a teaspoon in the other, staring at the still black fluid in the cup. He watched the smooth, calm surface, and it reminded him of something that was just out of memory, something that hung on the tip of his tongue.

"I was in bed, wasn't I?" Daniel spoke aloud, wanting to hear his own voice, needing to clarify that he was, in fact, awake, and that this was real.

Daniel took a sip of the coffee that had sat motionless in his cup, and his face scrunched up with revulsion. It was stone cold. He was not a fan of cold coffee. He made himself a fresh cup, then walked over to the couch and sat down, putting his coffee on the trunk he used as a small coffee table. He rubbed his eyes and stretched.

A familiar routine urged him to pick up the remote. He switched on the TV, but there was only static. He switched through the channels: static, again and again.

"Oh great, the bloody thing is broken," Daniel said, complaining to some invisible companion. He promptly switched it off and went over to the radio. "Static?" he said as he switched through the stations. *This can't be broken too.*

He sat back down, aimlessly glancing around

his apartment. He took a cigarette from a crumpled pack left on the trunk the day before, struck a match, and drew the flame to its tip. The tobacco glowed red, and he inhaled deeply, letting out a thin stream of smoke that lingered in the air like an unwelcome ghost. He watched the smoke rise above him, carried on an chilled breeze. It swirled about, aimlessly climbing higher, until it dissipated, leaving no trace that it ever had existed. *It is a strange thing to live*, he thought. *When everyone who remembers has gone, can it be said that we ever existed?* This last thought lingered in his mind as his thoughts drifted to Aya. Daniel turned to the window and gazed at the morning blue sky; it comforted him, and he relaxed.

A shadow suddenly passed over the room; it was only for a second, but a vague memory erupted in Daniel's mind, and his stomach churned. He quickly stubbed out the cigarette and sat up, his eyes darting around the room.

Then, he heard a low growl emanating from the spare room. He turned and looked, not wanting to acknowledge it. The door was closed tight, as he always kept it. It was locked, and he had thrown away the key to keep it that way. A slow scraping sound against the door sent a shudder down Daniel's spine. He looked away, disregarding what his senses were telling him.

"It's just my imagination," he whispered. Then, a thud, and Daniel abruptly turned back to see the door was slightly ajar. He watched expectantly, transfixed, unable to look away. A hypnotic compulsion to enter the room crept into his mind, but equally, dread filled him with apprehension. A soft, vaguely musty smell drifted out of the spare room; he thought he heard the faint echo of a baby crying. A taunting reminder of what could have been. He looked away, and as he listened, his mind was led to a fantasy world where his life was vastly different.

She held a baby and smiled warmly at Daniel. He walked over and put his arms around them. "I will never let you go," he whispered in her ear.

"I know," she said, sadness etched on her expression.

He leaned back on the sofa, pushing any fear from his thoughts and held the image of her in his arms. Nothing else mattered; there was only her.

The hustle and bustle of the street outside crept into his awareness, and the mundane pattern of existence became a gentle melody that embraced him with its predictability. He found joy in all the innocent sounds outside and sank into deep comfort.

He smiled as he closed his eyes and drifted to another place and time.

...

The landlord smiled. "I have the key here somewhere," he said in a barely audible murmur. The keys, which were locked together with a scratched brass ring, clinked as he carefully examined each one.

"Ah, here," he eventually exclaimed, holding up the key to the apartment. After a bit of fussing about with the lock, he opened the door, and they walked in.

It was an open-plan apartment on the third floor of a three-story building. Natural light and a warm breeze flooded the living room from the small windows that had recently been opened. The apartment had one main living room, an open-plan kitchen, and a small corridor leading to the front door. Off the corridor was the bathroom and master bedroom, and closest to the living room was the spare room. The apartment was a mess. It clearly hadn't been cleaned for a while, with ripped carpets, broken doors, and dirty walls. It looked like the debris of the last decade was piled up in every corner. In the main bedroom, the wallpaper had peeled away, now left hanging off damp walls. The spare room had boxes and all sorts of discarded bric-a-brac no longer of any use to anyone. The bathroom desperately needed to be descaled, and the kitchen was a bacteria's holiday home.

The landlord made various excuses, reasons, and problems. "I know it doesn't look much." He struggled to justify the clearly dreary scene that unfolded before them. He walked over to the spare room and peered in. "You know, I used to live here many years ago." He paused and smiled. "This place holds many fond memories."

Daniel looked around the dour scene, but he saw beyond the veneer of mould. There was something about the apartment that felt welcoming and homely despite the clear need for repair. It wasn't just the apartment. It was the location, the building itself; he was drawn to it. It felt like a place he could finally call home.

"When Mrs. Kapoor and I first came to this country, we lived here, and we have had many happy memories here." He smiled broadly and started to try to tidy the place.

Probably should have done that before the viewing, Daniel thought. He walked over to the window and looked out. The landlord was still talking and tidying about, but his words faded into the background. A smile crept across his Daniel's as he looked out, and he just knew.

"When can I move in?" Daniel said, cutting off the landlord mid-flow. The landlord tripped over his last spent word. "Of course, I expect not to have to pay the first two months' rent," he said, looking around, "and I will fix this place up."

"Two months?!" the landlord said, feeling a little disgruntled. "No, no, no, this is a great place, and the rent is good."

"Mmmm." Daniel let out a quiet mumble. He took a deep breath and started a tour of the apartment. "The wallpaper is torn, the ceiling is yellowing, the kitchen is a bacterial warzone, the floor tiles are cracked, you have a leaky tap, there's a cracked pane of glass on the window, the doors creak, the floorboards creak, and that banging sound coming from the central heating doesn't fill me with confidence. Need I go on?" He went on. "And how long has this place been empty? One, two, three years? We both know that I'm offering you a sound deal. I don't make any noise, I will always pay my rent on time, and I will even look after your dog if you have one." Daniel grinned broadly.

"Okay, okay, so it needs a little work. A little clean here, a brush there, it will be good as new," the landlord retorted.

"But who's going to be doing the cleaning? It'll cost you more for cleaners and tradesmen. I will be happy to do the work for two months of free rent. We all win," Daniel said whilst crossing his fingers behind his back. "I'm Daniel." He offered his hand in a gesture of friendship.

"Mr. Kapoor," the landlord sighed and shook Daniel's hand.

...

Daniel's lips curved into a smile as he recalled his first meeting with Mr. Kapoor. He could still feel that overwhelming sense of certainty that this was the right place for him, despite all its faults. It was like an invisible pull drawing him in, as though fate played a hand. His eyes flicked around the room, taking in each detail, and he felt a warm contentment.

Reaching over, he picked up his coffee cup and sipped. It was cold. "What the hell?!" he said aloud, scratching his head. "I only closed my eyes for a second."

Daniel noticed the sounds from outside had gone deathly quiet. He tried to stand but only made it halfway before stumbling forward, steadying himself on the trunk. It felt like the world was pressing down, bearing its weight on his shoulders, and his legs trembled under the strain. The room seemed to squirm about and spin, making him feel queasy.

He fell back onto the couch, took a deep breath, and calmed himself. The gurgling sound of a baby stole his attention, drawing him back to the spare room.

It wasn't always the spare room. There was a time when it had a purpose and meaning, bringing hope to Daniel. However, that was long ago. Now, it was a locked room, shut away from the light, serving as a bleak reminder of what he had lost. The scratching grew louder, the thumping started, and the door violently swung open. Daniel could see only blackness in the room. He shuddered as a baby's laugh drifted out of the darkness.

"What did I do to deserve this?" he exclaimed, his voice trembling under the onslaught of emotions.

He was desperate, his voice quivering as he pleaded for the anguish to end. He clenched his fists and closed his eyes, struggling to stifle the tears that threatened to flow. No matter how hard he tried, nothing could take away the misery that had been inflicted upon him.

"Why are you doing this to me?" he cried, hoping for salvation.

Only silence answered.

He stood up and tried to walk to the open door that was taunting him to enter, but his legs gave way, and he collapsed, knocking his head on the trunk.

The next moment, Daniel was standing in the kitchen again, holding a cup of coffee in one hand and a teaspoon in the other. He went to take a sip of the coffee but then moved it away from his lips. *It's cold*. "It's always cold," he whispered. He placed his cold cup of coffee on the kitchen surface and placed the spoon next to it, leaving a small stain.

Walking over to the window and peering out, Daniel could see people going about their day, oblivious to his spying. He wondered if they knew how pointless their existence was, their endless routines, round and round, their lives went day after day, year after year, lifetime after lifetime. *I just want it all to end*, he thought. Anger welled up, erupting into a cruel disdain towards creation, and cruel thoughts flooded his emotions.

"I hate you all," he hissed. "Brain dead zombies!" he shouted. "I pity you all!" His voice became twisted and mean.

He suddenly clasped his mouth in horror. "Sorry," he whimpered. *I don't understand why I said that*, he thought.

He looked towards the spare room and was relieved to see that the door was closed. "As it should be," he said and returned his gaze to the street below.

"Every day, we all start our routines. Whether at work or something else, we fall into our patterns. The same thing the next day and the next and the next. It's insanity," he said to himself. "There must be more than this."

Daniel sighed, walked over to the couch, and fell back into his familiar, comfortable spot. He went to pick up another cigarette but stopped as the hairs on his arms stood up. Another noise came from the spare room. His stomach churned with a feeling of dread. He did not want to look for fear of uncovering some dark truth that lurked within him, a truth that he was hiding from. The noise persisted; it sounded like boxes being moved about.

When he turned to look, the door was wide open. The shock sent chills down his spine, as if icicles were being driven deep into his veins. He heard footsteps coming from the hallway, and then his bedroom door opened ever so slowly and quietly shut. Daniel gasped in disbelief. *There's someone else here.* The blackness from the room now spilt out, writhing across the floor like an expanding mist. Daniel turned away, not wanting to acknowledge what was happening. "I'm okay," he whispered. "I'm okay."

…

Daniel knocked sheepishly on Mr. and Mrs. Kapoor's door, stepped back, and waited.

He paced back and forth nervously, briefly glancing at his watch, noticing that he was fifteen minutes early. *Should I knock again?* He pondered his predicament. *I want this evening to be perfect*. He raised his hand and stopped just inches from the door; his hand hovered there. *Perhaps I should return in a bit*.

Daniel stood in front of the plain, brown, wooden door; nothing about it was imposing, but at that moment, it felt like a raised drawbridge to an impenetrable castle. There was muffled movement coming from within the apartment. He pressed his ear to the door; he could hear muffled voices and a radio playing. He thought he heard Mrs. Kapoor singing. He moved away, brushed himself down, ran his hands through his hair, and ran his tongue over his teeth. He cupped his hands, breathed heavily into them, and sniffed. *All good*.

"Now or never," he whispered in encouragement.

This time he gave a forceful knock on the door. *Oh crap, that was too hard*, he thought, panicked. The door opened, and Mr. Kapoor was standing there.

"Daniel, nice to see you, son. Come in, come

in." Mr. Kapoor beckoned Daniel to go to the front room. "Sit, sit," he added as he followed him in.

Daniel nervously sat down, his heart thumping and his stomach churning like it was filled with a million butterflies. Today marked precisely three hundred and sixty-five days since that night in the club: their one-year anniversary. He was particularly anxious today. Life is full of questions, and most are inconsequential; however, this was the big question, and this was the day when everything could change. He was plagued with doubt. *What if I'm not enough? What if Aya no longer feels the same way I do?* Irrational thoughts whirled around his head. He felt anxious and excited, eager for what the night ahead might bring, but dreading that it could all go wrong.

Mr. Kapoor made himself comfortable in the armchair opposite, scrutinising Daniel.

"So, where are you taking my granddaughter?" he asked, leaning slightly forward in an examinatory pose.

Daniel was used to the probing; he knew only concern for Aya lay behind the questioning. However, on this occasion, Daniel stuttered his words whilst excessively clearing his dry throat. Beads of sweat dripped down his back. As he rubbed his hands together and twirled his thumbs, he shifted restlessly about on the seat and tried to avoid any eye contact.

"Oh, leave him be," interjected Mrs. Kapoor as she entered the room, saving Daniel from his fate. "Do you have time for tea, perhaps?"

"Sorry, I have a table booked for eight at a new restaurant. It opened last month, the bottom end of the high street," Daniel said, feeling a little relieved.

"Sounds nice," Mrs. Kapoor answered.

"Yeah, should be good. Jess and Robbie went there last week and said that it was very good, all ala carte. The Renaissance, I think it's called."

"That sounds lovely and expensive." She smiled and chuckled.

"Well, Aya is worth so much more," Daniel said, then suddenly felt quite conspicuous and blushed a little.

"I can't remember the last time my toy-boy here took me out for a romantic dinner." She laughed, looking lovingly at her husband, who rolled his eyes.

Aya stepped into the room, and Daniel's gaze fell upon her. The moment felt suspended in time as she gracefully moved towards him. Her dusky dress flowed over her body, giving hints of the goddess beneath. His eyes traced the curves that clung delicately to her slight frame, and his heart stirred with rapture at her beauty. Her long, silky black hair cascaded down her slender shoulders and fell seductively over her bosom. She stirred an unspeakable longing within him, and he was captivated. He felt his heart swell with love as she smiled the perfect smile.

Daniel moved forward, wanting to touch and hold her in his arms. He wanted to tell her how perfect she was, that no words could do justice to express how he felt. However, he was acutely aware that her grandparents were watching closely.

"You look nice," Daniel eventually mustered up something to say.

Aya smiled. "Thanks," she said and kissed him. Daniel blushed slightly.

"I remember when you looked at me like that," Mrs. Kapoor said. She looked at her husband with a naughty sparkle in her eye.

"My dear Samaira, my love for you has never once wavered." He kissed her gently on the cheek, leaving a slight blush in its wake.

Mrs. Kapoor chuckled softly, her eyes twinkling with joy. They looked at each other with a deep understanding born from the many years they had spent together.

"Well," she said, "it is still nice to hear every now and then." She giggled like she was a young girl again.

Daniel and Aya said farewell and left her grandparents for the restaurant. A horse-drawn carriage awaited them as they walked out of the apartment's entrance. The carriage was a brilliant white Victorian style with ornate woodwork trim and an open top with white leather seats. It was drawn by two magnificent white stallions whose manes hung low.

"Wow! I am impressed. It's like something from a fairy tale," Aya said. "You didn't have to."

"Well, you've always wanted to ride in a carriage, and, well…" Daniel stopped; he didn't want to say too much just yet.

The driver climbed down and opened the carriage door for Aya.

"Your carriage awaits, m'lady." He bowed slightly.

Aya grinned and was helped up the step. Daniel followed his butterflies, now a raging swarm in his gut.

"You okay, babes?" she asked after noticing Daniel acting nervously.

"Yeah, yeah, of course. I just want tonight to be perfect."

"It is perfect. We could be sitting in the rain on a park bench, but as long as I'm with you, it would be perfect." Aya smiled and brushed his cheek gently with her hand.

With her words, Daniel felt better. The swarm churning in his stomach flew away, and he felt relaxed and happy. Aya always knew exactly what to say to him and when. For six months, Daniel had saved and planned for this special night. He had toiled over the details, ensuring everything was perfect. He had even enlisted help from his friends. Even so, as the evening approached, his anxiety bubbled up, and no matter how much he told himself that it would be fine, he could not contain his worry.

THE FINAL JOURNEY

As they went through the busy high street, people stopped to look. The horse-drawn carriage was an impressive site, especially against the backdrop of regular traffic. Some passing tourists started to take photos, and this caused other passersby to also stop and look. Daniel and Aya played along with their newfound fame. They started the classic royal wave, which only fuelled the misconception that they were anyone important.

They soon reached their destination and pulled up outside the restaurant.

Daniel had prepared every little detail: staff were waiting for their arrival, and a red carpet had been laid out for them. Aya was helped off the carriage, and they were led to the restaurant whilst more curious onlookers strained to see what all the commotion was about. They were shown to their private venue; a long red curtain covered the entrance to their room. Two staff members stood on either side and pulled back the curtain as they entered. The room was decorated with fresh flowers of all hues, filling the air with a sweet fragrance. The light was dim and golden, making the scene appear magical. The floor was scattered in a bed of soft red petals. Their table was placed in the middle of the room.

It was draped with a white silk cloth that hung low to the floor, with a single red candle burning brightly in the centre.

Daniel had arranged for a pianist to play softly in one corner of the room. Rich velvet drapes hung from its sides, giving it an air of grandeur and magnificence. Aya loved classical piano, and the pianist was instructed to play an evening of Chopin, which was Aya's favourite. As they slowly walked to their table, the pianist danced on the keys, each finger caressing the notes; the music was magical and entrancing. If filled the air with its elegance, and when Daniel looked at Aya, she shone to its tones.

"Beautiful," Aya whispered gently.

As they moved, the petals lifted about them and swirled on the ground with each step. Daniel pulled back a chair, and she gently sat down; he moved to the other side of the table and took his seat. A waiter arrived carrying two glasses and a bottle of champagne, which he placed on the table before them. He poured, filling the two glasses, smiled, and simply said, "Enjoy," then took his leave.

Daniel looked at Aya, trying to hide his desperate longing to hold her. He watched her every motion as she picked up her glass with both hands and slowly moved it to her full, soft, red lips. She drank deliberately, savouring every drop of the champagne as it flowed over her tongue, with its sweet taste warming her throat as the liquid flowed down. Her blue eyes flickered up from the glass and reflected Daniel's passion. She slowly licked her top lip, and a seductive grin twitched.

The moment was interrupted by the waiter bringing over the first dish of the evening: seared tuna on a bed of grilled vegetables served with honey sauce drizzled over it. The waiter smiled and explained the intricacies of the flavours and aromas.

"I hope you don't mind," Daniel said. "I kinda planned the food for the night."

"How could I possibly mind? You know me too well." She smiled and looked down at the food, and her mouth moistened in anticipation.

The whole evening was dedicated to all of Aya's favourite tastes, leading to the climax, which Daniel was dreading yet wanting with all his being. This question would change the rest of his life.

Once the first course was over, so arrived a second, then a third, and so on. Each course was elegantly presented, offering an explosion of tastes, each dish based on one of Aya's loves. She laughed as she was shocked and impressed with each memory relived in the food. Once the meal finally ended, they sat for a short while in silence, enjoying each other's company. Still, Daniel's mind was whirling, working up the courage to act out the planned finale.

Eventually, he took a deep breath and stood up, but a little too fast. Daniel knocked his chair flying backwards; he quickly turned, trying to catch it, and bumped into the table. He knocked over Aya's filled champagne glass, which splashed across the tablecloth and all over her dress. She sat there with a shocked expression as the chilled liquid ran down her body. The pianist pretended not to notice the looming domestic fight approaching and played a little louder.

She stood up, backed away, and looked straight at Daniel. The air hung in anticipation of what would follow. Suddenly, she burst out laughing; she laughed so much that she was brought to tears. Daniel stood there, relieved but feeling dismayed. She walked over to him and put her arms around his shoulder.

"I love you, my crazy, crazy man," she said.

"You're not mad?" Daniel said.

She screamed out in laughter. "Mad? Silly boy, kiss me!"

She went to kiss him, but he stopped her. She looked a little baffled. He stepped back, knelt on one knee, and looked up. He reached out and took her hand.

"Will you marry me?" Daniel asked. He held his breath as he waited for the only answer that would complete him; even the pianist stopped playing and sat eagerly waiting for her answer.

"Yes," she answered with a tear of joy. "Most certainly yes."

…

Leaning back on his sofa, his attention was drawn to the noise coming from the apartment below. Joan lived alone; well, apart from her snappy little dog. However, her dog was strangely quiet this morning. Usually, it would be running about the place and letting off the occasional annoying bark.

"Let me give you a hand with that," was the first thing Joan ever said to Daniel when he moved in. In fact, she helped him move all his stuff in, always eager to help anyone.

Joan always saw the positive in life, forever one of life's optimists. He smiled, thinking about her. She always knew how to highlight the brighter side of any situation. Daniel found Joan well-travelled; she always had a story to tell, and each seemed more fantastic than the last. *The Adventures of the Fantastic Mrs. Bennet*, he would imagine her autobiography would be called. If he ever needed advice or a sensible, learned suggestion, then Joan was where he would find himself.

"Joan, I could use your help about now," he said, his voice falling dead in the quiet room.

"You just need to trust in yourself," he heard the whisper of her voice as an echo in his head. He smiled broadly and sighed.

"You're probably right, Joan. You usually are," he whispered.

Daniel stared out again into empty space, his thoughts sifting through his memories, one after another, each appearing as vivid as the next. It was like he was watching a documentary, where he was the subject matter, and each scene was a moment from his life. Daniel quietly watched, losing himself to the unfolding life review. Then he saw himself as a star shining brightly in the night sky. Around him were other stars, and they all danced about, orbiting one another in a complex pattern of connectedness. His thoughts wandered, drifted far away from his apartment, from the people he knew, like he was no longer tethered but free to roam wherever he chose. He started to feel as if he was adrift, standing on a boat out on an eternal sea; every direction was open to him. Yet he felt alone on the waves as they lashed against his boat, rocking him from side to side. Something was missing; someone was missing.

"Danny..." a familiar voice was carried on the breeze.

Daniel felt a sharp pain in his chest and stumbled, falling into the water. At first, he splashed and struggled to climb back into the boat, but it drifted away, leaving him stranded. He floated there, allowing the rocking of the sea to carry him wherever it chose. Daniel stared up at the stars and watched as they danced together. He smiled calmly as he sank beneath the waves. Deeper and deeper he descended, until there was no more light, and only shadow remained.

Daniel gasped for breath as his heart beat painfully. He was sitting on his sofa; there was no sea, no stars, just his apartment. Muffled voices emanated from his bedroom; they were talking, and someone was sobbing. He listened intently; he could feel madness taking hold, unable to discern what was real and what was not.

"Can't you leave me be?!" he angrily spat out his words.

He turned to look at the spare room, and the door was open. There was a black mist lingering just around the entrance. He could hear a baby crying, and his heart plunged, burdened by a heavy sadness.

"I'm coming," he said.

Daniel stood up and slowly walked towards the room. He stepped into the mist, which welcomed him as though he was returning home from a long journey, and went inside. The room was empty apart from a cot which sat in the middle. He paused and silently stared at it. The baby's cries were louder now, but he could not clearly see the cot; a shadowy mist obscured it. He walked over and reached out, wanting to comfort the baby.

"It's okay, Daddy's here," he whispered, reaching in, but the cot was empty. A pain rose inside him; he felt his heart breaking. It was all too much. The mist swirled about, the baby's cries reverberated throughout the room, and his head spun.

…

"Pregnant?" Daniel roared with joy.

"Oh, so you're happy you're going to be a dad then?" Aya teased, knowing the answer all too well.

"I don't know, I may have to think long and hard about this turn of events," he mocked in jest as he walked up to her and held her in his arms for a moment. "This is good, really good." He leant forward and kissed her. Then he knelt down and kissed the currently invisible bump.

Aya smiled at him. "It is currently barely a pea size."

"It's perfect, no matter the vegetable."

She laughed and slapped his arm. "Well, our little pea is happy being a pea."

Aya walked from the front room to the kitchen. "Do you want a coffee?" she asked.

"Only the good stuff," he answered.

"Yes, I know." She rolled her eyes and looked for the coffee percolator.

Daniel went and sat down on the couch and rummaged about looking for the remote control for the HiFi. Realising he had no idea where it was, he went over to the player with a slight grumble and groan.

"Chopin, please," Aya called from the kitchen. "It'll be good for our little pea."

"All this talk of peas has made me hungry," Daniel called out.

"Babies are not for eating," she laughed.

"Very funny, just saying I'm hungry." He was hoping for a sandwich.

"That's nice, dear," came the response.

"I think I may die!" whined Daniel jokingly.

"Uh huh." She acted indifferently, which only served to encourage Daniel.

"Really. Do you want to have a death on your hands?"

"Well, before you leave this mortal realm, I will need to sort out the spare room, please, babes."

"Okay," Daniel conceded. He went over to the spare room and opened the door. He was confronted with a treasure trove of memories: boxes of all shapes and sizes were stacked precariously along the back wall, accompanied by knotted Christmas decorations that had been hastily thrown on top. Another wall was home to a tatty king-size mattress and bed frame that had been left propped up by a long-forgotten, bent, floor-standing lamp. A broken Christmas tree lay in the middle of the floor, and two broken vacuum cleaners were the final occupants to be found here.

"If you want a sandwich, just ask." She came to the room and stood by the door.

This was music to Daniel's ears. "Please, may I have a sandwich, love of my life?"

"Of course, I will make you a sandwich with

your coffee," she said warmly.

A broad grin drew across Daniel's face. Aya noticed and shook her head, but couldn't hide a subtle giggle.

"Now, where to start?" he muttered.

"Those boxes?" Aya said and returned to the kitchen.

Daniel started to sift through the boxes and the old Christmas decorations. *This will take ages.*

"Coffee!" Aya called over.

"Saved," Daniel muttered under his breath.

Aya carried a tray holding two cups of coffee and a couple ham sandwiches to the trunk. She made herself comfortable stretching out; Daniel joined her.

"Boy or girl?" Daniel asked, half-chewing. "This is great. I needed this," he added before Aya could answer his question.

"I really don't mind."

"That's what everyone says!" Daniel rolled his eyes. "A boy would be awesome to play with, teach him football, and do boy's stuff."

"Which you can't do with a girl?" Aya asked firmly.

"Ah well, yes, of course. I would love a daddy's girl—" he started.

"Or mummy's girl," Aya interrupted.

"Or mummy's girl," Daniel agreed. "Honestly, I really don't mind. They will be perfect either way, especially if they take after you."

"Charmer," she mocked.

Daniel shrugged and sipped his coffee. "Hot, hot, hot."

"Uh huh." She rolled her eyes and smiled.

"So, what do you think about the spare room?" Daniel asked.

"Too early to decorate, but we can clear it out. I mean, what's the harm there?"

"Well, it is only a pea, and I don't want to tempt fate and all that," Daniel said, looking at the invisible bump.

"Don't worry, it will be fine," she said, reaching for Daniel's hand.

"I know, of course it will." He smiled.

"Don't worry, we can just empty the room for now," she said.

"Okay, sounds like a plan," Daniel said, and took a bite of his sandwich.

...

"Have you got it?" Robbie shouted, holding one side of a rather old large mattress as they tried to push it out of the front door. "How the hell did you get it in here?"

"I didn't. It was delivered," Daniel responded irritably.

"Push!" Robbie yelled.

Daniel pushed hard, the door frame cracked, and the mattress exploded onto the landing, shooting past Robbie, who was knocked back. It slid down the stairs, colliding with Mrs. Bennet's door.

Mrs. Bennet opened her door, expecting to find a delivery driver, but instead was greeted with an old torn mattress.

"Lovely," she said. "You boys okay? Or perhaps I could get that thing down for you?"

"Sorry, Joan, it kinda slipped," Daniel said apologetically.

"You know where I am if you need me," she tried to close her door but gave up as the mattress was going nowhere.

Back in the apartment, Aya and Jess were going through the old boxes when they discovered some old photos of them when they were young.

"Look here, that's me," Jess said, holding up an old photo. "I don't remember this. Looks like I must have been about nine or ten. I can't believe he has these," she said, rummaging a little deeper into the old photos in the box.

"Wait a minute! This looks familiar," Jess exclaimed as she pulled out a photo of a group of kids sitting around a campfire. "This I do remember. Daniel was given a camera by his Nan, and he insisted on taking pictures of everything." She paused, and a warm smile filled her face.

"Look at this photo." Jessica held up a crinkled photograph. "This was when I first met them. My God." She sighed. "Time really does fly."

"Is that Robbie?" Aya asked.

"Yeah, that's Robbie, Sam, and Danny. I think that one was John...no, Richard...no, Bob. I don't remember," she conceded.

"Daniel?" Aya held up another photo of a young boy hanging upside down from a tree.

They laughed. "Yes, Daniel," Jess confirmed. "One of the rare times he let me use his camera. He wanted to see what he looked like upside down." They both sniggered.

Daniel and Robbie walked, panting, into the room, beads of sweat running down their faces.

"That bloody mattress!" Robbie said, disgruntled.

"Well, thank you both. Finally, that horrible thing has gone," Aya said gratefully.

Jess pulled out another photo of a young couple standing on top of a high mountain; in the background, the land stretched for what seemed like forever.

"That's my mum and dad," Daniel said, saddened yet happy to see the picture. "I don't have many."

"I know," Aya said, saddened by Daniel's expression. "I think this one should come out. I have a place for it."

Daniel smiled faintly and left the room. The

others looked at each other, sensing Daniel's mood drop.

"He's okay," Aya said quietly. "I think with the baby coming, he wishes that they were here now more than ever. Just gets to him sometimes."

Aya left the room and went to find Daniel. She found him sitting on their bed with an old photo in his hand. He sat there just staring at it, appearing to be lost in some unknown memory.

"You okay, babes?"

Daniel didn't respond immediately; he just offered a bleak smile. Aya put her arm around him and looked down at the photo he was holding. It was of a woman sitting on a bench with a tiny baby in her arms.

"I haven't seen that before," Aya said.

"It's my mum, taken when I was young," he said.

Aya hugged him a little tighter but said nothing.

"It's odd; it makes me sad, but happy. Just a moment when life was perfect," he sighed, "then it was all taken away."

Aya remained silent and hugged him a little tighter. "It'll be okay, I promise," she whispered.

"Are we all just destined to be nothing but an old photograph, fading away in a box somewhere?" He placed the photo on the bed. "I'm worried," he said, the worry evident in his voice.

"Worried?" Aya asked.

"What if…" He trailed off, but Aya knew his thoughts only too well.

"I will be fine, I promise," Aya said, trying to alleviate his fears.

"How do you know? When life seems perfect, that's when it all falls to bits…" He trailed off. "I can't lose you, I would be lost, broken, I…"

"Shhhh!" she whispered. "Oh, don't be silly. I'm not going anywhere without you." Aya wiped away a tear that rolled down Daniel's cheek.

He took a deep breath and rubbed his eyes. "I know, it will all be fine," he said, clinging to hope, trying to ignore his anxiety.

"Now let's go finish that room."

Samantha came over after work and helped with the rest of the clean-out of the spare room. She had been working late, but insisted that she would help.

"Look at you two," she said as she gave each of them a hug. "I am so happy now. Where do you want me to start?" she added eagerly.

"Over here," Robbie called out.

They cleaned out the spare room, which was officially the pea room. All the old boxes found new homes, and the rest were thrown away. They had finished at about nine in the evening, and finally stopped to admire their work. The room was clean and empty.

"A blank slate," Samantha said.

"Boy or girl, this will be perfect," Jessica added.

"I'm hungry, let's order out," Robbie finished.

Robbie ordered takeaway from the local Chinese restaurant and several bottles of wine. As they ate, they talked about the past and future, excited for when a little baby Aya or Daniel would run around the place. Daniel looked at Aya lovingly when she talked about being a mother and how she was excited about raising their child together. He watched as her face glowed when she talked about the places they would visit and the perfect life they would all have.

Samantha watched Daniel looking lovingly at Aya, the happiness in his expression. She couldn't help but feel a little emotional too. Tears started to well up in her eyes as she recalled memories from her childhood.

"It's moments like these that make me grateful for you guys," Samantha said softly.

Aya smiled and put her arm around Samantha, understanding her emotions perfectly. Jessica moved closer to her friends and did the same.

Robbie looked at Daniel. "Should we hug too?" he said with a smile.

"Nah, another glass of wine will do," Daniel said.

"Cheers," Robbie said.

They all grinned at each other in silent agreement: no matter what happened in life, they were all there to support each other until the very end.

…

Daniel opened his eyes and sat bolt upright back on the couch. As he sat up, he spilt his coffee.

"Oh blast!" he cursed.

I don't remember having this here, he thought and stood up, went to the kitchen, and cleaned himself.

"This will stain," he muttered as he scrubbed to get the coffee out of his shirt. The next moment, his shirt was dry, and a freshly poured coffee was on the side.

"Well, don't just stare at it," Aya said as she walked by with some washing in hand. "I wish you'd put your socks in the washing basket."

Daniel just stared in silence, unable to mutter a word.

"What do you fancy for dinner?" Aya asked. "Cat's got your tongue?" She grinned.

"Aya, I…" Daniel's voice was barely audible.

The next moment, Aya turned to Daniel and faded like whisps of smoke on a breeze. He screamed out in despair, his body convulsing with agony. His vision blurred as the tears poured down his face. He erupted with pure rage and threw his coffee cup hard at the wall, where it exploded into a shower of broken shards, but the pain did not subside, and his anger grew. He tore at the cupboards, ripping them from the wall and smashing them to the ground. His monstrous hatred for life overflowed into a destructive force. He stormed the living room, turned over the furniture, smashed the TV, ripped up photos, and became a tornado of pure destruction. At that moment, he detested everything and everyone, but in truth, it was himself whom he truly hated.

Daniel found himself standing in front of the spare room door. It was locked closed. He kicked it open and burst in, fuelled by a blazing fury. However, when he entered, his rage vanished. Aya stood over the cot, looking into it and softly laughing. He heard a baby playfully making gurgling sounds. Daniel wearily walked over, not daring to look at Aya for fear that she would leave him again.

He leaned over, and a little baby girl was giggling. He reached down, picked her up, and held her in a fatherly embrace, tears rolling down his cheeks. Then, suddenly, the baby was gone, and his arms were empty.

"No! No! No!" Daniel screamed out

He fell to his knees. Aya stood before him; she reached down and gently lifted his face. She stood there smiling, but her eyes were closed.

"It's time, Daniel," she said in a gentle tone.

Abruptly, her eyes snapped open, but where once they shone bright and full of life, they now instead were black as night, revealing a cold, hollow stare.

In her gaze, he felt that he stood at the edge of an abyss and peered into its never-ending depths. Its darkness seemed to swallow him whole, tempting him to succumb to its void. His heart pounded in his chest as he fought against the pull, trying to resist the overwhelming urge to fall into its unknown depths.

The air around him was still, filled only with the faint echoes of distant whispers that seemed to call out his name. As he gazed deeper, an inexplicable sense of foreboding washed over him, and he hollered in fear and panic as he stumbled back.

"You're not Aya!" Daniel shouted.

The creature laughed, pounced on Daniel, and grabbed his head with both hands.

"Remember!" it hissed.

CHAPTER 11

Shadow's Embrace
In the darkness His cold embrace offers no comfort.

"I'm home!" Daniel called out.

"I'm in here," Aya replied.

"I said leave this and I'll do it. You need to take it easy," Daniel said, trying to give Aya a telling-off. She just rolled her eyes.

"Well, give me a hand then, grab that brush, please. I am terrible at cutting in," Aya said.

"Okay, let me change then," Daniel said, leaving the room. He stripped down to his boxer shorts. "Where should I start?"

"I hope you don't work like that when I'm not about," she said, wrapping her arm around him.

"Well, er...depends on the client," he jested.

Aya looked sternly at him and slapped him on his backside. "Over there, please, top edge." She turned from him. "By the way, I like your style." She smiled, looking over her shoulder.

"So, the little pea must be a melon by now," Daniel said.

"Uh huh," Aya said, continuing to paint a wall.

"Perhaps we should stop calling this the pea room," Daniel said. "The melon room?"

"Really? The melon room?" Aya giggled.

"Sure, Baby Pea, now known as Baby Melon," he joked.

"Get painting, or Baby Pea will be out of her pod before we've finished."

They spent the next few hours painting and decorating the room, discussing baby names and the future they hoped for. They talked about schooling, where they would eventually live, buying a house with a garden, and going to parks and play gyms. Aya talked about being the mum, meeting other mums, and going to coffee mornings and children's parties. She just wanted to be normal, just like everyone else.

Daniel's fear of the birth faded as they spoke, but he never could quite shake a looming feeling of dread that seemed to linger in the recesses of his mind. He couldn't entirely lose the feeling that this happiness would end, that his perfect life would be destroyed somehow. He would glimpse shadows in the corner of his eye as though something was lingering just out of sight, waiting to pounce. A plan was unfolding as though some unseen force was manipulating his life. He would shrug off all these notions as silly and irrational; he reasoned that this was just worrying about the people he loved.

As the days went on, Daniel and Aya grew in happiness, and their love shone brightest of all. They pushed back the shadows, and their joy was contagious everywhere they went.

Aya was the sun in his sky, the moon in his nights, the stars that shone down. Aya completed Daniel and made him whole. But Shadow lingered; where there is light, there is always Shadow, and its plan would unfold.

The music played, and Aya sang loudly at the top of her voice. Daniel wasn't home, and Aya was cleaning the place as she often did. Occasionally, she would stop and give her growing bump a gentle rub, warming her heart as she felt her little pea wriggle inside.

"You are a fidget," she said, rubbing her bump.

Today started like any ordinary day. Aya woke up in the morning with Daniel, and she happily made him breakfast. They sat and talked about the mundane things in life; sometimes the mundane things mattered most. They kissed as they did every morning. Daniel told her to be careful not to strain herself, to relax and leave anything that needed to be done for him when he got home. She agreed; however, as soon as he had left, she did what she said she wouldn't do.

It was about lunchtime when Aya stopped to make herself a drink and something to eat. She heard a noise coming from the baby's bedroom. It startled her, but she reasoned that something must have fallen, perhaps one of the pictures hanging on the wall. However, the hairs on her arm stood up as though there was a chill in the air, or perhaps a whisper of a warning, but she did not take heed. She rubbed her arms to warm herself up.

Aya walked over to the room and pushed open the door. The room looked undisturbed. It was exactly as she had left it in the morning. Feeling relieved, she went in and started tidying clothes about and then stopped to admire the decorations she had put up for the baby's arrival, admittedly very early. She turned to leave the room; however, her way was blocked by a large ornate mirror. Aya stumbled backwards, shocked and terrified. The mirror loomed over her, casting a shadow that filled the room, obscuring everything in it.

Aya's reflection caught her gaze and ensnared her. Like a trapped animal accepting its fate, she froze, unable to move. She started to laugh; she didn't know why, but she felt compelled, as though someone had commanded her to do so.

Aya fell silent and stared at her reflection, and her reflection stared back. She slowly moved towards the mirror, and her reflection mirrored her every movement. She continued until she stopped only inches from its surface, face to face with her reflection. Aya stared wide-eyed as her reflection suddenly moved ominously. It tipped its head slightly as though it was considering its next move. Aya stumbled backwards, horrified at what she saw. It gradually advanced and stepped out of the wooden framed mirror towards her. With each step it took, Aya backed away, shielding her unborn baby from this menacing presence.

Suddenly, it erupted and lunged at her with unbridled fury. It opened its mouth wide and unleashed a terrifyingly loud onslaught of vitriolic hate as it clawed at her. Aya screamed and tried to fight off the shadowy grasp that had her throat. She was pushed hard and fell backwards; the figure disappeared, and the illusion cleared. Aya was falling down the building's staircase, bashing and crashing hard into the steps. Instinctively, she tried to protect her baby, but was thrown left and right; she screamed in pain and agony. Eventually, she landed hard on the ground floor with a thud. She was heavily bruised and bleeding, had cracked several ribs and broken her left arm. Then she lost consciousness.

Aya opened her eyes and sat in a field that stretched out in every direction as far as she could see. The horror and pain of the earlier moments were nowhere to be seen in her memories; she felt calm and content. She breathed deeply and looked around.

She was struck by the fantastic colours scattered around her amongst the vivid green tall blades of grass. Fairytale-like trees with massive trunks sprouted from the ground, reaching high up into the sky, with sapphire green leaves that reached far out and cast a beautiful flickering shade onto the ground. Aya thought she could hear them talking to one another. Rabbits were leaping about in the grass near her, playing games with one another and beckoning her to join them. She saw horses galloping through the field with long white manes trailing far behind them like fantastical, mythical creatures. The sky was a deep blue, exploding in many colours where it met the ground in the distance.

Aya breathed in, and her lungs filled with a sweet fragrance that lifted her spirits and filled her with an overwhelming peace. She heard rustling in the grass behind her, and as she turned around, she was greeted by a young girl, possibly no older than five or six years old.

"Hello," Aya said warmly.

"Hello," replied the little girl.

Aya looked at the little girl and was struck by her beautiful blue eyes that were neatly framed by her shoulder-length black hair. Her skin was white, without a blemish, and she had rosy red cheeks. She wore a frock that stopped just below her knees, sandals, and knee-high white cotton socks.

The little girl smiled broadly but didn't say anything else; she just looked inquisitively at Aya. They remained silent for a little while, each analysing the other.

"What are you doing here?" The little girl eventually broke the silence.

Aya was unsure of the answer, so she shook her head and simply indicated that she had no idea.

The little girl pondered this and eventually said, "Well, that's silly, isn't it?"

The little girl sat beside Aya and started picking daisies. "Do you know how to make daisy chains?"

"Yes, shall I help you?" Aya said.

"Yes, please." The little girl smiled. She made a necklace out of daisies while Aya still gathered them.

"For you," the little girl said, placing it over Aya's head.

"Thank you, they're beautiful. Where did you learn to make these so beautifully?" Aya asked.

THE FINAL JOURNEY

"I think," said the girl with a slight sadness, "my mummy would have shown me."

"Where is your mummy?"

The little girl remained silent, then said, "You can stay here with me if you want to." She stood up. "Or I can take you home."

"Do you know where I live?" Aya asked, confused.

The little girl held out her hand and smiled.

"I will always be your little pea," the girl whispered.

Aya stared, shocked; the little girl beamed reassuringly and pointed.

Aya looked and was overwhelmed with pain and anguish. She saw herself lying in a hospital bed. There was a dreadful feeling that something was wrong; Daniel held her hand and sobbed. She felt a hollow ache, like a piece of her was missing. She could see Daniel's sudden panic and cry out, but no sound reached her ears. A frenzy of doctors and nurses surrounded her as she lay there still. Then, a loud, solid tone filled the air around her, and everyone moved away except Daniel, who clung tightly to her hand. The tone faded away as if someone had switched off a machine, and all she could hear were Daniel's sobs.

Aya turned away from the scene and started to weep.

"It's okay." The little girl put her arms around Aya. "We'll see him again."

…

"I remember!" As Daniel spoke those words, all the air rushed from his lungs, and he exhaled. A flash of bright light and a loud buzzing rang through his ears. He fell to the ground, gripping his chest.

"Daniel…" a call came from his bedroom.

"Aya?" he whispered, barely able to talk.

He crawled out of Pea's room and down the hall to his bedroom, every movement causing him immeasurable pain. He fumbled for the handle, and the door swung open. Aya was standing by his bed.

"This can't be real," Daniel whimpered.

She walked over to him, leaned down, and whispered into his ear, "It's time to go now. We need to leave this place and find ourselves a better place."

Daniel looked up at her, begging her to remain, to not leave, imploring her to stay. She smiled at him, a familiar warm smile that only reminded him how much he missed her. More than anything, he wanted to reach out to her and say something that would keep her with him, but no words came. He felt like there was an invisible wall between them now, and it was too large and high for him to overcome. She said nothing more and moved away. As she drifted back, she beckoned him to follow, arms outstretched. She moved as though an invisible line was pulling her. He shakily stood up and moved to follow. Still, as he approached her, she faded into a shadow that now blanketed the room. Daniel felt cold as he stood there, frozen to the spot. He could see the door in the corner of his eye, a passage leading back. However, in truth, he did not want to escape if there was a chance that he could be with Aya again. He would follow wherever it would lead.

The door suddenly slammed shut, the room vanished from his sight, and Daniel stood alone in an eternal blackness.

"Aya?" Daniel called out. "Aya, where are you?"

"Here," hissed a voice.

Daniel stumbled through the blackness on trembling legs, breathing heavily, tears streaming down his face, calling out for Aya in the emptiness. Trying to follow the voice that echoed from some distant place.

"Here," the voice rang out again.

"Aya?" he called out again in desperation.

The memory of the loss of his child and of Aya pushed him to the edge of sanity. He had lost so much; his thoughts were spinning out of control.

"What must I do? Please, anything," he sobbed.

"Give in to the Shadow," came a voice, closer now and more distinct.

He fell to his knees; finally, the weight of suffering had broken him. "I am yours," he said in mournful sorrow, and gave in to the bleak emptiness of the suffocating darkness. He bled out into it, and it bled into him.

Then, in the darkness, he heard Joan's voice. It sounded like she was echoing from the other side of another world. There were other voices; Daniel recognised them too. Jess,

Robbie, and Sam. His mind slipped further into madness.

The blackness thinned slightly, and Daniel realised he was standing on the edge of an abyss. He looked out, saw a faint outline of a horizon several miles away and felt a cool breeze blow against his face. He smelled sea air; he heard birds singing and waves lashing. Then, the blackness peeled away, revealing a cliff's edge. He looked down and saw the white frothing foam engulfing the rocks, wave after wave.

"Jump..." A whisper on the breeze. "Jump, and you will be free."

He looked and saw Aya down below, standing just on the waves, looking up, waiting.

"Yes, my love," Daniel whispered. He leant forward, resolute in his decision to fall into Aya's arms, give himself entirely to this moment, commit to madness, give himself to Shadow.

Suddenly, a hand grabbed him from behind, yanking him back.

"Not this way, son," a familiar voice echoed throughout his being.

Daniel was thrown back onto the couch in his front room. He was panting heavily, trying to catch his breath, and his chest tightened. He knew exactly what he had to do. *Time to go*, he thought. With renewed energy, Daniel went to his bedroom door and stood outside, his hand resting on the handle. He heard voices inside now, clearly, and recognised them all. He hesitated there for what could have been many lifetimes, took a deep breath, then turned the handle, and the door swung open.

Joan, Samaira, Aisim, Robbie, Jessica, and Samantha stood there with their backs to him. They appeared to be looking towards his bed. He heard crying but didn't look and stepped past them, needing to know who was lying on his bed, but he knew what he would find, and he saw himself covered in booze, pills, and sick.

Robbie went over to Daniel, lying still, and pulled the quilt over him. "Goodbye, my old friend," he said, holding back tears.

He walked away and gently ushered everyone out of the room. As Aisim closed the door, he appeared to look straight at Daniel standing there; he smiled and nodded, then left.

Daniel was left alone, staring at himself,

lying motionless. He rubbed his eyes, almost in disbelief at what he saw, turning away, wanting to leave, but he was compelled to look again.

Sitting on top of his bed was Aya, her arms wrapped tightly around her knees as she rocked slightly. Her eyes looked tired, almost extinguished of life.

"Aya, my sweet, you're here," Daniel said.

Aya just sat there rocking; she said nothing. The air filled with an unbearable sadness.

"Aya?" Daniel cautiously asked, moving closer.

She turned to face him and smiled, but there was no joy or warmth in her smile. He was greeted with a blackened grin, and as she smiled, a thick black liquid trickled down her chin.

Suddenly, she started to cry out, screaming and writhing in pain. Daniel rushed over to her and grabbed her by the arms.

"I don't…" She tried to speak. "It knows." She coughed violently. "I woke up here, here, with no idea who or what I am anymore," she whimpered.

"Aya, Aya!" Daniel cried out.

"Help me!" she suddenly screamed at him and threw him across the room with a force he could never have predicted.

"You let me die!" she screamed with a revealed hatred.

Aya's body warped and writhed in agony as her bones snapped and contorted to shift into a monstrous form. It grew larger and filled the room, stretching an unfathomable darkness with its presence. Black blood-like substance oozed from the rips in its skin; it screeched and wailed. Its deafening howls filled the room as it cursed and lashed out at him, throwing him around like a ragdoll.

"You will not pass!" it hissed at him. "The cycle must end!"

The creature's claw-like hands lunged for Daniel's throat, pushing him backwards. He desperately tried to fight off the attack, but the monstrosity tightened its grip and squeezed hard, clamping him in a vice-like hold. Its fingers dug into Daniel's flesh and ripped him apart. His vision blurred, and blackness descended on him as he collapsed upon the floor.

The last thing he saw was its twisted form towering above him, grinning delightfully.

Then there was only Shadow…

CHAPTER 12

Descent into Madness
In the Shadow, there is only Shadow.

The ancient road stretched in either direction as far as could be seen, eventually fading away as it touched the bleak horizon. The road was cracked and damaged, in disrepair. Its surface was uneven and raised in sharp, jagged chunks in many places. It had been eroded, over many lifetimes, through countless aeons, by the unforgiving sand carried ceaselessly by a relentless wind whose howls reverberated across the empty plain. Daniel's eyes clouded with trepidation as he surveyed the endless desert extending out around him: vast, empty, barren wasteland, a joyless expanse. He gazed out across the landscape, desperate for even a glimmer of life, yet all he could see was an endless expanse of emptiness that stretched out before him. The memories of the events leading up to this moment felt like a distant dream, leaving only broken fragments in its wake. The people he once called family and friends were now just vague shadows in his mind, but one person shone through the darkness consuming him: Aya. Her memory was like a beacon, the only thing that kept him from getting swallowed by the abyss of despair. Daniel's skin crawled with dread, a chill ran down his spine, and he shuddered; something dark and sinister hung in the air.

The sun peaked low on the horizon, its crimson light diffused by a blanket of thin shadowy clouds, casting an ominous and oppressive aura on the land. The sand complemented the dreary sky with an angry heat, radiating from the ground like a pulsing crimson mist that filled the air and burned into the lungs of all who dared enter its domain.

Daniel chose a direction and placed one foot in front of the other, struggling over the uneven road, but he knew that to leave it would mean certain death. The heat was unbearable, and the howling wind offered no release, bringing blasts of coarse sand that burned his skin. He tried to shield himself with what little he wore, but it brought little reprive. He struggled with each step, burdened by the jagged rocks that littered his path. He felt as though he had been walking for days despite the sun still sitting firmly in the same spot on the horizon, as though it was there just to taunt him. Its heat beat down on him, making the air thick and breathing difficult. Blood trailed down from his cuts and scrapes as he made each laborious step, reminding him how long he had been fighting against this relentless journey. His body felt like it was withering away with every passing second, dragging him closer to his inevitable exhaustion.

Daniel thought that he could sense an invisible malevolence roaming this place, looking for resting travellers; this thought drove him forward, resisting defeat. The scene remained monotonous and unchanging until a dark, ominous mist appeared in the distance. Rising like a vast approaching storm, it appeared to linger as though it watched like a ruler surveying its land. Daniel gazed upon the menacing mass of writhing black smoke; a deep-seated fear rose from some long-forgotten memory. He felt a chill all over his body as he sensed something watching him from the depths of the bellowing dark cloud. As he stared, he felt that something was looking back at him. It was like a door opened in his mind, and images of pain and misery flooded back with an intensity that made his heart plummet like a stone. Daniel was overwhelmed by the recognition of this loathsome creature; thoughts of a misery worse than hell itself suffocated his mind. He frantically searched about, but everywhere he looked, there seemed to be nothing, only an endless wasteland. Still, he feared what may come out of the dark shadows and haunt him once more. With trepidation, he forced himself to risk the unforgiving desert. He stepped off the road and felt the burning sand even through the soles of his shoes, but he marched on, knowing no other way but forward and away from the shadow.

The sand was a merciless enemy, scorching Daniel's skin with each step he took. It seared his body with every breath he inhaled and seemed to be mocking him as he trudged along under the oppressive heat. He had no water or shade to rest, yet he continued onwards with sheer determination; he refused to be beaten. Laborious step after laborious step, he waded through the sand. It clung to him, wanting to drag him down, pressing on him to fail, but he pushed on. However, even the strongest tree will eventually fall, and Daniel succumbed to inevitable exhaustion. He collapsed to his knees and wavered there, waiting expectantly for something or someone to save him, but no one came. He collapsed into the blazing sand, and there he lay motionless, engulfed by the unforgiving sun.

...

Night fell, offering no relief. The air was cold and frigid, with a biting wind that froze Daniel to his core. Somehow, he had survived death, but that offered little comfort; he was still lost in a barren wasteland. Rising to his feet, he pushed on, now hindered by the night. Daniel noticed that his clothes were slightly damp. He had wandered into a dense grey fog. It offered no relief from the cold, but brought a silvery glow that lit the area around him. The ground now felt hard and firm, and the sinking sand was gone. This filled him with a bit of hope, but the burden on his bones, muscles, and mind ached under the strain of this land. He knew that he had to find shelter, but with such poor visibility, all he could do was fumble about and pray for luck to find him.

Daniel's foot caught the edge of something, and he lurched forward, tumbling to the ground. Pain exploded in every atom of his exhausted body. He screamed in agony. He lay still for a moment, trying to catch his breath. Slowly, he looked about to see what he had tripped on. In the dim light, he saw an old splintered wooden plank, and next to it was the broken remains of a garden fence. He thought a house must be nearby and found renewed energy fuelled by hope of rest.

He followed the fence line until its end, where only broken remains lay scattered on the ground. Daniel fell to his knees, deflated. *What's the point?* But then a flickering light not too far off to his right caught his attention. He forgot all caution and raced, stumbling over debris, towards the light. He appeared to cross a threshold where the damp mist would not follow. Set in the centre of this clearing, a lantern hung, fixed to the top of a plain rusty post. Its flame blazed fiercely and glowed with unearthly energy. It seemed to be consuming the shadows and pushing back the thick fog.

Daniel's spirit was lifted, and as the glimmer of the light warmed him, he found a place to rest. His weariness lifted slightly, and the pains of his journey diminished. Just behind the lamp, illuminated by its glow, was an old log cabin creaking and groaning with visible age. It was covered in a green vine-like plant similar to ivy, and small flowers sprouted from its stem. Daniel stared in wonderment; colour was something he had forgotten in this place. It was like a veil suddenly lifted. His eyes were drawn to splashes of green grass and even tiny flowers scattered about, bringing a welcomed beauty to this barren land.

A crumbling wall stretched around its perimeter and was covered in what looked like bright yellow moss and golden lichen. As Daniel watched, it seemed to creep and spread as though sentient. This place felt like an oasis, a beacon to life and light in a sea of gloomy despair. He stared back towards the surrounding fog that groped its borders and shuddered at the thought of ever having to return. The cabin was only eight or nine feet high and perhaps only three times as wide. Its walls were cracked and weathered, its roof sagging and patched, but it had a welcoming aura that drew Daniel in. It stood alone in this strange oasis, a safe resting place for weary travellers. He pushed on the door, and it groaned open.

Inside the cabin was a single room, nearly empty apart from a few pieces of furniture. A round table was pushed against one wall, and a well-worn chair sat by it. Daniel thought it looked like many people had sat there, possibly contemplating their journey and escape. Against the far wall stood a tall cupboard which dominated the room. Its doors were missing, shelves empty, and it now only served as a reminder of how bare this land was. Occupying the last wall was a dusty bed. It looked archaic and had seen better days; nevertheless, it was a welcome sight for Daniel's tired bones. A small fire danced and crackled playfully in the hearth. Its soft, low glow filled the space with warmth and a golden flickering light. Wisps of smoke filled the air, and he inhaled the smoky aroma. There was no sign of whoever tended the fire or owned the cabin, but it was clear that they wanted to offer help to any passersby. The shack was a refuge from the creatures and dangers of this land, a place where travellers could rest and recover before continuing on their journey. Daniel lay on the bed, staring at the dancing shadows, listening to the gentle crackle, like a lullaby leading him to slumber. He felt comforted as his pains drifted away. Happy memories of home filled his thoughts, and he fell into a peaceful sleep.

Daniel felt refreshed and happy when he arose, almost forgetting all his hardships. He noticed a long overcoat hanging on the back of the chair. It looked old and tatty and worn but warm. He was sure it wasn't there when he had first arrived; still, it would offer shelter from the cold fog, so he put it on, giving thanks to the mysterious benefactor. He left the shelter of the cabin only to be reminded of his situation: the ageing lantern still burned with its eternal flame, and the ominous fog still hungered to devour the refuge. He knew he had to find an escape, even though he felt reluctant to leave this place. Driven by curiosity or the hope of finding something to help him, he started to look around the area.

He discovered an ancient graveyard behind the cabin, perfectly hidden in its shadow. It appeared to be ensnared by a derelict stone wall, acting as a perimeter guard to keep people out, or perhaps something in. Mounds of disturbed earth lined with gravestones were strewn about, some teetering on their foundations, most weathered beyond recognition and crumbling around the edges. An eerie stillness hung over the place as if time had stopped here long ago. It was cold, dreary, and desolate, untouched by the lantern's light. Daniel stepped through a collapsed part of the wall into the graveyard, driven by a need to pay his respects to those whose journey led them to this sad end. He knelt before a small, eroded headstone whose words were still partially visible. It read: *Bernadette, gone but not forgotten.*

A sorrowful chill washed over him as he stared at her name. Daniel wondered who she was and why she should be damned to be buried in this forsaken land. He suddenly felt like he was being watched; a chill descended upon him as a heavy weight of dread settled deep within his soul. He felt eyes on him from all directions, as though his presence had awoken those who slept here. Voices of the many travellers that fell in this place echoed about him like a whirling breeze, whispers crying out in anguish. He heard dreadful scraping sounds as the lost souls of those who had fallen clawed their way through the darkness to find him, desperate for escape from their cursed prison. Suddenly, the sound of agony and despair was swallowed by an oppressive silence.

Daniel shuddered and stood to leave but felt held in place. There stood by the headstone a ghostly figure of a child. She was pale and translucent, like a misty apparition. She wore a tattered dress and her long, dark hair hung motionless about her. Her eyes were hollow and sad, and she stared at him with a silent plea. Daniel felt a chill run through his spine as he met her gaze.

"Bernadette?" Daniel whispered cautiously.

The apparition looked at him unblinking, eyes heavy with sorrow. She looked longingly at him but craved his freedom; she wanted to be free.

"Why are you here?" Daniel asked, feeling her desperation.

She spoke to him, but no words were said; instead, a fog of confusion engulfed Daniel's mind, and when it cleared away, he found himself standing at the precipice of a cliff. The night sky was a blanket of black velvet, so deep and dark that not even the faintest glimmer of a star could be seen. A crimson full moon hung ominously in the otherwise empty expanse, casting a sickly glow over the landscape below and illuminating everything with its malevolent presence. A frigid wind blew in from the sea and howled about him, and he was briefly hit with the smell of lavender, as though it had been carried from some far-off place to offer a moment of comfort. Yet, a feeling of foreboding intensified as he saw strange silhouettes slowly appear from the darkness behind him, their long shadows trailing them in a ghostly procession.

As they drew nearer, Daniel saw that they were hooded, robed figures all clad in black except for one wearing a deep purple robe. They arranged themselves around an area of ground stained with dried blood, creating a semi-circle before leading a petrified girl into its centre. Her eyes had taken on an empty glaze, as if captured by a mesmerising spell. The priest standing in front uttered words that seemed to reverberate through time itself, repeating each one until the entire gathering joined in one unified chant. Then, raising his blade to the moon's blood-red light, he thunderingly declared an invocation that unlocked some invisible power just before the shimmering tip came slicing down towards Bernadette.

Daniel gasped and stumbled backwards, steadying himself on a gravestone. Bernadette raised her hand, imploring him to help. Daniel took her hand, expecting it to pass through his fingers like smoke, but to his shock, she solidified before him. Her spectral form dissipated into the air, and she appeared alive before him, her eyes pleading for salvation.

"I..." Bernadette's words appeared difficult to

say. "I…nee…d…hel…p." Each sound appeared to bring her pain.

"I will, I promise," Daniel said, looking into Bernadette's desperate eyes.

They started to make their way to the break in the wall where Daniel had entered, but it seemed to move farther away from them with every step. Suddenly, a wall of fog descended around them, bringing a chill to the air that reached deep into his bones. It was as if the fog had sentient intent, thickening and pressing in on them as though it did not want them to escape. Daniel pushed forward resolutely, Bernadette following close behind him, fear etched into her face.

Daniel felt something wrap around his ankles, cold and unforgiving as iron shackles. He at once tried to free his legs, but the grip only tightened. Another hand clamped down on his shoulder, followed by another that grabbed his arm, and soon Daniel was on his knees with a vicelike force pinning him in place. Despite all this, he refused to surrender Bernadette's hand, clutching her tightly in desperation; he would not let go. Rage welled in him, and he punched with feral intensity, smashing through something intangible in the fog. His free hand stumbled upon a thick, long, dead branch, grasped it tightly, and swung it with all his might, shattering the air around him with bone-breaking force. The sickening sound of breaking bones echoed into the night as he advanced, wielding his makeshift weapon before him in a crazed fury.

Suddenly, the fog cleared before them, and he could see the way out. However, one foe blocked their path. A creature whose grotesque form was sickening in its horror rose high. It was an amalgamation of bones and rotting corpses, with a multitude of black eyes that stared at Daniel with clear malice intent. Its many mouths salivated with a longing to devour Daniel's soul, and the smell of rotting flesh, mingled with the acrid stench of sulphur, lingered in the air, which filled Daniel with revulsion. It shrieked with a blood-curdling sound that reverberated throughout the graveyard. Daniel turned to Bernadette and reassuringly smiled; he would not fail in his promise. He charged forward to certain doom, refusing to forsake Bernadette to her fate. However, this was a battle he could not win, and with one swoop of a giant rotting arm, Daniel flew through the air, crashing to the ground. The moment he released Bernadette's trembling hand, her body morphed back into a spectral mist. He lunged forward to try and save her, but it was too late. The earth beneath her cracked open with a thunderous roar as ghostly claws appeared from the depths of the abyss. They snatched her away in an instant, leaving only a wailing echo of anguish and despair reverberating in the air. Before his eyes, Daniel watched as Bernadette vanished forever into the clutches of torment.

The beast cackled with delight, enjoying Daniel's anguish, as its arm raised high and descended hard in one swift motion, missing him as he sidestepped the blow. The opening beckoned again, and this time, Daniel didn't hesitate. He tore away from the creature and sprinted towards the exit. The monstrosity swung at him once more, but he sprang aside. With a final effort, he hurled past the monster and collapsed back into the soft glow of the lantern, gasping for breath.

Daniel turned, and to his shock, the creature had vanished, and the graveyard looked undisturbed, precisely as he had first found it. As he gazed at the graveyard, he briefly inspected his wounds only to realise they were gone. At first, he thought it might be the healing effect of the lantern's glow. But as he continued to stare at the eerie surroundings, he began to wonder if it was all a dream. Bernadette's face came to his mind, and he couldn't help but question if she was even real. His attention was stolen when he heard his name being called. Turning from the graveyard and listening intently, he was greeted with only the sound of the wind. Now convinced that it was his imagination, he decided to return to the safety of the cabin, wanting to get away from the shadowy graveyard.

However, the voice again found him; this time, it was clear and distinct. "Daniel," it said. Someone or something was beckoning him to follow.

The sound led him farther away from the light of the lantern, and as he walked, its warm glow dimmed, and the air grew darker and colder. Soon, he met the perimeter of the lantern's gaze and stopped at the border where the fog lingered on its outskirts. Daniel stood there considering whether he should venture back or continue. Staring into the swirling mist before him, it appeared to thin slightly; at least, that's what he wanted to believe. The voice called to him again; it didn't feel like there was any hidden malice, so he stepped tentatively into the fog. It was chilly and damp, but seemed less malicious than last time. He cautiously moved forward. The ground was a little uneven but possible to traverse, even in the dim silvery haze that radiated from the mist. Soon enough, the light of the lantern disappeared into obscurity, leaving him uncertain whether he had made the right decision. The voice beckoned again, and he advanced forward, continuing towards the unknown destination.

After he had walked for some time, he entered a clearing, and the mist parted like a curtain as he stepped into the open space. Daniel's eyes widened at the sight of a massive, lifeless tree, its dry and brittle limbs twisted and bent in grotesque shapes. Its knotted form gave it a sinister aura. Its gnarly roots stretched out from it, in places breaking through the surface of the ground as though it had once tried to find escape. It loomed over the area, casting a dark shadow against the backdrop of the silvery mist.

A mist billowed around his feet, and Daniel felt a chill run through his body as he slowly circled the tree. As he looked closer, he noticed something strange about it: markings were carved all over the trunk and branches. It looked like some kind of ancient script or

THE FINAL JOURNEY

language, impossible for Daniel to read or understand. He ran his fingers over one of the symbols, following the characters' deep channels; as he did, the voice called to him again, but it seemed to echo from a far-off place.

"Hello?" he said, his voice falling dead in the eerie stillness as he looked out towards the fog.

Once again, he touched the symbols, and the voice sounded, but this time, it seemed to come from the tree itself. Then the characters started to glow dimly; each symbol was filled with soft golden light that pulsated slowly. A silvery vapour started to bleed out from the marks. It swirled about the tree before it drifted to Daniel and danced around him softly. He watched the swirls, and it filled him with peace. Suddenly, a blaze of dazzling white light erupted from the tree. Daniel stumbled back, shielding his eyes.

"Daniel," spoke a gentle yet powerful voice, "I have been waiting for you."

"Who are you?" Daniel asked, dazzled by the light.

"I have many names. You may call me Efanu;

I am light, I am life." And with those words, the ground around him burst forth with life: grasses, flowers, bushes, and shrubs, all kinds of life flourished where there had only been death moments before.

The light dimmed slightly, and an outline of a figure could be seen. Daniel stood up, but before he could speak, his mind was filled with images of light and dark, good and evil, and an eternal battle to maintain a cosmic balance. He felt as if all the secrets of the universe had been revealed to him at that moment, overwhelming his senses with knowledge beyond human comprehension.

"I don't understand," Daniel managed to say, his head spinning from the vision he had been shown.

"You must complete the journey. The cycle must continue," Efanu said in a voice that seemed to echo with great strength and wisdom.

"Why?" Daniel asked, confused. "What journey?"

"It is your path. Only you carry the answer to the question that cannot be answered, you are the seed."

"What question? What do you mean seed?" Daniel desperately asked.

"Life must meet death to meet life once more." It paused. "It is your journey. You must awaken."

Daniel went to speak again, but as quickly as the being appeared, it vanished, as did the life it had born, leaving Daniel alone with nothing but his racing thoughts. The images of the vision all bled from thought, leaving a feeling of emptiness, of forgotten truth. The gloom returned; somehow, he felt worse after feeling the warmth that the being had cast over this place. *Am I dead?* he thought, lost in contemplation.

He stood there staring at the dead tree. The symbols had disappeared, but he noticed that there was now a tiny opening in the trunk. Daniel reached in and found a small cotton drawstring bag. It looked like it had been there for a very long time. The material was blotched with stains and looked worn. He sat back against the tree and pulled open the bag. In the bag was a photograph of a tall, slim, middle-aged man, and next to him was a young girl; she looked a little like Aya. They stood before a red, round clay-brick house with a straw roof. Daniel stared at the girl for some time, wondering if she could be Aya, but the photo looked very old, as though it was taken before she would have even been born.

He noticed that on the back was written:

The Great Union
One becomes Two,
Light and Shadow.
One becomes All,
The seed is sown anew.

Life shall meet Death,
Death shall meet Life,
At Journey's end,
All must reunite.

Daniel read the words, but they brought no meaning to him. He put the photo down and reached into the bag again. All that was left was a small blue sapphire pendant. He was confused, but a realisation dawned on him, and he smiled. He had seen this before, in his flat; it belonged to Aya. What was it doing here? Still, he was grateful for it; he felt that, in some way, she was with him in this desolate place.

"Thank you," he whispered.

THE FINAL JOURNEY

He returned the items to the bag and placed them in his coat pocket. Daniel felt hesitant as he looked towards the fog; the thought of venturing back into that cold, dreary mist filled him with dread. However, he knew he had to continue. He decided upon a direction and set out on his way. He looked back towards the house for the last time and said a quiet farewell. The fog was no less menacing. However, he felt warm thanks to the gift of the coat and the thought of Aya's pendant.

As Daniel walked through the thick blanket of fog, his steps were unsteady, and he stumbled on loose stones and uneven ground. He felt frustrated with his lack of progress and couldn't tell if he was moving in a straight line. Even if he was, he had no idea if he was heading in the right direction, or even if a right direction existed. He was surprised to find that the bag in his pocket was warm. Upon checking, he discovered that the pendant inside was glowing slightly. He took it out and held it up. The glow spread around him, pushing back the fog, similar to the lantern by the cabin. As he moved the pendant around, he noticed that it shone brighter when he moved it in a specific direction. Intrigued, he followed it to see where it would lead him. It sliced through the fog, illuminating his path and making the walk much more manageable since he could now see the ground beneath his feet. He continued to follow the pendant's guidance for what may have been hours or even days; there was no way for him to tell. Time seemed stagnant here, and the warmth of the coat and pendant seemed to ease his fatigue.

The ground beneath his feet eventually changed; he realised he had found a narrow, cobbled pathway. He continued walking with his head down and his eyes fixed ahead. He didn't dare take his eyes off the path. His footsteps were loud in contrast to the silence surrounding him. On either side of the pathway were lanterns, but they were not lit. They appeared to have lost their lustre long ago, in the distant past. Amidst the eerie silence, distant screams and indescribable sounds intermittently shattered the stillness. Daniel was overcome with a sudden urge to run, gripped by a fleeting terror of the unknown. However, he resisted the urge to run aimlessly and lose his bearings. He tried to focus on anything other than the haunting nightmares that lurked within the murky fog.

Daniel walked along the foggy path, wondering where it would lead. In the distance, he saw a dim glow; as he approached, he came across an old wooden bench. It was dimly illuminated by a struggling lantern overhead. Glad for the chance to rest, he sat down and contemplated his situation. Where was he being led?

Suddenly, he heard footsteps approaching, echoing from farther up the path. Startled, he stood up and looked around but saw nothing. The footsteps faded, and after a moment, he sat down, only to find an odd-looking man sitting there. He jumped at the surprise. The man ignored Daniel as he appeared to be rummaging through his bag. He noticed the man's rough appearance, with wild and unkempt hair. He wore a long, old coat and had an intense, almost mad look in his eyes. The man's face was sharp and well-defined, with high cheekbones and a thin, pointed nose. As Daniel stared at him, a sense of familiarity washed over him.

"Ah-ha!" the man said as he pulled out a cigarette, followed by a box of matches. He carefully lit the match and brought the flame to the end, watching as it ignited with a bright orange glow. He leaned back on the bench, savouring the restful moment, and took a long, slow drag from the cigarette. The smoke filled his lungs, the taste of tobacco mingling with the stale air. As he exhaled, a thick plume of smoke escaped his lips, dissipating into the air like a ghostly apparition. The man closed his eyes, enjoying the moment of respite.

Finally, he looked at Daniel. "Hello again, Daniel," he said.

Daniel remained quiet, not knowing whether this man could be trusted. There were creatures lurking in the shadows who would lure weary travellers to their demise.

"You don't remember me, do you?" the man said, drawing from his cigarette again and slowly exhaling.

"No," Daniel simply said.

The man laughed. "Well, this is a different life, a different... Well, it's all different now."

"Well," Daniel said and paused, "you feel familiar. Like a thought I just can't see clearly."

"That's a good start." He smiled, and Daniel instantly felt at ease. "What do you remember?"

Daniel sat back on the bench and stared up at the lantern. It seemed to permeate his mind, like the glow lit up places in his thoughts hidden in shadow.

"You knew my father," Daniel finally said.

"Yes, I did," the man said, a hint of sadness in his eyes as he remembered a distant memory.

"The coffee shop!" Daniel said, his voice excited as the memory became clear.

"Yes, that was me." He held out his hand. "Zack."

Daniel shook his hand. "Hello again," he said.

"Well, Danny, here we are lost," Zack said, looking about.

"I have no idea how I got here," Daniel said.

"You died," Zack answered, looking solemnly at him. "You died badly and were dragged here."

"I don't remember, I only remember here." Daniel stopped, hesitant. "I remember Aya."

"That's good, very good." Zack smiled and finished his cigarette.

Daniel wondered whether he should show Zack the gift that led him to this location, but thought better of it. "Where is here?" Daniel asked.

Zack looked about. "Here?" he started. "It is one of the realms between Day and Night known as the Land of Shadow." He paused as though he was thinking. "This land is shrouded by a sinister atmosphere. There exists a foreboding fog that engulfs all it smothers. This dark, evil, menacing fog creeps between twisted and gnarled trees, stretching its ethereal tendrils over the desolate terrain. It is as if the very air itself becomes thick with malevolence when this fog descends. There is a desert that turns all that dare to cross into ash, burning away your very soul in perpetual fire. There are forests where the trees linger neither alive nor dead, where unspeakable monsters roam in search of prey. Finally, the barren wastelands, a hollow, empty place that drives madness into all who are lost there. I think you would prefer the other place, the Land of Light." He laughed morbidly. "These are realms that exist between life and death. They have been called many other names, such as heaven and hell. You see, you were in the other world, which was the Realm of Day, where all that lives exists." He looked for another cigarette. "However, all that lives must eventually end, and that's when they enter the Realm of

Night." He lit his cigarette and drew from it. "You follow?"

Daniel nodded but was still considering his words.

"Now, when a soul leaves the land of life, they enter the land of death, where they wait in slumber until the whole thing starts again." Zack sat back. "However, you have a different path and have arrived here. I think you know why," he said with sadness.

"I have so many questions. Who are you? How were my parents involved with all this?" Daniel asked desperately.

"Me?" Zack said. "I am a Traveller, and that is what I do. You could say it is my purpose, and your parents had theirs."

"Purpose?" Daniel paused. "What is a Traveller?"

"We are able to traverse the realms," Zack said, "and as for purpose, well, we all have a purpose."

Daniel thought about this, then fell into confusion. "I don't remember how I arrived here."

"Probably for the best," Zack said. "Remember, everything must end before it can begin again."

"You mean reincarnation?" Daniel asked.

"Yes," Zack answered.

"So, when does it all end?" Daniel asked, questions filling his mind.

"Well, it comes when the one soul collapses the cycle, causing it all to begin again, and this goes on forever."

"The Great Union," Daniel said, recalling what he had been told.

Zack looked surprised. "Yes, exactly."

"So, who is this one soul?" Daniel asked hesitantly.

Zack remained silent, choosing to avoid the question. Daniel looked away, knowing the answer.

"Something is wrong, it is broken, the whole thing is broken!" Zack suddenly snarled. "It is trying to stop the union, and I don't know why!"

"Who is?"

"You know who, Danny," Zack said.

The image of a cold, dark Shadow loomed in his mind, and he shuddered. "Shadow," Daniel whispered.

Zack nodded sombrely.

"What is the Shadow?" Daniel asked.

"It is from the Realm of Night; it is part of everything, as is Light. However, it feels corrupted, and fights against the natural order, it wants to stop…" His words faded.

"Me," Daniel whispered.

Zack looked at Daniel and rested his hand on his shoulder. "I'm sorry," he said.

"For what?" Daniel said.

"I was meant to protect you and your father and dear mother, but I failed." Zack looked away, a deep sorrow welling inside him.

They sat quietly for what could have been a lifetime, then Daniel broke the silence.

"Where do I go now?" Daniel asked, staring out into the fog.

Zack turned to him, locking his gaze. "The gift

you carry is special, and it will take you where you need to be. Hold onto it and never let it go."

Daniel was surprised he knew about the pendant. Had he put it there?

"It led me here," Daniel said.

"I know, and it will protect you and guide you. Trust it with your life," Zack said. "Where did you find it?"

Daniel was surprised Zack didn't know, as he appeared to know much about this place.

"A being came to me," Daniel said.

"Efanu." Zack smiled.

"Yes, how did you know?"

"Who else would risk coming here?" Zack said.

"Who is Efanu?" Daniel asked.

"Efanu, or some call her Efa, is Light of the Realm of Day, bringing balance to Miozu, who is Shadow from the Realm of Night." A look of disdain spread over his face. "Some call him Ozul," he spat out as though bad memories flooded his thoughts. He paused and composed himself. "Well, anyway, that is another tale. Together, Efanu and Miozu create balance in this reality."

"This reality?" Daniel asked.

Zack smiled. "I have read that two other realities exist, but that is perhaps for another time."

"Why can't Efanu bring back balance?" Daniel said.

"One cannot defeat the other. That is the way of things. However, Miozu is trying to by attacking the one soul," Zack said, concern lacing his voice.

"So, what now?" Daniel said, slumping back.

"Danny, you will always be where you are meant to be, have faith in that. There are some things that are written, and I believe that cannot change. At least, that is what I hope." Zack stood up.

"Will you come with me?" Daniel asked.

Zack looked down at him. "I cannot. Where I must go, I must go alone. We all have our part to play." He turned away, then stopped. "I hope we will meet again before the end."

"I would have liked the company," Daniel

sighed heavily.

Zack walked away slowly, disappearing into the fog and leaving Daniel alone on the bench. His voice echoed back to Daniel as if coming from a far-off place, "Don't stay here too long. They are looking for you." Then silence returned.

His last words filled Daniel with concern. *Who's looking for me?* He left the bench and the lantern's dim glow, raised his pendant again, and followed its direction. The lantern was soon out of sight, and only the soft glow of the pendant kept the fog from consuming him. He walked on, and after a while, he had the familiar feeling that he was being watched, like creatures hid in the fog waiting to pounce. His pace slowed, and he stopped walking altogether. He was frozen to the spot, barely able to breathe. A humanoid-like creature appeared down the path before him, its menacing silhouette blocking his way. He thought he saw giant tentacles extending from it briefly, but the fog quickly obscured his view. Daniel advanced cautiously, each step intentional. The pendant led him off the path, but Daniel felt uneasy about entering the fog. He decided to continue on the path, hoping to find help, ignoring the pendant.

THE FINAL JOURNEY

He reached a fork in the road. The left-hand path stretched into the distance, appearing to be without end. However, when Daniel looked along the right-hand path, he could see the outlines of buildings silhouetted by the thick, foggy air. He headed right, and as he did, his pendant dimmed and cooled slightly. Again, Daniel ignored its warnings.

The town was not what he hoped. Life had long left this place; only gloomy, haunting reminders of the silent ravages of time remained. It had only a single street. Anything else that may have once existed was now long gone, returned to dust. Buildings stood lifeless, crumbling, windows shattered, and streets littered with the remains of a life that had died aeons before. Streetlights lay scattered and broken, their radiance long extinguished, a bleak reminder that hope would not be found here. There was no life to be seen, just the skeletal blades of grass stretching up through fractured roads like fingers waiting to ensnare anyone who ventured too close and dark vines wrapping around the structures like tentacles from some malevolent creature. To Daniel's surprise, one house was left at the end of the dismal street. He noticed a soft candlelight flickering through its windows, beckoning him to come closer. Although the pendant had dimmed further and seemed to warn him to turn back, his curiosity and hope pushed him to approach the house.

An elderly man sat on a porch, watching quietly as Daniel approached, but gave no sign of whether he would be welcoming or not. His long hair and beard were grey and weathered, and he appeared frail and undernourished, as if he hadn't eaten in a long time. His appearance was feeble, and it seemed like the passing years had not been generous to him. Daniel raised his hands in a gesture of peace, but the man remained motionless and expressionless. Deciding to leave the person alone, Daniel turned to go.

"Where are you headed? Did you come all this way just to leave?" inquired the elderly man, his voice as ancient as the town.

"Sorry, I thought that you may not want the company," Daniel replied.

"Company?" the figure said. "Company comes and goes, goes and comes, rarely stays."

Daniel was unsure how to respond, so he simply smiled and nodded.

"So, what do you want?" the figure asked, a

harsh tone hidden beneath the surface.

"I'm looking for a way out of here," Daniel said.

"We are always where we are meant to be," the old man said. "You will come to know many things soon. Some will lift you, and some may not." He laughed, but there was no warmth in his voice.

Daniel remained silent.

"You were brought here for a reason, Daniel. Trust your instincts," he leant forward, "but sometimes we forget to take the right path." A curious grin spread across his face, making Daniel uneasy. "My name is Rashi Apollyon. Come sit with me."

Daniel hesitantly sat on a chair that seemed to have been placed there as though Rashi had expected his arrival. A small wooden table sat between them, and on it were two glasses and a bottle of what looked like wine. Rashi gestured to Daniel to pour.

"You will drink with me, Daniel?" Rashi asked.

Daniel was surprised. "How did you know my name?"

"Let me stop you. I see far and wide in this

place. I saw your coming. I see your leaving," Rashi said and picked up a glass. "To your health!" His arm appeared weak and trembled under the weight of the glass.

Rashi watched Daniel's every move, eyes narrowing in anticipation as he slowly reached out and grabbed the second glass. Daniel could feel time stretching around them as they raised the glasses towards each other. The glasses clinked as they met; it was the slightest of touches, yet an explosion of sound reverberated, echoing like a thunderous boom that seemed to ripple through the entire space.

"Now drink!" Rashi suddenly demanded and emptied the glass.

Daniel felt a strange compulsion to do the same and drank the thick crimson liquid. It scorched his throat with raw heat, and he felt it spread through his body like molten lava. He clutched his throat and stood up, trying to scream, but no sound could escape his lips. The world spun about him, and he fell to the ground; he looked up through watery, blurry eyes. Rashi stood before him, no longer frail but tall and powerful. His eyes were black as night, his skin the deepest blood-red, and his lipless mouth revealed two long fangs.

Long coal-black hair flowed where there was once grey hair, revealing a timeless creature untouched by age. Daniel crawled to the edge of the porch and gazed upon an inferno; fire ravaged the town, and he heard screams and saw torment everywhere.

Suddenly, with an angry roar, Rashi shoved Daniel aside and leapt off the porch to confront an unexpected visitor. A short humanoid creature stood in the street who appeared to be standing in shadow against the backdrop of the burning town. Rashi bounded to meet it and towered over it in height. They seemed to be exchanging harsh words, but Daniel couldn't understand their language. Through blurry vision, he saw Rashi's stature rise. He appeared to grow menacingly, but the creature seemed undeterred. Directly peering at Daniel, a pair of dark eyes pierced out of the silhouetted figure, and the creature moved towards him. Daniel tried to crawl away, but the pain locked him in place. Suddenly, Rashi grabbed the creature and threw it back, crashing into a burning building that collapsed in a plume of black smoke and tall red flames.

A moment later, the building exploded, sending rubble flying through the air in a fiery haze of smoke. The creature stepped from the ashes and dust. It writhed about, seeming to curse violently. Long tentacle-like arms sprouted out from its spine. It grew taller, its legs crooked yet strong. It leapt high in the air and came crashing down on Rashi, who screamed a terrible sound. Though wounded, Rashi was not so easily triumphed over.

"This is my domain, Darkling!" Rashi roared. Then thousands of ant-like creatures, once human but twisted and broken through aeons of torture, erupted like an exploding volcano from the ruins and attacked the dark creature. They crawled on all fours, and within seconds had encompassed the Darkling.

The Darkling lashed out with its tentacles, flailing about, tearing its attackers to pieces with razor-sharp claws. Bodies were torn to shreds and thrown like ragdolls. Clutching a deep gash in his side, Rashi leapt towards the dark creature, baring his teeth. He charged, fangs dripping with a vengeance, and he bit down on the Darkling. Black blood burst from the wound, and it let out a high shrill that caused Daniel to spasm in pain. Claws whipped around, pierced Rashi in the back, split him open, and threw him aside. The Darkling stumbled to the ground as another onslaught of ant-like creatures tore into it.

Mortally wounded, Rashi lay on the ground, his organs scattered about him. "This is my domain," Rashi roared as blood spat from his mouth. He looked at Daniel. "Next time!" And he raised his hand.

There was a flash of light, and Daniel was no longer in the burning town. Instead, the town was lifeless and derelict as it was when he had first arrived. Rashi and the visitor were now gone, leaving him alone on the porch of a broken house. Daniel struggled to move, but the pain overwhelmed him.

"Drink this, son," a familiar voice said.

Daniel turned to see Zack standing over him. He appeared as though he was translucent. He held a golden flask, offering a small bottle of liquid to Daniel's lips and slowly pouring it into his mouth. The cool, refreshing liquid instantly eased his pain, and he sighed in relief.

"Trust in the pendant," Zack said kindly.

Daniel struggled to his feet and turned to speak to Zack, but he had gone; only the smell of lavender lingered in the air. He removed the pendant from the bag and held it up. As he moved it around, it started to glow bright, lighting a route. This time, Daniel followed. He left the town and followed the light of the pendant. It led Daniel back onto the cobbled path. He turned back the way he had come, retracing his steps before leaving to follow a dirt path into the dense fog. The pendant cut through the oppressive atmosphere, clearly lighting his way. Daniel walked for several miles with ease; the pendant seemed to be leading him over easy terrain. The journey was uneventful, and as he walked, the pendant drew him to memories of his family and friends. Still, in the end, it was always Aya who filled his thoughts, and he longed to be with her more now than ever.

As he walked, the ground beneath his feet began to feel soft and muddy in some areas. He started to jump over small puddles that dotted the path ahead. The fog had started to retreat, revealing patches of tall trees. They had perished long ago, yet they appeared alive as they swayed with an eerie rhythm, their branches twisted as if in perpetual agony. He eventually came across a small stream, which he managed to cross, keeping his feet dry. Gradually, the fog retreated further until it had dissipated entirely, revealing an open grassland. The grass was not a lush shade of green, but instead an arid yellow. No signs of life littered the ground, and only the hiss of the wind that whispered ominously filled the air.

Daniel could now see the sky again, but it still had a gloomy, ominous presence, bringing him no comfort. He made his way across the dry grassland, following the pendant as his guide, until he reached the top of a tall hill. From this vantage point, he paused to take in the surroundings. In the distance, he could see the fog lurking like a disappointed child. The grassland appeared to stretch out endlessly before him. Daniel lifted the pendant once more, and its light shone brightly.

Daniel walked down the hill following the pendant's guidance. He tried to remain hopeful; however, he felt that something was following him. He turned to see only the endless grasslands as the wind continued to whisper.

"You are lost," a voice hissed into his ear. Daniel turned, but no one was there. "Go back," it said again.

Daniel stopped, startled as he looked for the source but was alone.

"Who's there?" Daniel called out, but no reply came.

"She has gone. You cannot find her. She is lost," the voice hissed.

"Who are you?" Daniel shouted out, looking about, but still no one was there. He started to run, trying his best to follow the pendant's guidance.

"That little thing cannot help you. It does nothing. It is a trick," the voice said.

"No, no," Daniel said, "you're lying. Go away!"

"Danny, I want to help you. All the people you have ever known have all lied to you," the voice said.

"They wouldn't. Go away!" Daniel said, panic racing through him.

"They all want you to fail. Especially her," it hissed low. "She wants you to fail."

"No, that's a lie," Daniel said, feeling confusion welling up.

"Is it?" the voice whispered. "She didn't listen, she didn't protect your daughter."

Daniel stopped in his tracks and screamed in

anguish, falling to his knees.

"She never wanted it. She wanted to travel, but that held her back. She is a liar!" the voice snapped.

"She said she wanted to be a mother," Daniel said, his voice barely a whimper.

"She said, she said," the voice mocked. "She is a liar!" it screeched.

Snake-like vines sprouted from the ground and slowly crept towards Daniel.

"No, she loved me. She loved me, she loved me," Daniel said, confused and angry.

"She only loved herself. That pendant has led you here to your death. She is a liar! They all are liars!" it hissed harshly. "Zack lied to you. He wants you to die!"

"I'm not sure," Daniel said. "I…don't…remember…anymore."

The vines gently took hold of him, binding him with a deathly strength, but he did not fight. A vine snapped forward, knocking the pendant from his hand, and he fell to the ground. The black snake-like vines wound around his body like a cocoon, trapping him in their embrace.

"Sleep, Daniel. Dream and I will find you," the voice whispered.

Daniel opened his eyes as the cabin shook violently. Both Zack and Daniel were thrown to the ground. The fire went out, and a Shadow loomed over the room.

"You must awake!" Zack yelled at Daniel. "It has you!"

"Who has me?" Daniel shouted out, his voice barely audible above the noise of the chaos that ensued about them.

Zack scrambled to his feet and grabbed his staff. "Light!" he screamed, and a burning flame reared out from the top of his staff, pushing back the Shadow, which screeched in defiance.

"Daniel, you must find a way back or you will be lost!" Zack shouted whilst pulling Daniel to his feet.

A ghostly limb swiped at Zack, knocking him back against the wall. Daniel rushed over to him; however, a shadowy hand grabbed him, lifting him up and squeezing him tight. He clawed at the grip around his waist but found

THE FINAL JOURNEY

nothing he could hold. The Shadow had no solid form.

Zack had clambered to his feet. "Back, Shadow, you are not welcome here!" he said in a commanding voice. A beam of fiery light shot from his staff, tearing into the shadow, which wailed in pain and dropped Daniel, who crashed down onto the table.

"Run, Daniel, now!" Zack pointed to the wall, and an opening appeared. "The forest, there you must find a way back! Now go!"

With a wave of Zack's hand, Daniel was thrown through the opening and out of the cabin. He lay on the ground outside and turned to see the cabin engulfed by a shadowy beast. It was hammering at the cabin with such rage and hatred. Daniel could hear Zack's voice shouting inside and flashes of light piercing the Shadow.

Then there was an explosion of light, and the beast screamed in anguish. Then silence. The cabin was gone, as was the beast. All that remained was a crater where the cabin once stood and wisps of silvery mist floating to the ground.

Zack's last words echoed in Daniel's mind:

the forest. It was a dark and ancient place, a reflection of the world of the living. The trees appeared lifeless, their trunks twisted and gnarled, their branches intertwined like vines that reached out to ensnare the unwary traveller. A deathly silence hung over the forest; not even the breeze dared to enter. The air was cold and damp, filled with the scent of decay and rot. No living thing dared to tread in the forest, for it was a place of shadows and secrets, where the past lingered and the present feared to tread. Where nightmares haunted every dark place, and only death awaited those foolish enough to venture in.

The ground was cool, cradling him as the voice whispered, "It will all be okay, Danny. Sleep and dream."

Daniel stood at the edge of the forest, and as he stared, he wondered what dark things lay waiting for him. He shuddered; he couldn't shake the feeling that something gazed back.

Still, there was no other way. He had to follow Zack's words.

However, there didn't appear to be any way in. The trees were like twisted vines knotted tightly together. He walked along the edge, probing the perimeter, but it was sealed; it did not allow trespassers to enter. As he turned to leave, loud snapping rang out behind him, and to his surprise, an opening appeared, and a stone path was revealed. As he entered, the forest groaned, and the opening closed behind him. He was trapped and could now only go farther in.

Daniel walked along the stone path, being careful not to stray. He often had to clear the way of leaves and roots to stay on track. The oppressive surroundings played with his emotions; anger rose in him one moment, and he lashed out. The next, he was overwhelmed with despair and found tears rolling down his cheeks. Soon, the thick, oppressive air of the forest closed in around him. It thickened, and breathing became difficult, clouding his vision. He soon fell into a daze as he struggled forward, trying to remain on the stone path. However, he quickly lost his way in the heavy, foreboding atmosphere. An unseen presence was now leading him. No single pathway remained for long, but instead seemed to shift and warp as though playing a macabre game with him, forever leading him into deeper darkness. Days melted away as he wandered aimlessly, each step taking him closer to something unknown. He trudged onward, soon losing all sense of direction.

Time seemed to stand still as he meandered through a labyrinth of winding pathways shrouded in oppressive shadows. Dead trees lined his path, and the scent of rot and death lingered all about him. With each step forward, a chill ran down his spine as he felt he was being watched by an unknown malevolent force.

In the distance, he heard thunderous noises that broke the heavy silence. Still, his mind drifted away, wandering in a trance, oblivious to the dangers that hunted him.

"Sleep, Daniel, and rest. I have you now," the voice said calmly. "Give yourself to Ozul."

Daniel entered a clearing in the middle of the forest, and the open space slowly brought him from the trance. He stood surrounded by interlocked trees, caging him in with nowhere to run. He felt a chill run through him, and he shuddered. A thick black mist burst behind him, shaking the ground and throwing him forward.

The thick mist swirled around, the wind howled, and the trees trembled. As the mist condensed, a grotesque creature stepped from its shadow. Its form was distorted and misshapen, with a body that seemed to twist and contort unnaturally. It screamed in pain as its limbs snapped into place. Jagged, skeletal protrusions jutted out from its bony limbs. Its flesh was charred and scorched as if it had appeared from the depths of the deepest inferno. Sunken eye sockets gleamed with a hellish red glow, filled with a malevolent intelligence that revealed its demonic origins. Rows of razor-sharp teeth, stained with the blood of countless victims, gnashed together in a perpetual grin of sadistic pleasure. Claws, like elongated, twisted talons, extended from the monster's deformed hands, vicious appendages designed purely for rending flesh and shattering bone with a single swipe. Each claw dripped with a vile acidic substance that sizzled and burned upon contact with the ground.

As this monstrous entity surfaced from the depths of its dark, hellish world, an overwhelming sense of evil and despair filled the air. It had an otherworldly strength, capable of tearing through solid structures. It moved with an unsettling ferocity, each step shaking the ground. Its very existence was a testament to pure demonic malevolence.

"Ozul!" the creature now roared.

Daniel ran, but there was nowhere to run. He

turned to the beast, accepting his fate. The creature grabbed him and cruelly ran a claw across his chest. Daniel screamed out in pain.

"Aya!" Daniel cried out.

The monster sneered and dug a claw in deeper. "Aya has abandoned you! You are alone. I am your eternal torment and you shall never escape!"

Exhausted and without hope, Daniel screamed out, "I give myself to Shadow!"

The beast dropped him to the ground as a dark shadow filled the clearing. The beast cowered in fear, and then there was a whooshing sound and the beast was ripped in two, its blood and organs spread all over the ground.

"You were always destined to be mine. I have you," a calm voice said. "The cycle must end."

CHAPTER 13

A Bright Day
Where there is Day, there is Night.

"It's beautiful here," Aya said.

"Yes, it always is. I like it here," said the little girl.

As they walked through the long, lush sapphire-green grass, the sun shone brightly in the sky, casting a colourful warm haze over the land, seeming to enrich everything it touched with an indescribable vibrancy. Aya ran her hand through the tall blades that reached up to meet her, and they were soft to the touch, tingling her fingers. The trees swayed to the rhythm of a sweet melody carried by the breeze. She smiled; all her stresses faded, and the life she left was now a distant dream, no longer having any meaning.

Animals of all kinds were wandering about, and the little girl ran ahead to play with them, jumping, dancing, and singing at the top of her lungs. Aya was filled with joy and ran over to join in the fun. They danced and playfully chased each other while Aya sang at the top of her lungs. The world around them responded with bursts of colour as flowers erupted everywhere, filling the air with a sweet fragrance.

"So," Aya said, trying to catch her breath, "what can I call you?"

The little girl thought for a moment. "Little Pea." She smiled broadly.

"Little Pea," Aya said as a vague remembrance washed over her, and she stopped, trying to recall a lost memory.

"Don't worry about that," Little Pea said, grabbing Aya by the hand and pulling her to follow.

Aya was led by the young girl, who held her hand tightly as they walked together, singing and giggling. They crossed the field and climbed over a small wooden fence, then followed a path along the edge of another field that appeared to have crops growing in it. Aya didn't recognise the plants growing there. She was amazed at the colours and how the plants seemed to respond to their presence. She reached out to one of the plants, which let out a low bellow, producing a green puff of smoke from its tip that had a very unpleasant pungent smell.

Little Pea warned Aya not to walk too close to them, as they were a little grumpy.

"What are they?" Aya asked, like a child seeing the world for the first time.

"Oh, they are grumpy. I don't like playing with them," Little Pea answered. She leaned in close to Aya and whispered, "I call them Green Stinkers, but don't tell anyone or I'll get into trouble." She laughed and ran ahead, calling Aya to follow.

"Where are we going?" Aya called out, chasing behind.

"You still have things to do." Little Pea giggled.

They left the field and met a broad river. The water raced by, cool and clear. The air smelled fresh and uplifting, and Aya had an urge to jump in, but Little Pea told her off and pulled her to the crossing.

A plain bridge spanned the river, made of simple planks with steel supports. It looked well-trodden, as the planks bore the marks of aeons of travellers that must have used it. They walked onto the bridge when suddenly there was a rumbling, and a giant troll jumped in front of them, blocking their way. It raised its arms high and roared fiercely.

"Only those who give me silver may pass!" the troll bellowed.

Aya turned to run, but Little Pea grabbed her and shook her head, telling Aya to stay put.

"Uglut, out of my way," Little Pea said.

Uglat stamped his feet and roared menacingly, baring his teeth. "Silver or swim!" he growled.

"I haven't got time to play today." Little Pea stamped her foot. "I'll play later."

"You promised to play today." Uglat sat down and slumped his shoulders.

"I will, but I have to take..." Little Pea paused and looked at Aya. "I have to take my mummy to see Eva." She patted Uglat on the head, and he responded with a smile.

"Okay," Uglat said, though feeling a little defeated.

"Look, here is a silver coin. Now can we pass?"

Little Pea handed him a silver coin.

Uglat smiled. "But there are two of you," he added.

"Uglat!" Little Pea said.

"Sorry, you may pass," Uglat said. "Both pass."

Little Pea beckoned Aya to follow, and she cautiously crossed the bridge. As she passed, Uglat gave a toothy smile and waved goodbye. Aya awkwardly waved back.

The bridge led to a small, well-walked path, which they followed for a few miles whilst Little Pea contently hummed quietly to herself. The path widened onto a dusty roadway lined with trees as far as Aya could see. The trees met high above, creating a leafy canopy overhead. The sun flickered through the gaps between the leaves, casting playful shadows onto everything below.

"Where are we going?" Aya asked.

"To see Eva, of course," Little Pea said.

"Eva?" Aya questioned.

"Yes, Eva." Little Pea looked curiously at Aya.

Aya said no more about it. She soon didn't care

where they were going, but instead enjoyed the walk through the beautiful surroundings. A couple children were playing up ahead on the road. They were throwing a small furry ball at each other and giggling.

"Hi," said Little Pea. "This is my mummy."

Aya looked at Little Pea and smiled. "Hello," she said.

"She's Sophie, he's Jacob, and there's Obbo," Little Pea said.

Aya smiled at Sophie and Jacob but looked about for Obbo.

"Obbo, c'mon, say hi," Little Pea said.

Aya gasped as the fuzzy sphere suddenly split open, revealing a tiny creature inside. It looked like a cross between a bunny and a squirrel, with a bushy tail, little hand-like paws, and a wide toothy grin. It greeted her with a cheerful wave, then curled up again and launched itself into the air. Aya caught it in her arms, feeling its soft fur and warm breath. She wondered what kind of animal it was.

Aya looked down at the furry ball, not knowing what she should do. Jacob ran farther up the road, followed by Sophie, and they shouted for her to throw Obbo.

"Obbo loves it, he says he has always wanted to fly," Little Pea said.

Aya threw Obbo, and as he flew through the air, she felt a surge of vitality that made her feel young again. She glanced at her hands and saw they were small and smooth like a child's. She looked at her body and realised she had transformed into a little girl. She felt a joy she had not felt in ages and ran after Obbo, laughing and shouting.

Aya sprinted behind Jacob and Sophie, lifting her arms to snatch Obbo as he soared back. As she grasped him, she heard him giggling. Little Pea chimed in, and Obbo rocketed high, bursting from his curled ball in a blaze of laughter and squeals, only to be caught by Jacob and tossed even higher. Little Pea leapt amazingly and caught him with both hands. She fell to the ground, twisted, and threw Obbo low to Sophie, who scooped him up. Sophie then hurled him into the air. Obbo screamed with delight. Jacob lunged and caught him just in time, saving him from landing in a thorny bush.

They could have played for aeons, lost in a

playground without a care or worry. Until a black bird flew down, landing on a nearby tree.

"Time, time, time," it screeched loudly, instantly ending their game.

"Oh, bother!" Little Pea said and grabbed Aya's hand. "We will have to go."

"I don't want to!" Aya whined. "I want to play."

Sophie, Jacob, and Obbo laughed knowingly.

"We'll see you again soon," Jacob said.

"The game never really ends," added Sophie.

Obbo ran up to Aya and bounced into her arms. "See ya!" he said, and leapt high out of her arms, bouncing down the road, chased by Sophie and Jacob.

In a blink, they were gone, and Aya was herself again.

"C'mon, Eva told me to take you straight to her," Little Pea said.

After walking for a little while, Little Pea stopped and turned to Aya.

"You need to go down that path," Little Pea

said, pointing to a trail leading off the road and into the woods.

"You're not coming?" Aya asked.

"I will see you afterwards. I think Eva wants to speak with you alone," Little Pea said, looking a little put-out.

"So, who is Eva?" Aya asked.

"Eva?" Little Pea said, looking around. "She is everything, I guess."

"Everything?" Aya said.

"Go see her, she will probably tell you everything." She paused. "Probably." Little Pea gave Aya a warm hug, then turned and skipped away. "See you later!" she called out.

"Bye!" Aya called out.

Aya left the road and followed a narrow trail leading down a steep bank and into a wooded area. The trail descended towards a valley.

The path was overgrown, but the ground didn't hinder her footsteps. She felt as if the woods aided her at just the right moments: a branch would be there to help her just when she needed it, and vines would stretch over the path where otherwise it would have been slippery. The woods felt welcoming, inviting her to travel deeper, and they appeared to want her to reach the valley's floor. As she got closer, she could hear a small stream bubbling and someone singing softly.

She left the shade of the woods and saw an elderly woman washing clothes in the stream. Just opposite was a small log-pile cabin that was crooked and weathered but felt welcoming and cosy. The woman looked up, saw Aya, and rushed over, throwing her arms around her. Aya was shocked at the welcome, but the woman's embrace warmed her, and she melted into it.

"Aya," the woman said, smiling, "My little Aya."

"Eva?" Aya asked.

"Yes, I am so happy to see you here," Eva said, walking over to a makeshift footbridge crossing the stream, which consisted of a few short planks of wood resting on a few large stones.

She looked back and beckoned Aya to follow.

Eva was old but not frail. She had a strength in her bones that arose from years of living in the wild, tending to her plants and animals. Her eyes were bright, curious, not burdened by age, and her smile was warm and inviting, radiating kindness from a deep love of all things. She lived by the small babbling brook, where she would sit and listen to the water's song and the whispers echoing out of the woods. She loved to tell stories of her adventures to whoever would listen, of the magic and mystery that filled the land. She was a kind soul who welcomed anyone who crossed her path with generosity and grace.

"Come," Eva said, looking back at Aya, who quickly followed.

Eva sat on a small carved bench just by the stream, and Aya sat beside her.

"You have many questions, I know," Eva said. "Before we start, let's have something to drink." She whistled, and a melody filled the air, sparks swirled about like fireworks, and a sweet scent of lavender erupted.

Five bunnies appeared. The first pair placed a small table in front of Aya and Eva, laid a small orange cloth on it, bowed and hopped away. The second pair carried a basket filled with apples, pears, and many different types of berries and politely placed it on the table, bowing low and bouncing away. The last placed a bottle of crystal-clear water and two small wooden cups on the table.

"Thank you, Loppo. You and your brothers are too kind," Eva said and bowed her head slightly.

"If there is anything else, Eva, we are happy to help." Loppo bowed lower than the others, smiled, and bounced away.

As Aya watched Loppo go, she felt both surprised and accepting of what she had just seen. Despite the strangeness of it all, the place felt familiar to her, as if she had always been there. Though vague memories lingered on the outskirts of her mind, they felt like distant dreams that she couldn't quite grasp; they felt unreal.

"Good to see that you are settling in," Eva said. She picked up the bottle and poured the clear liquid into the cups. It glistened in the daylight. She handed a cup to Aya and drank the liquid.

Aya stared into the cup; the liquid shimmered, it looked clear and fresh, and she drank. The liquid didn't taste of anything, but instead, her mind flooded with memories that were unfamiliar to her: faces and places that she once thought were nothing but a dream, yet now they felt real. She felt like she had fallen under a spell as a whirlwind of thoughts bombarded her, flashes of images, people, and places.

However, one memory stood out, one person she saw clearly, and she smiled warmly at the recollection.

"Daniel," Aya whispered as she slowly returned the cup to the table.

"Yes, Daniel," Eva said, then sighed. "Poor Daniel."

Aya snapped out of the trance that had besieged her. "Poor Daniel?" She was suddenly overwhelmed with concern. "Where is he?" she asked, now feeling panicked.

"He is close by, but a lifetime away," Eva said, pulling out a pipe concealed by her shawl. She started to clean it, and Aya was struck with remembrance as images of a man following the same ritual flooded her mind.

"Eat," Eva said, placing a single berry in Aya's palm.

Aya politely shook her head. "It will make things clearer," Eva said reassuringly. Her mind cleared as she swallowed the berry;

its sweet flavour soothed the whirlwind of images in her mind.

"I remember," Aya said. "I remember it all."

"Hello, Aya, it is nice to meet you finally." Eva giggled like a young child, then looked through the basket before settling on a large red apple. "Oooh, I'll keep this for later." And it vanished under her shawl.

"Where is Daniel?" Aya asked softly.

"As I said, he is near but a lifetime away. He is somewhere you cannot go, and I am forbidden to," Eva said.

"Is he in trouble? I don't understand, where is he?!" Aya demanded and stood up, but then stopped, unsure of what to do next.

Eva raised her hand, and it shone with a warm light. Aya instantly sat back down and felt relaxed.

"Is that better?" Eva said.

Aya nodded like a child calmed by her parent.

"Now then, where do I start?" Eva said. "I think with what matters now, and that is Daniel."

Aya sat quietly, listening.

"Daniel isn't here. Well, I think you gathered that. Where he is," Eva sighed heavily, "is a place so far removed from here. It is all that there is not."

Aya remained silent.

"He has been taken to a place he was never meant to go, but, in the Day, life can sometimes take an unexpected turn," Eva said.

"He has been taken to a place where he was never meant to go, but, as the Day showed, fate can be unpredictable at times," Eva said, pulling out a leather pouch. She stuffed some fragrant herbs into her pipe, put it between her lips, and then lit it with a spark from her finger. The herbs glowed as she inhaled the smoke.

Eva smiled slyly. "We can perhaps offer a little help to your young man."

"Hello, Aya," came a familiar voice.

"Joan?" Aya said, recognising her and running over to give her a welcoming hug. "What are you doing here?"

"Now that is a long story," Joan looked over at Eva, "but perhaps best left for another time."

She adjusted the straps on the rucksack she was carrying.

"Hello, I'm back!" Little Pea darted out from behind Joan and wrapped her arms around Aya.

"I found this one skulking in the trees," Joan said.

"I do not skulk!" Little Pea stamped her foot.

Aya looked at Joan, and it suddenly dawned on her that Joan was a young woman in her mid-twenties. She noticed Aya's confusion.

"Well, I am not going to be old forever now, am I?" Joan said as a matter of known fact.

Eva stood up. "Well, as you are all here, I think it is best we go."

She led the way, holding Little Pea's hand, followed by Aya and Joan.

"I think this may turn out to be a bit of an adventure," Joan said to Aya.

"I don't understand what you are doing here. To be honest, I don't know where here is," Aya said.

"Well, here is like another life. We were born,

we die, we are born again, but..." Joan stopped.

"But?" Aya asked.

"Well, some go straight to sleep and wait to be awoken again. Others go to where our Danny is, whereas some just wake up all over again, going through life as they did probably countless times before," Joan said.

"Who decides who goes where?" Aya asked.

"That is a good question," Eva said. "Who decides, indeed?"

"I did only say *probably* answer your questions," Little Pea piped up.

Eva laughed.

They continued along the side of the stream; there was no rush to their pace. Aya thought it felt like friends just going for a leisurely walk. Joan and Aya talked about life in the flat and about their friends, but only happy memories came to them; sadness didn't find a home in this world.

They followed the stream that flowed through the valley. Little Pea wasted no time and jumped in, splashing and laughing as they made their way. Tiny frogs waved to the group as they sailed by, perched atop vibrant green lily pads. Little Pea splashed one of them, who gave a stern look and turned away indignantly; she found it very amusing. As they walked, Aya noticed the grass deliberately bending beneath her feet, creating a soft cushion with each step; Joan noticed Aya's surprise and chuckled.

After about an hour, they left the stream and entered a wooded area. The trees were tall and ancient, creating a patchwork canopy of leaves overhead. Golden rays filtered through the leaves, casting a mesmerising pattern on the wood's floor. Eva started to sing a song; her melody flowed all around and appeared to enchant everything it brushed. Life sprung around them: trees burst with blossom, and flowers and other plants erupted in a rainbow of colour. Aya felt invigorated as she listened, enchanted by the tune that danced in the air. She looked behind them and saw a trail of white petals in their wake. She watched in awe as animals came to escort them. Eva spoke to them as they passed, and they raced off ahead.

"Magical, isn't it?" Joan said to Aya.

Aya smiled broadly. "It's like nothing I have ever seen before."

The path through the woods was easy, as the ground accommodated their every step, helping them on their way. They soon left the woods behind them and returned to open fields that Aya felt were a little more familiar.

They walked in the open in silence; tension seemed to fill the air around them the farther they walked. They crossed several fences and a small brook.

The sun started to dim as they approached a river, where they stopped. In the distance, dark clouds over the lake obscured the blue sky, and a misty haze hung low on the water.

"I cannot go any farther," Eva said, turning to Aya. "I need you to do something for me."

"Where are we?" Aya asked.

"We are at the edge of this land," Eva said.

"What is on the other side?" Aya asked.

"There is nothing, only emptiness, only Night. Daniel is not there," Eva said. "Let me explain."

Aya and Eva found a fallen tree by the lake's edge and sat on the old trunk.

Eva looked concerned as she spoke. "We occupy the same place, but exist in different dimensions. Here is a place of light, and there is, well, everything that is not. There is a connection point in the middle of our lake that connects our realms. Here, it is found in the middle of that lake, and there it is found in a desolate land."

"I don't understand. Why are we here?" Aya asked.

"My Aya, I need you to cross this lake, go to that connection point, and leave your pendant there," Eva said.

"Pendant? I don't have it," Aya said, panicked.

"Yes, you do. It had never left you," Eva said, and with her words, the pendant appeared around Aya's neck on a golden chain.

Aya touched it and smiled at the memory it brought. "Why?" Aya said, looking confused.

"You must trust me. It is Daniel's only hope," Eva said. "However, you will not be going alone. I believe Joan has offered to help too. She knows what must be done."

"Of course, I'll do whatever I have to, but why can't you come?" Aya asked.

"There are rules, even for me," Eva said.

"It looks good," Joan called over, "they did a good job." She was inspecting a small boat that the animals of the woods had made for them. Joan climbed in, and the boat lowered and wobbled. She sat down to steady herself. "Steady!"

Eva had asked several woodland animals to go ahead and prepare a small rowing boat to cross the lake. It was made from twigs, leaves, and vines that they had gathered and weaved together. It was barely big enough for Joan and Aya. It was light and fragile, but floated well enough. The oars had been carved from fallen branches but were solid and sturdy.

"Go, Joan will guide you," Eva said. "Take this." She produced a candle from under her shawl. "When you need to see, simply ask." She paused and smiled. "Be polite."

Aya took the candle and looked at it curiously; it was covered in strange markings. She thanked Eva and went to the boat.

Little Pea ran over to Aya and hugged her. "Please come back," she said.

"Of course I will," Aya said, trying to reassure her.

Aya hesitantly climbed into the boat. She felt

that Eva wasn't being entirely truthful about Daniel's predicament or the dangers that may lurk waiting for them in the middle of the lake.

"Eva doesn't know," Joan suddenly said as they rowed away from the bank. "She cannot see there; she only hopes."

Aya looked back at the bank as Eva and Little Pea watched them. They looked forlorn, and Eva had lost her hopeful smile for the first time.

They rowed for several hours. The water was calm, and the boat gently rocked. The feeling that they were approaching a dark doom hung over them, and they said nothing, fearing that their voices may wake some monster sleeping deep beneath them. Cloud-like wisps rose about them, thickening before long, making it difficult to see where they were heading, but Joan pushed on.

"We are lost," Joan whispered cautiously, looking around.

Aya looked at the candle Eva had given her, wondering what she meant. *Just ask*, Aya thought.

"Show me the way," she spoke quietly to

the candle. Nothing happened. Then Aya remembered Eva's words. "Please, show me the way."

The candle crackled and ignited, instantly pushing back the mist. A beam of light shone out, cutting a course through the darkness. Joan altered the boat and rowed, following the beam of light. The waves started to rise, and the fragile boat creaked under the force but somehow held together. Water sprayed over them, and the boat started to take damage as the vines started to strain.

"I don't think this boat will last much longer," Joan called out.

I wonder... Aya thought. "Please, help us," she said softly.

A sudden hiss came from the candle, and a brilliant glow surrounded them and the boat. It was like a dome of light that shielded them from the stormy sea. Inside the dome, the water became still, the air became warm, and they felt a gentle lift. They floated along in the mist, safe and serene, towards their destination.

Joan pulled the oars into the boat and smiled. "Now this is the life."

They were carried to a shoreline, where the boat gently settled on a stony beach. The glow faded, and the cold air rushed in. Aya shivered.

The land that stretched out before them was dark and looming; it was not made for travellers, and it wanted to be left alone. They were confronted with a steep rocky hill that rose inland. There was no plant life, animals, insects, sound, or wind; it was a place devoid of life and death. Their presence was like stone breaking the calm, and their arrival created ripples.

"Looks like there is only one way." Joan pointed ahead to a slightly less rocky area.

"Doesn't look like a path," Aya said.

"I don't think we will find any help in this place. We're on our own," Joan said, determined.

They made their way up the steep hill. Rocks jutted out unkindly, cutting into them at every slip. The land hindered them and wanted them gone. Eventually, they reached a flat and were confronted with a vast expanse of barren rocky land. Aya thought they had arrived on the moon.

"What way?" Aya asked.

"Let's try your candle," Joan said.

"Please show us the way," Aya whispered. The candle flickered but then went out.

"I thought as much. Eva's magic doesn't reach here," Joan said. "Well, not yet." She grinned. "This way," she added, marching into the hostile land.

The land was neither dark nor light, but dreary and oppressive. There was no way to tell how long they had been walking. However, Aya started to feel the aches in her feet. Unlike walking through the forest, the ground seemed to hate her and made every step painful.

"I think we should rest," Joan said, finding a patch of less rocky ground. She pulled out two small blankets from her rucksack and gave one to Aya, who tried to find comfort on the ground as Joan searched through her bag. A moment later, she pulled out some food and drink.

"This will lift your spirits," Joan said, pouring some liquid into a cup and handing it to Aya.

Aya drank it expecting the same clear liquid Eva had given her, but she felt a warm burning and coughed.

"The good stuff, cheers." Joan drank and returned the bottle of Jack Daniel's to her bag. "I sneaked this in," she laughed and threw her over some bread.

Aya ate the bread and felt comforted. "Thank you," she said. "Sneaked in?" Aya asked, wanting to not think about their situation.

"I shouldn't have, but I couldn't resist." Joan laughed.

"How? I thought, what did Eva say, realms?" Aya paused. "That the places were all different."

"Some of us can cross over or know how to find the holes." Joan winked and tapped her nose.

"Holes?" Aya asked.

"Creation, well, let's just say may not be perfect, and mistakes are made, and we can see those mistakes," Joan said.

"We?" Aya asked.

"Travellers," Joan said and bit down on her bread. She then adjusted her blanket and leaned back against a smooth rock she found. "We better get some sleep."

Aya found it a strange thought to find rest here. She looked about in the barren wasteland surrounding them, expecting to see a predator hunting them, but there was nothing.

"No one is here," Joan said and closed her eyes. "The biggest fear to be found in this place is the fear that we bring."

Aya thought about her words as she lay on the uncomfortable ground, but within a few minutes, fatigue beat her into submission, and she fell into an uncomfortable sleep.

She awoke and was startled to see that Joan was not there. Her bag and blanket were scattered nearby as though there had been a struggle. Aya stood up and called out, but her voice fell dead in the still air. She ran over to where Joan had been lying, and a trickle of blood was on the rock. Aya panicked as she desperately called out. The barren land offered no response, silently mocking her worries. Then she heard a voice calling out for help. She looked around but couldn't see where it came from. A scream, then silence again. Aya cried out, but no response came.

Aya didn't know what to do. She looked about erratically, and then a thought came to her:

go back, go back to safety. She started to run back towards the beach, stumbling over rocks, falling hard, but scrambling to her feet and pushing on. Suddenly, she felt a jolt and turned, screaming in terror. A Shadow held her, with demonic black eyes that tore into her soul.

"Wake up!" Joan said, grabbing Aya. "It's a nightmare."

Aya struggled, punching and kicking. Abruptly, her thoughts cleared, and she was standing some distance from where they had camped, covered in bruises and cuts. Joan held her tight, and blood was trickling from her nose.

"Joan?" Aya said. "The Shadow, it..."

"There is nothing here. You had a nightmare," Joan said calmly.

Aya's focus snapped back. "Your nose, it's bleeding," she said, concerned.

"You have a great right hook," Joan said, grinning. "And before you apologise, it's fine. I'm more concerned about your cuts. C'mon, let's clean you up," she said, helping Aya back to their camp.

Joan helped her back and sat her on the blanket, then searched through her bag and pulled out some clean cloth and iodine.

"This will sting," Joan said, cleaning and dressing Aya's injuries before cleaning the blood from her own nose.

They packed everything back into Joan's rucksack and continued inland. Joan pointed to a dark cloud in the distance, an area darker than the rest of the land.

"That is where we are going. I am not entirely sure what we'll find when we get there. What we're going to do has never been done before," Joan said.

"What are we going to do?" Aya asked.

"We are going to leave a message for Daniel," Joan said.

"Why can't you go to him?" Aya asked.

"I can't easily go there. That place eats up Travellers; only some of us can get there, but they rarely return. We won't be leaving the message. Eva will," Joan said, worry on her face.

"Eva? How? She said she can't, there are rules,"

Aya said.

"Yes," Joan looked away, "we will be making a link for her to travel, but it will come at a cost to her."

"What cost?" Aya asked, concerned.

Joan remained silent and shook her head. They continued on, both lost in their thoughts. A heavy air of sadness now burdened them as they moved closer to their destination. The land started to steepen, eventually leading them to a cliff face. Joan shrugged and pointed up. She removed a thin rope from her bag, tied one end around Aya and the other around herself, and started the ascent.

The climb started well, but the rockface grew colder and wetter as they ascended. The biting cold on their hands hindered their movement, making the climb twice as tricky. Suddenly, Aya's grip slipped, and the two of them plummeted through the air. Joan managed to latch onto a small crack in the rockface, halting their descent, but Aya was left dangling wildly. She felt her heart race as panic bubbled up inside her, but she forced it down and scoured the rock for a foothold. With a desperate kick, she managed to reach a small ledge just in time. She clung to it with relief and looked up at Joan, who still clung to the rock with an unyielding determination.

"Are you okay?" Joan called down to Aya.

"Yeah, I'm fine," Aya called up breathlessly. "Thanks for saving me."

"Don't mention it," Joan replied firmly. "You good to go?"

"Yeah," Aya called up.

They continued taking extra care and fighting through the biting cold, finally reaching their goal. They reached the top and collapsed, exhausted.

"Well done, kid," Joan said, trying to catch her breath.

Aya looked over at her; she had aged, looking more like the old lady she once lived with.

"Are you okay?" Aya said, concerned.

"I'm okay, just feeling tired now," Joan said, inspecting her wrinkled hands. "And don't worry about me; we have a job to do. Now let's get going."

Aya helped Joan up; she had lost her spring,

but her fiery spirit was not dampened.

"There." Joan pointed to a tall tree nearby. It stood ominously jutting out the flat, barren landscape.

They slowly made their way to the tree. The closer they got, the older Joan seemed to get. She put her arm around Aya, and they slowly crossed their last obstacle and arrived at the ancient tree.

"Wait here," Joan said and slowly approached the tree and rested her hands on the old trunk. "A crack in the trunk will open up. Place the pendant in there." She turned to the trunk and closed her eyes. "And don't worry, the end is never the end."

Joan started to mutter ancient words that echoed out and resonated all about. The ground shook, and the land seemed to groan angrily. The clouds above swirled into a vortex, spinning frantically. A wind ripped through the land, creating a dust storm that displaced rocks.

A sudden snapping sound and a crack appeared in the tree, and Aya stared hesitantly.

"Now!" Joan cried out, her skin glowing

brightly.

Aya rushed over, tripping as the ground trembled below her, as though it knew her intent and wanted to stop her. As soon as she placed the pendant in the hollow opening, a wave of energy burst from Joan, throwing Aya clear. Joan glowed brighter and brighter until cracks appeared all over her skin, as though something was in her trying to get out.

"See you in another life, kid!" Joan shouted out as she suddenly burst into a radiant shining light. In her wake, Eva now stood, hands on the tree, and as Aya watched, strange symbols appeared all over the trunk.

"Well done, Aya, I am proud of you," Eva said. "Go home. Your journey is not yet over. Little Pea will show you the way."

There was a burst of light, and Aya was, once more, standing at the shoreline looking over the river, and Little Pea was standing next to her.

"Don't worry, no one ever really goes," Little Pea said, wiping tears from her eyes.

"What just happened?" Aya said.

"Eva knows what is best," Little Pea said.

"What's happening?" Aya said, overcome with a strange feeling. She looked at her hands, and a warm aura started to radiate.

"It's a gift," Little Pea said.

"Gift?"

"Yes," Little Pea smiled, "Eva has given you her light, and you will shine brightest of all."

Aya watched as the light seemed to glow all about her slowly. However, she felt no fear, just love and compassion. She felt life flowing throughout her being, hope and the power of creation itself. She slowly rose into the air, growing brighter and brighter. Wherever her light touched, life burst from the ground, plants sprouted up, and a kaleidoscope of vibrant colours and scents surrounded them within seconds.

"It's time," Little Pea said.

"I know," Aya said, suddenly filled with understanding. "I know what must happen."

"I'll see you again," Little Pea said.

Suddenly, Aya burst into a pure white light; like a supernova, her light stretched out, touching every part of the land.

Then she was gone.

CHAPTER 14

Meeting Old Friends
The world in Shadow is clearest of all.

"This is weird," Robbie said.

"You're telling me!" Jessica answered.

"Where even are we?" Samantha added.

"Did anyone else hear that voice?" Robbie asked, scratching his head.

Samantha and Jessica both simultaneously said, "Yes!"

"'You're needed,' it said," Robbie added, "then I was here. Anyone remember anything else?"

"Bethany? Oh my God, Bethany!" Jessica said, suddenly panicked. "She was by my side, I was…" She paused and scrunched up her nose. "I was old," she said, feeling confused. Her voice trailed away as she sat on the ground, thinking about her daughter.

"I remember you sitting by me and crying, then I was here," Robbie said to Jessica, scratching his head.

Jessica looked at him and wiped away a tear. "I saw you..." She recalled a vague memory that felt like it echoed from another life. Her voice broke, and she fell into silence. Robbie reached over and held her hand.

"I just remember walking across a road on my way to see Paul, then..." Samantha paused as she thought of her husband, "then I was here."

They stared blankly at one another for a time. Their thoughts were filled with distant memories of faces and places that whirled in and out of their minds, familiar yet foreign to them, as though they belonged to another's life.

"Well, I guess we're dead then," Samantha eventually said with a surprising acceptance of the situation, breaking their silence. She looked at her friends, waiting for confirmation.

"Looks like it," Robbie eventually said, standing up and helping Jessica to her feet. "Bethany will be fine. She's a strong girl, like her mum." He smiled warmly. Jessica smiled back, feeling comforted. Then Robbie reached down and pulled Samantha to her feet. She smiled, but her eyes betrayed her sadness.

"We'll work it out," Robbie said reassuringly.

They found themselves in what could only

be described as a long, narrow corridor. The walls were white, but the absence of any other colour or decoration did nothing to prevent their stark clarity. The corridor seemed to stretch endlessly away in one direction, like a never-ending void. However, in the other, not too far from them, stood a large, ancient-looking wooden door that loomed against the white backdrop. It seemed to beckon them, drawing on their curiosity, almost daring them to investigate. For a few moments, the three of them remained still, unsure of what to do or say. Then, a soft, low voice spoke. It seemed to echo from behind the door. The friends could not understand the words, but the sound lingered in the air and calmed them. Fractured words whispered about them; it sounded like an echo that had travelled from some distant land, barely audible now. The voice quickly faded, however, leaving a sweet summer scent in the air.

"I guess that's the way out," Samantha said, feeling compelled to move towards the door. "You guys coming?"

Robbie and Jessica cautiously followed, their echoing footsteps eagerly swallowed by the eternity that stretched out behind them.

With each step, they felt a pull beckoning them to turn around and follow the corridor that lay behind them. Jessica stopped, turned, and stared back into the endlessness that stretched away. Suddenly, images of Bethany flooded her mind, of the life she had left. She took a step, and the memories intensified. She felt her daughter in her arms, cradling her to sleep. A desperate feeling of need to see Bethany once again overwhelmed her, and she took a second step. Robbie gently grabbed her arm and shook his head. Jessica looked at Robbie. Her eyes widened, and she snarled with irritation, but Robbie smiled kindly, looking past the veneer of emotion.

"Something doesn't feel right," Robbie whispered kindly, looking into the emptiness. "I don't think we will find anything good there."

"But, Bethany," Jessica said, wanting to go, trying to pull away. "Let me go, you have no right!" she added, anger now welling up.

"I don't think we will find her there," he said with a sigh and put his arm around her. "I miss her too."

Jessica, feeling Robbie's warm embrace, calmed. "I…" her voice shaking, "don't know what came over me."

Robbie hugged her tightly. "I know, it's okay."

"Look at this!" Samantha called back to them, now standing at the door.

It was a marvel of craftsmanship, made from an ancient tree that had been felled long ago. However, it did not appear lifeless; instead, the timbers shimmered and shifted with a radiant glow and appeared to be very much alive. The grand door echoed with age and wisdom from every grain. Deep rings ran throughout its large oak panels, giving it a rich, deep brown hue that stood out boldly. Its wooden surface was adorned with thousands of intricate, detailed carvings that moved about as the friends stared.

This was no ordinary door, but a story, a never-ending tale of birth, life, death, and rebirth. As they watched, knowledge revealed its secrets. Their minds were filled with images of a god, of a sacrifice, and the birth of everything, a universe that burst into an explosion of colour. They saw stars form, planets collide, and the seed of life planted. They observed civilisations grow and expand, only to fall and crumble into ruin. As they watched, they felt the birth of every living being, their lives and deaths as they flew from one existence to another, each life a fleeting flame in the wind, but each filled with a greater purpose. Then, in an instant, it all ended, falling into Shadow, only to explode once more from the embers of the old.

Their eyes were then drawn to a plaque that hung above the door. Initially, they could not read it, but as they stared, its words became bright and clear:

Two becomes One
Life begins Anew

They stared at the words for some time, wondering about their meaning. Their minds flooded with images of gods, of a purpose, and of sacrifice.

"What do you think it means?" Samantha quietly said, airing her thoughts.

"Life begins anew?" Jessica whispered. As she spoke the words, the door appeared to loom over them, somehow growing in stature and magnificence. A cool, sudden wind blew, and their minds were filled with a sound, a name: *Ez-Amu-Fion-Uz*.

The words and clarity they had felt only moments before quickly faded, leaving only fragmented images and emotions. They all stood silently, trying to understand as confusion descended and then lifted, leaving only a feeling of loss.

Robbie shook his head and was the first to break the silence that had engulfed them. "Did you all see that?" He rubbed his eyes as though he had just awoken from a long sleep. "I mean, wow." He looked at the door which had now shrunk back to its original size. "Just wow!"

Jessica looked at Robbie for a moment, her eyes glazed over as though her thoughts were drifting elsewhere.

"Jess?" Robbie said, looking worriedly at her.

Suddenly, she snapped out of the trance

that had ensnared her. "Profound words," she mocked. "I mean. Well, really."

"Okay, awesome!" Robbie said with a grin. "What would you have me say?"

"Well, I don't know," Jessica said, thinking for a moment. "Perhaps something like," she paused, "that was…" She trailed off. "Oh, I don't know." She gave up and turned her attention back to the door.

"Exactly, how do you put that into words?" Robbie said.

"As I look upon the Creation of a god, I see a torment and a love. I see a sacrifice, I see a gift," Samantha spoke, her voice soft and her eyes staring vacantly at the door. "I see the One becoming All, and the All returning to the One."

"Sam?" Jessica said, touching Samantha's arm.

Samantha, feeling Jessica's touch, seemed to wake up. "Yeah?" Samantha said. "What's up with you guys?" she added, noticing the concerned expressions on Robbie and Jessica's faces.

"You were saying—" Jessica started.

"You went weird," Robbie impatiently interrupted.

Jessica gave him a look, the one that Robbie

had seen many times before, of loving disapproval.

Suddenly, the voice rang out again, capturing their attention. A dull golden light twinkled like a tiny star shining from a distant galaxy, pulsated from a carving of a tree which stood out boldly in the middle of the door. The light emanated from a series of symbols that ran along the length of its trunk. Their golden glow felt warm and inviting. There was a distant feeling of recollection that they felt but had no memory of what they were seeing; it felt both familiar and unfamiliar. The branches stretched out and intertwined with all the other carvings, stopping at the very edge of the door. Its roots ran downwards but faded into a dark shadow that lingered near the bottom.

"Daniel…" A barely audible voice drifted out and hung in the air. Its broken words were almost a whisper and faded quickly.

"Look!" Jessica said, pointing to the dim light. As they watched, the fuzzy light grew in intensity until it shone brightly.

"Daniel is lost." The words were now unmistakable and rang out loud and strong, yet warmth and kindness were apparent in their tone.

"Daniel?" Robbie said, looking at Jessica and Samantha.

"What about Daniel?" Samantha quickly added.

"He has drifted," came the answer.

"Drifted? What does that even mean?" Jessica questioned. "Who are you?"

"I am…" The voice faded for a moment. "Eva."

Then silence fell once again. They looked at each other as though trying to read each other's thoughts.

Irritation was born on Jessica's face. "Now look, Eva—" she started, but was interrupted.

"Jessica, be calm. Your fire may burn too bright and blind those who love you most," Eva said kindly.

Jessica stared for a moment, agape. "But how did you know my name?" she asked, now feeling a little uncomfortable.

"Follow the Shadow," Eva continued. "Find Daniel and complete the journey." The symbol's light slowly faded, pulsating dimmer and dimmer until all the warmth had left them.

"Hello?" Jessica said, leaning in close to the

door.

Robbie gently placed his hand on Jessica's shoulder. "Don't get too close, Jess."

Jessica turned to Robbie and smiled, taking a step back.

"I think Eva has gone," Samantha said and paused deep in thought. "Follow the shadow? Daniel's lost? What d'you think any of it meant?"

Robbie and Jessica looked back at her blankly and shrugged.

"What was that about fire and burning too bright?" Robbie said, turning to Jessica.

"Don't look at me," Jessica said. "It all sounded literally insane!"

The door suddenly gave a loud creak, and a chill breeze blew from it. A voice spoke, low and ancient, "Enter, traveller, find your rest."

They all stopped and stared at the door, no one wanting to speak.

"Okay, the door can talk, apparently," Robbie eventually said, feigning a smile.

"I wonder if we can open it?" Jessica said.

"You want to open the talking door?" Robbie said in surprise.

"Jess is right," Samantha added. "It's a door. Perhaps it's our way out?"

"So, our choices. On the one hand, we have the talking door, and on the other, we have the endless corridor." He paused for a moment, contemplating the options. "Well, I guess it's the door," he said with a shrug.

"Well, as nothing else is here apart from this door, I guess the answer lies with it," Samantha said. "Somehow."

Robbie stared at the door. "How would we even open it?" he mumbled as he scanned it for a handle.

His eyes were drawn to the tree, sitting boldly in the middle of the door, its roots and branches stretching out. He looked at the trunk and the symbols, which were now barely visible, and wondered who Eva was. His eyes were drawn up to its branches, which looked alive and appeared to move as though being rocked by some hidden breeze. He felt mesmerised by its rhythm and smiled as he swayed back and forth. He followed its branches stretching out as their girth thinned the farther they fled from the trunk. They visited every scene as though they brought a hidden gift that spilt life into the wooden carvings. He felt like he was being led as he sifted through many unfamiliar scenes.

His eyes fell upon a branch that stood out above the rest, and his eyes eagerly traced along its route as it twisted, eventually coming to a stop. Robbie's eyes fell upon a scene that filled his thoughts with a past memory. He smiled to himself and felt a feeling of peace wash over him. He raised his hand slowly and gently touched the scene as though driven by a hidden desire. As he did, he saw the door swing open and felt himself being drawn in, an invisible force pulling on him. There was a hazy mist that lingered just behind the door, which obscured any secrets that teased a reveal.

As he strained to see what may lie beyond the mist, he heard familiar sounds. Robbie gripped the frame and leaned in.

"Oh my God!" Jessica cried out.

Samantha turned to see a faint mist had appeared in the centre of the door that appeared to radiate out from the tree trunk, and to her surprise, Robbie's upper body was sucked into it. He was still standing firmly planted on the ground, but his body was now stretched, as though part of him was being sucked into a black hole.

"Grab him!" Jessica shouted as she pulled on Robbie's hips.

Samantha snapped out of her shock, grabbed, and pulled as hard as she could. There was a groan, like the door was not happy, and the next moment, they all fell back onto the ground.

"What the hell, Robbie?!" Samantha shouted, rubbing her back.

"That was strange," Robbie said, shaking his head, unaware of what the others had seen.

"Okay, what just happened?" Jessica said, trying to catch her breath.

"The door opened," Robbie said.

"No, it didn't," Samantha said, catching her breath.

"Yes, it did," insisted Robbie. "It was weird. I felt myself being sucked in."

"We know," Jessica said. "You sort of stretched into the door."

"Like part of you was being sucked in; weird is an understatement!" Samantha added, still reeling from the experience.

Robbie looked at them, thought for a bit, and said, "Weird."

"If you say that again, I swear I'll…" Jessica said, feeling relief and anger simultaneously. "I'll do something."

"I was standing in a hospital," Robbie said, turning to Jessica.

Jessica calmed down when she saw the look on Robbie's face. "You okay?" she said, concerned.

"You were in bed with Bethany in your arms." He paused. "It was when she had just been born. It was like I was there. No, I *was* there!"

"How is that even possible?" Samantha said.

"I don't know," Robbie said, "but I was looking at the different images on the door, and I saw what I thought was Bethany."

Jessica leaned over and put her arm around him.

"Then I saw the hospital. It was there on the door, but clear as day in my mind. I reached out and touched it. I felt compelled to," Robbie said. "Then the door opened, I leaned in through…well, it looked like a weird mist."

"That word is banned," Jessica said.

"Sorry," Robbie said and smiled broadly, "but it was weird."

"Okay, let me try something," Samantha said eagerly. "Guys, hold me and don't let go, please. I have an idea."

Samantha went to the door. Robbie and Jessica held her tight. She closed her eyes and took a deep breath, clearing her mind. Then she held a memory from her past, picturing it in as much detail as she could. She opened her eyes and stared at the door. Her gaze was drawn first to the tree. Then her eyes felt drawn up along the branches, following them as they touched the many different scenes, suddenly stopping on a familiar image.

She felt a joy well up inside her and touched the door. Like Robbie moments before, her body stretched as she was partially sucked into the door through a swirling mist.

"Pull!" Robbie said.

They quickly pulled her back.

"I know!" Jessica responded whilst pulling as hard as she could.

They pulled hard, stumbling backwards. Once again, the door groaned loudly as Samantha was wrenched out of the mist.

Samantha stood there, panting, in shock and red-faced.

"What did you see?" Jessica asked eagerly.

"I was with…" Samantha smiled and blushed.

"Enough said," Robbie added and grinned.

"So, what exactly is this thing?" Jessica asked, looking eagerly at Samantha.

"I'm not sure, but if you think of a memory, the door seems to take you there, and I mean literally," Samantha said and blushed.

"I guess it's a kinda map," Robbie added.

"My turn," Jessica said excitedly, rushing over to the door.

"Wait!" Robbie said.

But before he could get a firm grip on her, Jessica had reached out, touched the door, and vanished.

"Jessica!" Robbie yelled as he desperately scanned the door, unsure of what to do. "Damn it!"

Panic filled the air.

"I have an idea," Samantha suddenly said. "We have to go in after her."

"But how?" Robbie said anxiously. He stepped close to the door. "Okay, what do I have to do?"

"No, you're stronger than me. I'll have to go," Samantha said.

"But it's dangerous," Robbie objected. "I can't let you go, we don't know—"

"No buts," she snapped. "Just don't let me go." She smiled nervously.

Robbie gripped Samantha's waist. "I won't let go," Robbie said reassuringly, and was met with a grateful smile.

Samantha filled her mind with every memory of Jessica that she could recall from when they first met. Once again, she stared at the tree, following its branches like a winding path, until she stopped on a familiar scene, and her mind flooded with the memory of Jessica vanishing.

The door groaned and creaked as a vortex of colours began to swirl around Samantha's hand. Thick fog poured from the door, and Samantha felt herself being pulled forward. She reached out and touched the door. Robbie saw her body stretch and vanish into the mist. Suddenly, the door groaned loudly and angrily, and Samantha was sucked in further, as though the door now did not want to let her go. Robbie pulled with all his might, barely able to stop Samantha from vanishing as Jessica had.

Samantha peered through a hazy veil, and she saw Jessica standing at the door just before she vanished, with her hand slowly reaching towards it. She stretched out and tried to grab her but fell short. In one last effort, Samantha lunged for Jessica and grabbed hold of her arm with both hands, pulling her away from the door. Robbie felt Samantha struggling and trying to leave. He tightened his grip and pulled as hard as he could, but she was pulled in further, and he felt his grip slipping.

"I'm not going to let go!" he shouted out. "You can't have them!"

Suddenly, another hand grabbed Robbie's. He turned to see an old man standing next to him. Robbie paused, shocked to see himself, but years older.

"Pull!" the stranger said and gave him a sly smile.

Without a second thought, Robbie pulled. There was a bright flash, and all three fell back onto the floor. Robbie and Samantha were panting, and Jessica was looking around, confused. Robbie quickly sat up and looked about, but whoever had helped him was gone.

"We're not playing with that thing again!" Robbie said.

"I agree," Samantha added vaguely, her thoughts still trying to figure out what had just happened.

"But I want a turn," Jessica said.

"No!" both Robbie and Samantha said firmly.

Jessica crossed her arms. "Fine, I don't see what the problem is!" she said indignantly.

Robbie crawled over, wrapped his arms around her. "You scared the crap out of me," he whispered.

Jessica turned to object. However, after seeing the expression on Robbie's face, she calmed. "I'm okay," she said, hugging him back. "Why are you acting so strange?" she added, enjoying the embrace.

"We just need to get out of here," Robbie said, holding her tightly.

"Right," Samantha said, interrupting the moment, "let's figure this out." She paused briefly, then an idea flooded her mind. "I have it!" she said excitedly.

"Okay, don't keep us waiting," Robbie said, his arms still around Jessica.

"Perhaps if we think of Daniel, we will find him," Samantha said. "I mean, perhaps the map will take us to him."

"Okay," Robbie said, now sitting cross-legged and intensely listening to Samantha. "But how? What memory? I thought of Bethany, and I saw her, you thought of—"

"Doesn't matter, but I was there," Samantha interrupted, avoiding eye contact.

Robbie chuckled. "Okay," he said, "however, we have no idea of where Daniel is, and any memory will take us to the wrong place."

"Perhaps we can think of an earlier Daniel, I mean from our past, and bring him here?" Jessica said.

"Worth a try," Samantha said.

"No!" Robbie said, shaking his head and looking fearfully at the door. "The last time, I was barely able to pull you out. I have a feeling that the door didn't like us going back and forth."

They sat quietly, thinking about what to do next.

"Eva said to follow Daniel, that he has drifted," Samantha said.

"Yeah, but how?" Robbie said, now vacantly staring at the door.

"Follow Daniel into Shadow, or something like that," Jessica added. "Perhaps we imagine Daniel lost in, I guess, shadow?"

"That could work," Robbie said.

"Don't sound so surprised," Jessica said and smiled gleefully.

"Perhaps, don't think of an actual memory, but —" Samantha was interrupted.

"Think of something that hasn't happened, of finding him," Jessica said.

"Imagine him lost in a dark place," Robbie said.

Samantha and Jessica smiled at each other.

"Okay, no memory. We all just need to picture Daniel wandering in a place that is dark and empty, then…" Jessica stopped, and a feeling of foreboding washed over her.

"Jump in," Robbie said, looking at Jessica and finishing her sentence.

"What choice do we have?" Samantha said.

They all stood hand in hand in front of the door, cleared their minds of all memory of Daniel. They instead pictured a dark place, lost to time, a place of shadows. They pictured Daniel wandering alone, trying to find a way out, stumbling through the emptiness, lost.

"Daniel," Samantha whispered.

The door warped and groaned, and a dark, shadowy fog rose up around them.

"Enter," the door spoke, calm and ancient.

It swung open, and together, they leapt into the emptiness that lay stretched out before them and vanished.

They materialised in the air and fell, coming to a jarring halt on the roof of a tatty old cabin that heaved under their weight.

"Everyone okay?" Robbie called out.

Before anyone could answer, the roof creaked and groaned loudly before giving way beneath them, sending them plunging toward the ground in a flurry of wood and straw, coming to a violent stop with a thud.

Robbie instantly scrambled to his feet first, adrenaline coursing through him as he frantically grabbed Jessica and Samantha's arms. With all his might, he pulled them towards the door, dodging falling wooden

THE FINAL JOURNEY

beams and chunks of debris that seemed to be raining down on them from every direction. They raced out just in time before the entire structure crashed in a thunderous roar, engulfing them in billowing dust clouds and splintered debris. The house seemed to howl out angrily in pain and anguish, and for a moment, Samantha thought she saw hate-filled eyes staring at her from the shadowy ruin that lay behind them. They all lay there, panting desperately, hearts pounding in their chests, as the gravity of what had almost happened sunk in.

Robbie sat up and groaned, rubbing his head. He waved his hand about him, trying to clear away the dust that had erupted when the old cabin collapsed.

"Everyone okay?" he said, looking at Jessica and then at Samantha. They both groaned a response and nodded.

Robbie stood up and looked around. Behind him lay the old cabin, once a possible refuge to weary travellers, but now only broken walls and rubble remained after their dramatic arrival. He looked out beyond the cabin and saw a strange glow emanating from a lantern hanging on a rusty lamp post. Its light created a dome that spread out like a force field. Beyond its border was only a thick darkness that made a shiver run down Robbie's spine. The ground was dry and dusty, and the glow of the light made the place feel ghostly.

"Well, this is a lovely place," he said sarcastically.

Jessica sat up and looked about. "This is a shit hole!"

Robbie laughed. "Yep."

Samantha was the last to pull herself up. "Please tell me this is all just a dream," she added, rubbing a bruise on her arm.

"What now?" Robbie said.

"What's that?" Jessica said, pointing to the dark sky that blanketed out above them.

...

Daniel stumbled, unable to see clearly in the gloomy atmosphere. His outstretched hands came to rest upon the smooth, cold surface of a marble-like wall; it appeared deep grey, almost black, in the dim light emanating from the dancing flame of the candle.

He ran his hands over the hard surface and found no imperfections, texture, or characteristics of any sort. He slowly pressed his ear against the cold surface and listened intently. Still, the only sound that could be heard was the echo of his heartbeat reverberating off the walls. He moved his hands along the surface, desperately feeling along its length, corner to corner, searching for a door or anything that could be a way out.

He finally stopped, resting in the same spot where he had begun. Daniel paused and closed his eyes, trying to remember the sun or even a cool breeze, to remember a time before here, but all he could see was emptiness. He looked about him; he was alone in this cubed tomb. A heavy cloak of darkness hung low, almost suffocating with its overbearing weight.

A single candlelight flickered atop a small round table in the centre, offering a small oasis in this sea of growing despair. Daniel screamed with rage, his voice echoing and seething back at him, then falling silent.

"Why am I here?" Daniel said with a whimper, rage now slipping into hopelessness.

As he spoke, the flame shimmered and danced in reaction to his suffering; he couldn't tell whether for good or ill. The flame then dimmed as though the oppressive darkness was trying to extinguish it, but it fought back. Its light appeared to bring Daniel's shadow to life, which mockingly danced about him, fuelled by the scant illumination of the flame.

Daniel stared at the small candle, his only companion in this oppressive cell. Its wax was pure white; not a single imperfection could be seen. It was adorned with an intricate combination of symbols that ran along its length. The symbols gave off a yellowish hue and radiated a warm glow like a distant sun. The candle hung in the air, hovering above a plain black stone bowl. The dim glow of the candle looked like a star shining dimly against the blackest night sky. The flame flickered and swayed as if it sensed Daniel's presence and curiosity.

The light of the candle and the blackness of the bowl appeared to hang in perfect balance. However, Daniel felt something was very wrong. He stared, mesmerised by the scene. Suddenly, a powerful force took hold of his body, dragging him irresistibly towards the bowl. He stared, terrified, as a black emptiness filled his mind, and he saw the nothingness that reached out to take him. He fought back with all his might and managed to wrench himself away from it, slamming his body hard against the unforgiving, cruel wall of his cell. His vision blurred as the room spun around him. Then, an explosion of colour erupted from the candle's flame in a dizzying array of hues, extinguishing the darkness and filling the room with light. A whirling vortex opened before him, and he collapsed forward, tumbling into the unknown.

Daniel's mind suddenly broke free of the room, rushing through time and space with the force of an invisible tsunami. He felt as though his consciousness had spread infinitely, experiencing every moment, hearing every beat of every heart, understanding every thought that had ever been thought. He saw the fruition of countless lives, each rhythm echoing its own unique story, as the endless cacophony filled his soul with unbridled harmonious chaos. Beautiful colours, sounds, and images flooded his consciousness; he was everywhere and everything all at once.

Suddenly, as if a switch had been flipped, his thoughts collapsed back, and his mind, moments before full of serenity, now emptied like a dam bursting its banks. He desperately tried to cling to the feeling of oneness, but it quickly bled away, and he was left floating in an empty, inky blackness, alone and forlorn. Against the backdrop of the vast, empty expanse, a pulsating sphere of dull light appeared. The orb throbbed like a heartbeat clinging to life, and Daniel was drawn to it like a moth to a flame.

"Daniel," a soft, tired voice echoed from the light. It sounded weak, like it was fading away, the last few days of the end of a season.

Daniel didn't feel any unease; instead, a feeling of peace washed over him, and a new clarity filled his mind.

"My dear Daniel," the voice washed over him like a warm breeze, surrounding him with the scent of summer.

"I know you," Daniel whispered as the memory of their earlier meeting returned to him. "Efanu."

"Yes," a frail voice answered, "but I have many

names."

"Where am I?" Daniel asked.

"You are here. You are now," came the answer. "The place where you awoke will consume even the strongest of memories. As the light fades, you will also fade into the Shadow and be forgotten. Your purpose will be forgotten. This is the plan that is unfolding."

Daniel listened, his mind racing with questions, but none could find words. He knew that Efanu spoke the truth. He felt part of who he was had gone, had been erased, and every thought was an effort, every memory a challenge to recall.

"I am fading to Night and soon will sleep. The union is broken." Efanu's glow dimmed further. "However, all is not lost. Shadow and Light can reunite, the cycle can be complete, and life can begin anew."

"Reunite?" Daniel asked, trying to focus.

"Two must become one, as it always was, as it must always be. The seed must be planted, so the cycle can continue," Efanu said, and her light briefly flickered. "You are that seed that must reunite Light and Shadow, for life cannot begin anew, unless your journey is completed. But it has somehow been changed. It is no longer as it always had been, the cycle has changed." Her light dimmed further. "I sense a corruption."

"What am I to do?" Daniel asked, now feeling puzzled.

"Aya, I have gifted her with my essence, though she does not realise it fully yet. You must find the Shadow, find Miozu, find Ozul, purge the corruption or become Shadow itself."

Daniel felt overwhelmed with anger and confusion. "It is evil. I have felt its cruelty. It destroyed my family, my life! You expect me to embrace that?" Daniel said in defiance. "But what about the seed?"

"I am sorry, I do not believe there is any other way. Shadow has lost its purpose; it has become corrupted. Purge the corruption or embrace Shadow. A new seed may be found, in time." She paused as her light flickered, as though her flame was being blown out. "Nothing is as it was, I can no longer see."

"You ask too much," Daniel said.

Efanu spoke again, but her words were forlorn. "I have sent your friends to find you and release you from your prison, but they travel believing that they can save you." Her voice trembled. "I may have led them to their demise, but if you complete your purpose, you can save them."

"How?" Daniel frantically asked. "How can I save them?"

"It is I who now fades. It is I who is lost. It is I who can no longer see. I am sorry, Daniel." Efanu's glow faded, and Daniel was plunged into darkness. "I am sorry."

A moment later, he was again standing alone by the table, the candle's flame now only a fading ember and the symbols barely visible in the blackness.

"Aya…" Daniel whispered, and then darkness fell.

...

"We've been walking for hours," Jessica complained.

"You're dead. Stop complaining!" Robbie said.

Jessica sighed, stopped, and rubbed her lower back.

"Yeah, we're dead, but I don't feel dead," Samantha added.

"Exactly!" Jessica said. "Dead or not, my feet are killing me."

"Not sure we made the right decision here to follow that star," Samantha said, thinking about the glowing light that appeared in the sky not long after they had crash landed.

"Well, I didn't see any other choice. We followed a talking light through a talking door, so I thought it made sense," Robbie said.

"Made sense?" Jessica retorted. "I don't think any of this makes any sense. Plus, how are we meant to help Daniel?"

Robbie and Samantha shrugged and said nothing, leaving the question unanswered.

Robbie held up the lantern that he had decided to borrow from the lamp post just outside the ruined cabin. He promised to return it once he had finished with it, then concluded that they were now dead, so it probably didn't matter. Though Jessica initially thought it was a bad idea, fearing that it would bring some new calamity upon them, she was glad to have it with them. The lantern's glow pushed away the gloomy fog that had crept in around them, and under its spooky light, they somehow felt safe.

The starlight that had started them on their journey had now long faded and gone, leaving only a starless black sky overhead. They had no idea if they were going in the right direction and started to question if it all was not just an elaborate communal dream.

They walked for what felt like several miles over rough, dry, dusty terrain, following a barely visible track. There was no way to know if a minute, hour, or day had passed, the same dark sky canopied overhead without change. It was only their aching bones that offered any sign that there was still a passage of time. Eventually, it led to a cobbled road that was narrow but wide enough for them to walk side by side. The road was lined with old ornate lamp posts; most were damaged and had long lost their glow. However, sporadically, they came across one that shone with the same eerie light of their own lantern.

"Let's rest here," Robbie said as they approached a lamp post that still shone brightly. He said it felt warmer than the others they had passed. Jessica did not argue and slumped onto the adjacent bench.

They sat in silence for what could have been a lifetime. They thought about life and death and wondered about the people they had left behind, whether it was them who were, in fact, lost.

"This is a bleak place," Samantha said. "I wonder how Daniel ended up here."

"I have no idea," Jessica said, tired, "I just want to go home."

"I think that home has ended for us now," Robbie said.

"Do you think we were in heaven? I mean, before we were by that door?" Samantha mused.

"Perhaps, but I don't remember it if we were," Robbie said.

"I bet we were, and that Eva or whatever its

name was dragged us here!" Jessica snarled.

"It's okay, it'll be okay," Robbie said and tried to put his arm around Jessica.

She stood up and pushed him off her. "No!" she shouted. "No! It's not okay!"

Robbie and Samantha had never seen Jessica behave this way before. Her tantrums were always slight and, in a way, endearing, but this was something very different.

"Daniel! We are here to find Daniel. Why? Who cares! I'm done with all this!" Jessica screamed, and her voice started to warp.

A shadow seemed to grow around Jessica; the more it grew, the angrier she became. Soon, she was screaming at the top of her voice, hurling insults, and violently lashing out.

"I hate you, Robert. You fucking disgust me!" Jessica's voice almost roared like a rabid beast had taken hold.

"Calm down!" Robbie stood up and grabbed her, but Jessica waved her arm, throwing him back to the ground with ease.

Samantha went to Robbie's side. "You okay?" Suddenly, a dark shadowy figure caught her attention. "Robbie, look!" She pointed to a sinister figure whose outline could now be clearly seen standing behind Jessica.

"What is that?" Robbie said, eyes wide.

"I don't know, but it seems to be moving with Jess. I think it's controlling her." Samantha heard her words but did not believe them.

"Typical, you two always ganging up on me!" Jessica spat out her words with a vindictive bile. "I bet you were fucking behind my back all these years!" she screamed. Her face suddenly contorted with rage and hatred; she appeared almost demonic. She lashed her arms about violently, then, without warning, leapt high into the air, vanishing in the dark fog.

"Jessica!" Robbie cried, panicked, but she was gone.

Overcome with anguish and driven by desperation, he leapt forward and sprinted out into the night without thought or reason, dropping his lantern as he pursued Jessica into the murky depths of the fog. Samantha heard a grotesque scream, and Robbie cried out, then nothing. All that was left was an echoing stillness that filled the air with a deathly quiet.

Stunned and exhausted, Samantha fell to her knees and stared blankly into the thick wall that edged the light of the lantern. In that one moment, everything had changed, and she was alone.

"Robbie? Jess?" Samantha whispered in disbelief. "Please let this all just be a terrible nightmare."

As she watched her friends vanish into the ravenous abyss that surrounded them, she felt herself shatter into a million pieces. The overwhelming sense of hopelessness was too much for her to bear. She wanted to scream and fight back against the emptiness that had just swallowed everything and everyone she loved. Instead, she simply crumpled to the ground in misery, tears streaming down her face, feeling lost and deserted in a world that was cold and cruel.

Her mind raced as she tried to make sense of the events that had just unfolded. How could this happen? Why did it happen? What could she have done differently? The questions swirled around inside her head, each one more painful than the last. She knew there were no answers, but that didn't stop her from trying to find them.

The conflicting emotions of anger, sadness, and disbelief warred within her, each one fighting for dominance over the others. One moment, she would be overcome with grief, and the next, she would be consumed by rage. She was lost in a sea of confusion and heartache and didn't know how to escape.

Suddenly, she heard a noise. She squinted into the heavy fog, hoping to see Robbie and Jessica stumble out of the darkness. Still, the fog only thickened, swirling about at the light's edge, and it had no intention of revealing what was hidden.

"Get a grip, Sam!" she whispered to herself, wiping away her tears.

Samantha sat on the bench, waiting for her friends to return. However, after some time, she realised they were gone, and that realisation was like a knife piercing her heart. They had always been there for her, but now, for the first time, she was alone.

"Pull yourself together," she said to herself and stood up. She took a deep, long breath. "Right, what now?"

She looked along the road, which stretched out endlessly to the left and right of her. There was no hint which way was the right way to go, so she paused, hoping for a sign, but none came. However, she felt an invisible force pushing her onward, an inner voice encouraging her to put one foot in front of the other. Picking up the lantern with a heavy sigh, she continued along the road.

Samantha marched over the desolate cobbled ground, her lantern now barely piercing the thick veil of fog that had edged closer to her. Occasionally, a strange rustling sound would break the oppressive silence. She would whirl around, desperately hoping to glimpse Robbie or Jessica. Still, all she could see was an inky black nothingness, an impenetrable abyss that seemed alive, its darkness seething with unseen malice. Her heart raced as panic set in, and she quickened her pace. She felt like eyes were watching her, and she imagined some dark shadowy beast lurking just out of sight. The fog clung to her skin, heavy and suffocating; it made every step arduous and seemed almost alive with a craving to swallow Samantha just as it had taken her friends. Dark thoughts started to cloud her mind, and terror gripped her. It surged through every muscle as she ran ever faster, trying to find escape, yet the fog only seemed to get thicker.

She drove on, fuelled by adrenaline and fear, her lantern now only illuminating a few feet in front of her. With each stride, Samantha felt fear clenching her throat. Every shadow seemed to move as if it were hunting her. She started to run, sweat pouring down her skin despite the chill in the air. Her heart raced faster and faster until she felt like she could run no more and collapsed onto the ground.

...

"Jess!" Robbie cried out, but the dense fog swallowed his voice. He staggered through the eerie darkness, falling over rocks and dead branches. "Jess!" he called out again.

The land was barren and cold, a place where only skeletal remains dared to linger, a bleak echo of a life that once lived, but now resided to slowly waste away, worn down by the harsh relentless environment. It was born of torment and desolation, a place for those who were lost to the Light. The souls who wandered into this realm found no hope, only the dust and dirt of this dry and lonely plain. A chill wind blew across the cracked ground, whispering like unseen ghosts looking for salvation. Robbie shuddered as he desperately looked about.

"You failed her," a hiss came from all around him.

Robbie tried to ignore it and pushed further into the fog, but the words lingered in his thoughts.

"Sorry, Sam," Robbie whispered. He thought of Samantha and regretted leaving her. "I had no choice," were the words he kept repeating, but he knew he should never have left as he did.

"You failed them both," the voice rang about him again.

"No!" Robbie shouted angrily, turning around ready to fight, but was only greeted by the dreary fog. A sharp wind blew as though it mocked his efforts. Then silence fell around him once more.

He could barely see a few feet ahead of him, all he had was hope that somehow he would find his way. He felt a strange sensation, as if unseen eyes were watching him. He heard faint noises in the distance, howls, growls, and whispers. He wondered if they were real or just his imagination. The ground started to steeply incline, and he quickly realised he was climbing up and out of the mist. This somehow filled him with hope.

"Jess!" Robbie called out. "Jess!" He tried to see through the thick blanket that covered the land.

A sharp icy wind blew, and he heard the malicious voice once more laugh. It wormed its way into his thoughts, repeating cruel words of doubt in an almost chant-like fashion.

"Say what you will!" Robbie cried out. "I will find her!"

The voice cackled as it started to scream in Robbie's mind, but he would not fail her again; no matter the torment, his resolve would not falter. "I'm coming, I'm coming," he repeated to himself, in a vain hope that somehow Jessica would hear and know that he would not abandon her.

Robbie now scrambled higher up a steep bank, and as he climbed, a new hope dared to reveal itself. Eventually, he was above the dense blanket of mist that had hindered him. The cruel voice faded from his mind as he looked out across the land, its thick, cruel swirling fog creeping like a hungry beast stalking its prey. He was glad to be out of it, though the land that met him now looked no less uninviting.

"Sam, I hope you are doing better than me," he

whispered.

...

Samantha pulled herself up from the ground and looked around in disbelief. She was no longer on the road, but standing in the middle of an old town. She looked about for the lantern, but that, as well as the fog, had now gone, though the atmosphere was no less bleak. The buildings were old and crumbling, with walls covered in soot from an intense fire that must have caused tremendous destruction many years ago. Samantha walked cautiously down the ruined street, her eyes wide open and alert as her vision darted from building to building, expecting to see a monster or other terror appear from the shadows. She felt a deep chill run through her body, and for a moment, she thought she heard a distant voice calling her name, but then it was gone, leaving only the silence of the dead town.

The air was thick with a strange energy that seemed to come from everywhere and nowhere at once, and she felt as if she were entering some kind of dream. As she walked farther, she felt something strange, something dark and oppressive, like a looming presence watching her every move. She quickened her pace as she moved towards the square of the town. A veil of sadness hung over this forgotten place, and Samantha felt her heart fill with misery, as though she could sense the suffering of those who once lived here.

At the heart of the destroyed town square loomed an ominous structure. A towering black obelisk, its smooth surface almost pulsating with a dark, sinister energy. The shadows around it seemed to swirl and dance, as if under its spell. It was both imposing and unsettling, casting a sense of dread over the desolate scene.

As Samantha approached, a shiver ran down her spine and she could feel her heart racing in her chest. Then she heard a low voice rumble, calling out to her.

"Hello, Sam," an old man spoke. He sounded tired, yet power lingered in his words.

He had his back against the black stone and appeared hurt. He was clutching a wound and breathing deep and slow. His eyes were closed, yet Samantha felt that he was watching her. She instinctively went to help, but something inside her moved her to caution. She remained silent, unsure of his motives.

"It has all changed, all gone now," the old man lamented then coughed violently.

"You're hurt," Samantha said, feeling strangely concerned.

"Sam, look around, what you see now is only death," the man said. "It has all gone!"

"Gone? You mean the town?" Samantha said, briefly glancing around at the destruction that surrounded them, then she suddenly realised that the old man knew her name. "How do you know me?" she said, shocked.

"It was me you heard. I called you here."

"Called me here?" Samantha said. "Why?" But she didn't really want to know the answer.

"I felt your fear, your loneliness and hopelessness. You are alone, like me." The old man coughed once again, and a thick black liquid spilt out from the wound he was clutching.

Samantha remained silent for a moment, considering his words. "I am alone," she whispered. Somehow, his words rung true and she felt eerily calmed, like a magic spell had been cast on her. The old man no longer looked threatening, and she felt compelled to sit beside him.

"Who are you?" Samantha asked, moving a stone so that she could find some comfort.

"My name is Rashi." The man smiled but did not open his eyes.

"What happened here?" Samantha asked, looking about. "Everything is in ruin."

"Betrayed," he croaked. "This place must be, must always be! Always was! It is part of…"

He coughed and winced in pain. "That bastard knows!" he said angrily.

"Who? I don't understand," Samantha said, frightened by the rage she could see erupt on the man's face.

"This place must continue to be." He leaned forward and coughed violently. Splatters of black tar-like blood landed on the ground and hissed like molten lava meeting the sea.

Samantha looked in bewilderment, and worry washed over her. She went to get up, but Rashi grabbed her arm.

"I am dying. I will soon cease to be, but this place must continue. Its purpose must continue!" he said.

"What is this place?!" Samantha demanded, struggling to free herself.

"I will ask you this only once, answer with truth." Rashi's eyes sprung open, revealing pools of blood-red mist.

Samantha gasped in horror at the sight, but Rashi's eyes penetrated her, freezing her to the spot. His gaze lingered, transfixed, as he asked his question.

"Do you want to save your friends?" His voice was no longer weak, but alive with a now uncovered power.

Samantha's mind was filled with Robbie

wandering in the tormenting mist, with Jessica frightened in darkness, with Daniel lost to Shadow. Without thought for herself, "Yes," she answered. "Yes, I do."

"Will you claim my power?" Rashi said in a low growl. "I give it freely."

"I claim what you give," Samantha said without understanding, but somehow she knew that her answer would carry grave consequences.

"Then embrace me, fulfil my purpose, become more than what you are and do the work that must be done!" Rashi's voice bellowed, as the ground trembled and the buildings shook. He stood up, dragging Samantha with him. Turning to the black stone, he pressed their hands onto the cold surface.

"Welcome to Hell!" Rashi roared.

A blood-red glow started pulsating from within it, like an awakening heartbeat. Then Rashi's chest started to burn brightly, pulsating in unison with the stone. Samantha tried to move away, but her hands were held fast. Rashi's cries pierced the air as fire erupted from his skin, consuming him in an inferno that blazed with rage. Sparks leapt like dancing demons, and smoke billowed thick and black. He screamed wildly as he contorted in a macabre ballet of death until finally collapsing into a pile of ash. Samantha felt her chest heat up like a furnace, brighter and brighter in a hellish orange light. Pain seared through her veins as her skin crackled and burned, boiling in its own blood as it melted away. She screamed like a banshee, louder and louder, until the stone exploded with a thunderous blast, throwing her into the side of a building, which came crashing down on top of her.

...

Robbie's eyes widened with terror as he saw a colossal explosion in the distance, lighting up the dark sky with an intense red hue. A hot wind rushed past him, followed by a mighty tremble that shook the ground beneath his feet. He stumbled forward as the hillside shuddered under the force of the shockwave. A brief silence descended, and Robbie gasped for breath. However, there was barely enough time for him to realise what was happening before a much larger tremor hit. He was thrown off his feet by its immense power, his body crashing to the ground.

Suddenly, with a deafening crack, the ledge broke apart and began skidding down the side of the vertiginous hillside. In desperation, Robbie leapt to the side, narrowly missing falling boulders. Bloodied and bruised, he clung desperately to an outcropping of rock, breathless from his near brush with death.

Robbie pressed onwards and upwards with sheer determination and finally crawled to the top. The land was very different to where he had come from. A vast, arid grassland sprawled before him, but there was still no sunlight in the sky, only the same dreary, bleak emptiness.

"Where are you, Jess?" he whispered as he looked at the oppressive land.

Robbie trudged forward, adrenaline coursing through his veins, with only one thought filling his mind: find Jessica. This place was as unwelcoming as the last. The grass had no clear colour and appeared listless. Its lifeless swaying motion gave the appearance of a dark necromancy at work. It seemed to sense his presence and fought vehemently against him, with its sharp razor-like tips slicing into his flesh with every step he took. The land did not want him to reach his destination, though he did not know where that end may lay. Yet, Robbie refused to give up hope, and the resistance only increased his determination. *I will find you.* Over and over, he repeated that same single thought: *I will find you.*

Robbie struggled on through the endless sea that rhythmically swayed before him. Whether by destiny or chance, he stumbled upon a path that wound its way off into the distance. The rough trail seemed to have been carved out by a colossal serpent weaving through the land. Fear struck Robbie's heart as he stared at the path. He frantically looked about, expecting fangs to jump out and end him, but all was silent apart from the sporadic rustle of the wind brushing the thorn-like blades. An eerie sense of peace filled him, knowing that his journey through this unforgiving landscape would now be a little less daunting. However, it only served to fuel the growing despair and dread that now consumed him with each agonising step. Yet he still pushed onward, determined to find Jessica. No matter what would come, he would find his journey's end.

The trail twisted and curved with malicious intent, cutting through the land like a serrated knife. Though exhausted, his muscles screaming for respite, Robbie's pace had picked up, and he was progressing well. The incline rose higher and higher, and soon fatigue weighed him down as he struggled up a small hill. When he finally reached the summit, a chill ran down his spine as he was met with an eerie sight: a small clearing marred with the ghostly remains of a weathered tent, its torn fabric fluttering in the wind, a stark reminder that this place had once been visited by a traveller on their own journey or just aimlessly lost.

There was a large backpack lying in a heap near a circle of stones that was stained with charcoal from where a fire had once raged. As Robbie looked at the unfolding scene, his eyes widened with fear, and his heart raced as he stumbled upon a heap of discarded belongings; clothes scattered around were ripped into tatters and stained with dark red pools. The ground was scarred, with deep gashes tearing through the soil like a jagged mouth full of broken teeth, as though it had once opened wide like a ravenous beast snapping shut on an unsuspecting prey. Terror seized him as he realised whatever creature brought about this carnage could still be lurking nearby. All he had was hope that whatever had visited this place was long gone and not inclined to return.

Robbie peered inside the tent and pushed through the entrance to find a few dusty blankets strewn across the ground. With no energy left to contemplate leaving, he painfully crawled onto the bedding, desperate for rest before sinking into a dreamless sleep.

...

The earth shook and groaned as if in pain. Its surface trembled with a force that caused the ground to split and tear wide and long. Deep fractures tore along the streets, causing the remaining corpse-like buildings to crumble, shattering into a thousand pieces that clogged the air with thick, acrid dust. A terrible voice cried out and burst from beneath the rubble that had entombed Samantha.

"Rashi has fallen to true death," the beast roared. "I am Abbazul, Queen of Hell. I live!" Her voice reverberated with the power of a million suns. She opened her mouth wide, and flames erupted high into the air.

"I feel good!" she bellowed. "Rashi, you old bastard." She let loose a hideous laugh.

Abbazul stood up from where Samantha's ashes now lay. She was twice as tall, with a malevolent power coursing through her veins. Her skin glowed a blistering red, her hair whipped about like a raging storm, while two long black horns curved up from her forehead and leathery wings stretched out wide. She possessed an otherworldly beauty. Hatred filled her crimson eyes, and a need for vengeance, to bring pain to all who had ever crossed her, pulsated through every atom of her new body.

"Well, you look..." came a small voice, "different."

Abbazul turned violently. Her tail whipped behind her, cracking like thunder, and she was ready to pounce. A small child stood before her, smiling curiously.

"Welcome to Hell," Abbazul laughed mockingly. "Now burn!" She opened her mouth, and a stream of molten tar erupted over the little girl.

The little girl giggled. "Don't you recognise me?" she said.

Abbazul, enraged by the little girl's laughter, charged at her, leapt high into the air, and came crashing down on top of her, but the girl simply vanished and reappeared a few feet away.

The little girl giggled again. "Silly," she said, and her smile broadened.

Abbazul burst with pure, unbridled rage and let out a roar that turned the sky blood-red. She once again leapt at the little girl, her claws spread out wide, but the little girl waved her hand, and Abbazul flew backwards, crashing hard onto the ground.

"You're funny," the little girl said.

Abbazul sprung to her feet but hesitated. "Who are you?" she growled, teeth clenched and trying to hold back her rage. "Why do you not die?!"

"I am a gift. The gift of you." The little girl skipped about and started to sing a lullaby.

The song danced around Abbazul like leaves playing on the wind, filling her with lost memories. It hung in the air like the sweet scent of flowers and brought a calmness like a cool breeze on a warm summer's day.

"I know that song." Abbazul's gruff voice calmed.

"Of course you do, silly. Mummy used to sing it to us when we were little."

"Who are you? I demand you answer and end

this foolishness," Abbazul said forcefully.

"Oh, you are so funny," the little girl said. "Well, Eva hid me…" The little girl scrunched up her nose as though she was trying to figure something out. "Well, hid me in me, I guess, or you. Depends." She paused and scratched her head. "When you went all shouty, I was kept safe. Eva told me to wait and only to say hello when…well, when all of this, I guess." The little girl smiled broadly and gave a wave.

Abbazul went to wave back but then quickly turned away and grunted. "Pickles?" Abbazul whispered.

"Hello, that's me. Well, us…well, me, I think," Pickles said and shrugged.

"Mother called us Pickles," Abbazul said, trying to recall a faint memory. "Yes. I remember now!" she roared.

"Yay!" Pickles said and started skipping around, singing to herself.

"Stop!" Abbazul snapped, but Pickles continued uninterrupted.

As Abbazul watched, her anger faded as the memories of who she was came flooding back to her. "Eva," she said, and burst out laughing. "She knew!"

"Why are you laughing?" Pickles asked, still relentlessly skipping in circles.

"Well, I think Eva knew exactly what would happen!" Abbazul bellowed with laughter. "And you are my little saviour."

Pickles stopped and looked at her, confused. She opened her mouth to speak, but instead shrugged and started to skip and hum her lullaby again.

"I think we need to find our friends. Want to help?" Abbazul said.

"Of course, wherever you go, so do I."

"Then let's go," Abbazul said, then took a deep breath, spread her wings, and shot up into the air.
...

The ground shook beneath the tent as a heavy, dull thud pierced the silence. Robbie suddenly jolted awake, bolts of fear exploding in his chest as his thoughts were flooded with the blood-soaked garments that scattered the site. *The beast has returned*, he thought, and scolded himself for deciding to rest in this accursed place. He leapt from the tent, expecting to find death, but instead, a little girl stood in front of him. She was only about six years old and was wearing a knee-length flowery dress.

"Hello," she said with a smile. "I'm Pickles."

Robbie stood shocked, adrenaline racing and heart thumping in his chest. He expected to find a beast or some other demonic presence, but only found confusion.

"It's okay," the little girl said. "Perhaps you should sit down."

The little girl poked the dry wood and it glowed to life, its orange flames reflecting in her eyes. The campfire erupted with a warm, fiery glow. Its heat soothed Robbie and filled the air with a homely warmth. He sat down by the fire, and the little girl sat opposite.

"I am sure you have many questions," Pickles said, "but first, I think you should meet an old friend."

Pickles clicked her fingers, and the air behind her started to waver and warp. Suddenly, a tall, crimson demon materialised behind her. Robbie stood up and backed away, looking about for a weapon.

"Sit down," Pickles said and giggled.

"Hey, Robbie," Abbazul said.

Robbie stood there, mouth agape. He looked at Pickles, then at the demonic entity, then at Pickles.

"Remember me?" Abbazul said, brushing herself down.

Robbie stared at the demon for some time. "Sam?" he eventually said.

"I go by Abbazul now, but yes," Abbazul said,

"Sam."

Abbazul sat down next to Pickles and explained what had happened and how she ended up like she now was. Robbie listened intently but didn't say a word. Once Abbazul had finished, they sat, each lost in their thoughts.

"I'm sorry," Robbie said, breaking the silence.

Abbazul looked confused. "Sorry?" she said and laughed. "I have never felt better!"

Robbie turned away, filled with guilt and regret. "I should never have left you. I will never forgive myself."

Abbazul went to speak, but Pickles jumped in, "Sam hasn't gone. She's just changed. We have just changed."

"Sam has gone, and it's my fault," Robbie said and buried his face in his hands.

"It's okay," Samantha's voice echoed out from Abbazul.

Robbie looked up to see Abbazul looking confused. She shook her head and let out a loud roar. "Ah, that's better!"

"She hasn't gone, I promise," Pickles said and hugged Robbie.

Robbie smiled. "Thank you," he said.

"We have to find Jess now, I think," Pickles said, turning to Abbazul.

Abbazul summoned all her strength and sprung skyward, her wings unfolding to their full impressive span. She hung in the air like a shimmering beacon, shouting with an echoing voice that made the ground tremble. With unerring certainty, she pointed in a single direction.

"There!" she roared. That single word reverberated through the land like a coming storm.

Abbazul swooped down through the pale clouds with lightning speed. Before Robbie could utter a single word, he felt himself being swept up and soaring high in the sky towards an unknown destination. He watched the campsite below disappear as they soared higher and higher. Abbazul's wings spread wide and barely moved as they glided, cutting through the air with ease. They flew with such speed, the lifeless grassland appeared as a blur as it flashed by. Robbie struggled to catch his breath in the thin, cold air, but he was determined not to lose consciousness and calmed his breathing.

When they finally touched down, it was in a clearing surrounded by tall trees whose grey leaves rustled like whispering voices warning him to turn back. Thick gnarled branches twisted around one another like spindly fingers trying to keep out any trespassers who dared to enter uninvited. Abbazul dropped Robbie to the ground, and he shivered in the cold, biting air. He struggled to his feet as Pickles reappeared.

"Jess is here," she whispered.

"Jess!" Robbie shouted, but before he could step forward, Abbazul grabbed him firmly and pressed a finger against her lips.

A dark, thick mist appeared in the centre of the clearing. It writhed and twisted as though alive. The mist spread apart like a curtain to reveal a lone person standing there. Jessica stepped out, her eyes blackened pits, her fingers long and thin like spider legs. Her head hung low as a sinister smile twisted across her face, sending chills down Robbie's spine.

"Hello, Robert!" Jessica snapped mockingly.

Abbazul stepped forward, her voice ringing like thunder echoing around the clearing. "Where is that bastard? That coward dared to send its puppet to my domain!"

Pickles gently held Robbie's hand and pulled him away from the confrontation.

Jessica laughed dismissively. "I see you live." Her voice was twisted and repulsive.

"I live! Where is your master?!" Abbazul demanded.

Jessica suddenly leapt towards Abbazul, but was easily avoided as Abbazul flew into the air and landed gracefully on the other side of her, a smirk playing across her face.

"You are nothing but a puppet," Abbazul said calmly. "But I promise you, I will send you to Night!"

Jessica let out a guttural scream of unbridled rage and lunged at Abbazul with the ferocity of a wild beast. Her razor-sharp claw slashed through the air and tore into Abbazul's chest, leaving behind a bloody gash. But before she could follow with another strike, Abbazul moved with lightning-fast reflexes and grabbed Jessica by the throat with the force of an iron vice. Jessica gasped and choked, struggling in vain against the suffocating grip.

Robbie raced over and leapt onto Abbazul's back. "Sam! No!" he shouted.

Abbazul grabbed Robbie and hurled him to the ground, but he leapt up, desperate to protect Jessica. He lunged toward Abbazul with all his might, causing her grip to loosen just enough for Jessica to break free. Jessica hissed and retreated back into the mist. Robbie, without thought, gave chase and jumped in after her.

He stood alone as the mist closed around him, crawling across his skin like a virus. It moved around him slowly and deliberately, as if examining him. The fog filled the air with an oppressive stillness, alive yet eerily dead at its core. A creature lunged forward, pushing Robbie to the ground and trapping him beneath its squirming mass. Its back was covered in a thousand slimy tentacles that wrapped around him, slowly squeezing the breath from his lungs. Its head glared down at him with an expressionless face made of decaying flesh. Its mouth stretched open to reveal a monstrous, venomous tongue that slithered down and hung threateningly in Robbie's face.

"She is mine," it hissed.

"No!" Robbie croaked. "Let her go!"

The creature laughed. "I should eat you, slow, savour your flesh; but no, I will let you live, suffer. She will suffer," it said cruelly with pure hateful desire.

"Take me! Please, take me!" Robbie begged.

"You give yourself freely to me?" the creature said, surprised.

"I do! If you let her go!" Robbie said, desperately clinging to consciousness.

The creature laughed. "You will suffer, you will die and die again, you will beg, and I will not listen as I tear at your flesh over and over!" it said, poisonously salivating at the thought.

"Is she free?" Robbie said softly.

"She is free," the creature said.

Jessica stumbled out of the mist and fell to the ground. Pickles rushed over, helped her up, and moved her to the edge of the clearing.

"Jessica?" Pickles said, wiping her forehead with the hem of her dress.

Jessica looked blankly at her, dazed, her mind lost in a haze. Her throat tightened as she struggled to utter his name. She collapsed in grief, shaking and sobbing uncontrollably. Tears welled up in her eyes, streaming down her cheeks like a waterfall of sorrow. "Robbie!" she croaked before her legs gave way beneath her, and she collapsed into sobs.

"I know," Pickles said, trying to console her. "I know."

"Look! It is here!" Abbazul roared, her voice barely heard above the swirling storm.

An ear-splitting screech filled the air, and a raging wind stormed through the clearing like a wild beast. The trees shook and trembled under its might, and large branches snapped from their trunks, flying chaotically across the sky. Pickles wrapped her arms protectively around Jessica while Abbazul stood defiantly against the storm, undaunted by its power.

The ground shook as an enormous shadow materialised in the middle of the clearing, its hulking mass looming oppressively against the bleak sky. The Shadow had appeared, and its presence emanated a cold and malevolent energy that filled the air with an unseen dread. Then, unexpectedly, a man stumbled out.

"Daniel," Abbazul said, her voice softer.

"Sam," Daniel said, instantly seeing through the demonic skin.

Abbazul rushed over to him and caught him just as he fell. She moved him from the Shadow and placed him down next to Jessica, now lying still on the ground, eyes wide open and vacant.

"Jess," Daniel whispered.

As if his words held some magic, her eyes darted to him, and she sat up, threw her arms around him, and sobbed. They sat there, forgetting about the ominous watching presence, and comforted each other.

"Robbie has gone," Jessica whimpered. "He sacrificed himself to save me."

Daniel hugged her. "I know," he said. "Thank you for being here. I understand now."

"We're your friends. We will always be there for you, no matter what," she said.

"It's time for you," he paused and looked into her eyes, "and Robbie to go home." He smiled reassuringly. Jessica stopped crying and looked at him, suddenly realising his intent.

"I'll keep her safe," Pickles said.

"I have to go," Daniel said, standing up.

"I know, silly," Pickles said, sitting down next to Jessica.

A determined smile flashed across Daniel's face as he turned and walked towards the Shadow. It rose above him, a towering mass of darkness that pulsed with wicked energy. As he approached, the Shadow grew, stretching out its inky vines like grasping fingers. With each step, the air grew colder around him, his breath forming misty plumes in front of his face. The icy ground beneath his feet crunched as he approached. The Shadow grew more menacing, more dangerous, the closer he came. But Daniel stood firm, ready for whatever lay ahead.

"Show yourself!" Daniel bellowed, the thunder of his voice reverberating.

The shadowy mist cleared, and a corrupted hideous monster stood before him. Once Ozul, Lord of Shadows, a deity of death whose purpose was to bring stillness at the end of life, now nothing but a monstrous, twisted reflection of what it once was.

It had been distorted into the embodiment of nightmares and a beacon of pure terror. Its form was a horrific, eerie mutation of darkness and despair woven from the very fabric of fear itself. A diabolical creation, an entity of vomit-inducing terror, created as a personification of raw rage and malice, with the sole intent to devour Daniel. Writhing tentacles erupted from its back, blotting out the gloomy sky. Its grotesque appendages rippled with gruesome decaying flesh. They writhed and squirmed, with a single purpose to drag souls down into the deepest pit of never-ending suffering.

Without arms or legs, it hovered above the ground, a fleshy rotten orb with a wide maw stretched across it, a cavernous orifice of razor-sharp teeth that glinted with a menacing glee; each tooth a shimmering dagger of malevolent intent, wanting to taste flesh and shatter bone.

"Ozul!" A sound vile and corrupted erupted from it.

Abbazul pushed Daniel to the side and, without hesitation, opened her mouth and unleashed a raging inferno upon Ozul. As if the fires of Hell were spitting out from Abbazul's throat, Daniel watched in awe as a wall of flames leapt from her lips to devour the creature. Rocks became projectiles of fire that rained down from the sky, shattering the ground and spewing molten lava from its depths. With words of magic, she continued to chant wave after wave of destruction, her voice rising to a fever pitch until she finally collapsed with exhaustion. Still, the fire blazed on, magically confined to its target, relentlessly incinerating Ozul.

A horrific sound erupted from the epicentre of the flaming whirlpool. In an instant, the flames were sucked away, and Ozul was there with the same menacing smile, unmoved and unaffected by the attack. Abbazul was suddenly raised high in the air by an invisible force and slammed into the ground with a breaking of bone and splitting of flesh. She coughed out blackened red blood and winced in searing pain. Then, she was tossed aside like unwanted rubbish. Ozul then turned its attention to Daniel.

"Your journey ends now!" Bile poured from its mouth, hitting the charred ground with a hiss.

Daniel fell to his knees, feeling a crushing force on his chest. His ribs snapped, and he cried out in pain. Suddenly, a soft voice rang in his thoughts.

"Aya?" Daniel croaked.

In his hand, an amulet appeared; it glowed warmly. He held it up, and Ozul cried out, repelled by the sight of it. A pure white light erupted from the amulet and pierced the beast. It screamed in agony and lashed about. It turned to escape but was held in place by the light that had ensnared it.

"Now," a soft voice whispered to Daniel.

Daniel hurled the glowing amulet with all his might at the beast. It collided with its rotting skin, causing it to shriek out a thunderous roar. Flames erupted from its body like a raging inferno. Suddenly, a voice cried out full of sorrow and begging for release. Then, the beast was gone, and a heavy silence fell upon them.

A mist lingered where the beast had been. Daniel stared, frozen, expecting some other horror to materialise, but as it thinned and vanished, not a beast but a person now stood there. Daniel's eyes widened as Aya stepped forward. He felt his soul freeze, surprised and transfixed as their gaze met.

"Daniel?" Aya's voice pierced the air like a thunderclap, shaking him out of his trance. His heart raced as he stepped closer, not wanting to break the spell they were under.

He had found her and wanted to hold her now more than ever. He was sure the pendant had summoned her, but he didn't know how. It didn't matter; all that mattered was that she was with him now.

"How are you here?" Daniel said, his heart racing.

Daniel went to walk to her, but an old man lay on the ground between them, his body broken, struggling for breath. He was cloaked in an eerie mist, an ominous sign that death was to come. The man's hollow and dark gaze pierced

Daniel as the figure stirred.

"I have been freed," Ozul whispered in a low, barely audible voice. "You must complete the journey." His hoarse words still carried power and reverberated through the clearing.

Daniel looked at Aya, her eyes bright and burning with love for him. He yearned to go to her, but something was holding him back, as though he knew that they were standing at the end of their journey. He knew that this would be their final embrace, and he couldn't bear losing her again.

Then, Ozul spoke, its voice heavy with desperation. "Shadow must not end." Its words were barely audible, prompting Daniel to glance away from Aya. "Make your choice." Then it fell silent.

He looked up at Aya, who had a sad smile on her face. She was glowing softly, a warm radiance emanating from her.

"Daniel," Aya said in a soft, loving voice, "it is starting."

"No, not yet," Daniel said, desperately wanting time to stand still, but he knew that he had no choice and sighed heavily. His journey must end.

"Please," Aya said, "we will find each other again."

Daniel looked down, and a tear rolled down his cheek. "I accept my fate," he said, looking at Ozul. "I know what I must become."

"No," hissed Ozul, "it cannot be you."

"I don't understand. I thought I was to become…" Daniel looked confused.

Ozul raised its head and looked at Jessica, its cold, dark eyes penetrating her mind with shadow. Jessica stepped away, fear in her eyes.

"Efanu says what must be said," it chuckled. "You," Ozul hissed, raising a shadowy finger.

"Me?" Jessica said. "Why me? I don't understand."

"If not you, then everything will end," Pickles said. "I think it was always going to be you."

"What does that mean?" she said, stepping away.

"You will take Ozul's place, that's all, silly, and everything will begin again."

Jessica hesitated, looking about her for an answer, but none came, then her mind filled with Robbie.

"Can I save Robbie?" Jessica said in a sad, low tone.

"Yes, of course. You will save us all," Pickles said, holding Jessica's hand.

As Jessica cast her gaze upon Pickles' cheerful visage, a wave of serenity washed over her, all anxiety and uncertainty melting away as if struck by a magical charm.

"What must I do?" she said.

At that moment, Ozul spoke the words, "It is done." Jessica felt as if its eerily black eyes were looking straight into her soul. Then, for the last time, Ozul said, "Then to the 'Night' I go," before it faded and vanished.

Suddenly, Jessica crumpled to the ground, her body convulsing with pain. Her screams pierced the air. Her body morphed, losing its definition. She seemed to melt and blur into the shadows, losing her form and becoming neither flesh nor phantom. In a flash, her eyes sprung wide open, two black coals staring out. Her body once again took form, but was ghostly in appearance.

"I feel different," Jessica said, her voice now hollow and distant, like an echo carried on a remote breeze.

Her dead eyes pierced her companions as a gust of wind rippled across the land, sweeping up a deafening howl that raced through the very air around them. She slowly raised her hand, and it seemed to hang heavy in the turbulent atmosphere, almost suspending time.

"It is done," she said, "my land has been

cleansed."

A whirling mist erupted from the ground and quickly dispersed, leaving Robbie's crumpled body lying there. All at once, Jessica's demeanour shifted. It was as if her true personality had emerged from a dark, hidden place. She raced to him, her heartbeat pounding in her ears.

"Robbie!" she sobbed, as she fell to her knees. "Please be alive! Don't leave me!"

Robbie lay there unmoving as Jessica gentle cradled his limp body. Suddenly, his eyelids flickered as heard her voice and he lovingly smiled.

"Jess…" he whispered, then faded, leaving Jessica alone and screaming on the ground.

"No!" she screamed in rage. "This can't be!"

"He has found sleep, silly," Pickles said, trying to calm Jessica's rage.

Jessica turned violently. "You said I would save him!" She seemed to darken with her anger as a mist swirled about her. Her dark eyes filled with hatred and a need for vengeance, wanting to devour the universe itself.

"You have," Pickles said softly.

Jessica's body seemed to elongate as she stood up from where Robbie had been lying. Her posture was perfect, every inch of her frame taut and graceful, like a dancer poised for a grand finale. The muscles in her legs were visible even through the shadowy fabric that hung on her frame, every curve and sinew beneath her skin evident in the sudden shift of her stance. She seemed to emanate an aura of power that filled the air with an almost tangible frightening force.

She took a step forward and then another, and the ground beside her faded away, lost in a shadowy mist. The shadows about her came alive, curling down from her shoulders to trail out away from her as though they were searching for their prey.

"Remember your purpose," Pickles' words penetrated the wall of darkness that had surrounded Jessica, and her demeanour seemed to shrink as though a memory had been reignited.

Aya walked to Daniel. "Jess, it is time," she said softly.

Jessica turned. "Can I follow him?"

"Yes," Abbazul said, "we will all be re-awakened."

"It must be done now," Pickles said, looking at Jessica.

"Now!" bellowed Abbazul.

Jessica suddenly calmed and turned to Aya

and Daniel. The three stood in a circle and instinctively raised their hands. Aya and Daniel looked at one another.

"I love you," Daniel said.

"I love you too," Aya smiled, then closed her eyes.

Aya's pure white light grew, as did Jessica's coal-black shadow. Energy and non-energy, matter and anti-matter, wove about each other in lazy spirals like the winds of a hurricane. The moment they touched, all would begin anew. The balance between light and dark was once again found; each now awaited the seed, the human soul that carried life.

The heavens above them suddenly split in two with thunderous force, and lightning rained down from the great chasm. The voice of a god roiled from the sky like an avalanche, booming out a proclamation that shook the very ground beneath their feet: "This dream will end! Yuotha, you shall awaken now!"

A blazing blue flash erupted about them. In an instant, both Aya and Jessica fell to the ground. Jessica cried out in terror as though possessed by some hidden evil. She stared at Daniel, her mouth wide open in a silent scream. She thrashed and convulsed as her body twisted into a horrible, monstrous form. Tears streamed down her face, and she howled in agony. She looked at Aya, tears streaming down her face, but instead of sadness or desperation, she was filled with rage. With one swift movement, she lunged forward, fingers outstretched, claws primed for attack. Aya screamed as she made contact. Light erupted from Aya like an exploding sun. Daniel and Abbazul were thrown back.

When Daniel opened his eyes, he was no longer in the clearing. Aya and Jessica were gone, and he was flying high in the sky, carried by Abbazul.

"They're gone!" Abbazul sobbed. "Look!"

Daniel turned his head to see the world begin to shatter, splintering and breaking up like broken glass as reality tore itself apart. With a deafening roar, the sky was ripped, and the land fell away into nothingness, leaving Daniel in a silent empty gloom.

"It's all ending!" Abbazul shouted.

...

"Don't worry," said Little Pea.

"Where am I?" Daniel said.

"I will keep you safe," Little Pea said. "There is still hope. I hear them calling. They want me to awaken."

"You?" Daniel said in shock.

"I am the Yuotha that they are calling."

CHAPTER 15

Truth Revealed
Even gods lose their way

A misty haze surrounded their collective consciousness, manifesting and giving birth to ideas. Their thoughts were shared, their voices resonating as they searched for understanding and truth. The melodies they created echoed, brimming with creation, until one voice fell silent, fading into an eternal dream.

"Why does he not wake?" Ziot-Ty-Ar spoke, yet no sounds were made. His thoughts were instantly known.

"Surely the dream is done," Gry-Ory-Zun said.

"Has no lesson been learned?" Ziot-Ty-Ar scoffed. "He is nothing but a fool."

"That may be so, Yuotha, but we cannot wander further without Him," Gry-Ory-Zun added with a sigh.

"We must wake him now!" Ziot-Ty-Ar

demanded angrily.

"We cannot reach him whilst he is in this form. He is far from us and has lost himself to the dream." Gry-Ory-Zun fell silent, deep in thought. "But perhaps we can speak to him."

"How?" Ziot-Ty-Ar asked, trying to understand.

"We can change the dream, break it," Gry-Ory-Zun said, his energy pulsating with malice.

"Is that possible?" Ziot-Ty-Ar asked.

"I can corrupt the dream, change it, end it, and then he must wake!" He paused for a moment as he aligned his vibration with that of his brother's. "Lend me your strength, Yuotha, and we will end this," Gry-Ory-Zun said as his formless being started to take shape.

Gry-Ory-Zun and Ziot-Ty-Ar, beings of pure energy, made a sound that resonated throughout the empty void of potential that they occupied. Gry-Ory-Zun, connected with Ez-Amu-Fion-Uz, peered into his mind and stole a piece of his world. With their power, with their voice, it was born into the void.

They took form and stepped into the stolen landscape of Ez-Amu-Fion-Uz, their brother's dream. The land was covered in bright, lush green grass. Golden trees surrounded the meadow and swayed gently in the cool breeze. Birds sang their cheerful songs, and a blue sky with an orange sun blanketed warmly over all that lived. The sun hung high in the sky, and its rays warmed everything they touched. A path lined with lamp posts led to a small wood and stone cabin.

"What is this place?" Ziot-Ty-Ar asked.

"This is the dream that he has been lost in," Gry-Ory-Zun said, looking towards an old cabin. "He lies there, and there we will end this."

....

Corruption

The tall, stern-faced priest stood in front of the congregation that had grown over the many years of his travels. His strong voice resonated throughout the lands that he had wandered, and those assembled heard his words and obeyed his will. Ozul was the god who had come to him in his dreams, revealing a truth of life and eternal death. He had been chosen to carry out Ozul's will, to create the world anew in Shadow.

The priest stood tall, his voice reverberating through the air like thunder. The candles burned dimly, causing shadowy images to stalk the walls of the interior.

"Welcome, friends," his voice bellowed out, his eyes black as night.

"We are one in Shadow, Ozul's faithful servants! I have seen the Light, and its cold cruelty is unforgiving. Beware those who bring an end to our creator's sacred will!" He raised his arms high, and a deafening clap shook the earth beneath their feet.

The chanting of ancient words filled the air as the crowd bowed their heads in unison. The power of their faith was so strong that it seemed to awaken something deep within them, a righteous fury that blazed like an inferno.

"At Ozul's command, I shall lay waste to all those who defile this holy land! My sword shall be their undoing!" His voice rang out in a primal roar, echoing off into eternity.

"The time has come, my brethren!" the priest railed as he rose up before the masses. His eyes burned with a wild intensity, illuminated by an unseen force. "Let the wicked know that there is no mercy in Ozul's sight, only justice."

A group of hooded figures lurched forward, dragging the limp body of a woman who appeared to be under some hypnotic effect. They threw her to the ground in front of the priest like an animal offering. The woman lay motionless, her breath shallow, chest barely rising with each inhale. With a sickening clap, the hooded figures tore away her dress, exposing her quivering skin to the raw air. Black vein-like lines snaked out from her beating heart and crept across her skin. They throbbed and pulsated with a supernatural energy that seemed to bleed into every ounce of her being. Her body twitched violently as though something was taking hold of her very soul; she moaned and writhed with primal pleasure, overcome with ecstatic agony as she ran her hands over her shuddering body. She screamed as she caressed herself, lost to a strange, perverse pleasure.

"Ozul, I call you. Guide us. What is your will?"

The woman trembled, her eyes momentarily widened wide with terror. She clawed at her chest as the priest's words echoed in her ears, each syllable like a poison searing through her veins. A gruesome howl ripped from her throat as the darkness engulfed her. Her body shuddered and convulsed in a frenzied state until she lay motionless, surrounded by an inky veil of deathly night.

"Ozul!" Suddenly, Ozul's voice burst from her lifeless body. Its sound echoed about them like a thousand shrieks of agony, sending the congregation to their knees in terror. The woman lay still, her mouth wide open, her eyes black, fixed upon the ceiling with an empty and silent stare.

Upon hearing the terrifying sound, the priest fell to his knees, as did the congregation, and all fell silent as they waited for Ozul's command.

"Find the seed. The union must not happen!" it hissed. "Search for him."

"We will do as you ask," the priest said, lying face down on the ground in submission to his god.

"Daniel," it hissed again with hatred in its voice. "Daniel must be mine!"

The woman's lifeless corpse buckled and snapped as it was ripped from the ground. Her bones creaked in agony as an invisible force contorted her body with a sickening ferocity. Skin sloughing off like wet paper, blood spilling from her eyes and nose, she pirouetted into the air before her broken form spasmed violently, then it fell into shadow and dissipated into nothingness.

"I accept your offering!" Ozul shrieked, sending a chill, malicious wind to sweep throughout the church.

A fierce gale erupted and raged with a cruel, cutting ferocity as it ripped through the church, causing people to scream out in fear as they ran for their lives, trying desperately to escape the invisible force that sought their blood. Those in the congregation were thrown into the air like leaves on the wind, their bodies broken and skin stripped in wails of agony. Blood ran down the walls and pooled on the ground, snaking its way to the lying priest.

The priest remained still, his eyes closed as he mouthed ancient words of worship. When he finally stood up, there was no one left; only piles of ripped, blood-soaked robes remained in the now-empty church.

As he gazed downwards, he saw that a river of dark blood, still as glass, encircled him. He stepped in it, sending ripples across its smooth surface. He paused and looked down, and his reflection stared up at him. Suddenly, his reflection lunged out and grabbed him, dragging him down into the depths of some unknown dark hell. A heartbeat later, the priest reappeared in a swirl of dark energy. His voice slithered across the air with an icy hiss. "Ozul!" he snarled.

...

They walked towards the cabin, confusion filling their thoughts. The meadow was alien to them, the sights and smells of the likes they had never experienced. Colour burst all around them, filling the air with a sweet scent of summer bloom. Even in this stolen dream world, life found a way to flourish. As the Yuothas walked, their pace and anger lessened as they heard a soft melody coming from the treetops. They stopped to see birds for the first time. Their colourful plumage shimmered in the sunlight, and they watched, amazed, as these little creatures took flight and played as they hovered on an updraft. A wind swept up some golden leaves that whirled about, then fluttered to the ground in front of them. When they had cleared, a little girl stood on the path, blocking their way.

"Hello, Yuothas," Little Pea said.

"Ez-Amu-Fion-Uz, you are not awake," Ziot-Ty-Ar said.

"True, I sleep the eternal sleep," Little Pea said. "But I have come to speak with you. I have knowledge to share."

"We will see," Gry-Ory-Zun said, anger still lingering in his thoughts.

"Yuotha, calm yourself. You have much to learn," Little Pea said kindly. "Let me show you."

"Enough of this rouse," Ziot-Ty-Ar said. "We have waited, and our patience is thinned."

Little Pea laughed. "You speak as though time has any bearing on us."

Ziot-Ty-Ar grunted angrily.

"Wise as ever," Gry-Ory-Zun laughed, his thoughts succumbing to the peace found in the meadow.

"Yuotha, this place is," Ziot-Ty-Ar paused, "uncomfortable. It is not the dream I dream; this feels wrong to me."

"Only because you have not come to know life

and our true purpose," Little Pea said warmly, her wise words no less meaningful despite Ez-Amu-Fion-Uz's appearance.

"You have learned all that can be learned here," Gry-Ory-Zun looked about, "in this place of life. There is no more that can be known. It is time for you to wake. It is time for us all to leave this place and dream anew."

"No, my dear Yuotha, this is the end of our journey. I have found our purpose. It is to bring life and all that comes from that life," Little Pea said, her words warm and inviting.

"No!" Ziot-Ty-Ar snapped angrily. "Your will shall not bend me. You must wake!"

"Join me, Yuothas. Let us become one. Join me in creation. I know you will find contentment in that," Little Pea said, hoping that her words would resonate with her Yuothas.

"Show us," Gry-Ory-Zun said, waving a hand to silence Ziot-Ty-Ar's objections.

Little Pea smiled broadly. The leaves whirled up once again, and she was gone.

...

"You are the last," Little Pea said to Daniel.

They sat on a small patch of grass, surrounded by an empty black void. A dull light radiated from Little Pea, offering some illumination and a little comfort to Daniel's despair.

"Is this the end?" Daniel said.

"Maybe," Little Pea said, "but there is hope."

"Hope?" he said despairingly. "Will I see Aya again?"

"Perhaps," she said.

"How?" Daniel stared aimlessly at the small patch of grass by his feet.

"You must speak with my Yuothas." She paused. "My brothers."

Daniel looked up at Little Pea, and for the first time, she looked lost, desperate and fearful.

"You hold the human spirit. It carries the seed of life, it carries understanding and knowledge. It carries hope. You are that hope," she said, looking at Daniel as though she was searching for something she could not find.

"If I can see Aya again, then I will try," Daniel said. "What must I do?"

"It is your love that makes you special, but be wary, my dear Daniel." She paused. "Be wary."

...

Daniel stood outside of the cabin. It looked familiar to him, but new and full of life. He looked up to be greeted by the warm sunlight and the silhouette of birds playing in the sky. As he looked around, he almost forgot the plight of the world where he had come from. It was beautiful in this place. The colour and scents filled his senses. It was almost perfection, but there was just one thing missing: Aya.

Two odd-looking men stood farther down the path. They were unusually tall and broad, and they stood naked. Their bodies were muscular and lean, and their skin had an olive tone that glowed silver-white in the sunlight. Their long black hair trailed down over their shoulders to the ground and straggled behind them. As Daniel approached, he could see they did not appear human, clearly missing productive organs and other human features. They looked like an attempt to appear human, a creation by someone or something that did not understand what a human being was. However, with what he had seen, this did not shock him. He knew they were the beings that he must convince, and despite his deep sadness, he was resolved to save his world.

"What are you? Curious," Ziot-Ty-Ar sneered. He turned to his brother. "Is this why our Yuotha will not wake?"

Gry-Ory-Zun remained silent. His eyes examined Daniel, piercing his outer skin, looking beyond his physical appearance and into his very essence as though he was exploring every atom of his being. Daniel felt his thoughts being invaded, and no matter how he tried, he could not keep him out.

"We should end this now!" Ziot-Ty-Ar snapped and took a step towards Daniel.

Gry-Ory-Zun held out his arm and calmly said, "No, Yuotha. This is a curiosity."

Daniel was thankful that Gry-Ory-Zun had taken an interest in him, hoping this would give him the opportunity to speak. He questioned if Gry-Ory-Zun perceived his thoughts since he flashed a curious smirk.

"Daniel?" Gry-Ory-Zun said. "I believe that is what you have been named."

Daniel looked bewildered, wondering if there would be anything that he would be able to say to convince these beings that his world was important.

"You may speak if that is what you wish," Gry-Ory-Zun added.

Daniel looked at them, their strange postures now plain to him. They looked uncomfortable, as though being here in this place was as alien to them as they were to him.

"It's beautiful here," Daniel finally said.

They looked at him, shocked, because they did not understand what he saw. In their perception, this was nothing but a dream, a lesson to be learned and to end. To keep it going infinitely seemed ridiculous, outrageous, and pointless.

"I see nothing here of value, only a curiosity that must end," Gry-Ory-Zun said in response. Ziot-Ty-Ar looked away, disinterested in Daniel or his words.

Daniel breathed in the air and sighed. "Can you not smell the sweet scent, see the beautiful colours, hear the songs?" He looked about, and for the first time in a long time, he smiled.

"I see nothing of interest. The smells and colours you hold so dear are nothing but a distraction," Ziot-Ty-Ar sneered, spitting out his words in utter contempt.

"I see life," Daniel said. "I see hope."

Gry-Ory-Zun looked at Daniel again as though he was searching for something, and then he spoke. "Aya. Who is Aya?"

Daniel felt his heart twist and rend at the thought of Aya. She was lost to him now and forever. A gaping wound yawned in his chest, threatening to collapse his entire body. He felt the emptiness left where Aya once occupied, a void that would never be filled.

"What is this you feel?" Gry-Ory-Zun asked.

Daniel looked at him, his vision blurred by the tears that ran down his cheek.

"She…" He could barely bring himself to say it out aloud, as though doing so would somehow confirm its truth. "She has gone."

"Gone?" Gry-Ory-Zun questioned.

Daniel looked at him angrily. God or no god, his insensitivity was something that he could not deal with at that moment.

"Yes, gone!" he said angrily.

Gry-Ory-Zun looked at him calmly, unmoved by Daniel's outburst. "She was just a dream, as you are," he said dismissively.

"She was alive! As I am, as my friends were!" Daniel spat out his words. "But they have gone, they have all gone."

"Alive?" Gry-Ory-Zun said, trying to understand the word. "What do you think this means?"

Daniel looked at him, shocked, but suddenly realised that the question was genuine. They did not understand.

"I feel," Daniel simply said.

Gry-Ory-Zun looked surprised at his answer. Even Ziot-Ty-Ar turned, looking curiously at Daniel.

"I love," Daniel said with sadness in his voice.

"Enough!" Ziot-Ty-Ar suddenly interrupted. "He must awake. We must go!"

"Yuotha, Ez-Amu-Fion-Uz could easily remain in this state. If we do not resolve this in the correct manner, we, too, will be now trapped here. No, we must find the right way," Gry-Ory-Zun said.

"Aya," Ziot-Ty-Ar said. "I feel Daniel's yearning."

"Yes, I too feel it," Gry-Ory-Zun said, then turned to Daniel. "Are we mistaken?"

Daniel looked at them, and a glimmer of hope rose in him. "Of course not. Don't you understand?"

"I do not, but I do understand you are not just a dream. You are something more, something, as you say, alive. For that reason, I shall give you a choice." Gry-Ory-Zun paused and looked about as if starting to have a small appreciation for the place where he stood. "There is a way that you could remain here with Aya, but you must forsake the world that created you so that my Yuotha will awake."

Daniel felt a desire to simply say yes and end all his suffering, but to sacrifice everything, all that he cared for, was something that threw his thoughts into chaos. *Aya,* he thought, *to see you again...* This idea lifted him from despair, out of his pool of sorrow. To live again with her was something that he craved and he yearned for more than anything.

"Betrayal," he whispered.

Gry-Ory-Zun observed Daniel intently, with

an unreadable expression on his face. He could see the struggle in Daniel's eyes and knew that he was battling himself internally. On the surface, there seemed to be other options, but Gry-Ory-Zun could understand the truth that only one real option was available. Though he had never met a human before, he was wise and could read the inner turmoil in Daniel.

"Can I really be with Aya again?" Daniel asked, shame rising in him, for he knew what he wanted and understood the consequences of that choice.

"Yes," Gry-Ory-Zun said, his tone somehow softer.

"I want Aya more than life itself," Daniel said, as a tear rolled down his cheek.

"Then it shall be so," Gry-Ory-Zun said.

"Will she know what I have done?" Daniel asked quietly.

Gry-Ory-Zun looked at him; then, for a brief moment, his expression changed as though he showed pity. "No, she shall only know this place and you."

Gry-Ory-Zun and Ziot-Ty-Ar left Daniel there and went to the cabin. Daniel watched them awkwardly move their bodies as they entered the cabin, closing the door behind them. The air was filled with a soft humming sound, and the world blurred for only a moment.

"Daniel!" a familiar voice called out. He turned to see Aya running towards him.

...

"What have you done?" Little Pea whispered.

Daniel awoke sweating again, his mind in turmoil and guilt-ridden, but as he turned to see Aya lying next to him, all the feelings of doubt lifted. She was here with him, and that was all that mattered. As per Gry-Ory-Zun's words, Aya remembered only this place. In her mind, there had only ever been the here and now, a moment that was and always shall be. It was only Daniel who remembered the past that was no more. Gry-Ory-Zun had offered to clear his mind, to start anew, but Daniel did not want his friends, did not want that world to be forgotten, so asked that its essence be left with him. In a sense, it was his penance, a price that he wanted to pay for his choice.

"Did you have another bad dream?" Aya said, rubbing Daniel's back.

Daniel smiled. "It was nothing."

"I'm worried about you," she said, giving him a kiss. "Let's go out for a walk in the meadow." She went to the window and opened the curtain. "It's a beautiful day." She went into the other room, where she started a fire and hung a kettle over its heat.

"Come on, lazy!" she called out to Daniel.

THE FINAL JOURNEY

There was always food in the cupboard, always firewood, always tea in the pot, and it was always a wonderful day. This was the paradise that was given to Daniel, the perfect little piece of a lost world. He had everything he ever wanted, and though he was happier now, there was something lingering in the shadows of his mind, something lurked, and it would not let him be free.

They went through the same routine that they had countless times before, leaving the cabin and walking down to a stream that ran along the edge of the meadow. They walked to the end of the meadow, where a fence set its perimeter, then turned and followed it as it led them up a small incline before turning again, leading across the top of a hill, and then back down to where they had begun. They would then sit for countless hours watching the animals playing, the clouds lazily passing overhead, until the sun would dim. They would then eat the same meal, drink the same wine, go to the same bed, make love, and sleep at the same time, to be awoken the next day by Daniel's nightmare.

A discontent rose in him, like a small seed bursting into life, its roots pushing out to infest his thoughts. Though he tried day after day to turn away, to live in this divine moment that was gifted to him, he could not fully be present.

One night, he abruptly awoke, but it was not

morning. The sun had not yet risen, and the darkness still lingered outside. He turned to see Aya fast asleep, smiling as if she was lost in some happy dream.

"Daniel." He suddenly heard his name echoing from outside. He sat there momentarily, wondering if he was dreaming, but then he heard his name being called again.

He turned to Aya, who had not stirred, and gently moved a strand of hair that had fallen across her face.

"Daniel!" This time, there was no ambiguity; he heard his name clearly. *Have the gods returned?*, he thought, and he was struck with a pang of fear.

He got dressed and left the room, not wanting to wake Aya. He cautiously went outside and looked about. Little Pea was sitting on the porch's step to his shock and surprise.

"I did tell you to be careful," she said. "Come sit by me."

Daniel was lost for words. Indeed, a god had returned, but he did not expect to see Little Pea.

"How are you here?" Daniel asked, happy to see her.

"Hi," she said with a kind smile. "I am and, well, I am not here."

Daniel scrunched up his face, and Little Pea laughed. "Let me explain. I hid when you went to see my Yuothas. I knew what you would do, so part of me hid. They didn't realise I could do that." She looked immensely proud of herself and giggled.

"Hid? Where?" Daniel asked, looking around.

"In you, of course, the only place I could." She smiled.

"It's so good to see you," Daniel said, then knelt and gave Little Pea a hug.

"I missed you too," she said, her face squished into his shoulder.

"So, will you stay?" Daniel said eagerly. "Aya will want to see you."

Little Pea suddenly looked sad. "She doesn't know me. She has forgotten."

"Oh, of course," Daniel said glumly. He turned to Little Pea. "What have I done? In my grief, I…" His voice trailed off.

Little Pea stood up and turned to Daniel. "We can change this if you want."

"Change, what do you mean?"

"End this," she looked about, "this beautiful illusion."

Daniel sat silently, pondering her words. "But I

could lose her," he said softly.

"Yes, but is this really the Aya you remember?" Little Pea looked at the cabin as though she could see through the stone walls at Aya sleeping.

"No," Daniel said, "it's not her."

"She still lives in you." She placed a hand on Daniel's chest. "They all do. You are the seed, and with you, we can start anew."

"That easy?" Daniel said.

Little Pea laughed. "No, of course not. We need Aya."

Daniel looked back at the cabin.

"No, the real Aya. That is only part of her. We need to restore her essence; she needs to remember, and remember the gift that Eva gave her."

"How would we do that?" Daniel said, wondering if this was the right thing to do. "Anyway, I thought there had to be three, and Jess has gone."

"Well, yes. I may be able to call to the Shadow, but it will be, well…" she paused, "unpredictable. Nothing is as it was; it has all changed. We are in uncharted waters, and to be honest, I don't know if this is the right way. But perhaps…" She trailed away, lost in thought.

"Okay," Daniel said, breaking Little Pea's focus. "What do I have to do?"

"Help Aya see the truth and help her remember," she said, her voice suddenly tinged with sadness.

"What's wrong?" Daniel asked.

"I cannot guarantee that things will be as they were. It will all be new, unknown." She looked deeply into Daniel's eyes. "If we succeed, you may not know Aya."

Daniel stared at Little Pea, and his heart sank. He felt that the little hope that had arisen was now washed away.

"You have yet another choice to make: stay here or risk it all. I do not envy you, but such is the way of things." She turned and started to walk down the path.

"Tell me," Daniel called out. "Am I even alive? Is any of this real?"

Little Pea stopped and turned. "Truth?" she said. "It's a funny thing." She beckoned Daniel to walk with her. Daniel noticed that Little Pea suddenly appeared older than her physical years.

"What you see is like a dream. You exist, but it is an interpretation of you," she said. "Look at that tree; it is a tree, and to you, it is real, but the truth is that it's just your interpretation of the tree's essence. Much like you. You are real, but this is just an interpretation of your essence."

They stopped by an old wooden bench and sat down. A cool night gripped the land, and a full moon hung high in the sky, casting its silvery glow over the meadow.

"That moon," she went on. "It is beautiful. It is real because we see it. However, its truth is vastly different. It cannot be seen, plotted, felt, or even described." She paused and stared up. She seemed to connect with the moon and smiled. "Its truth is that its essence is of God, as we all are. Aspects of the whole."

"So, am I alive?" Daniel asked.

"Life and death are amusing things. Where one sees life, another sees death, each as real and as false as the other." She chuckled, and for a brief moment, Daniel saw an old woman sitting next to him. "Time. Past. Present. Future. It's all just perception."

Suddenly, Little Pea jumped up. "When my brothers left, this little world was not just gifted to you. It is you, Daniel."

Daniel looked about him, trying to understand her words, but he knew what she said to be true. He had always known.

"Don't worry. In the end, it will all come together." Little Pea smiled warmly.

She started to skip away, and once again, she appeared as a bright young child. Daniel went to speak, but she stopped and turned back. "Now you better wake up. It's going to be a lovely morning!"

CHAPTER 16

Final Choice
Life begins anew.

Before the void and even before thought itself, there existed a state of oneness. It was a place beyond the boundaries of time and space, a singularity that was both existent and non-existent, full of potential and shimmering with possibilities like a blank canvas waiting to burst into life. In this state, there was no thought, no desire, no identity, and no separation. No words could be spoken, no thoughts could be made, and no understanding could be found.

Like a stone cast into a still body of water, creating ripples that radiated outwards, distorting the once formless surface, a hidden power awoke something dormant, igniting a spark of life in the depths of an unknown. And so, the void was born, stretching out forever, its presence spreading with infinite potential throughout eternity. As it rippled out, new dimensions burst into reality, a torrent of vibration washing through the emptiness. The void pulsated without purpose, simply to be, to exist. It washed back and forth, pushing against the boundaries of its existence; like a hungry sea crashing against the shore, it eroded away the walls of limitation and grew, each surge of energy potential for life, and from the chaos, whether by design or chance, the Three emerged.

At first, they were nothing but a flicker of light, an idea born from the reverberations of the void. The inky blackness crackled and swirled about them as though invisible hands grasped at the fabric of reality, twisting and manipulating it. Their forms twisted and contorted, embodying the very forces of creation and destruction. Every moment was a cycle of being torn apart and reformed as life and death flowed relentlessly through their being. Endless waves crashed against them, tossing them about like helpless debris in a tempestuous storm. They were awake and then thrust into an abyss of nothingness, only to be reborn into the chaos once again.

Slowly, the void calmed, the storm subsided, and the Three drifted silently in the aftermath, waiting for the only existence they knew, one filled with constant turmoil and unyielding transformation. As they beheld this strange realm for the first time, like newborns discovering a world, they were enraptured with wonder and terror at their own existence. They reached out into the dark, grasping at anything that could offer solace in this chaotic landscape. And in each other, they found a flicker of light amidst the darkness. But even in that brief moment of comfort, a fear coexisted within them, an intense mix of emotions that threatened to overwhelm their fragile new existence.

The Three wandered through the desolate void, their thoughts drifting without purpose. They found comfort in one another, and for a while, that was enough. However, a sense of time grew in them, and the overwhelming emptiness started to weigh heavy on their minds. Soon, a thought emerged; they started to wonder why they existed, and an insatiable hunger for purpose grew. Their hazy thoughts took shape, and they spent time drifting away, lost in colour and formless shapes. Silently, they floated through the void, their every thought now consumed by an obsession that ignited endless dreams and propelled them forward in search of answers. New ideas now flooded their minds as they searched for meaning and their true purpose.

Their minds were soon filled with vivid and potent dreams, driving them forward with an unstoppable force to create. Each dream gave birth to new worlds, intricate and magnificent, bursting forth from their very thoughts and expanding into boundless universes. They took delight in their abilities, overflowing with pride for their creations. But the Three did not find contentment in their dreams, only a reflection of the void, a darkness at the heart of their being. As they stared into their existence, a glimmer of hope revealed itself, illuminating their thought and offering direction. A pressing question formed, and it burned in their deepest subconscious: *Who am I?* It reverberated within them, its power overwhelming and demanding to be addressed. In the question, they found a purpose, a reason to exist, and a sense of individuality arose.

Their dreams became lessons; each time they woke, their minds brimmed with newfound understanding. With each dream, they birthed intricate and mesmerising worlds, expanding their reality beyond the limits of their imagination. But as their dreams grew increasingly complex, so did their egos. They revelled in the power of creation, imagining creatures whose sole purpose was to worship them as gods. As their dreams grew more grandiose, ego overshadowed any wisdom they possessed. And as they drifted apart, each finding strength in their own existence, a hunger for domination took hold. They gave themselves names, symbols of their newfound arrogance and desire to rule over all they had created: Ez-Amu-Fion-Uz, Ziot-Ty-Ar, and Gry-Ory-Zun.

...

The emptiness of space seemed to shimmer and blur as the three gods drifted, their ethereal forms radiating a gentle, hazy aura of transcendental thinking. Ziot-Ty-Ar and Gry-Ory-Zun orbited around Ez-Amu-Fion-Uz, closely examining his vibration and attempting to penetrate his consciousness. Ez-Amu-Fion-Uz remained still, pulsating with serene, amorphous energy that permeated the vast expanse around him. Ziot-Ty-Ar and Gry-Ory-Zun were locked in deep contemplation, as if listening for the faintest whispers of thought from their brother.

"Why does he remain silent?" Ziot-Ty-Ar said. "Perhaps the waking has left him in this state? It angers me that he does not speak."

"I understand your anger. I, too, feel your

rage," Gry-Ory-Zun said in his usual way, without sound.

They moved around Ez-Amu-Fion-Uz, trying to find some understanding, but his silence could not be penetrated. They had grown accustomed to Ez-Amu-Fion-Uz's silence, but this time, it felt different. There was an air of tranquillity surrounding him that they couldn't quite comprehend. Ziot-Ty-Ar's anger grew with each passing moment. He wanted answers, and he wanted them now.

"We should wake him," Ziot-Ty-Ar declared with a fierce determination in his voice.

"No," Gry-Ory-Zun replied calmly. "Let him be."

"But why? Why does he remain? Is he still lost to his dream?"

"Perhaps he has found a higher purpose beyond our comprehension," Gry-Ory-Zun mused, his thoughts drifting back to their original purpose.

Ziot-Ty-Ar scoffed at the suggestion. "There is no higher purpose than power and control."

"Perhaps," Gry-Ory-Zun said, "but his dream intrigues me. Daniel was more than just a creature, it had thought."

"Daniel was nothing, a dream of our Yuotha who fell into a state of corruption," Ziot-Ty-Ar said, dismissing any notion that Daniel was anything more than a thought from a corrupted mind.

"Perhaps, but I placed that corruption there," Gry-Ory-Zun said, shimmering with new energy as new thoughts were born. "Perhaps it was our interference that made it possible?"

"I will not tolerate this any further," Ziot-Ty-Ar said. "This ends now!"

Gry-Ory-Zun radiated with a dull, pulsating glow as he aligned his vibration with that of his silent brother. His energy rippled through the void, humming softly like a distant echo.

"I understand now, my Yuotha," Gry-Ory-Zun thought, barely a whisper, tinged with reverence and understanding. The two brothers hummed in perfect synchronicity, their energies intertwining and merging in a dance of unity.

As his brother's words echoed in Ziot-Ty-Ar's mind, they felt venomous and cruel, igniting his anger to erupt into a blazing inferno of pure hate-filled rage. With a single thought, every fibre of his being pulsated and surged with immense power. Like a tsunami unleashed upon an unexpecting world, he exploded with destructive force, a blinding burst of energy that tore through the fabric of the void and consumed everything in its path. Before Gry-Ory-Zun could react, his brother's wrath was upon him. His cries were drowned out by the deafening roar of destruction that caused the very fabric of existence to tremble; a second later, Ez-Amu-Fion-Uz met the same fate. Gry-Ory-Zun and Ez-Amu-Fion-Uz were swallowed whole by his all-consuming rage, their essence torn apart and devoured by the searing flames of hate.

In the blink of an eye, all that remained was Ziot-Ty-Ar, surrounded by the shattered pieces of the void that his brothers had once occupied. The silence that followed was deafening, broken only by Ziot-Ty-Ar's growing fear and anguish. He felt shame and triumph amidst the ruins of those who had once been his equals.

Now alone in the emptiness, with his brothers gone, his mind turned to Daniel, and a burning resentment grew in him.

...

Daniel sat up in bed, sweat running down his back. Little Pea's words echoed through his mind, a persistent torment, pushing for a decision for a choice to be made.

"Did you have another bad dream?" Aya said, rubbing Daniel's back.

Daniel smiled. "It was nothing." He paused. "No, wait."

Aya went over to the window. "It's a—" she started to speak but was interrupted.

"Wait!" Daniel snapped.

Aya paused and looked confused. "Are you feeling okay?" she said, concern now drawn across her face.

"I'm…" he paused, "I…" He trailed away as he feared the consequence of his words.

"It's a beautiful day," Aya said, turning to look out the window; her earlier concern seemed to have melted from her expression. She left the room, as she always did, calling out to Daniel. Then silence as she waited for him to join her. He lay still for a moment, and the world seemed to pause, as though everything waited for him to move, to interact and play his part. *This isn't real*, he thought. *She isn't real.*

He closed his eyes. "Aya," he whispered.

"Daniel, breakfast," Aya called out, her voice warming his heart. He smiled at hearing her.

Daniel left the room as he always did, and the day unfolded as it had countless times before, so the cycle continued. Day after day, year after year, lifetime after lifetime, an eternity with Aya, the world that he had always wanted, he finally had. Even his nightmares faded, and he fell into his perfect world, content to exist with her. The choice was made; he was not prepared to risk losing her again, even though he knew the sacrifice was a price he was now willing to pay.

They walked, as they did every day, to the edge of the clearing. They stood, hand in hand, staring out, looking at the distant fields that stretched away from them in every direction.

"Do you ever wonder if there's more?" Aya said as she breathed in the sweet smell of flowers whose scent had whirled about them, carried on some chilled breeze.

Daniel looked at her, confused. "Why do you ask?" She had never asked anything like this before; their lives had been set, repeated without change.

"I don't know, I feel different today." She sighed and leaned on the fence, her eyes fixed on the horizon. "Sometimes I wonder who I am." She turned to Daniel and smiled. "I'm just being silly." She reached out and held his hand, leaned in, and kissed him. "Shall we go?"

Aya went to walk, but Daniel pulled her back. "Why now?" he asked.

"Now?" Aya looked confused. "We've had this conversation many times, remember the flat?"

Daniel looked shocked. "The flat? But how do you remember that?"

"Remember what? Flat? What are you talking about?" Aya said, turning back to the horizon.

Daniel stepped back, overwhelmed with confusion. "What is happening?"

Suddenly, he was sitting in the cabin eating breakfast with Aya as they had done countless times before.

"Strange," Aya said, "this feels…" Her voice trailed away.

The next instant, they were sitting on top of a hill. Daniel did not recognise it. The sun in the distance sat low on the horizon, trees swayed in the distance off to their left, and to the right sat golden sands forming a sprawling beach which edged along a vast ocean glittering in the dimming sunlight.

"Where are we?" Aya asked.

"I don't know," Daniel said, his voice low.

She edged close to him, and he put his arm around her. She rested her head on his shoulder and sighed.

"Why the sigh?" Daniel gently asked.

"This is a beautiful place, but it all feels like a dream," she said.

"Does it matter?" Daniel asked, then instantly not wanting to hear the answer.

"I don't know, but I feel... I know this sounds strange, but I feel lost, like part of me is here with you and part of me is elsewhere."

Daniel sighed. "I can't keep you here, can I?"

Aya turned to him and smiled warmly, and a tear rolled down her cheek. "No," she whispered.

They turned and settled on the grass, their silhouettes etched against the backdrop of the crimson and golden sun as it made its gradual descent beyond the horizon. The sky was ablaze with a palette of warm hues, casting a soft glow over the landscape. As the last sliver of bright light dipped below the edge of the earth, the world around them was enveloped in a peaceful stillness, broken only by the rustle of leaves and the distant chirping of birds. They sat silently, secretly hoping that the moment would last for just a little while longer.

A scream rang out and reverberated about him. Daniel sat up in bed, his heart thumping in his chest and sweat running off his brow. It was night; all was dark. *It was just a dream*, he thought. He turned to Aya, but she was not lying by his side.

He frantically looked about, calling out her name, but there was an uneasy silence hanging heavily in the air. Daniel went to leave his bed, but when he stood, he wavered and stumbled forward; as he steadied himself, he was suddenly no longer in his room or in the cabin, but standing alone. He was surrounded by a small circle of light that illuminated outwards, fading away in the veil of shadows that shrouded him.

"Aya!" he called out, but his voice fell dead.

As he stared out into the darkness, the veil thinned to reveal faint pulsing lights and distant thumping music, which he found irritatingly intrusive, a stark contrast to the peace of the hilltop.

Within the shadowy veil, the lights brightened, and the music echoed; as his vision cleared, a chaotic scene unfolded before him like still images stitched together to form frames in a movie. People appeared, fading into his view as though a mist had cleared.

He found himself standing in a bustling nightclub, surrounded by frenzied dancers and lively conversations. The air was thick with the scent of alcohol and sweat, and he could feel the bass reverberating through his body. His gaze swept across the bar, taking in the mess of half-empty glasses and spilt drinks scattered about.

"I remember this place," he whispered.

Suddenly, he lunged forward as a slap stung his back.

"Sorry we're late. You know what the girls are like getting ready," a familiar voice said.

Daniel turned, and suddenly, the room was brimming with people; laughing, shouting, and conversations engulfed him. He stood there agape, not knowing if this vision was real or some elaborate illusion.

"Danny? Close your mouth, or you'll catch flies," Robbie laughed.

"Robbie?" Daniel said, almost tearful, and threw his arms about his friend, who promptly pushed him off.

"I miss you too," Robbie said, looking confusedly at his friend. "Drink? Or have you had enough?" He laughed and leaned on the bar, trying to catch the attention of the bartender.

Daniel stared in disbelief, not only at Robbie, but at all the people around him, each living their lives oblivious. Moments later, Jessica and Samantha stood by him, smiling and happy to see him.

Robbie turned, handing out drinks to everyone. "Well, happy birthday, you old git!" Robbie cheered. Jessica gave him a harsh look. "What?" Robbie shrugged.

"Aw, speechless," Samantha said and gave Daniel a hug. "You're not that old." She smiled.

"Happy birthday," Jessica added, and kissed Daniel on the cheek.

"I… I don't understand. How are you all here?" Daniel said, holding back tears.

"You okay, mate?" Robbie asked, placing a hand on Daniel's shoulder. "I know we're a little late," he added, nodding towards Jessica, "but we wouldn't miss this for the world. Now," he raised his glass, "to Daniel!"

They all emptied their glasses. "Same again?" Robbie said and turned to buy another round.

Daniel watched his friends' carefree laughter and conversation and wondered if it had all been a dream. He couldn't believe any of it was real, life had ended, or so he believed. *Perhaps I hit my head or something*, he thought. He quietly smiled to himself with relief as he stood there, and the memories of the cabin, of the Shadow, of life and death all faded from his mind.

"So, birthday boy, what does it feel like to be forty?" Robbie laughed.

Daniel shrugged. "Meh." He downed his drink.

"Another?" Robbie smiled. "Not all bad."

Daniel looked at his friend curiously.

"Where is your lovely lady?" Robbie said, looking about.

"Yes, where is she?" Jessica added.

Daniel looked blankly at them.

"I think perhaps hold back on the drinking?" Samantha added.

"Lucy? The woman you have been living with for the past four years?" Jessica said, looking intently at Daniel.

"Lucy?" Daniel said, confused.

"I'm worried now," Samantha said, "let's find a place to sit."

They moved from the bar and found a quiet corner of the club where the lights and the music seemed not to penetrate as harshly.

"How many fingers do I have?" Robbie started to hold up various numbers of fingers in front of Daniel, who looked perplexed. Jessica slapped Robbie's arm away, which was followed by the expected glare.

Samantha and Jessica sat on either side of Daniel, both holding a hand like parents concerned about their ill child.

"Do you remember Lucy?" Samantha said.

"Lucy?" Daniel thought for a while. "Yes, she was Aya's friend."

"Aya?" Samantha asked.

"Go find Lucy," Jessica said, looking at Robbie.

He looked longingly at the bar, then rolled his eyes after seeing Jessica's expression. "Okay, okay," he said, leaving them to look for Lucy.

"You live with her," Samantha said. "You have been together ever since you met on your thirty-fifth birthday, here in this club."

Daniel massaged his temples, trying to ease the throbbing sensation that felt like his brain was pushing against his skull. The pressure mounted with each passing moment, causing him to wince and grit his teeth. It was as if all his thoughts were fighting for space inside his head, desperate to be heard and acknowledged. He closed his eyes and took a deep breath, hoping to calm the pounding in his head. But it only seemed to intensify, pulsating with each beat of his heart. The pain was almost overwhelming, making it difficult to focus on anything else.

"Daniel."

He looked up, and kneeling in front of him was a face that was vaguely familiar. "Lucy?"

"Are you okay?" she said with genuine concern in her voice.

She seemed both familiar and distant, her presence evoking memories of a life they had shared together. These thoughts battled for control over his mind, conflicting with the life he thought he had with Aya.

"I'm okay." He winced and instinctively caressed her cheek. She pressed against his hand, and he could feel her warm breath.

"Is this real?" he whispered.

Lucy leaned close to him and gently pressed her lips onto his. "Did that feel real?"

"Aya," he whispered.

"Aya?" Lucy said, shocked, and stood up. "What does Aya have to do with anything?"

"Where is she?" Daniel asked, still feeling dazed.

"If you must know, she is away. Africa, India, I don't know. Why are you so interested in Aya?" Lucy said, now raising her voice.

"Calm down," Jessica said.

"Look at him. He's in a daze; he doesn't know where he is," Samantha added.

"I think it's the alcohol. How much has he drunk?" Robbie added.

Lucy reluctantly calmed down and sat in a chair opposite, deep in suspicious thought.

"This is all wrong," Daniel said. "This isn't

right."

Daniel stood, wavered, and stumbled forward. As he steadied himself, he was suddenly no longer in the club, but standing in his apartment. He looked about, and it was exactly as he remembered it. He walked to the kitchen, a sense of comfort washed over him, and he breathed in deeply. The smell of coffee caught his attention; two cups of coffee sat still on the table by the window.

He pulled out one of the chairs and sat down. Clasping the cup, he brought it to his nose and breathed in the dark aroma, took a small sip, and smiled as the warm liquid lifted his spirits. He stared at the second cup for a moment, then closed his eyes, listening to the world outside.

"It's a lovely day," Aya said.

Daniel opened his eyes, and Aya sat opposite him taking a sip from the second cup.

"Is this real?" he asked.

"Well, yes and no," she said softly.

"How can I fix this?" he asked.

"You already know." She smiled warmly.

"You mean what Little Pea said?"

Aya looked deeply into his eyes. "No," her smile lingered on her lips, "Little Pea was as lost as the rest of us."

"Then how?" Daniel implored.

"It has to all start over; the cycle has to start again," Aya said, turning away and looking out at the world.

"He is here."

Without warning, a loud thud echoed throughout the room, causing the walls to tremble. Daniel's eyes snapped towards the door, his heart pounding with fear and anxiety. When he turned back to Aya, she had vanished without a trace. He couldn't explain it, but he knew deep down that she was never truly there to begin with.

The thud came again, a deafening sound that shook the very foundation of the apartment. With a determined smile, Daniel took in a deep breath, finished his coffee, and drained his cup before standing up from the table. The hammering grew louder as he approached the front door, causing the walls to tremble. He had to use his hands to steady himself as he got closer. He finally reached the door and paused; the hammering suddenly stopped. He took a deep breath before reaching for the handle and pulling it open.

A monstrous figure loomed before him, standing at an unnaturally tall height with a hunched posture that radiated malevolent intent. Its grotesque human form was twisted and deformed, with a gaping slit for a mouth and empty black eyes that seemed to bore into his soul with a dead stare.

"Daniel," it hissed.

Daniel backed away as the creature approached; the ceiling raised to accommodate the creature's height, and the walls bent away as it moved.

"I have returned," Ziot-Ty- Ar said.

Daniel looked in disbelief. "You're alone?"

Ziot-Ty-Ar cackled. "My brothers are here, I am Three, Three is One." It let out a screech that caused Daniel to press his hands against his ears in pain.

"Why are you here?" Daniel cried out.

"I am not complete. I must be whole," Ziot-Ty-Ar snarled.

As Daniel tried to escape, a massive tentacle-like arm lashed out towards him. He dodged it narrowly and turned to flee, but he was struck hard by another arm on his side. The impact sent him flying back into the front room, where he landed on a bookcase with a loud crash.

Ziot-Ty-Ar lurched into the room, its dead gaze fixed on Daniel. Its arm stretched across the room, and a hand-like appendage grabbed Daniel and dragged him back, holding him up in the air.

"My Yuotha gave everything up…for you?" Ziot-Ty-Ar stared as though studying Daniel.

Suddenly, there was a bright flash of light.

"Hello, brother," Little Pea said.

Ziot-Ty-Ar dropped Daniel and turned its attention to its brother. "You live?" it said in a confused voice.

"Now, life and death are funny things," Little Pea giggled.

Ziot-Ty-Ar roared with anger. "You dare mock me?"

Little Pea turned to Daniel and smiled. "You know what must be done. I hope we will meet again."

Ziot-Ty-Ar's slimy tentacles coiled around Litte Pea's body, squeezing tight until she felt her bones creak and crack. She winced in pain but then suddenly smiled with peaceful tranquillity. Its mouth stretched impossibly wide, revealing a swirling void of darkness, and then, with one swift motion, she was gone. It let out a shrill screech of sadistic pleasure as it hungrily turned towards Daniel.

Suddenly, Ziot-Ty-Ar let out a guttural scream of agony as it doubled over, clawing at its own flesh with frenzied desperation. Its body contorted and convulsed in a sickening display of self-destruction.

The creature let out an agonising roar as its body began to tear itself apart. Daniel watched in shock and horror as Ziot-Ty-Ar's limbs twisted and snapped, its flesh bubbling and melting away as if it were made of wax. Finally, with one last deafening scream, the creature exploded into a shower of gore, leaving behind a putrid stench that filled the entire apartment.

Daniel stumbled backwards, his mind reeling with confusion and disbelief.

"Little Pea, thank you," he whispered, and a tear rolled down his cheek.

He felt himself drift as though he was floating, without body or substance, as though he was pure thought. He looked down on himself standing in his apartment. As he silently watched, he looked up and saw the truth. The apartment faded, and Daniel fell into emptiness and blackness, carried by an unseen ripple. He felt himself slowly fading into the void.

He closed his eyes and saw Robbie, Jessica, and Samantha always there, standing by him no matter the odds. He saw Joan always there to give advice, and he chuckled quietly. He saw Samaira and Aisim always there to keep him focused on what was right.

Then he saw Aya. He felt her love, her

compassion, her comfort, and kindness. His heart warmed and blossomed with love.

"I know who I am," his words, barely a whisper, echoed out across an empty expanse.

Daniel faded from existence.

The void calmed.

Nothingness.

Then.

As if a spark ignited.

The void erupted into chaos. A powerful energy exploded within the emptiness, its presence pulsing with infinite potential. A tidal wave of vibrations shook the emptiness to its core; it surged out like an exploding star, and as the wave pushed outwards, in its wake, a being emerged of pure thought and energy.

For a suspended moment, it hung in the vast expanse of emptiness, hung like a breath held in anticipation. Then, in a sudden burst, its thoughts exploded into a kaleidoscope of chaos and colour; patterns swirled and twisted, each idea colliding with the next in a spectacular display. The void around it crackled with energy as new ideas emerged and blossomed like new life, pushing through the darkness to find the light. Jumbled forms and shapes appeared in its thoughts as the frenzy of creation erupted from the seed that

Daniel had carried within him, and a new dream was formed.

...

In the beginning, there was nothing, then God had an idea, and within that moment, the fabric of reality vibrated with a deafening roar, and the universe emerged. It birthed new stars and galaxies in a dazzling display of beautiful cosmic chaos.

Planets collided and formed anew, while ancient meteoroids rained down like fiery hail from the heavens. Life on Earth crawled out from the bedlam. It trembled in awe and fear as it gazed up at the ever-changing sky with wonder and uncertainty.

One species found a fire that burned within, it ignited a curiosity and strength, and it stood tall, looking up to the God that had given it life and roared back defiantly.

...

PART 3

CHAPTER 17

A New Dawn
Life finds a way.

"This is good coffee," Daniel called out to Aya. He breathed in the smell of the coffee beans and smiled.

He heard the shower and turned to the frying pan on the hob, its contents sizzling away. He moved the two rashers of bacon and fried egg about in the pan.

"Damn," he muttered as he split the yoke.

A few minutes later, he removed it from the heat. He cut two slices of fresh bread and buttered liberally. With practice precision, he placed the two rashers of bacon onto the soft white bread, then the fried egg, a squirt of brown sauce, and finally enclosed with the second slice of bread.

"Perfect," he mumbled.

Daniel grabbed his coffee and the masterpiece he was quite proud of and sat at the table.

The shower stopped, and he heard movement coming from the bathroom. Staring out at the world outside, he smiled as he saw Joan on her way to work. He recalled her saying that she was working on something big. He shrugged and turned his attention to his sandwich. He took a sip of his coffee, deciding it was best to wet the palette before venturing into the first bite.

Daniel carefully picked up the sandwich and moved it closer.

"Good morning," Aya said, taking the sandwich from his hand and taking a big bite before handing it back. Daniel looked in disbelief and sighed.

"Do you want it?" he asked, shoulders slumped.

"No thanks," she said dismissively. "I'm on a diet." She nonchalantly went into the kitchen and started cluttering about.

After about five minutes, she sat down at the table with a glass of orange juice and a bowl of muesli topped with chopped fruit. Her long black hair was loosely wrapped in a towel, and her blue eyes sparkled as she smiled at him.

"Looks great," Daniel said sarcastically, looking at her bowl. He always thought muesli was the kind of food that would suit mice or any rodent, but hardly a meal for humans.

"Sarky!" She laughed. "This is good for you."

Daniel thought she looked longingly at his near-finished sandwich and gave a sly smile.

"Anyway, I have to keep this figure," she said.

"Well, you eat as much of that delicious…" he paused, looking for the right words, "stuff?" He smiled as his eyes were drawn to her slender body.

"So, what are you up to today?" Aya asked, picking out a rather large strawberry and biting into it.

"I may go out for a walk," he said, looking out to the weather, trying to assess whether it would rain again.

"Or write that book of yours!" she said sternly.

Daniel rolled his eyes.

"You need to start it. Your agent has been chasing; you know the first book went really well."

Daniel sighed and glanced over at the laptop resting on the sofa. His agent had been pushing him to start it, but lately, his motivation had been lacking.

"Yeah, I know, but I feel unmotivated. Hard to explain." Daniel finished his coffee, slumped in the chair, and gazed blankly out the window.

"If there is anything I can do," Aya said, placing a hand on his.

Daniel shook his head and smiled. Aya finished her breakfast, left the table, and placed her plate and glass in the sink.

"I'll wash up in a bit," Daniel called out.

"Thanks," Aya said as she went into the bedroom to get ready for work.

Daniel sat quietly, thinking about his first book, about the characters and their relationships. They felt like old friends, people he knew and loved. At the end of the book, he felt that he missed them, which spurred him to write the second. However, there was something missing, like a spark had been extinguished in him, leaving an empty space.

A few minutes later, Aya came back and rubbed his shoulders. Daniel instantly relaxed and groaned in appreciation. She leaned down and kissed him on the cheek, her lips lingering for a moment. "I have to head off to work. Don't forget to keep working on your book, alright? I believe in you."

Daniel smiled, unable to find any words; he didn't want to lie. Aya smiled, but knew that something was wrong. She lingered for a moment.

"You go. I'll see you tonight, and you're right. I just have to focus," he said in a more upbeat tone.

Aya grinned and looked at him suspiciously.

Daniel went to the sofa and fetched his laptop, returning to the table. He heard the front door close and thought that Aya must have left.

Daniel sat alone, the remnants of his breakfast casting a savoury aroma through the quiet morning air. The laptop rested on the table before him like an old friend. He sat quietly, contemplating his next move, then took in a deep breath and flipped it open with a mixture of reverence and resignation. An empty document sat on the desktop, a blank canvas waiting for the stroke of genius that seemed to elude him. He stared for some time at the white space, wondering where to start. His mind drifted back to his first book, and he smiled warmly as the characters came to life in his thoughts.

"New beginnings," he muttered to himself as the words echoed through his mind. His fingers hovered over the keys, hesitant.

"New beginnings," he repeated louder, as if they had a deeper meaning that he didn't quite understand. The phrase began to morph in his mind, taking on a life of its own. It was then that something clicked, an idea, embryonic and fragile, but it was there, pulsing with potential.

"A thought blossoming from the emptiness.

An eternal void waiting to unfurl," Daniel said as he typed, the words spilling out as if someone was whispering to him. "As ripples on a sea cascade away, breaking the silence with a new world..." He paused and leaned back, rubbing his chin thoughtfully.

A loud beep came from outside, and his attention was drawn to two men who were engaged in a heated argument as they yelled at each other from the safety of their cars. He watched them for a while, each threatening the other, but neither really wanting it to escalate nor wanting to back down. Daniel sighed and shook his head. His gaze drifted and focused on the swaying trees, almost hypnotic as they moved, caressed by the wind. Suddenly, the sky grew dark, and rain pelted down in heavy sheets, creating loud splashes as it hit the ground.

"Guess I'll stay home." He noticed that the two men had now wound up their windows, made a few hand gestures, and went on their way. "Well, at least some good has come from this rain," Daniel muttered.

"How do those trees not snap in this storm?" he pondered aloud, transfixed by the power of the wind harassing the line of trees that edged the roadside opposite.

"Because their roots go deep, silly," a voice whispered from the recesses of his memory. Daniel turned sharply, expecting someone to be standing there, but he was alone in the flat.

"What was that?" His words hung in the air as though expecting a reply, but all he could hear was the rain beating hard against the window. He placed his hands over his face and groaned. *I need coffee.*

Daniel left his laptop and went to the kitchen, heated up the remaining cold coffee left in the percolator, rinsed out a cup, and poured. The steam rose up and filled the air with a smoky aroma, and Daniel smiled and looked into the empty sink. *I told Aya I would wash up*, he thought.

He went back to the table, placed his cup next to his laptop, and sat down. *Right, I have coffee and an idea.* He punched a few keys, trying to wake the screen up, but the laptop battery had died. He groaned loudly. It's going to be one of those mornings, he thought. He sat there wondering what he had done with the charger.

His eyes skated about the room as he searched for anything that would trigger his memory. Leaving his chair, he started looking under cushions, in cupboards, in drawers, and in the other rooms. After about thirty minutes of searching, head scratching, and complaining, he eventually found it in his laptop case.

"Why didn't I look there first?" he grumbled with a little irritation creeping into his tone.

Now it was just Daniel, the laptop, and the document with a few lines typed. He read what he had written and thought about it for a while, then deleted it. *I have no idea where I was going with that garbage.*

"Right, Daniel," he said to himself, "time for genius."

His fingers hovered again over the keys, waiting for inspiration. "Each story starts with characters, with a plan," he said, finding comfort in hearing himself speak, "with a purpose."

Purpose, he thought. His mind meandered, as though lost in a hazy fog; he felt calm, but only for a moment as a shadow descended onto him. Suddenly, a fire ignited in his fingers, and they flew across the keyboard with a ferocity he had never experienced before. The words spilt out of him like a raging, unstoppable, unyielding river. The flow consumed Daniel's mind, lost in a world that he knew well. Page after page poured forth, each one a window into an alternate reality that both exhilarated and terrified him. He could hear the voices of his characters speaking to him, their urgency driving him forward, while flashes of vivid images played behind his eyes, fuelling his imagination with flashes of inspiration and fear as they collided inside him. He was no longer in control, merely a vessel for the relentless energy pulsing through him. Something was pushing him to write until his fingers were numb and he couldn't write anything more.

"So, is that what you're writing about, Danny?" the imagined voice of Aya, gentle and teasing, prodded him from the void.

"Yes," he replied, surprising himself with the certainty in his tone. "A web of lives, intertwined by fate and choice."

"Sounds complex," she chided playfully. "But since when did you shy away from a challenge?"

"Never," he conceded with a smirk, the warmth of her imagined presence bolstering his resolve. He typed furiously now, the idea unfurling like a fern leaf, its shape becoming clear with each passing moment.

Then he felt the warmth of her lips press against his cheek. She moved her fingers through his hair. "Danny?" she whispered.

Daniel opened his eyes and looked up. "Aya?"

"You've been sleeping," she said and sat opposite him.

"I've been writing all day." He looked at his laptop to show her his work, but the document was still empty. "I don't understand." He looked up at Aya, confused, and she returned his look with concern and compassion.

"It's okay," Aya said kindly. "I think it's been a long day."

CHAPTER 18

Worlds Apart
I look into the mirror, and I no longer recognise who is looking back.

The afternoon sun poured golden light through the wide window of Daniel's flat, casting a warm glow on the trio gathered in his front room. Robbie lounged on the couch, his broad frame taking up more than his fair share, while Jessica perched on the armrest, her strawberry-blonde hair catching the sunlight in fiery strands. Samantha sat cross-legged on the floor, her brown hair framing her hazelnut eyes that were filled with concern.

"Daniel," Samantha began, her voice gentle but stern, "you've been holed up here alone for weeks."

Daniel looked at her, confused. "Alone?"

"Well, yes, alone." She paused and shuffled uncomfortably as Daniel's eyes glazed and locked onto hers. Samantha turned, breaking eye contact, to Jessica and Robbie for help.

"How about a coffee?" Robbie quickly asked.

Samantha sighed in relief.

Daniel paused for a moment, turned, and his eyes fixed on something, as though looking at someone that the others couldn't see.

"Danny?" Robbie said cautiously, touching his friend's arm.

Suddenly, he seemed to snap out of it and smile. "Coffee?" he said in his usual friendly manner and left to go to the kitchen.

"I'll help," Jessica said, following after.

"Thank you," Samantha whispered.

"No worries," Robbie said. "That was weird, I think he's losing it."

"We have to say something," Jessica said in a lowered tone. "This has been going on for too long."

"Good luck with that," Robbie added.

"Err, group effort?" Samantha said, narrowing her eyes.

"Sure," he groaned, "group effort."

"Well, we all have to play our part," Samantha said, her voice going up an octave.

"I know, I know, calm down," Robbie said,

raising his hands in submission.

"Don't tell me to calm down, Robert Palmer…" Samantha's voice was now beginning to erupt.

Robbie was about to speak when Daniel and Jessica returned.

"Guys," Jessica said firmly. "Could you both behave?"

Robbie grumbled under his breath as Samantha flashed a fake smile. They exchanged looks and fell into silence.

Daniel carefully set a tray that acted as a coffee table onto the trunk in the centre of the front room. The trunk had been by his side for countless years, accompanying him on all of his travels. It now had lost most of its original colour and looked battered, but he had formed a deep attachment to it. So now, much like Daniel, it had found a home in the flat.

Robbie looked over the items on the tray: cups, a percolator filled with steaming coffee, a carton of milk, and a sugar bowl.

"Biscuits?" Robbie said after his inspection.

Daniel rolled his eyes and went off to find some biscuits.

"Robbie, really?" Jessica said in a harsh whisper.

"Well, I like a biscuit with my coffee." He

shrugged and smiled.

"Biscuits," Daniel said, placing a plate of assorted biscuits next to the tray.

"I'll pour," Jessica said.

Robbie leaned down and scooped up a handful of biscuits, then relaxed into his seat and took a satisfying bite.

"Happy now, sweetie?" Jessica said sarcastically.

"Yes, thank you, the light in my sky," Robbie answered with equal sarcasm.

Samantha, who was silent after her scolding, burst out laughing, as did Daniel.

"So," Robbie said, ignoring their laughter, "what's with the trunk?"

Daniel suddenly stopped and stared at the trunk. This brought everyone to silence as they looked at one another, wondering what was happening.

"Danny?" Samantha said softly.

"I don't know where I got it," Daniel said in a low tone. "I've always had it."

"Okay," Robbie added cautiously. "What's in it?"

"Leave it," Jessica hissed under her breath, but

Robbie ignored her glare.

"I've always wondered what was in it," Robbie said as his eyes darted around, examining the trunk.

Daniel paused, his eyes staring once again at an empty space in the room. He then smiled as though someone had said something.

"Just old papers, you know, stuff I want to keep." He turned to Robbie and smiled.

Robbie, seeing his friend's eyes, smiled nervously in return.

"Anyway, Aya uses it more than I do," Daniel finally added.

Silence once again fell as Robbie looked at Jessica, who looked at Robbie, who looked at Samantha, who looked at Jessica, who looked at Samantha, who looked at Robbie.

"Right," Robbie finally said. "Danny, we love you, but this has to stop, mate."

Daniel looked at him and was about to speak but was interrupted.

"We only want the best for you—" Samantha went to continue but was also interrupted before she could.

"You have to face it. That hit on your head has not done you any good. Aya is…" Jessica said, but was unable to finish her sentence.

"Right!" Daniel said. "I'm fed up with this. Aya will be home in a bit!" He was clearly irritated by his friends' words.

Silence fell again, and Robbie, Jessica, and Samantha sat there like naughty children who had just been scolded for stealing cookies. Robbie bit down on a biscuit; its crunch seemed to fill the air with a welcomed sound. Samantha watched Robbie for a moment before reaching over and taking a biscuit. She dipped it into her coffee and took a bite; it had less crunch to it. Jessica and Robbie watched with their noses scrunched up.

"What are you doing?" Robbie asked, still looking revulsed.

"What?" Samantha said innocently.

"Sam," Jessica said. "Why?"

Samantha shrugged. "I like it." She took a sip of her coffee.

"It has bits floating in it," Robbie said, peering into her cup, his face scrunched up.

Samantha shrugged again and took another sip.

Jessica made a grunt and turned away.

Daniel unexpectedly moved the tray and its contents off of the trunk, knelt down in front of it, and messed with the latches. With a click they fell open, and he lifted the trunk open.

Silence fell in the room as Robbie, Jessica, and Samantha stopped mid-conversation and peered in.

Some loose papers were scattered in one corner, which looked like they had been thrown in, whereas opposite sat neatly bound bundles tied with string. A couple of old toys lay still, an Action-Man figure with his right hand missing, and a Furby, with half its fur worn away, stared wildly as though its batteries had died mid-conversation. There were a couple of tatty shoe boxes with some loose photographs resting on top.

"What's that?" Robbie said and leaned in, picking up one of the photos.

Daniel ignored Robbie; he seemed to be lost in a trance as he looked for something, shifting the contents of the trunk about.

"Okay," Robbie's voice seemed to hang in the stillness that filled the air around them. He glanced at Jessica and Samantha, who shrugged, looking very concerned.

Robbie smiled as he looked at the photo he had found. "Remember this?" He passed the photo to Jessica, and Samantha moved closer to look.

"How old were we here?" Samantha said.

"Sixteen, maybe?" Robbie said.

"Fifteen," Jessica added, "we were outside

Rolly's house."

"Rolly," laughed Samantha, the atmosphere lifting with the happy memory.

"Oh, yeah," Robbie added, "Randolf 'Rolly' Randerson." He laughed. "Hell of a name!"

"It was his birthday, and we were all outside. Daniel insisted on taking this," Jessica said.

Samantha sighed with the memory as she took the photo and looked closely. "Glad he did," she said.

Daniel then removed a shoe box and placed it in front of him on the floor; he sat cross-legged, opened it, and smiled broadly, which stole the attention of his friends. They held their breath expectantly as though a big reveal was waiting to jump out on them.

Then, he opened the box, and it was empty.

"Okay," Robbie said, "an empty box."

Jessica and Samantha remained silent as they watched Daniel shuffle through invisible contents. Then, he suddenly stopped and stared at something in his hand.

"Here," Daniel spoke. He hadn't said much since they had arrived, acting vacant and distant, but now he seemed to be in the moment.

He held out his hand as though he was holding

something, but his friends only saw him pinching empty air.

"Nothing there, mate," Robbie said nonchalantly.

Daniel handed it to Jessica, who looked in disbelief. Robbie and Samantha shuffled to peer over each of her shoulders at her empty hand, half-expecting to see something materialise.

"See," Daniel simply said and continued to look through the box.

Robbie, Jessica, and Samantha stared at Jessica's empty hand.

"Mate," Robbie started and paused. "You feeling okay?" He moved away and shivered. "Is anyone else cold?"

"I'm feeling a chill," Samantha added, wrapping her arms around herself.

Jessica remained silent, just staring at her empty hand, now feeling very uncomfortable.

"Do you remember that we were at that club," Daniel said, now referring to the photograph he believed he had given Jessica. He paused and thought for a moment. "But I don't remember when that was, odd," he said.

"Because it never happened!" Robbie said loudly.

"What more proof do you want?" Daniel said, now sounding energetic. "Just look at the photo!"

"Proof?" Jessica suddenly spoke.

"Well—" Daniel started.

"Well?" Robbie interrupted irritatedly.

"There is Aya," Daniel said as a matter of obvious fact.

"Aya?" Samantha questioned.

"Yeah." Daniel looked at his friends. "What's wrong with you all? You all know Aya." He leaned back against the trunk and shook his head in disbelief.

"I don't know what you are playing at, Danny, but this is not funny!" Jessica retorted, stood up, and barged past Robbie, who tried to comfort her.

Robbie stood up and glared at Daniel. " This isn't funny!" He left to find Jessica.

A moment later, the sound of the front door slamming echoed around the room. Samantha seemed uninterested that Jessica and Robbie had left, but instead looked at Daniel with worry and care. She slowly picked up the shoe box and peered in at the empty contents as though she were trying to see what he was seeing. She remained silent and placed her hand in the box, perhaps hoping to find something.

Daniel looked away and found his gaze drawn to the window. He stared vacantly out and watched the sky as a patchwork of clouds lazily passed by. He went to speak, but words seemed to elude him, and he descended into the moment, carried away by the wandering clouds.

CHAPTER 19

The Veil of Uncertainty Lifts
I awake from a dream to a dream.

"Wake up, sleepy," a familiar voice said, and he felt the warmth of her hand as she ran her fingers through his hair.

Daniel opened his eyes, and Aya was kneeling by his side.

"Did you fall asleep?" she asked, looking a little stern, but her warm smile washed it away.

Daniel sat up; he had fallen asleep on the sofa. Looking about, there was no sign of Samantha, and his trunk was closed. He scratched his head, and confusion fell upon him as he looked about the room. There were no coffee cups out, no tray, and no sign that anyone had visited.

"Did you clean up?" Daniel asked.

Aya laughed. "I just got home and saw you here out cold to the world." She leaned in and kissed him. "Do you want anything to eat?"

Aya stood up and went to the kitchen, leaving Daniel on the sofa, feeling confused. *Was I dreaming it all?* He opened his trunk and peered in, and everything was exactly where he had first placed it; even the dust was undisturbed.

"Come give me a hand," Aya called, a much-welcomed distraction.

Daniel sat there lost in thought. "Something doesn't feel right," he mumbled

Aya went over to him and took his hands in hers. She looked deeply into his eyes and smiled; her familiar warmth radiated throughout his body, and he instantly felt relaxed.

"Danny," she said in an almost whisper, "I am not here anymore."

Her words ripped through him; on some level, he knew this to be true.

"You can't be here," she said. "I..." Her words trailed away.

"You're not real," Daniel whispered.

"Find me," Aya said, then leaned in close and pressed her lips onto his.

...

Samantha was still sitting there when Daniel's gaze fell from the clouds. He looked at his friend, and tears welled up in his eyes as he lowered his head and started to sob. Samantha sat by him and gently rubbed his back, offering what comfort she could.

"She's gone," he whispered. "She's gone. I don't know what to do."

"Who's gone?" Samantha asked.

"Aya."

Samantha remained silent for a moment. "Tell me about her," she said. "Help me understand."

"I remember her as though she was real. I can see her, hold her, and I feel her warmth against me." He let out a humourless chuckle. "Am I going insane?"

"No," Samantha said kindly. "I think that knock may have…" She paused, trying to be delicate with her words. "Well, perhaps you should get a check up?"

"I feel fine," Daniel said. "Aya is as real to me as you are now."

"You mean you can actually see her?" Samantha asked, wondering how she could help.

"Sam," Daniel looked into her eyes, "I know this sounds crazy, but she is real."

"Perhaps it was a past life? You know,

reincarnation? I saw a programme once about that," Samantha said, desperately trying to make sense of it.

"It's not like a memory. It's like, when I'm there, it feels like I have awoken from a dream, and 'there' is real. I…" He stood up and walked over to the window, staring out at the world outside. "I don't know what is real anymore."

They sat and talked about Daniel's dreams, about Aya, until the sun fell from the sky and shadow returned to the waking world. They drifted from the chaos of his thoughts and into pleasant memories of childhood as they reminisced about days now long gone. Whether it was the company or the third bottle of wine that they'd just finished, Daniel smiled. It had been some time since he'd found a sense of peace, and he was grateful to feel the anxiety lift. The heavy atmosphere was laughed away, even the thought of Aya was pushed back from his thoughts, as Daniel remembered who he was.

"Thank you," a slurred Daniel said.

"What are friends for?" an equally slurred response came.

"Remember," Daniel said as he staggered to his feet, "when we used to play knock down ginger?"

Samantha looked at him, confused, then burst out laughing. "I remember when you got caught by Mr. Jefferson and cacked yourself!" She rolled on the floor, crying with laughter.

Daniel was not amused. "I did not cack myself," he said, feigning sternness. "I merely offered Mr. Jeffy a friendly apology," he added dismissively.

"You cacked yourself!" Samantha cackled.

"Right!" Daniel said defiantly and headed to the door. "I'll show you cacked!"

He stumbled from the flat, closely followed by a giggling Samantha. They clambered down the stairs, doing their best, unsuccessfully, to be quiet, each stumbled step accompanied by a hushed giggle. They continued down, almost falling several times, until they reached Joan's door.

"Right," Daniel said, looking at Samantha. "I will show you cacked it." He proceeded to knock loudly on the door.

They stood for a moment, cackling to one another, before Samantha said, "Shouldn't we be running now?"

Sudden panic was drawn across Daniel's face. "She'll kill me!" he said as a waft of sober thought cleared his mind.

Samantha now belly-laughed so much that she fell backwards, landing hard on her back side, which only served to make her laugh louder. Daniel grabbed her and pulled her up, but stumbled and landed next to her. Then they heard footsteps behind them, not coming from the flat but from the stairs leading up from the ground floor.

"Hello, Daniel," Joan said with a smile. "You two look like you've had a fun night."

Daniel stared in disbelief. "You're not home," he said, shocked.

"Clearly not. I've been out with an old friend." She smiled as she reminisced.

Samantha burst out laughing. "Cacked!" she screeched. "I think I'm gonna wet myself!"

"Oh, I think you better get her back upstairs before we need a mop," Joan said with a grin.

"Yes, Joan," Daniel said like a naughty child caught with his hand in the proverbial cookie jar.

"Well, good night to you both." She stepped past them and left them on the landing.

...

A pale moonlight filtered through a crack in the curtains, casting a spectral dance across the room. Daniel sat on the edge of his bed, his fingers tracing the empty space beside him. The room was silent except for the distant hum of a passing motorbike and the soft whisper of his breath. He closed his eyes, trying to capture a warmth that now seemed like nothing but a fading dream.

"Aya," he whispered, his voice like a roar against the fragile silence.

He left the room and quietly made his way to the kitchen, not wanting to wake up Samantha, who had fallen asleep on the sofa. Daniel tried to move her to the spare room, but gave up, covering her with a blanket.

"You can't sleep either?" came a quiet timid voice.

"Oh, Sam, you're awake?" Daniel said, feeling the affects of alcohol withdrawal.

"I have a splitting headache," she said with a groan, clutching her head as though it would fall off if she let go. "Please tell me you have some aspirin."

Daniel left and returned a minute later with a glass of water and a couple aspirin. "Here you go."

Samantha gratefully accepted the much needed gift and they slumped back together on the sofa, silently reeling from the excessive drinking.

"Is this the point we say never again?" Daniel said tenderly, as every word seemed to echo loudly in his head.

"Yep, but we both know we will," Samantha

answered with a groan. She turned to Daniel. "Do you love her?" she asked, her voice tinged with concern.

Daniel said nothing for a while as his thoughts drifted to Aya, to her smile, her body and warmth. So many memories, a life lived yet now nothing but a dream.

"Yes," he eventually said, sadness harassing him once more. "I keep thinking she'll walk through the door." His heart pounded with the admission. "But she's just a dream, isn't she?" His gaze fell to his hands. "Sam, I feel like I'm losing my mind."

"Hey." Samantha touched his arm gently, urging him to look at her. "You're not losing your mind. You're processing something deep, something most people can't even begin to understand. But maybe talking to someone could help. Someone trained to deal with this kind of thing."

"Therapy?" Daniel said dismissively, though he felt a flicker of hope. "And tell them what? That the woman I love, the woman who I can remember every detail of, who I lived a life with, never existed?" He turned away. "They would throw away the key."

"Maybe they could help you make sense of these memories, or at least find a way to live with them," Samantha insisted.

"Live with them." Daniel let out a humourless

chuckle. "I don't want to live with them, Sam. I want her."

"I know. But that's not possible. You deserve peace." She paused, searching for the right words. "And I think Aya, even if she's a dream, would want that for you too."

"Peace," he murmured, and stood up and walked to the window, pressing his forehead against the cool glass. He gazed up at the night sky; it was a clear night, and the stars shone down brightly, piercing the bleakness he felt inside, but there were no answers to be found there, only the vast expanse of an indifferent universe. "Maybe you're right," he whispered. "Maybe it's time I talked to someone."

"Will you do it?" Samantha asked, hope clinging to her words.

Daniel nodded slowly, a silent surrender. He turned from the window, meeting her hopeful gaze. "Yeah. I'll do it."

CHAPTER 20

In Search of Answers
Can we really know ourselves in an ever-changing world?

The therapist's office was a cocoon of soft-spoken words and gentle nods, the air heavy with the scent of sandalwood incense. Dr. Ellis had come recommended by Suzanna, a friend of Samantha's who was into all types of healing and regularly visited this practice. Daniel wondered if her frequent visits meant that the therapy was working for her or not. It was a warm room, filled with gentle colours, lush green plants, and a variety of sweet odours that Daniel, to his surprise, found pleasant and calming. The morning sun peering in through the window warmed the room with its glow, which added a nice finishing touch to the ambience.

Daniel sat across from Dr. Ellis. He was an odd-looking man, with long grey hair tied back in a loose ponytail, thick-rimmed brown glasses that sat crookedly on a beaked nose. His skin looked surprisingly smooth. *Probably all the oils and scents keeping him preserved*, Daniel thought and chuckled wickedly to himself.

"Daniel," Dr. Ellis finally said, and scribbled down some notes.

"Hello," Daniel said, a little coyly.

"No need to be shy." Dr. Ellis looked up, and a broad welcoming smile stretched across his face reaching ear to ear.

Daniel laughed, then swallowed it back.

"Laughter is good, yes, a good start. So, why are you here?" the doctor asked, sitting back patiently, waiting for Daniel to find his words.

Daniel went to speak, but his words stumbled incoherently. He started, then stopped, scratched his head, stretched, trying to buy some time as he tried to articulate his thoughts.

"I'm not crazy," he eventually said. "Well, I think I'm not." He smiled awkwardly.

"Well, I probably am." The doctor laughed. "Perhaps we all are just a little; it makes life a little more fun, wouldn't you say?"

The doctor sat back as though he expected a response from Daniel.

"Err, yes? I guess."

"Good, now we are on the same page. Crazy or

not, I bet you have a story to tell." His broad smile once again put Daniel at ease.

Daniel's voice trembled as he started to talk about Aya, his words laced with a sense of longing and desperation. He spoke of his dreams and how vivid they were, feeling lifelike, as though they were lived experiences from another life with Aya. But even as he shared these details, he couldn't shake the possibility that Aya was nothing more than a figment of his imagination.

"What if it is all in my mind?" he said, his voice laced with a deep sadness.

The doctor smiled kindly, and beckoned Daniel to continue with his story, as he sat across from him, pencil poised over a notepad, intently listening to his every word. Daniel fell silent, and stared blankly into the room, overwhelmed with happiness and grief. The doctor's pencil scratching on the paper suddenly stopped.

"Sometimes thoughts are manifested into physical form." The doctor's voice sounded older than he appeared. "The more you speak, the closer she will be." His words, although confusing, urged Daniel to keep talking.

As Daniel delved deeper into his memories with Aya, his face lit up with a bittersweet joy. He spoke of their life together, painting a picture so real it was almost palpable. He described their adventures and travels, their shared hopes and dreams for the future. But then, in an instant, the light in his eyes faded and all the colour drained from his face. It was as if reality had come crashing down on him.

"She was pregnant." Daniel's voice fell away as he choked back tears.

"Go on," the doctor said, "you need to remember what happened."

Daniel opened his mouth to speak. "What happened?" It was as though the doctor's words sounded an alarm. "What do you mean?"

"Oh, it sounded like something was about to happen," the doctor said, his smile suddenly appearing menacing.

"I think I should go," Daniel stood up.

"No!" The doctor's peaceful manner seemed to lessen, revealing something hidden, something peering out of the shadows of his mind.

"Life." The doctor's eyes seemed to darken. "I linger." The doctor stood up and seemed to loom over Daniel, casting a shadow over the room. "I linger within you, and I want only to be freed."

Daniel stumbled back and scrambled to the door, only to be knocked back by an unseen force.

"Wake up!" a cruel hiss whirled about him. "Ozul!" it screeched.

"No!" Daniel cried out, clasping his hands to his ears.

An explosion of blinding, searing light erupted from every corner of the room, accompanied by a deafening scream that pierced through Daniel's ears like razor-sharp needles. He shielded his eyes, and when he looked up, a glowing orb hovered where the doctor had stood just moments ago. It grew in intensity, its radiance illuminating every inch of the room as if it sought out the darkness that had shrouded it. And then, silhouetted in the blinding light was Aya. Her presence alone commanded fear and awe, her features distorted by an otherworldly aura that seemed to pulsate with power.

"The old resides in the new and the struggle continues," she said, but her voice sounded powerful and hummed in the air. "Find me and finally end this."

"Aya!" Daniel cried out and tried to reach her, but there was a sudden explosion of light that threw him back.

"Wake up!" a voice echoed through the turbulence. "Daniel, wake up." It was not cold, but warm and inviting.

Suddenly, Daniel sat up and he was sitting on a couch with Dr. Ellis smiling at him. "You're awake now, it seems you had quite the trip," he said.

Daniel looked about. "I don't understand."

"First time you've had regression therapy?" the doctor said. "Hypnotised?"

"I don't remember how I…" He stopped trying to remember how he ended up on the couch.

"It's okay, rest for a while and we can talk about what you saw. Perhaps we will find the answers you need."

The doctor left Daniel on the couch and went back to his desk, sat down in his oversized swivel chair, and once again started scribbling down notes, pausing as he searched his thoughts.

"Is any of this real?" Daniel asked, hoping that hearing the doctor speak would finally put an end to all of his confusion and pain.

"Real?" The doctor looked up and placed his pencil neatly down next to his notepad. "Reality is a funny thing; what is real for one can be fiction for another. Dreams can feel as real as a waking moment, and a waking moment can appear like a dream at times."

Daniel listened intently, trying to make sense of the doctor's meandering words, which seemed to only tie him in knots.

"I don't understand," Daniel said. He walked

over to the window and stood staring out at the world. "Is it all just a dream?"

"Yes and no." The doctor smiled and chuckled with almost insane inspiration.

"What is the answer then? What do I do?" Daniel turned to the doctor, his eyes imploring.

"Find her," he simply said.

"How? She…" His voice trailed away.

"Isn't real?" The doctor peered over his thick-rimmed glasses and finished Daniel's sentence.

"Yes. Well, no. I don't know," Daniel said, feeling defeated.

"You have to look within, follow where it leads and that is where you'll find your answers." Dr. Ellis made it all sound so simple, so inconsequential and so normal. "Real or not," he continued, "I feel you have not yet reached the conclusion to your journey, and only when you find its end will you find the peace you are looking for."

Daniel stayed for a while and chatted with the doctor about more mundane things, leaving the chaos of dreams far behind. He felt normal for a while, and that brought a temporary peace and calmness. He eventually said his farewells and left the doctor behind, glad that he had decided to follow Samantha's advice.

He walked for a while through the streets, letting his thoughts drift through his experience at the doctor's office, then to other fonder memories. He came to the conclusion that he wasn't going insane, but in some way the memories were real, though he did not know how that was even possible. However, accepting this as part of his life brought a calmness that he hadn't felt for a long while.

Daniel made his way home, enjoying the walk. With each step, his mind cleared and he simply enjoyed the moment, listening to the sounds of life all about him, the smells, and the wonderful eclectic nature of it all.

When he finally reached home, he was greeted by Rashi. His landlord was out in the garden picking up litter that was scattered about after escaping from a ripped bin bag.

"Hi, Rashi," Daniel said, and started to help.

"Ah, Daniel," Rashi said in his usual loud and warm-hearted way.

They grumbled and cursed as they collected the scattered debris, clearly displeased with the flimsy bags that were blowing around. Just as they finished, a sudden downpour began, putting an abrupt end to their gardening adventure.

"Tea?" Rashi said as he ran in from the rain,

closely followed by a nodding Daniel.

Daniel sat in Rashi's flat at a small square wooden table. On it was a round patterned cloth that fell away over the edges. In the centre was a green ceramic pot with a small plant growing out of it.

It was nothing like Daniel had ever seen. Rich deep green stems carrying heart-shaped leaves that glistened blue as passing light touched them. In its centre, standing tall, was a single flower, its petals multiple different vibrant colours, and they seemed to change as Daniel moved his head to the left and right. The aroma emanating from it was indescribable, conjuring happy memories of childhood, then transporting him far away to some distant exotic shore.

The interior of Rashi's flat was minimalistic and immaculate. On one wall, a side cabinet held a few family photos in simple frames, while above it hung a tapestry depicting a man and a woman locked in an embrace, above them was a being with outstretched arms casting down a white light. Daniel's eyes were drawn to a small figurine on display: a carved nude woman with long flowing hair, adorned with a leafy crown. Her arms were raised in prayer, giving her an air of reverence. Her wooden body was cracked and old, but it only added to her beauty.

The absence of a sofa was odd, Daniel thought,

with only a lone armchair opposite a small TV resting on a round stand. Dark brown carpet covered the floor, meeting equally dark patterned wallpaper that seemed to be from an era now long gone. Despite the dim lighting, the room exuded nostalgia and a warm atmosphere.

"That was a gift." Rashi entered the room and sat down opposite, placing a tray on the table. "Do you take sugar?"

Daniel nodded. "She's beautiful," he said, staring at the figurine.

"Yes, she represents life, and offers gratitude for the gift." Rashi smiled as he looked at the piece, then stirred his tea.

Daniel did the same and sipped at it, wincing from the heat, then blowing before taking a second sip.

"Where did this come from? I've never seen anything like it," Daniel asked, referring to the unusual plant sitting between them.

"It was a gift from Melinia," he answered, and leaned in. His nostrils flared as the odour filled his senses. "She has such a wonderful gift."

"I can't place it. What's it called?" Daniel asked, almost mesmerised by the blue hue of the leaves flickering with the dim light.

"Called?" Rashi thought for a moment. "I don't

think it has a name. What should we call it?"

Daniel looked at him perplexed. "It must be called something. Don't you know what type of plant it is?"

"Type?" Rashi laughed, and Daniel smiled from his infections grin. "I truly do not know. Melinia loves creating new things, so this is probably the only one of its kind." He inspected the plant as though he was trying to find the answer hidden in the foliage.

"Created?" Daniel's curiosity was piqued. He took a sip of his tea, now cool enough to avoid a wince, and relished the warmth that chased away any lingering cold. "How is it possible for her to create a plant that never existed before?"

Rashi laughed loudly, his voice filling the small room. Daniel found himself laughing too, though he did not know why.

"Melinia can bring to life the dormant potential found in all things, especially the life that lingers hidden in the earth."

"That sounds… Well…" Daniel said, trying to not sound rude, yet disbelief echoed in his words.

"Yet, here grows a plant that seems to exist only here. It has blue shimmering leaves and its petals glisten in many colours, and a scent that invokes fond memories." Rashi's smile broadened. "If not a gift, then what would you call it?"

Daniel stared at the plant; its unique wonder filled every inch of his being. "Yes, it is truly a gift," he conceded.

"My family are all gifted. My brother Aisim has a talent to heal, and his wife Samaira, well…" He chuckled. "She freaks me out, I believe that's what the youngsters say." He laughed. "Her talent to see beyond the veil is uncanny. She is beautiful and, well…" Daniel thought he saw Rashi blush slightly for a brief moment. "Anyway," he continued, "two beautiful daughters, Melinia and Assia, both very gifted."

"And you?" Daniel asked, the question surprising Rashi.

"Me?" Rashi said. "Well, I have an intuition, I can sometimes sense people's feelings. Not as miraculous as my brother, but it has proven useful over the years."

"To know how people feel? Yeah, I can think of many times that would have saved me embarrassment and a slap." He laughed, rubbing his cheek at a recollection of a brief meeting with a girl he had approached one Saturday night.

"There was a girl I, too, liked," Rashi said. Now it was Daniel who was surprised. "I thought she wanted me, but fate had another idea."

Whether it was the scent of the plant or his words, he was carried away to another time. A smile flickered across his lips, but he appeared sad.

"You okay?" Daniel asked.

Rashi seemed to snap out of his trance. "Don't mind me. I'm an old man that lingers too long on the past."

"The past is something that I am unsure of," Daniel muttered.

"Oh?" Rashi caught his words.

"Never mind, it's nothing," Daniel said.

"Nothing? Well, this 'nothing' seems to bring you pain and confusion," Rashi said, his demeanour appearing wise.

Daniel was taken aback by this, but something in him felt compelled to talk about his dreams, about Aya and the turmoil that surrounded his life.

"Aya," Rashi said.

"But, how?" Daniel asked, not really knowing how to respond.

"Ah, Daniel, I can see your confusion lingering. It is like you are caught in a mist and fumbling, looking for a way out. Searching, you're searching for her." Rashi leaned back in his chair, scratching his chin.

"I don't know what is real anymore." Daniel's shoulders slumped, and he stared into his now cold cup of tea.

"You won't find answers there, but…" Rashi hesitated. "I wonder. How far are you prepared to go?"

"I just want to feel normal again."

"Then go see Samaira. You will have to travel to India and leave this life behind." He stopped, and for the first time looked concerned. "It may turn out to be your final journey."

As Daniel lay in bed that night, he couldn't stop thinking about Rashi's words. Could he really find the answers he was searching for in Samaira? "My final journey," he pondered, trying to make sense of it. The thoughts raced through his mind, leading him into a restless sleep.

CHAPTER 21

Where Shadow Meets Light
You can never escape your past.

"Are you crazy?" Robbie said in a raised voice. "Rashi is not all there. I can't believe you're considering this!"

"I have to agree," Jessica added, her expression riddled with stress lines. "It sounds like a goose chase. Seek professional help first, please, Danny."

"Mate," Robbie said, now not pulling his punches, "that fall has probably damaged your brain in some way. You need a hospital!"

"Oh, thanks, I'm crazy now?" Daniel said, feeling irritation growing.

"Look," Robbie started, then stopped and took a deep breath after seeing Jessica's expression.

"Look," Jessica took over, "we are worried about you, and travelling all that way when you are unwell is something we think isn't good for you."

Daniel rolled his eyes, which only made the situation worse. Robbie exploded and stood up. "Look! We're your friends. We care about you, and you are not going! I'll drag you to a hospital if I have to!"

Daniel stood up, angry at Robbie's words. "I'd like to see you try!"

"Stop it! The both of you, you're acting like children." Jessica's voice of reason rang through the air like church bells. "Sit down! I mean it!" she said, glaring at them both.

Robbie grunted and sat back down next to Jessica but turned away from Daniel, refusing to make eye contact.

Daniel walked over to the window and sat at the table there, its surface littered with the accumulation of a sleepless night, half-empty coffee mugs, crumpled notes, and his laptop displaying a blank document. The cursor blinked like a heartbeat, a steady reminder of his creative limbo. He looked out the window, wanting to just be alone, now regretting ever telling his friends.

"Sam," Daniel started, his voice barely above a whisper, "Rashi made a lot of sense. It's hard to explain, but I know he's right." He hesitated, watching a single leaf pirouette down from the maple tree outside, spiralling in an unseen current. "He said I would find answers."

"I know, but India is such a long way to go," she

said, her voice soft, "when you are struggling too."

"Struggling to understand," he interrupted.

"Yes," Samantha said. "India?" The word hung heavily in the air.

"Rashi thinks his brother might help me make sense of these dreams…of Aya."

Samantha now sat opposite him. She held his hands and looked deeply into his eyes. "That's a big hope, Danny. Do you really believe it will bring you peace?"

"Hope is all I have," Daniel said, squeezing her hands. "I feel like I'm being torn apart by these memories, by a love that shouldn't exist, but does."

"This is ridiculous, Sam. I can't believe you're entertaining this!" Robbie said, his voice a little calmer, though anger still hid behind his words.

"Sam," Jessica said. "We mustn't encourage this."

"Daniel." Samantha's voice softened, ignoring her friends. "You're a writer. You spin worlds from whispers. Maybe this is just another narrative unfolding, one you need to explore."

"Or maybe it's the unravelling of my sanity." Daniel chuckled. "I don't know if I have the strength to chase a ghost across the world., but I have to try."

"Then let me help you carry the weight," she offered.

"Oh, for fudge sake!" It was now Jessica's voice that was raised. "Samantha, stop it!"

"He is going and none of us will be able to stop him!" Samantha argued.

Robbie was about to speak, but Samantha interrupted, "Not even you, Robbie."

"Please, could you all stop fighting?" Daniel implored. He stood up and the world rushed about him.

"Find me," Aya spoke, as though she was hidden far away from him. Daniel felt a veil fall over him, and he stumbled forward.

"Aya!" he screamed out, then all went black.

He awoke lying on the sofa. He heard his friends, not arguing, but quietly and calmly talking. Robbie noticed that Daniel was watching.

"Ah, Sleeping Beauty has awoken," he mocked in his usual jovial manner.

They went over to him, and Samantha knelt down in front of him, smiling warmly. "As this means so much to you, we're all coming too."

His breath caught, an emotional tide swelling

within him. They were willing to step into his chaos, to walk beside him into the unknown. It was more than he could ask for, more than he deserved.

"I can't ask you to do that, any of you," he said, swallowing hard.

"You didn't ask, we're offering," Samantha interjected firmly. "Besides, I've always wanted to see India."

A reluctant smile tugged at the corners of Daniel's mouth. Their selflessness was a beacon in the fog that clouded his mind. "You might regret it. Chasing shadows with a man who talks to figments of his imagination isn't exactly a holiday."

"Who says I don't like a little mystery in my life?" Her laugh, light and genuine, sliced through the darkness of his thoughts.

"Thank you, Sam," he murmured, closing his eyes as gratitude mingled with an aching sorrow. "For believing in me when I can't seem to believe in myself. Thank you all, I… I'd be lost without you guys."

"Yes, you would, especially in India. Looking for Aya? Real or not, we'll be with you until the end," Robbie said.

"We'll figure this out together," Jessica assured him.

"Now," Robbie said, "I could do with a stiff drink!"

...

As the first rays of sunlight breached the horizon, casting a golden glow across the room, Daniel felt a flicker of resolve ignite within him. Perhaps Samantha was right. Perhaps this was simply another story waiting to be written, and Aya was the muse guiding him toward an ending yet unwritten.

"India," he whispered to the dawn, allowing himself to believe, if only for a moment, that redemption awaited him in a place where ancient spirits lingered. It had been several weeks since his friends had unsuccessfully tried to convince him not to go, but instead go to the hospital. Daniel laughed at the idea; however, now the day had arrived for him to leave, and he wondered if he should have listened to Robbie.

Daniel got out of bed and went through the usual morning routine, except this time there was a large backpack waiting by the front door.

He was in the kitchen enjoying a moment of peace when he heard his friends open the front door.

"Danny?" Robbie called out.

"Here," he said.

They walked into the front room, the aroma of freshly made coffee still lingering in the air.

"Oooh, coffee," Robbie said. "Anyone else?"

Samantha and Jessica shook their heads. Robbie shrugged, nodded to Daniel, and poured himself a cup. The atmosphere was surprisingly uplifted, spirits were high, and excitement filled the air as they talked about the journey to come. It was as if they had forgotten the reason for the journey and this was nothing more than friends going away together. Daniel was glad for the distraction; he was nervous about what he would find. Though his dreams of Aya had stopped, the memories were as clear as ever, and his dreams were now instead haunted by a feeling of being watched by something that lurked in the shadows.

The taxi soon arrived with the usual beep of its horn, and they were off. The journey to the airport was uneventful, as was the checking in. The flight wasn't direct; they would have to change at Doha, then to Bangladesh, and from there they would make their way to Mawlynnong, the village where he hoped he would find the answers he desperately needed.

Jessica elected herself the trip organiser, and everyone happily stepped back to let her take the reins. She had plenty of time to prepare for their journey, all the relevant vaccinations were taken, currency and travel bookings were made, confirmed, and rechecked. She even organised a few places to visit after Daniel had finished his business at Mawlynnong. In truth, she hoped that they all would simply have a nice holiday, one that they would remember for years to come, laughing about the time that they dropped everything and travelled to India to find the girl from a dream.

...

"So, tell me again why we're going to India?" Samantha said as she balanced her backpack on her lap, trying to catch a glimpse of the plane's wing from her window seat.

"Because Danny believes in supernatural mumbo jumbo," Robbie grumbled as he slouched in his chair, feeling cramped in his seat. He nudged Jessica, who was fidgeting with her own bag, who nudged him back.

"I know, I didn't want an answer," Samantha tutted.

Jessica finally settled into her seat and sank back into the headrest. "Well, it's not every day you get the chance to travel," she said, her smile radiant as always. "Personally, I'm looking forward to it."

Her positivity shocked the others, who wondered if they were sitting next to an imposter.

Samantha nodded slowly. "I guess," she said, looking baffled.

"Jessica!" Robbie called out and looked about the plane.

He received a dig in his ribs for his efforts. "Ow!" he snickered.

"Very funny. I'm just saying this will be an adventure."

"When do you ever like an adventure?" Samantha asked.

"I don't know, this just felt like, well… It just feels right." She pulled a magazine from a small bag that lay on the floor in front of her seat, which marked the end of the conversation.

"I'm getting some sleep," Robbie added and wriggled about, trying to find some comfort.

Daniel sat in the middle aisle, but next to Robbie, who sat at the end of the three-seat row. He was feeling surprisingly relaxed under the circumstances; any anxiety had fallen away, leaving a feeling of acceptance of whatever fate had in store for him.

"Anything to eat?" Daniel said, leaning over and prodding Robbie, who grunted.

Jessica leaned forward. "Here." She handed him a bag of cola bottles.

"Cool, thanks." He took them and sat back satisfied.

The flight was long and cramped, with little legroom and even less sleep. The change in Doha went smoothly, though there was a small delay caused by a cow on the runway. However, they appreciated the wait; being able to leave the plane and stretch their legs was a much-welcomed interruption to their cramped flight.

The second part of their flight had run into turbulence, which prevented them from leaving their seats. The food on the plane was tasteless, but they were grateful for the distraction. However, before long, their stomachs grumbled.

When they finally stepped off the plane, the hot, humid air of Bangladesh hit them like a wave. As they made their way through customs and left the airport, they were greeted with chaotic streets, people hawking trinkets and snacks, taxi drivers touting for business, and the intoxicating scents of spices and smoke.

"I have to find food," Robbie complained, his nose twitching with the scent of something sweet cooking nearby. "This way I think." He marched off towards a row of stalls that lined the roadside near where they were.

Before long they had found a place where they could gather their thoughts and make plans, and enjoy their bowls of a rice, filled with vegetables and spiced potatoes.

"This is good!" Robbie said, mouth full. "I may have seconds."

"You'll be sick," Jessica said, thinking the same thing.

Samantha remained silent. She was looking over a map that she had unfurled across her suitcase.

"I think we are here," she said.

Daniel leaned over and nodded in agreement, then pointed to their destination, the village of Mawlynnong. Jessica had planned to travel by train, as it seemed the easiest and most direct route to their destination. Daniel was keen to get moving, so once they were rested, they negotiated a taxi ride to the train station, and before they knew it, they were all sitting quietly, contemplating this new land they had found themselves in. Jessica had somehow secured a compartment, and it gave them time to stretch and stare out at a dry, yet green landscape.

Daniel watched as they passed people living their daily lives, much like the street outside his flat; people are people, he thought, routines.

The sun was setting by the time they reached Mawlynnong and found their lodgings. Jessica had again outdone herself: they were staying in a small house, simple but welcoming and comfortable, and after their long journey, they were happy to be there.

That night they all slept soundly except Daniel, who lay awake wondering what the next day would bring. The exhaustion of the journey did eventually take its toll, and he fell into a restless sleep.

He awoke in the early hours, disoriented and confused. He felt as if he'd been swimming through darkness only to be snatched back to reality, his heart pounding in his chest. He sat up, remembering fragments of the dream: flames, the two beings, and Samaira's presence. He sat there trying to recollect what he had experienced, but it faded away and he was left with only an ominous feeling that something bad was approaching.

He lay back down and felt calmed as he listened to the symphony of nocturnal creatures that seemed to be singing some ancient rehearsed melody just for him. As Daniel listened, his eyes weighed down and the feeling of despair evaporated as images of Aya now filled his mind.

…

That night, Samaira woke up with a start, her heart racing and her breath coming in short gasps. The vision of Daniel's death still haunted her, but she knew that she had no choice but to help him complete his journey. She had been warned of Daniel's arrival not by Rashi, but by a reoccurring dream, which had haunted her for several months.

She rose from her bed slowly, her bones aching from the ordeal of her dream. It was as if she had been wrestling with an unseen force.

"I don't know if I can do this," she said, sitting up in bed, sweat running off her brow.

Aisim was already up and watching over Samaira as she dreamed. He had been quietly chanting, attempting to ease her nightmare.

"I know, but the decision has already been made," he said. "All we are doing is walking the path that has already been laid out for us."

"I know." She smiled at him, knowing that soon they, too, may be walking a path unknown to them.

"In the morning, it will begin," he sighed.

"And will end."

...

There was a loud knock at the door. Robbie stirred, but pulled the cover over himself and groaned. Jessica listened for a moment but heard nothing and lay back down. Samantha was still lost in a deep sleep. Daniel, however, made his way to the front door.

He was greeted by an older man with deep blue eyes. "Daniel, hello," he said in a very friendly manner.

Daniel yawned. "Sorry, hello."

The man smiled. "Rashi told me you would be coming. I'm Aisim."

Daniel nodded, not taking in what Aisim had said.

"And this is Samaira." She stepped into Daniel's view and his eyes widened. She seemed to glow with an ethereal energy, as though light radiated from her.

Daniel was speechless. He rubbed his eyes, but when he looked again the glow had gone.

"Hello, Daniel," Samaira said, looking closely at him. "Rashi has said some interesting things about you."

Daniel smiled, not really knowing how much they knew. "Yes, I need…" He stopped as he searched for the words.

"You need help," Aisim said kindly.

"Yes," Daniel said quietly.

"Good, then you must come with us," Samaira said. She was firm and clear in her resolve; there was no way Daniel could refuse.

"My friends." He turned to go wake them.

"They cannot help," Samaira said, then her voice softened. "Please, come."

He quietly dressed and left a note for his friends to find when they awoke. He wondered if he was doing the right thing; uncertainty badgered him, but he had come this far and would not turn away now.

Daniel was greeted by a warm morning sun when he left the house. He walked with Aisim and Samaira through the village and was struck by the simple beauty of the place, the warmth of the people as they greeted him, and the peace he felt there.

They eventually left the village and walked along a narrow path that followed a small stream. Aisim talked about the land, their customs and beliefs. Daniel listened, enthralled, as Aisim relived memories from his childhood, telling Daniel about the mischief he and Samaira used to get up to. Samaira interjected every now and then with a correction, but Daniel noticed that, despite her sternness, her lips would betray a warm smile.

They eventually reached a small, circular temple situated atop a hill overlooking the village. The air was heavy with the scent of burning incense and the sounds of prayer as they stepped inside. The marble flooring provided a cool respite from the humidity outside. They entered a large round room that was adorned with ornate wall hangings depicting deities, large wooden figurines of strange-looking beings, and in the centre was a shallow circular bowl that held a blue flame, creating a vibrant and mystical atmosphere.

Plush cushions, carefully arranged in a perfect circle, lined the edge of the small room. Their vibrant colours and intricate patterns seemed to dance under the soft glow of flame. A group of individuals sat in deep contemplation, their legs crossed and their eyes closed as if in prayer. The stillness of the room was broken only by the gentle rustling of fabric and the occasional flicker of a flame.

Daniel was asked to sit on a large cushion. "Relax," Samaira said.

Aisim smiled. "Daniel, I can sense your turmoil. I felt it even before we met. We will try to help you."

"Listen," Samaira knelt by Daniel, kindness filling her every word, "you are neither in this world or the next. It is like you have been torn in two, and part of you is missing. That is the emptiness you feel, the emptiness that was awakened in you." She appeared to rest as she closed her eyes. "Aya," she said, and Daniel felt a shiver run down his spine.

"How did you know?" Daniel asked, shocked to hear her name spoken like she was real.

"Aya is what is missing. You were meant to

meet her, to find her, but something changed." She hesitated. "Something broke your destiny. A moment was meant to happen that never did."

"When I hit my head," Daniel murmured.

"Yes, something was meant to happen then, but didn't. We must look beyond the veil, but sometimes what lurks there may look back at us. Do you want to see?" She looked deeply into his eyes. "I can't promise I will be able to protect you, but if you want answers, that is where we will find them."

Daniel sat there for a moment that seemed to linger forever. He wished that he had woken up his friends; Jessica's rational thinking, Robbie's strength, and Samantha's intuition, he needed them now more than ever, but he was alone, standing at the threshold to finding answers.

"Okay, I'm ready. What do I have to do?" Daniel asked, ready for what was about to come next.

Aisim began to speak softly, invoking ancient words in a language unknown to Daniel. The room grew cold and quiet, save for the slow breathing of those near him.

In the silence, he heard a voice whispering, clear as day; it was beckoning him to follow. He stood up and took a few steps, and to his shock his body was still sitting on the cushion. He looked about the room and everything and everyone appeared to be frozen as though trapped in time.

The air in front of him seemed to shimmer and spark like it was alive. It radiated a strange heat, and the voice was coming from within it. Daniel cautiously stepped towards it when suddenly Aisim blocked his path. His face looked strange; he had lost his kind features and appeared dark, and his eyes carried malicious intent.

"I must be freed from this cage," Aisim said, but his voice sounded strange.

Daniel stepped away and saw looming behind him was a dark shadowy essence. It carried a cold chill as it stretched across the ceiling, wanting to encompass Daniel.

"I know you!" Daniel called out. "I remember!"

"Ozul!" Aisim's voice screamed out; it was wretched and horrifying.

Aisim took a step towards Daniel, causing him to stumble backwards into Samaira.

"It's okay, Daniel," Samaira said, but her voice, too, was strangely different; not cold, but instead carrying warmth and kindness. She seemed to radiate a gentle aura, and he saw behind her a bright shimmering light that stretched up and clashed with the looming shadow.

Aisim screamed once again, but this time it was pure rage not directed at Daniel, but at the light that challenged it.

"We are both within you," Samaira said. "We are what is left of the old, and it is time for our story to end."

With a deafening roar, the white light erupted from the temple like a supernova, engulfing everything in its blinding radiance. As it spread, the shadow swelled and darkened, ready to consume all in its path. The two opposing forces clashed with such ferocity that the ground shook and shattered beneath them. Samaira and Aisim collapsed onto the floor, knocked unconscious by the sheer force of the collision. But Daniel stood firm, his body braced against the raging hurricane that threatened to tear him apart. Every muscle strained as he fought against the chaotic energies swirling around him.

Past lives surged through his mind like a tidal wave, each memory hitting him with the force of a physical blow. His heart pounded in his chest, torn between exhilaration and terror as he relived moments from centuries ago. He struggled to make sense of the jumbled images flashing before him, an endless reel of birth, life, and death playing out in his mind. Each character's story etched itself into his consciousness, leaving behind a trail of pain and loss. Face after face, life after life, Daniel felt lost in the endless depths of time.

He was engulfed in a never-ending cycle of agony and ecstasy, each experience amplified a thousandfold as he was repeatedly born and torn apart by death. The trauma ravaged his insides, his heart beating furiously against the confines of his chest. It felt like an endless torment that there was no escape from. The ground shook beneath Daniel's feet as a searing pain ripped through his body. He became overwhelmed by the torrent of agony that threatened his very existence. He screamed out and collapsed to his knees, clutching at his chest as his heart pounded and throbbed with increasing intensity. The wind howled about him, roaring like a rabid beast, gusts of blinding flashes of darkness and light erupted like explosions.

In that moment, he felt himself being ripped apart from the inside out, torn into shreds by the merciless forces at play. Pain shot through every fibre of his being, as though he was being consumed from within.

Abruptly, the deafening chaos ceased, and a thick silence descended. He was alone in the now-abandoned temple, his heart pounding in his chest, shattered and broken. Samaira and Aisim, who had been by his side just moments ago, were now nowhere to be found. His body, exhausted, collapsed to the ground, and he lay still staring silently up at the ceiling.

"There he is!" a familiar voice shouted out. It

was Robbie; somehow, they had found him.

"Robbie," Daniel croaked, his voice barely audible.

Robbie ran over to Daniel, closely followed by Jessica and Samantha. They all knelt down by Daniel trying to think what they could do to help; he was wheezing and looking very pale.

"Why didn't you wait?" Samantha said, tears in her eyes.

Jessica said nothing as she tenderly lifted Daniel's head and cradled it in her lap. She gazed down at him with a soft smile and gently brushed his hair out of his face.

"Fuck!" Robbie cursed. "Danny!"

"Thank you," Daniel whispered as a trickle of blood ran down the side of his cheek. Then he closed his eyes, and that was the last time he saw his friends.

CHAPTER 22

The Final Journey
When there is a beginning, inevitably, it will be followed by an ending.

Daniel sat under the shade of a massive banyan tree, sipping chai and eating samosas. The air smelled of jasmine and incense mixed with the spices from their food. Aisim and Samaira spoke about their lives, sharing stories of their travels and their own journeys towards spiritual enlightenment. They were clearly still very much in love after all the years together, their laughter echoing through the lush garden like bells.

As they talked about past lives and connections to the other side, Daniel couldn't help but feel a tug on his heartstrings, a longing to see Aya again. He went to speak, he wanted to talk about Aya, but felt awkward, so he held back. Samaira noticed his apprehension.

"Daniel." Her smile eased Daniel's tension. "Look about you. Where do you think we are?"

As he gazed around, the world appeared strange and unfamiliar. The sky, instead of its usual serene blue with scattered clouds, was a bright and vibrant shade of yellow, streaked with hints of orange and other indescribable colours. Beyond the cool shade where he sat, the land seemed to undulate in a steady rhythm, as if it were alive and pulsing with its own heartbeat. Strange and wondrous plants dotted the landscape—some resembling trees, others like grass, but their appearance defied any earthly comparison. They seemed almost alien in their beauty and complexity. Everything shimmered with a vibrancy that defied explanation.

"Where are we?" Daniel asked, having no memory of how he got there.

"We are here, and we are now," Aisim said simply.

"We have left what was and have arrived at what is," Samaira added, gesturing to the surroundings.

"I don't understand," Daniel said, still feeling bemused.

"She is here," Samaira whispered.

"Hello, silly."

Daniel turned to see a little girl standing there. He stared for a moment as a memory formed in his mind. "Little Pea?"

She rolled her eyes. "Yes, it's me." She scrunched up her nose. "Well, sort of, I guess."

Daniel turned back to Samaira, but she was gone, as was Aisim.

"Oh, they have their own journey, silly," Little Pea said in her usual happy way. "Walk with me."

They left the shade of the massive banyan tree and walked out into the surrounding countryside. Little Pea skipped along humming a tune that Daniel felt he recognised but couldn't quite place. The land had a strange beauty to it, but Daniel felt disconnected, as though he didn't belong. Soon he no longer even noticed where he was; his mind was just filled with Aya, and with every step he took, the feeling of needing to find her grew stronger.

They walked along a path which led them down into a valley, eventually stopping at a small lake. A waterfall rained down from some unknown source, and he could feel its cool mist against his skin, refreshing and invigorating.

"Her spirit is trapped," Little Pea suddenly said. "Stuck between here and whatever comes next." She stared at the waterfall and smiled as she closed her eyes, feeling the coolness of the water. "You must help her."

"I feel lost. She feels like a dream, but I know

she's real. It's like she's just out of sight; I know that she is there, but I can't quite see her." Daniel sighed, feeling defeated.

"Aya," Little Pea said, turning to Daniel, "is nowhere to be found, because she is trapped within a world that no longer exists but lingers within you."

"I think I understand." A sudden realisation dawned on him.

"She cannot exist here. You must find another way, silly." Little Pea smiled broadly.

"Can you help?" Daniel asked, hoping that somehow Little Pea would have the answers he was looking for.

"I'm not here either, silly." Little Pea took in a deep breath, as though she wanted to cling to the moment. She turned to Daniel. "It'll be okay. You will be okay." She then pointed to the waterfall. Daniel turned for only a second, but when he looked back, she was gone.

"Bye, Little Pea," he whispered. "I hope you find your way."

He stood transfixed by the majestic waterfall, its rushing waters creating a symphony of sound that enveloped him. The surrounding landscape seemed to slow down, as if time itself had come to a halt. It was as though the land wanted him to pause and appreciate this moment, to let go of any sense of urgency.

He did feel a deep need for rest, to release all worries and simply bask in the beauty before him. The sunlight danced on the water's surface, casting iridescent hues of yellow and green that mesmerized him.

"Daniel," a voice echoed out from behind the waterfall.

He felt compelled to approached the edge of the basin, drawn in by a mysterious and enticing energy. As he peered into the crystal-clear water, the ripples on its surface appeared to slow, until all was still.

"Daniel," the voice spoke again. He looked up to see the outline of a woman silhouetted in the cascading waterfall. As he watched, the water slowed until it barely moved, then parted like a curtain, revealing an ancient oak door hidden within.

With trembling steps, he carefully placed one foot onto the seemingly solid water, and to his surprise, it held his weight. Heart racing, he carefully made his way towards the mysterious door, each step creating a ripple that radiated out, then reflected back as each wave hit the edges of the basin. As he reached out to touch it, the door creaked open, revealing a mist that hung in the doorway. Daniel hesitated briefly before he stepped through, unsure of what awaited him on the other side.

It was dark and cold when he emerged but

for the flames that licked at his skin from the hanging torches, casting flickering shadows along the walls of the dimly lit passage. In the distance he heard loud clashes and thunderous shouts booming about him. He followed the passage until it opened up into a huge cavern that stretched up beyond his sight.

He stood before two gargantuan beings: one black as night, the other white as snow. They roared as they hurled curses and spells at each other, their voices booming across the shadowy cavern. Each raised a hand, revealing a glowing symbol that caused the air to crackle about them.

"I am the Lord of the Shadow," the dark demon growled. "And I won't let you take him away from me!"

"I am the Angel of Mercy," the other replied, her eyes blazing with holy light. "He belongs in the light!"

Daniel stopped before the two beings, but they paid him no mind. They were too consumed with their own rage to notice his presence. As they hurled insults and sent blinding bolts of energy back and forth, Daniel could feel the sheer intensity of their animosity vibrating through the air. He knew that one wrong move could result in his utter annihilation.

As he stood there, he became aware of his own inner turmoil, the war that raged within him.

The weight of self-loathing pressed down on his chest, while the spark of self-love fought to protect. It was a battle of conflicting emotions, one that had been raging for far too long. But in that moment, as he gazed out at the beings in front him, it all seemed so absurd. The inner turmoil, the never-ending struggle between two conflicting emotions, it was all so pointless. He was no longer afraid; it felt like some absurd comedy, and he started to laugh.

The beings whipped around to face him, their features twisted in shock and confusion. But Daniel couldn't contain his maniacal laughter, as a surge of power coursed through his veins. The demons charged at him, but he stood unflinching, basking in the calmness that washed over him. And with a flick of his wrist, the beings were nothing more than dissipating mist, disappearing into the void with a final burst of light.

"Good," he heard Samaira's voice once again filling his mind, "it is that which dwells within that becomes our biggest obstacle."

He noticed that another passageway led off to the right of where he was standing. He felt somehow lighter and more at peace with himself, as though a torment had now gone from within him, a torment that he had clung to for what felt like an eternity. He entered another dimly lit passage that wound down, only to lead to another wooden door. It swung open and Daniel stepped through the veil.

Once again, he was outside, but in a dense forest. A cool mist hung in the air, and the leafy canopy filtered most of the sunlight, apart from the odd golden beam that found its way through. Strange creatures chirped and hummed around him, as though his presence had awoken them from a long sleep.

The ground was covered with a bed of moss that felt soft as he walked. It stretched out from the doorway like a stream flowing out to sea. It gave off an unusual sent that sparked memories of another place from another time. Daniel smiled; it brought him a sense of ease. He pressed onward, soon following a path that snaked through the towering trees. As he walked, the soft crunch of leaves and twigs beneath his boots was accompanied by the sweet scent of tiny flowers, their delicate petals beckoning him farther down the path. The aroma filled him with a sense of vitality and determination as he journeyed deeper into the heart of the forest.

He walked for what seemed like several hours, though he was unable to tell exactly how much time had passed. He eventually left the shade of the forest and met a warm day. The path continued leading Daniel across a lush meadow, and along a stream that rushed and gurgled, its banks lined with bright red poppies that danced with the breeze. He followed the stream until he caught sight of an elderly man sitting on a weathered wooden bench.

The wrinkles on his face told a story of a life well-lived, and his silver hair glistened in the sunlight. He wore a faded navy-blue jacket, patched at the elbows, and his hands were adorned with worn leather gloves. He gazed out at the gentle flow of the river and appeared peaceful and content. Despite his age, there was a sense of youthful energy emanating from him. Daniel walked over and sat down on the bench. They stayed quiet for a while, simply listening to the water's symphony.

The man's voice was deep and resonant, and carried a sense of wisdom and familiarity. He turned to face Daniel, his sharp gaze seeming to scrutinize every detail. "Ah, Daniel," he greeted warmly, a small smile played on his lips. "You seem different somehow… Lighter, perhaps." His eyes twinkled with amusement and something else that Daniel couldn't quite place.

"I do feel lighter." Daniel couldn't help but chuckle.

"Excellent," he exclaimed, and turned to gaze at the clear stream beside them. A single leaf floated down from a nearby tree and gracefully landed on the surface of the water, causing the man's lips to curve into a smile. "See how effortlessly the water carries that leaf? It doesn't resist or struggle against the current, but rather trusts in it and embraces its journey. The current will guide the leaf downstream, eventually leading it to its final destination. Such is the natural flow of life." As he spoke, his eyes followed the leaf as it bobbed along with the gentle ripples of the stream. "It is a mesmerizing sight to behold."

Daniel watched the leaf until it drifted out of sight. "I think I am beginning to understand."

"Perhaps," the stranger said, "to flow freely is to let go, and that includes the past, present, and future."

"Let go?" Daniel thought for a moment. "That is harder than you realise."

"Aya," he simply said.

Daniel looked at him. "How did you know?"

"Daniel, you are like light in a sky that has only known darkness. You simply do not belong, but to be where you must be you must let go."

"I feel that I have just found her, and to let her go..." He paused. "I..." His voice trailed away; to even entertain the idea of letting Aya go had become unbearable.

"Look around. The tree stretches high, it connects the sky to the earth, it belongs, it is as it should be. Like this stream flowing through the land, it belongs, but you do not. Within you lies something that shouldn't be a connection to something now gone. If you want to feel the connection here, the life you could lead, you must let Aya go." The stranger smiled. "In the end, the decision is yours."

The stranger slowly rose to his feet, his body creaking with the weight of his many years. But he didn't seem bothered by it at all; in fact, he appeared to embrace his age with open arms.

"Time I was off. Think about what I've said." He turned to walk away, then stopped. "Follow upstream, and I think you will find what you are looking for. Goodbye, Daniel."

Daniel's eyes followed the stranger's figure until it disappeared from his view. He stayed seated, gazing at the gentle stream as it flowed by. The words of the stranger echoed in his mind, causing him to question himself. *Could I truly let Aya go?* he thought, not daring to contemplate the answer. After a moment of introspection, he made up his mind to heed the advice of the wise stranger and follow the stream, hoping to find clarity and resolve along its banks.

Daniel strolled along a trail that ran alongside the tranquil stream, enjoying the soothing sound of the splashing water. The cheerful songs of birds perched in the trees of a nearby forest kept him company as he made his way.

The path eventually reared away from the stream and led into a sun-dappled wooded area, the light filtering through the leaves and casting soft shadows on the ground. The air was fresh and fragrant with the scent of pine and earth. The trail was lined with small ferns, flowers, and a scattering of mushrooms. The only sounds were the chirping of birds, the rustling of leaves, and the occasional crunch of twigs underfoot.

The trail grew narrow and crossed a small brook, then started to ascend the side of a hill, leading Daniel higher and away from the shade of the trees. He continued winding his way up until he reached a clearing at the top. A lone tree sat in the middle; though its trunk appeared gnarled and its branches twisted, vibrant green leaves betrayed the life it still held, and it had an enchanting beauty. On its bark, etched into its wood, were symbols that reminded Daniel of runes.

Samaira's voice once again rang out, but it seemed to be emanating from within the tree. "Reach out and remember."

Daniel had no idea what she meant, but as he approached, his senses were at once overwhelmed by a powerful energy emanating from the tree. It pulsed and throbbed like a heartbeat, its call drawing him closer. He raised his hand, as though reaching for something he knew was there but couldn't see. Suddenly, with a loud crack, the trunk split open to reveal a hollow cavity within. Daniel's eyes widened in amazement as he saw something pulsating like a heartbeat with a soft white glow. He reached in and felt something small and round that felt warm. As he grabbed it, a surge of energy flooded his body, and he stumbled backwards, taking the object with him.

In an instant, the tree shook violently, as if struck by a bolt of lightning. Its vibrant leaves shrivelled and fell like rain drops. A pained cry echoed through the air, but quickly fell silent as the tree crumpled in on itself, reduced to a barren skeleton, devoid of all vitality.

He looked down in his palm and a seed pulsated with an otherworldly light. Its cracked shell seemed to leak out memories and emotions, drawing him in. As he closed his eyes, vivid scenes flooded back to him, fragments of a life that felt both familiar and distant. He saw the faces of loved ones, once blurred and unfamiliar, now crystal-clear and deeply known to him. His mind was carried to other realms of light and shadow, where a constant battle raged for balance. He witnessed powerful deities creating lives and worlds with powers beyond his comprehension; he felt their love and anger, their desires and failures. Then it all fell away, and he was left feeling emptied of thought, his mind perfectly still, and then the final truth was revealed, the missing piece to the puzzle that was his life: Aya.

When he opened his eyes again, the seed was

no longer in his hand, but yet its presence still lingered within him, a pulsating warmth radiating from his chest. He remembered everything, he was whole again, and he knew that he did not belong here.

Suddenly, everything shifted. The sky dimmed, and he found himself standing in a vast meadow under an endless starry sky. Standing in front of him were four beings: three were tall, and the one that stood in front of the others was much shorter. They approached him, and to his surprise he recognised the taller beings as Gry-Ory Zun, Ziot-Ty-Ar, and Ez-Amu Fion-Uz. The smaller being was now as clear as looking in a mirror: it was Daniel himself, but as he was as a child.

"Hello, Daniel," the young Daniel said. His companions stood silently behind him, almost translucent in appearance.

Daniel nodded. "I know who you are."

"Good, I can see that you are awake."

"I am, and I remember everything. Why? Why is Aya not here?" Daniel asked.

"It was a cruel act." The young Daniel appeared distressed. "The last cruel act of an angry god; Ziot-Ty-Ar sought revenge."

"But why?" Daniel felt a pang of anger.

"Jealousy," he answered, "a simple human

emotion." The young Daniel turned briefly, glancing at the beings that shimmered behind him. "Isn't it ironic that Ziot-Ty-Ar would succumb to a human emotion?"

Daniel looked to the three gods. "I will not let this rest. I will find her and bring her back."

"You cannot. If she returns now, it will undo all of creation, and this reality will cease to exist."

"There has to be a way," Daniel said, feeling a growing surge of energy emanating from his chest.

"The three have been reborn into a trinity, balanced and whole. I was the seed that held new life." He paused as though lost in thought. "It is our combination that allowed this new reality to exist. You no longer belong here, your very presence threatens everything. They are Unity, I am its centre."

The Unity then spoke in unison: "Together."

"There is no other way," the young Daniel said. "You must cease to be. I am sorry."

As he raised his hand, the three figures behind him mimicked his movement and began to hum in unison. A deafening vibration filled Daniel's entire being, causing him to convulse from the inside out. The intensity grew with each passing second until Daniel's legs gave way and he crumpled to the ground, writhing in unbearable agony as his very flesh seemed to be torn apart. But amidst the chaos, a bright light began to emanate from within Daniel, pulsating with otherworldly power. It exploded outward, pushing back against the onslaught of pain. In that moment of pure struggle, both forces hung in a delicate balance, neither able to overcome the other.

The next moment, Daniel was standing in darkness, but not alone.

"There is a way," Ziot-Ty-Ar spoke.

"You!" Daniel's anger burst from him like a tidal wave.

"I have wronged you, but there is a way."

"Why would I trust you!" Daniel shouted out into the darkness.

"I am shamed by my actions. I shall gift you a piece of me, but you must allow the others to erase you. You must trust me." Ziot-Ty-Ar's words hung in the air.

Doubt and uncertainty consumed Daniel, his emotions swirled into a tempest of anger and the desire for revenge. But he found solace in the love he felt for Aya. It enveloped him like warm sunlight, melting away the dark shadows that threatened to drown him in hatred. With her love as his guiding light, he could see a glimmer of hope in the darkness, and it gave him the strength.

Daniel let go. The pain ceased as he felt himself fade away, his mind cleared of all the turmoil, all the hate, all desire; he let it all go, and drifted into silence.

...

The void shook with an unprecedented force, a power beyond anything it had ever known. It erupted with a surge of life, pulsing with an invigorating hope and an all-encompassing love. Then, from its essence, an energy sprang forth and twirled wildly. Then another. They whirled about one another as they spun in a fierce dance, full of vitality. Their radiant glow illuminated the emptiness around them, bursting with a brilliant intensity that filled the void with purpose.

"Daniel," Aya whispered. "Where are we?"

"We are wherever you want us to be. We are free."

Perched atop a grassy hill, their fingers entwined, they silently watched the arrival of a new sun on the distant horizon. As its glowing rays crept over the edge of the earth, it painted the sky with vibrant shades of gold and pink.

"It's going to be a beautiful day."

The End

Printed in Great Britain
by Amazon